FREUD'S MISTRESS

. . .

FREUD'S MISTRESS

...

KAREN MACK &

JENNIFER KAUFMAN

AMY EINHORN BOOKS

Published by G. P. Putnam's Sons

a member of Penguin Group (USA) Inc.

New York

AMY EINHORN BOOKS
Published by G. P. Putnam's Sons
Publishers Since 1838
Published by the Penguin Group
Penguin Group (USA) Inc., 375 Hudson Street,
New York, New York 10014, USA

USA · Canada · UK · Ireland · Australia
New Zealand · India · South Africa · China

Penguin Books Ltd, Registered Offices: 80 Strand, London WC2R 0RL, England
For more information about the Penguin Group visit penguin.com

Library of Congress Cataloging-in-Publication Data

Mack, Karen.
Freud's mistress : a novel / Karen Mack and Jennifer Kaufman.
pages   cm
"AMY EINHORN BOOKS."
ISBN 978-0-399-16307-4
1. Freud, Sigmund, 1856–1939—Fiction.
2. Psychoanalysts—Fiction.   3. Austria—Fiction.   I. Title.
PS3613.A272548F74   2013   2013004036
813'.6—dc23

Printed in the United States of America
1   3   5   7   9   10   8   6   4   2

Book design by Gretchen Achilles

TO MOLLY FRIEDRICH AND
AMY EINHORN

. . .

FREUD'S
MISTRESS

. . .

1

. . .

VIENNA, 1895

The season for suicides had begun.

The young woman sat at the writing desk by the window and dipped her pen into black ink. It scratched across the paper like a raven's claw. Outside, the sky was ashen gray. Since early November, the air had been bitter cold, and patches of ice had spread over the breadth of the Danube. Soon the river would be frozen solid until spring. Just the other week, she had read in the *Salonblatt* about a wealthy young aristocrat, dressed in bridal gown and veil, who jumped her steed off Kronprinz-Rudolf Bridge. The beautiful filly sank like a stone, and the woman's body washed up on the shore, shrouded in white satin.

She never thought it would come to this, but now here she was, at her sister's mercy, asking for help. She finished the letter at dawn, just as the bells of St. Stephen's rang out across the city. She sealed the envelope and placed it in the letter box outside the front door. She would remember this day. It was the beginning.

TWO DAYS EARLIER

The sky was raining ice, but the woman hurrying down the boulevard wore no coat or hat. She was carrying a bundle wrapped in stiff, coarse blankets, and the heavy load hampered her gait, causing her to favor one leg, then the other. Strands of long, wet hair lashed across her mouth and eyelids, and every few minutes she would pause, shifting the weight of her bundle onto one arm and hip, and exposing her free hand to brush the sleet off her face.

She crossed the Ringstrasse—the broad, tree-lined avenue that circled Vienna—then passed a row of massive apartment buildings, their exteriors casting glazed shadows on the cobblestones. The storm was getting worse, a constant downpour. Blinded by the wet, she continued on, splashing through puddles in her good leather boots, crossing Schwarzenbergplatz, the invisible boundary between the aristocracy and everyone else. A few hundred yards away, a row of opulent homes blazed with lights.

Earlier, in her haste to leave, she couldn't be bothered to run upstairs to get her woolen overcoat and gloves, and now she sorely regretted this rash decision. She was chilled to the bone. Idiot, she thought. My boots are ruined.

She slowed her pace and swept through the ornamental iron gates of the baroness's residence, heading around back to the servants' entrance. She rang the night bell and then knocked loudly, cursing softly and swaying with impatience. Open the damn door. There was a dull, aching pain in her side as a gust of icy wind drove her slightly off balance. She shifted the load over her shoulder, her fingers throbbing as she pounded on the door.

When the night maid finally appeared, Minna brushed past her in a fury. Took bloody long enough, she thought, but murmured a perfunctory "Good evening" and descended a dimly lit stairway to the basement kitchen. She carefully placed her bundle on a cot near "the Beast," the enormous black furnace by the scullery. A frail, drowsy child emerged from the blankets and sat there silently as Minna pushed the cot closer to the furnace, slid the thin mattress back on its frame, and settled the child beneath a feeble candle flickering on a wooden shelf.

"Fräulein Bernays, you're wanted upstairs. The mistress has been ringing for over an hour," the night maid said, adjusting her starched white cap. "Everyone suffers when you run about . . ." she added, sighing heavily as she bent over and wiped a mud print from the stairs. "I told the mistress you went for a walk, but she wasn't having any of it, said you must have gone somewhere . . ."

"If you must know, we've been out gargling gin. Haven't we, Flora?"

"Yes, Fräulein," Flora said, with a weak smile. "And *then* we went to the doctor."

"The child's delirious," Minna said. "Cover up, dear, it's freezing in here."

There was a draft coming from somewhere that made her long for dry clothes, and her head was pounding. She put her hand in her skirt pocket and fingered the brown paper parcel of medicine. Thank God—still there.

Earlier that day Minna had discovered Flora in a terrible state, attempting to do her chores but coughing so hard it brought her to her knees. Several times, Minna had dunked the pathetic little thing, wailing and hiccupping, in a cold bath to break the fever, but nothing seemed to work. The child was doomed, her cheeks shining with fever, the sweating sickness getting worse and worse. Minna could stand it no longer. She bundled her up and, without a word to anyone, set out to take the child to the doctor.

"My throat hurts," Flora whimpered, struggling for breath, as Minna rang the bell at the physician's office.

"He'll take care of you," she answered with an air of conviction she did not feel. "You're the baroness's charge, and very important."

An elderly gentleman appeared in the doorway, blotting his mustache with a linen napkin. Minna could see a woman sitting at the dining table across the room, and there was an aroma of boiled beef and wine.

"Herr Doctor, my employer, the Baroness Wolff, wishes immediate treatment for this child. She is most concerned."

The doctor hesitated a moment as Minna pushed by him, launching into a litany of the child's ailments: fever, coughing, nausea, loss of appetite. There was little reason to doubt her authority. Even without her overcoat, and despite the muck on her clothes, she was an elegant woman—willowy with a straight back, smooth skin, and perfect diction. In addition, she was a most convincing liar.

"Could she possibly have scarlet fever?" Minna asked, as the doctor led her to his offices in the back.

"Unspecified infection . . ." he concluded after an examination. "Bed rest for at least a month . . . linens changed twice a week . . . lozenges for the sore throat and Bayer's Heroin for her cough . . ."

Minna listened, nodding her head in agreement, all the while knowing what the doctor advised would be impossible to carry out in this household. In any event, how in heaven's name did Minna ever think she could get away with this? Her days, her evenings, even her Sundays belonged to the baroness. She was expected to serve at the pleasure of her employer, and tardiness often meant instant dismissal.

Minna thought of Herr Doctor's orders as she laid her hand on Flora's clammy forehead.

"Don't leave me," the child said, slightly bewildered, her voice hoarse and strained. She was ten, but looked six, and she clutched Minna's skirt, sensing a departure. Minna gave Flora two spoonfuls of the sticky, sweet-smelling syrup and whispered something in her ear. The child lay back down and turned her head to the wall.

The night maid eyed Minna as she pinned a few damp wisps of hair into her small bun, pointedly wiped the heels of her boots with a rag, and left the kitchen with no comment. She climbed back up the narrow stairwell, making her way through the marble-floored entrance hall, and then hurried down a vaulted corridor lit by a series of imported electric lights. She stopped briefly just outside the crimson drawing room and caught her breath, then knocked softly.

"You may enter," a voice called.

The baroness's inner sanctum looked like the kind of room that no one ever visited. Rich, heavy damask chairs and sofas, stained-glass shades, Persian carpets, and a collection of porcelain that included pug dogs, poodles, and exotic birds. There was a bowl of lilies on an inlaid side table, and in the corner near the window, a writing desk with a silver tray filled with tea cakes and snow-white sandwiches. Outwardly, Minna was calm, but her face was flushed and her heart racing, as if she had just broken a valuable vase. Also, the smell of the baroness's tea cakes reminded her that she had not eaten a morsel the entire day.

"Good evening, Baroness."

"The others are talking about you," the young woman replied abruptly, her voice pinched and refined. She was sitting in her perversely torturous corseted dress and examining Minna with a gaze that could sear the skin off a rabbit. "Would you like to hear what they're saying? They talk about your peculiarities—your constant reading and your walking about and such. Things I put up with at great inconvenience to myself. Things I've managed to ignore. You're late. Where have you been?"

"I went to the chemist. Flora is sick," Minna said.

"You think I haven't noticed," the baroness responded, beckoning Minna to sit down across from her. Minna hesitated. Her skirt was still damp and would leave a mark on the sofa's delicate fabric. She sat gingerly on the edge, extricating a silk pillow and pushing it aside.

"I'm not a monster, after all. I myself told Cook last week to give the little creature daily doses of camphor."

That would have been the first decent thing the baroness had ever done for her, Minna thought. The unfortunate Flora had been hired from the country to work as one of the general servants in the large baroque residence. Even upon her arrival, the little girl was thin and pale, too fragile for this kind of employment. She had straw-colored hair, eyes the color of sherry, and spent the better part of her day in the basement kitchen, choking on thick black clouds of fumes and smoke. Her duties ran from cleaning the boiler and emptying the fireplaces to scraping pots and cleaning privies. At night, Minna had frequently seen her crying herself to sleep.

"The camphor's been useless. She needed—"

The baroness held up her finger in warning, cutting Minna off. "I'll decide when my staff needs medication. And, by the way, when I had my sore throat last week, I didn't notice you running to the chemist for me."

There was a tense pause as the baroness adjusted the fringed pillows on her Empire sofa. "I must say, I've never had much luck with you people. I rarely hire anyone from the Second District, but you came so highly recommended. . . ."

Minna did not contradict her. She had never lived in the Second District, Leopoldstadt, where most of Vienna's middle-class Jews resided, but she had often felt the sting of anti-Semitism. When she was a child, she sometimes took revenge upon schoolchildren who taunted her with a barrage of bigoted slurs, one time hitting a boy so hard she bloodied his nose. But as she grew older, she found it was something best to ignore, although she still felt a chill at the nape of her neck every time she encountered it.

"Rest assured, my only concern is for the child," Minna said in a low, firm voice.

"Your concern should be for your employment. You're a lady's companion. And as far as I can tell, you haven't had any medical training."

"But I have. I was employed by a doctor in Ingolstadt."

"What's his name?" the baroness asked, skeptically.

"Herr Dr. Frankenstein," Minna shot back in a blithe tone.

The baroness stared at Minna for a moment in surprise and then smiled slyly as she registered the joke. She stood up and walked to the fireplace, gathering her basket of needlework. "Now, Minna," she continued, in a conciliatory tone of voice, "you must apologize so we can carry on."

"I apologize," she said promptly, although the sentiment wasn't there.

"I accept your apology," she said. "In any event, the girl has never been quite right. Weak and consumptive."

The baroness gazed into the mirror over the mantel and touched her elaborately upswept hair.

"What do you think of this hairstyle? It's the same as Clara's. She wore it to the Imperial Palace last week."

"It suits you," Minna replied, staring at the ridiculous bouffant pompadour and wondering if anyone on the face of the earth would be able to keep a straight face looking at it.

"Good, then, I'll keep it for now," she said with a dismissive wave, settling herself back on the sofa with her needlework on her lap.

The light was fading and shadows darkened the room. Faint sounds of horses' hooves and carriage wheels on cobblestones drifted through the heavy, swagged draperies and an occasional servant's voice echoed through the halls. The baroness's smooth white hands moved quickly as she concentrated on the pastoral scene she was embroidering on linen. Pale verdant greens, lush lavender sky, and a shepherd tending his flock.

Afterward, Minna climbed the two sets of stairs to her room, immediately pulling off her wet muslin skirt, flannel petticoat, woolen stockings, and unbuttoning the twenty buttons of her white cotton shirt. Her bone-crushing corset was pressing on her rib cage, and she exhaled thankfully as she unlaced it, tossing it on the floor. She needed to dry off. She was beginning to smell like wet dog. The room was dark, matching her mood—the walls an unhealthy shade of arsenic green. She put on her nightdress and carried a candle to the dressing table, her shadow following her.

Minna leaned her head back and began brushing her thick auburn hair, gathering it into combs. In her youth, she had been conscious of the wealth of her hair and her tall, slim figure. But over the years vanity had disappeared. The fine planes of her face and neck were still in evidence, but even in the candlelight she could see delicate lines around her eyes.

She never imagined that at this point in her life, at almost thirty years old, she would be standing by silently while a young woman, barely her age, scolded her and nearly let a poor child die like a dog. Minna would have been married by now, like her sister, Martha, if life had turned out differently, if her father hadn't lost his money and dropped dead on the street, if her fiancé hadn't died. If, if, if . . .

There was no sense going back over it. She had been on her own for years. No one else in the family could support her—Martha had a growing family; her brother, Eli, had married and moved away; so she fell back on the only options remaining to her—lady's companion or governess. She had to make her own way in this world, and it looked as if she would be moving on again soon.

She wrapped her shawl around her shoulders, hugging her body and pressing her fingers into her upper arms. She was tired. And her neck hurt. She drifted over to the balcony and looked out the window to the north.

A shot of gin would be nice, she thought, but she'd settle for a cigarette. She lit one of the thin Turkish smokes she kept in her bottom dresser drawer. The downpour had subsided into a slate-colored gloom and she inhaled deeply.

Often, late at night, when her duties were done, Minna would read until the candle drowned in a pool of fat. A hefty chunk of her wages went for books, but not the silver fork novels about maids fornicating in the attic and randy masters with roaming eyes. And not the eternally boring memoirs, the "remember me" books that she'd save until after her eyesight was gone. No, she preferred the big books, wading through Thomas Carlyle's *The French Revolution*, which was better than Edward Freeman's *History of the Norman Conquest*, but not especially enlightening. She struggled with turgid passages from Darwin's *On the Origin of Species* and works by Heraclitus and Parmenides—the heart of which wrestled with questions of existence.

And then there was Aristotle, whom she threw aside after discovering that he considered women one of nature's deformities—*an unfinished man*. She sold that volume with no regrets. Plato wasn't much better on the subject, insisting that women were less competent than men. Then again, she couldn't dismiss every philosopher simply because of his narrow-minded convictions. After all, Nietzsche, whom she adored, viewed women as merely possessions . . . a property predestined for service. And Rousseau believed a woman's role was primarily to pleasure men. It was dispiriting, actually.

But there was nothing to aggravate her in literature. In fact, it was the perfect antidote for those feelings of boredom, dread, and loneliness. She chose Goethe's epistolary *The Sorrows of Young Werther* and Shakespeare's *Henry VI* (Part Two, not Part One, which was more of a historical treatise and one of Shakespeare's weakest dramas, in her opinion). For sheer entertainment it was Mary Shelley's Gothic thriller *Frankenstein*, which she'd consumed in one sitting. And then there was that avant-garde Viennese author named Schnitzler, who had given up his medical practice to write plays about aristocratic heroes and their adulterous affairs. No irony, no moralizing, just a frank, unemotional study of the phenomenon of passion. She'd never read anything quite like it. An acquired taste, this Schnitzler—like olives or caviar or Klimt. But this was not a night to lose oneself in gin, tobacco, and biblio-mania.

She pulled on her boots under her nightclothes, not bothering to fasten the tedious number of buttons, and made her way back down to Flora's claustrophobic little nook. The child was curled up on the cot, clutching her rag doll.

Normally Minna would sit with Flora and tell her stories, but at the moment, Flora was in no mood. She wanted what any child her age would want. She wanted her mother and she wanted to go home. Minna sat down next to her and held her in her arms as Flora snug-gled in, laying her cheek against her chest. She gently stroked her hair and hummed softly until she saw Flora's eyelids flutter and then close. Minna breathed a sigh of relief when the child finally fell asleep.

The next morning, the baroness received a note from her doctor inquiring as to the child's health and explaining that "after-hours" calls were charged at a premium.

"You're dismissed," the baroness had said with a petulant frown, looking away as she informed Minna that all wages would be garnished. The usual nastiness associated with an infuriated employer and an unrepentant employee wasn't there. Minna stood justly accused. No vehement protestations. There would be no point. Especially in light of what Minna intended to do next.

An hour or so later, after the baroness left for the day, Minna packed up her bags and left them by the servants' entrance. Then she informed the staff that she and Flora had been "let go," and took the bewildered child to the Wien Westbahnhof. She was send-ing Flora home.

Flora was from a small village outside Linz, where the winters were long and the people worked at hardscrabble jobs in iron foundries, mines, or factories. There was, in Flora's life, privation and tragedy—a sister had died of diphtheria, a brother was imprisoned, and no one knew anything about the father, a general laborer who had disappeared long ago. But Flora clearly adored her mother. "She has golden hair," she told Minna one night, "like a fairy."

Minna wrapped her arms around the girl's small body and they huddled on the platform, half frozen, watching travelers gather at the gate—women with embroidered fur-collared jackets and fancy traveling valises, children with curled hair and warm overcoats. The girl seemed calm now, relieved.

When the train pulled up, Minna and Flora walked past the uniformed porters who were standing by private first-class cars with elaborate sitting rooms and electric lights. She helped the child into the third-class cabin, settling her on a hard wooden bench between two matrons, one of whom had a sleeping baby on her lap.

"Don't come back," she had wanted to say, as she brushed Flora's warm cheek with a kiss, and pressed a few kronen into the matron's hand, getting her assurance that she would see the child home. But she knew Flora would be sent off somewhere else in a few months. That was her fate. Minna felt a visceral charge of longing and regret. She would have liked, at the very least, to have felt she was setting Flora free.

Minna watched the train lumber away and stood alone on the empty platform as the severity of her situation finally hit her. There would be no recommendation from the baroness, that was for certain. Her money was woefully depleted, and she had no hope for future employment. She hailed an omnibus and rode along the jumbled, cobblestoned streets, trying to ignore the panic building up inside her. She was beginning to think that finding the perfect position was never going to happen. It was exhausting trying to sustain the feeling that she was just one step away from happiness.

She checked into a modest pension near the Danube, but sleep did not come easily. The hours drifted by, she dozed, she read, she paced. The clock ticked loudly on the dresser as she sat down finally to write to her sister. There was no one else. Not even her mother, who barely got by on her widow's pension. She was facing another failure.

She had been fired several times before and she had quit more times than that. With every setback, Minna would insist that she was fine, she liked her independence, her freedom, her time in the café reading and talking. And with every setback, her sister would turn to her in pity and pat her consolingly on the arm.

"Poor Minna. You know you never get a moment's peace when you work for those people. . . ."

She wanted a bath and a change of clothes, but her bags were still at the baroness's house—probably dumped in the alley by now. As soon as the day porter came on duty, she would send for them. She finished the letter to her sister and sealed it. For years, Martha had indicated that her husband, Sigmund, couldn't afford another person in the house. Now, according to her sister, things had turned around. His medical practice had improved. He had more patients. There was a sixth child. Mathilde, Martin, Oliver, Ernst, Sophie, and now Anna. Maybe they needed her.

Minna hoped Sigmund would be in favor of the situation. Their relationship had always been cordial. No, more than cordial. During the past several years, they had shared a lively correspondence concerning subjects of interest to them both: politics, literature, and his scientific work.

Minna closed her eyes and imagined Martha opening the letter and sending for her immediately. She held that image in her mind. And she, who had never been dependent on relatives, felt the immense relief of the ignorant.

2

. . .

Minna stood on the frozen, grimy curb, shivering in her coat. Her fingertips burned with the cold as she hailed a hansom cab, her spirits buoyed by the thought of settling somewhere. "Come home at once, my dear Minna," her sister had said in an entirely persuasive manner. "The children miss you terribly. We'll expect you before dinner."

The sky was overcast, the wind blowing off the river, another brutally cold November morning as Minna set out to join her sister. The spindly coachman was initially courteous when he first pulled over, but then glowered as she stepped aside to reveal her belongings lined up on the sidewalk, as if she'd been evicted. He grumbled as he hefted her bags into the luggage compartment of the carriage, and now, as she rode through the empty streets, the man's clucking sounds were nearly as loud as the clopping of the stepper's hooves.

Wie lange dauert's? she had asked. How much longer? He seemed to be taking the "scenic route" around the Ring, passing every neoclassical, Renaissance, and baroque building and pointing out each one's distinguishing features. "The Hofburgtheater was founded by the Emperor in 1874. . . . The Hofoper was inaugurated by His Highness not that long afterward, and the Hofmuseum. . . ." Perhaps he's angling for a bigger tip, she thought, as she looked out at Vienna's wedding-cake skyline, with its snow-capped, pointed turrets and Gothic flourishes.

Martha's words had been reassuring, it was true, but Minna was coming around to the unfortunate fact that this was a rescue, not an invitation. It had not been her choice to impose on her sister, who could hardly say no. How demoralizing at this stage in her life to be in this position. On the other hand, for the moment, this home was a sanctum for her depleted spirits.

Minna nervously looked at the little gold watch dangling from her mother's bow pin. She knew how her sister felt about tardiness. Dinner, the *Mittagessen* meal (soup, meat, vegetables, and a sweet), was always served precisely at one, and not a minute later. People did not drift in and out of Martha's dining room. And all chores were performed with military precision. Martha's rules. She would be living under Martha's rules. As was fitting. This was Martha's house, Martha's husband, Martha's children.

The Freuds lived in the Ninth District on a steep, unprepossessing street. One end bordered a respectable residential neighborhood, while the lower end swept down to the disheveled Tandelmarkt, huddled near a canal of the Danube.

The coachman reined in the horses, and his mouth. One more description of a *Hof* palace, a *Hof* theater, or a *Hof* anything, and Minna would have wrung his *Hof* neck. When the carriage finally pulled up to Berggasse 19, she paid him (including a decent tip—it *was* freezing up there) with the last of her savings. She arrived at her sister's house without money and without a plan.

She always thought her sister's apartment building had an

ennobling facade—high ornamental windows, baroque and classical features, an air of grandeur to it if one didn't look at the stores on the ground floor. On the left of the entrance leading into the apartment was Kornmehl's kosher butcher shop and on the right, Wiener's co-operative grocery. The Freud children were bundled in coats and crowded on the front stairs, waiting to greet her.

"How long are you going to *sthay*, Aunt Minna?" asked four-year-old Sophie, a pink-cheeked, curly-haired cherub with an impressive lisp, who couldn't quite manage a smile. The rest of the children surrounded Minna as she climbed out of the carriage, a few of them sniffling and rubbing their eyes.

Before Minna could answer, she heard seven-year-old Oliver call back to his mother, "Mama, where is she going to sleep? I thought Papa said there was no room."

Martha appeared in the doorway, shooing the children aside like pigeons.

"Darling Minna. Here you are," Martha said, rising on tiptoes and kissing her sister on both cheeks.

"Martha, I can't tell you how much . . ."

"Stop. Don't say another word, my dear. We're the lucky ones."

Minna put her arms around her sister and then stepped back and looked at her. She hadn't seen Martha since the birth of Anna and was somewhat unnerved by her appearance. Her lusterless hair was parted down the middle and pulled back in an uncompromising bun, her expression tense and edgy. She looked like someone who had just come out of hiding—her puffy, red-ringed eyes pouched with purple bags, her usual meticulous attire rumpled and slightly askew. Martha had always been "the pretty sister," blessed with a gentle, oval face, pale complexion, and a Cupid's bow upper lip that gave her demeanor just the right amount of allure.

But now, after six pregnancies, she seemed blurred around the edges, and the only overall impression one got of her was fatigue.

"I've been so worried about you," Martha said, as she clasped Minna's hand and led her into the apartment. Sophie, Oliver, and yet more children herded behind them, loitering in the hallway and shoving one another aside, trying to lead the way.

They walked slowly through the stolid bourgeois apartment, past rosewood consoles, Biedermeier tables, fatigued Persian carpets, and draperies that trailed on the floor. There was a light smell of furniture oil and floor polish. The children followed behind, their sense of decorum gradually disintegrating. Oliver and Martin tore through the drawing room like little hellions, toppling a chair, while the girls yanked Minna's sleeve, vying for her attention.

Minna's bedroom was small and oddly shaped, the former dressing area of the master suite with a long, narrow window over the bed. A jug of water was placed beside the washbasin, a gas lamp was on the dresser, and fresh, laundered sheets were laid out on the bed. There was a small fireplace, bordered with decorative tiles, and an ornate wooden wardrobe was squeezed into the corner.

Martha led her into the room and pulled back the white muslin curtains, letting the soft afternoon light flood across the shiny wood floor. She poured a glass of water and handed it to Minna.

"You look thin, my dear. Are you eating well?" Martha asked, watching her sister thoughtfully as she sat on the edge of the bed.

The two sisters still resembled each other—their eyes the same dark color, their noses straight, and their hair thick and wavy, although Minna inherited her father's lean frame, while Martha was becoming the image of their plump, matronly mother. In their youth, the difference in their stature was not as apparent, but over the years, it had become more pronounced.

There was a banging at the open door as eight-year-old Martin, the eldest Freud son, struggled in melodramatically with her suitcases. He might be handsome in a few years, Minna thought, but at the moment, he was gawky and slightly chubby, with a pronounced bruise under his right eye. Martha had often complained that the child was always getting into trouble, constantly coming home with skinned knees, black eyes, and ominous notes from other children's mothers.

"What happened to your eye?"

"Nothing," he said. "How long are you staying?"

"Just through dinner," Minna answered.

"Really?" he replied hopefully, giving Minna the distinct impression that the matter of the "maiden aunt" hadn't yet been settled between his parents.

3

. . .

I t's lovely," Martha said, admiring the fine fabric of a silk dinner gown that Minna was unpacking.

"A gift from a former employer. Well, not exactly a gift. The baroness thought it was outdated and told me to get rid of it," Minna said, smiling. Then a childhood memory washed over her. She and Martha were planning for the first social event of the season. It was a different time and place, and it all seemed so frivolous now.

Martha was eighteen, and, in the eyes of her many suitors, female perfection—five feet two; a small, pretty face; dainty hands and feet. On this particularly splendid fall day, she had the rosy glow of a morning walk still on her cheeks and she looked pristine in her soft gray suit and matching boots. She and Minna made their way across the broad Ringstrasse, past St. Stephen's and the opera house, and into the heart of the old city, where the family dressmaker had a small shop. The first "smart" party of the season was still months away, but Martha had already decided on the material for her gown: seven yards of extra-wide yellow brocade (no crinoline—too vulgar and old-fashioned) that would be measured, cut, and sewn into a tightly corseted, tyrannizing shape, emphasizing Martha's tiny waist and modest derriere.

The shop was located on a crooked, dark street with medieval cobblestones and was sandwiched between a perfumery and a fine cabinetmaker's studio that reeked of lacquer. As the two girls entered, they were instantly marooned in silk. Scores of fat, luscious fabric bolts leaned up against the walls, blocking the aisles and windows, along with boxes spilling over with trimmings, bows, feathers, and fringe. Minna fingered the rich French weaves, the intricate Italian prints, the satin velours in jade and garnet and shimmering gold. But where were the prices? she wondered. Not a tag in sight.

"Martha, how much do you suppose . . ."

"Oh, Minna, look. It's Prussian blue velvet," Martha replied, transfixed.

"Your friends will be Prussian green with envy," Minna said with a grin.

At fourteen, Minna was taller than her older sister, almost unfashionably so, with abnormally long legs and neck, and collarbones that stuck out from her blouse. She did not yet go to socials, like her sister, nor did she even own one grown-up party dress. She glanced at herself, then at her sister in the dressing-room mirror. She did this on a regular basis, hoping her image would magically shrink down to that of her sister's, but, alas, it was not to be, something that made her glad in the years to come.

Minna, however, was comforted by some things. Both she and Martha had the same fine-boned Bernays profile and their skin was white and spotless. But her feet were gargantuan compared to Martha's, and by the time Minna was eight, the two couldn't even share boots or slippers. Then there was her hair, always falling out of its braid and ending up in unruly wisps around her face. And the matter of her handwriting. It was smudgier than Martha's, the tutor never failed to point that out, while grudgingly conceding that Minna was the "student" in the family.

After the fitting, the two sisters walked arm in arm past the architectural infinity of the Ring and the ornate facades of apartment houses, and then along the Kärntner Strasse, past the cathedral. Those days, one could hardly go anywhere without seeing military officers in full regalia, and a group of them smiled at the sisters and touched their helmets. Then it was just a few more streets down to the canal and the wholesale merchant mart, where they bought hot, sticky cream cakes in paper cones and waved at the people in passing boats. At that moment their world was secure and uncomplicated, and they were thankful in a way most young girls were not. The past had been a nightmare.

Ten years earlier, when the family lived in Hamburg, their father, Berman Bernays, was sent to jail for bankruptcy fraud. He had been wrongfully accused, of that Minna was certain. Nevertheless, for years there was a lingering tinge of embarrassment that blighted family gatherings and other social events. While he was in prison, Minna's mother assumed a haughty air of contempt to counteract the disgrace; and her older brother, Eli, dropped out of school, abandoned his friends, and went to work for an uncle from Kiev who peddled dry goods up and down the countryside. Eli would disappear for weeks on end to God knows where, then reappear dispirited and drained of energy, wearing rumpled clothes and smelling of sausage and cabbage. He would rail about the filth and disease of the villages, the crowded rooming houses with no lavatories, but most of all, he hated the life of an itinerant peddler. (Ah, well, thought Minna, he showed them all, moved to America with his own family, richer now than any of them.)

She would never forget the day her father finally came home. He stood in the doorway, looking half-dead, his hair grown gray and wispy, his beard matted on his chin. His appearance hit her like a stone, and stunned the rest of the family into silence. Martha recoiled when he drew near her, so he turned to Minna.

"My little *shana madel*," he said, using the endearment he had called her since she was born, "my beautiful girl." He threw out his arms and hugged her close, and she could feel his bones through his sweater.

Later that evening, as they lit the Sabbath lights, the family was quiet, careful, but Minna's mother's voice assumed a tone of anger mixed with anxiety that, even years later, never went away. Her resentment increased when Minna's father found a new position as a secretary to a well-known economist and moved the family to a modest house on the outskirts of the Jewish district of Vienna. There was a solid Jewish middle class there, he had argued, and many of his friends had grown wealthy and powerful under the Hapsburg monarchy. Hundreds of Jewish families like their own had streamed into the city in those days, escaping the growing movement of anti-Semitism in the countryside outside Hamburg, and seeking opportunity and culture unequaled in Europe. But his reasoning fell on deaf ears. Emmeline missed her native Germany and blamed Berman for their disgrace and economic hardship. After all, her family had been socially prominent, if not wealthy, and the calamity of his imprisonment had taken away their good name.

"Vienna oppresses me," she said peevishly. "The noise from the street is unbearable. And all those ugly steeples!"

"I like it here," Minna would respond, cool and defiant, indirectly defending her father. "It's so boring in the country. There's nothing to do in Hamburg."

While her mother went on and on, listing her grievances about the city, "the jaded avant-garde, the damp weather, the shabby synagogue . . ." her father would retreat to his chair, smiling wanly. Later on, Minna would sit by his side, and they would play cards or read. She would often think of these moments, when it was just the two of them.

The night before he died, Minna and her father went out for their usual evening stroll. There was always a burst of vitality and life on the streets of Vienna, and Minna loved to look at the handsomely clad men in silk top hats and the women in elaborate feathered hats, fashionable gowns, and glossy fur capes as they gathered in the grand entrance of the Hotel Imperial and the popular Café Central. She would watch sleek black carriages arrive at restaurants filled with people smoking and laughing and drinking bitterbrewed *Kaffee mit Schlag*. The air was filled with mist and light and music. And, Minna thought, as much as my mother hates this city, this is how much I love it.

She could remember the exact moment when she got the news. She was back at the dress shop, discussing which of Martha's many suitors would fill up her dance card, when a white-faced Eli burst through the door. Berman had been crossing the Ringstrasse at a busy intersection when he collapsed in the middle of the street. According to passersby, he had stood still for a moment, clutching his arm, and then dropped in a heap on the cobblestones, a carriage swerving suddenly to miss him. He was just fifty-three years old. Dead from a massive heart attack.

For the next few days, everything was focused on arranging the burial, which according to Jewish tradition, had to take place two days after the death. Emmeline was inconsolable and even more sharp-tongued than usual. She sat in the drawing room, alone at the end of the sofa, her needlework untouched on her lap. Curtains were drawn, mirrors covered with black crepe, and clocks stopped at the time of death.

"We are left with nothing, girls. Nothing."

Emmeline's anger was matched by Minna's unimaginable disappointment. She was astounded at the loss, at the cold, dark silence filling the space that once was his. The universe seemed so unjust, so empty and thin.

In accordance with Jewish law, the family sat shiva for seven days. No bathing or showering. They wore torn black ribbons on their lapels and listened as the rabbi, who stopped by several times a day, led them in the mourners' Kaddish. Minna couldn't stand all the consoling visitors with moist eyes. She couldn't stand all the food and wine and socializing. In her fourteen-year-old brain, it felt as if everything had turned to dirt.

Their mother, Emmeline, used this tragedy to further her campaign to leave Vienna for their former, more modest home in the countryside outside Hamburg. Neither sister wanted to move, but their mother persevered. During this period, they lived on the generosity of aunts, uncles, and Eli, their older brother, who was now making a good living as a businessman.

In those days, the girls were confidantes, allying themselves against their mother. But eventually Minna became the stronger one, more outspoken, able to fight the necessary battles to ensure what little pleasures they had left. When they wanted to go out, it was always Minna who braved their mother's temperamental moods and voiced the request. Consequently, Martha became the favorite, a fact their mother did little to hide, and Minna did little to pretend she didn't know. Martha was dutiful, soft-spoken, and acquiescent, while Minna was independent and fearless. Those were their appointed roles, and it was really no different now, even though Martha was married and Minna had been on her own for years.

I s this alcohol, Tante Minna?" Martin asked.

"No," she lied as she stashed the bottle along with the cigarettes in the bottom drawer of the dresser.

He continued to hover like a vulture as she opened the smaller of her cases and pulled out a small portfolio of her correspondence and a photograph of her mother in a widow's cap.

"I could stay and help if you want," he said, watching with sharp, bright eyes as each item was pulled from the valise.

She wished she had something to give him. In the past, she had always brought little things for the children, fancy bags of glass marbles or postcards with pictures of Emperor Franz Josef or Prussian soldiers with elaborate helmets and sabers. (There were also a few postcards she knew he'd like of the emperor's mistress, a famous Viennese actress draped in a diaphanous gown—Hapsburg Cheesecake, everyone called it. These she *wouldn't* give him, even if she had the money.) Nevertheless, the Flora incident had been expensive, and she was forced to send Martin on his way empty-handed.

She watched him walk slowly down the hall, then sat on the bed, even more disappointed than the child. She could hear the distant sounds of bustling, midday crowds at the Tandelmarkt, cries from boatmen on the Danube canal, jingly bells of a parish church, and the clattering and rinsing of saucepans from the kitchen. From across the hall came the shrill noise of squabbling children and a howling baby.

Martha smiled sympathetically at her sister.

"You know, Minna. It's very important—very, very, important—to be surrounded by one's family."

"I agree," Minna answered with a slight grin. "As long as it's not Mother."

Martha laughed appreciatively.

Both of them knew that their mother had been on an active campaign to marry Minna off. After all, she only wanted what all practical-minded mothers wanted—her aging, not-so-eligible daughter safely married. How many times since her fiancé's death had Minna heard her mother tell her she needed to be less haughty with her words, less imaginative? Minna had paid a penalty for her nature, Emmeline argued, and as a result she would remain single. Also, she was too bookish, too biased, and intolerant of people who disagreed with her. The last time Minna visited Hamburg, her mother had advised, "You should talk less of Gounod operas and more of other subjects, or better yet, talk less in general. Most men don't appreciate a bright wit, unless it's their own."

To Emmeline, women like Minna were marginalized, surplus daughters with mediocre prospects, never fitting in, as if constantly suffering from a mild illness or having a physical disfigurement. This was an argument that Minna could never win. It was a good thing she wasn't Catholic. Her mother might have stabled her in a distant convent.

"Now don't get angry . . ." Martha said, hesitating, "but you know she only has your best interests at heart."

"All she cares about is one thing. . . ." Minna said, pulling her few remaining books from the suitcase and setting them on the dresser, using the Dickens and the Kipling as bookends.

"Well, one must be somewhat realistic. A woman alone . . ." she said, running her fingers through her hair, a habit Minna remembered since childhood, whenever Martha thought she might offend.

"So what are you saying? That I should have married that friend of Eli's, that salesman from Hamburg?" Minna asked, digging through her valises.

"No, not him. Wasn't he the one you kept calling the Merchant of Venice? What are you rummaging around for?"

"A husband," Minna teased.

The two sisters laughed, their faces bending toward each other as if they were gossiping at a tea.

"Well, if that's the case, Sigmund has a colleague I'd like you to meet. Dr. Silverstein. Socially prominent. A lifelong bachelor. But at this age, there's always something . . ."

"Martha, please. Let me settle in a bit before you start all this."

"Start what?" Martha asked innocently.

"It's just that . . ."

"It's *always* just this or that. You must admit, there were others . . . after Ignaz died. Respectable others. You were too busy . . . or too . . . I don't know. . . ."

Martha had always believed that Minna could get married anytime she wanted. She just needed to be more pliable, or at least pretend to be. Men weren't amused by women who were unconventional—straying from the norm and bringing chaos into their lives.

Minna, on the other hand, had always believed that marrying merely for security sentenced one to a lifetime of boredom. But she looked into her sister's worried face and decided to appease her.

"All right, my dear," Minna said indulgently, "the next time you see Prince Charming, send him my way."

4

. . .

M inna dear, sit next to Sigmund," Martha said, motioning
to two empty chairs at the far end of the table. "Where are
those children? I ask you, how difficult is it for everyone to be on
time?"

Minna looked around the somber dining room. She had never
liked the crimson-flocked wallpaper and oppressive velvet curtains, which gave the room a stuffy, funereal atmosphere. If she
could pull down the drapes, she would, and, she thought, she'd also
refinish the beef-colored mahogany table. But all of this, including
the elaborate rosewood sideboard, was de rigueur in every proper
dining room. The only unique touch was the couch, placed for no
apparent reason at the far end of the room and smothered in Persian carpets. What they used it for was a mystery.

"Light the candles, will you, dear?" Martha asked, fussing over
the flowers. She disappeared into the kitchen as the children saun-
tered in unhurried, and headed toward their assigned seats—Oliver
next to Sophie, with Martin and ten-year-old Mathilde across from
them. Mathilde was the oldest child and the acknowledged beauty

of the family. It didn't take her more than two minutes to start bossing the others around.

"Wipe your nose, Oliver. Have you no manners? It's disgusting. Sophie, hurry up!"

The baby, Anna, was with Frau Josefine in the upstairs nursery, and six-year-old Ernst, as Martin told Minna, was still at speech therapy. Ernst had a lisp even more pronounced than that of his sister Sophie, and after years of erupting with incomprehensible phrases, he was now seeing a specialist.

The children all had that scrubbed-behind-the-ears look: neat pigtails and lace pinafores for the girls, and crisp linen sailor shirts and knickerbockers for the boys. Minna attempted to talk with each one, but they were all so animated and impossibly fidgety that she found it difficult to follow the different strands of conversation, particularly when they were all speaking at the same time. As the noise level rose, Martha flitted back and forth into the kitchen, checking on the biscuits, the beef, getting this child a glass of water, that child a napkin, removing an elbow or a leg from the arm of a chair, and, at one point, bending over and picking up a wad of lint from the floor.

"What on earth . . ." she murmured to no one in particular, then sighed and sat stiffly in her chair.

Minna smoothed her high-necked, white silk blouse, thinking that the room smelled like Sunday. She had taken off the jacket of her traveling suit and loosened the hair from her bun when she was upstairs in her bedroom, but now she felt suddenly underdressed compared to the formality of the dining table. Lace tablecloths, silver candlesticks, good china, vases of flowers. Martha straightened her place setting and fixed her eyes on the door.

"Sigmund's lecture must have run over again. . . . I simply don't understand it . . . talking endlessly to his students when he knows we're waiting . . . or maybe he took the long way around the Ring . . . he's sure to catch his death."

A uniformed maid, carrying a steaming soup tureen, marched in from the kitchen as Sigmund simultaneously appeared through double doors. It certainly wasn't the first time Minna saw him, but it felt that way. He walked into the room and gave her a curious smile. He was handsomer than she remembered, with a heftier build and finer clothes. In fact, he was impeccably groomed, wearing a pinstriped, three-piece wool suit and a black silk cravat. There was a simple gold chain, a chain that had belonged to her father, that was attached to his watch, secured through a button-hole, with the excess length draped across his vest. In one hand, he was holding a small antiquity, a solid bronze figurine, and in the other, a cigar. His hair was thick and dark, slightly graying at the temples. And then there were the eyes. Intense. Dark. Appraising.

Minna thought back to when she first met him, a new suitor for Martha. He was standing in the parlor of their home in Vienna, a poor Jew from the wrong side of town, whose family had neither social standing nor wealth. He was looking at Martha, and Minna was looking at him. It was twilight, the time when day and night slur together at a certain moment and then all the colors of the day fade to black. Her sister had been introduced to him a month before, but by the end of this particular visit the stage was set for both of them. Martha was almost giddy when she talked about him. But not their mother, a woman from a distinguished German Jew-ish family who deemed the young doctor hardly worthy of her daughter. Nevertheless, two months later the couple was secretly engaged. Minna remembered thinking that Sigmund's wild infat-uation and pursuit of Martha didn't seem quite real. As if they were playing at being in love, the courtship taking place in both of their minds. The progression of it all was baffling, at least to Minna.

During these first visits, her sister hardly talked. Martha was a soft, delicate little creature filled with hope. And Minna was a different version of herself as well. Back then, she was tall and thin, all angles and tangled hair. Too much enthusiasm, too much talking, and far too clever. In those days, Sigmund got exactly what he wanted: an old-fashioned sweetheart, not a woman with opinions who engaged in serious conversations. Minna's role was clear from the beginning, and she was ever mindful of that fact. Minna was the intellectual and Martha was the intended. And now here they were, Martha and Sigmund, married, six children, married, married, married.

He stood there for a moment, watching Minna. She met his gaze and he gave her the same look he used to give her years ago, making her feel that it was more than simple recognition. Then he crossed the room and took his seat next to her empty chair, placing the antiquity on the table in front of him and stubbing out his cigar in a small brass ashtray.

"My dear Minna," he said, "to what do we owe this great pleasure?"

"To my getting dismissed," she said, smiling demurely. "Again."

He laughed, but her joke came at the cost of revealing her situation, which, under the circumstances, she meant to avoid. She colored slightly as she leaned over the table and lit the candles.

"Tante Minna got sacked?" Martin asked, his mouth twisted in disbelief.

"Martin, your language. Who uses such a term?" Martha said.

"Again? Has she been dismissed before?" chimed in seven-year-old Oliver, whom Sigmund had named after one of his heroes, the great puritan Oliver Cromwell.

"What would you like to drink, Minna?" said Martha. "Quinine? Beer? Wine? Sigmund, what shall we serve Minna to drink?"

"But who would dismiss Tante Minna?" Oliver persisted.

"What did you do?" Martin asked.

"No more questions," Martha said, cutting them off. "Eat your soup. Did you say wine, dear? It's wonderful to have Tante Minna here with us, isn't it?"

"Yes," Sigmund added, standing in a polite gesture as Minna finally sat down in the chair next to him.

"How fortuitous that *she* landed here. Tell me," Sigmund asked, looking straight at her, "how did we get so lucky?"

"Well, *she* happened to be working for a beastly woman who hadn't the common decency of a, I don't want to say a blood-sucking rodent, but I suppose that would be a fair comparison. Wine sounds lovely."

His eyes met Minna's for a moment with an appreciative glint. Then he looked away and leaned back with his arms crossed, just the way she remembered when she and Martha used to meet him at the café with a group of friends many years ago. He had finished his neurological training by then, and was living in a cramped, one-room flat at Vienna's General Hospital. Minna's fiancé, Ignaz Schönberg, one of Sigmund's closest friends, was also part of this little band. He was a Sanskrit scholar and a philosophy student at the university and his outbursts of Sanskrit trivia struck Sigmund as so much poppycock.

"You see, the title of this piece is *Turanga Litia*. Two thoughts, really. *Turanga* and *litia*. *Turanga*, that means 'time.' And *litia*, 'play.'

Time Play. It's a good deal more involved than that, of course. . . . One could say that . . ." Ignaz said with intensity.

"One could certainly say that," Sigmund interrupted, in a mocking tone. "Could you hand me that newspaper?"

It was the two men's habit to meet most afternoons, with Martha and Minna frequently joining them. They all had just enough money to buy one coffee each, and they nursed it for hours. Martha would mostly listen, but Minna felt no such reticence as they talked of poetry, the meaning of life, recitations of Goethe and Shakespeare, politics, and the ever-growing wave of anti-Semitism in Vienna.

On one occasion, they were arguing about Darwin's theories, the way students often did when trying to impress one another. Freud had loaned Minna his prized copy of *On the Origin of Species*, which Ignaz had already read and which Martha had no interest in whatsoever.

"Men from monkeys. Ridiculous!" Ignaz said. Poor Ignaz.

"How completely shortsighted! Do you also believe the world is flat?" Minna challenged.

"You didn't realize you were about to marry Kate," Freud said, sitting back in that exact same way he was now and folding his arms with an ironic smile.

"Kate?" Martha asked Minna.

"Yes. Your beloved Sigmund has just called me a shrew."

"No offense intended, my dear," Sigmund responded. "You know how fond I am of that particular shrew, her disagreeable demeanor notwithstanding."

"No offense taken," Minna said, secretly enjoying being compared to the heroine.

"I find that character so foul-tempered and sharp-tongued," Ignaz had said.

"Ah, but that's her great charm," Freud replied, and then recited long passages from *The Taming of the Shrew*. She could still see him as he was in the café, challenging everyone, his head raised, chin thrust forward as though his genius had dared be questioned. Even then he was impatient, filled with random, eccentric thoughts, and had an air of being the smartest person in the room. Initially, Minna would sit back and let him dominate the conversation. But then he would look for her reaction, and the two of them would end up in a dialogue of their own.

They had, in fact, for years shared a lively correspondence. It began, oddly enough, shortly after he and Martha got married. Initially, it was all about books. As a child, growing up with six sisters and an overbearing mother, Sigmund read to escape his poverty and his chaotic home life. And Minna delighted in having someone who considered her an intellectual as opposed to a strange duck.

She remembered their early letters, discussing the Romantic Lake District poets, Wordsworth and Coleridge. The classic thinkers were next. He would write about Homer and Dante, flaunting his mastery of Greek and Latin. She would have her own opinions, reading the German translations and questioning his interpretations. They both loved Dickens and the Russian writers Tolstoy and Dostoevsky. Also Shakespeare, whom, he boasted, he began reading at the age of eight.

He was passionate about the poets Schiller and Goethe, quoting long passages from both. And fascinated with the ancient worlds, extinct civilizations, gods, religion, and myths, including the story he kept going back to, *Oedipus the King*, the Sophocles play that he had translated from the Greek for his final examination at the gymnasium. Sprinkled in between, he'd complain about his practice, his colleagues, the children's constant ailments, and his inability to stop smoking. Although his letters in that regard were overwrought and filled with drama and self-pity.

"I gave up smoking again . . . horrible misery of abstinence . . . completely incapable of working . . . life is unbearable. . . ."

"Your Achilles' heel," she'd respond, then ask him about his latest research. He would send her pages detailing his "break-through" psychoanalytic techniques, including his theories about hysteria and a treatment called "the talking cure." He compli-mented her, telling her that she was a detailed and perceptive reader of his work. She had learned early on to be careful in her responses because he could be pugnacious and took offense easily.

In the past few years, she had attempted to include Martha in their literary discussions, but to no avail. Sometimes, Minna thought, rather uncharitably, but there you are, Martha had noth-ing in the way of an observed or even active inner life. She rarely read novels anymore or even the newspaper, and she still felt Shakespeare, in translation, was impossible to decipher. Except for the sonnets, which she liked. Perhaps a reminder of her early courtship, during their four-year engagement, when Freud would send them to her on a regular basis. In those days, there were at least a few authors she favored, especially Dickens, but all that seemed to fade after the children.

Martha entered from the parlor, carrying a carafe of red wine, and stopped when she noticed the boys had left the table and were wedged behind the sofa, fighting over what looked like a little toy soldier.

"Oliver, Martin, back to the table! Sigmund, where is the claret that was on the top shelf, you remember, the one the patient gave you who couldn't pay? All I could find was this *vin ordinaire*."

He shrugged, seemingly focused on his small statuette. The figurine's left arm was raised to hold a spear (now missing) and she was wearing a breastplate embossed with the Medusa's head. It was Sigmund's peculiar habit to bring one of his favorite antiquities to the dinner table, leaving the silent statue standing in front of him, like an imaginary friend. Thank goodness he didn't converse with it, Minna thought.

"First century?" Minna asked.

"Second century, Rome. Athena, goddess of wisdom and war," he replied.

"Roman, not Greek?"

"Very good. After a Greek original, fifth century, B.C.," he said, leaning to the side as Martha stood between the two of them and poured Minna a glass of wine.

"Aunt Minna?" asked Oliver. "Would you like to hear what I learned today?"

Without waiting for an answer, Oliver plunged into a detailed description of the geography of the Danube River, including all the countries it flowed through.

"The Blue Danube, which, by the way, isn't really blue. Muddy yellow is more like it. It's the longest river in Europe after the Volga, two thousand eight hundred fifty kilometers. It starts in the Black Forest and then flows east through Germany, the Hapsburg Empire, Slovakia, Romania, and Bulgaria."

"Very impressive, Oliver," Minna said, giving the precocious child free rein to continue in what became a relentless stream of names and numbers.

Minna listened attentively as Oliver then listed the cities, wondering where he might be going with all this. At some point during his recitation, the others at the table affected disinterest, as Minna grew more and more weirdly fascinated by the scene unfolding before her. Something told her there was no getting to the end with Oliver.

"There are those who think he ought to be shot," his brother Martin piped up cheerfully at one point. "He can really get on your nerves."

Oliver, ignoring Martin, continued his ardent and detailed dissertation, blithely oblivious, blurring the line between exhaustive and excessive. Meanwhile, glaciers were plunging into the sea and tree trunks grew another ring. Finally, Martha interrupted.

"I had quite a day with one of our domestics," she said. "You remember Frau Josefine's sister? The dark-haired one? She was filling in today, and first thing dropped one of our good crystal goblets. And never mind her dusting. So inefficient, I had to send the chambermaid back through. A complete disaster. My God, you don't have to be a genius to know that a dirty house breeds diseases: cholera, typhoid, diphtheria. Isn't that right, Minna?"

Minna nodded politely with a barely perceptible grimace, dreading what was coming next.

"Oh, yes," Martha continued, "household dust contains mud from the streets, horse manure, fish entrails, bedbugs, decaying animals, debris from dustbins, and—don't listen, Sophie—vermin."

Martha needn't have worried. No one was listening except Minna. No one *ever* listened when she went on and on about dirt. Minna felt obligated to show some interest, but it was exasperating, not to mention embarrassing. Oliver was still squabbling with Martin and the girls had their heads together, chattering over some secret something under the table. Freud glanced at Minna, his eyes flickering, revealing a thinly veiled annoyance, as the serving maid delivered the Viennese stew along with Tyrolean potato balls and cabbage.

"Sigmund, I gather things are going well with your practice?" Minna ventured, trying to change the subject.

"Actually, quite well. Although one can always use more patients. . . ."

"And the university? Martha tells me the lecture halls are filled. Would Herr Professor Freud mind if I listened in sometime?"

"Oh, no, no, no. He's not a professor. . . ." Martha said.

"Thank you, Martha. Thank you for reminding everyone," Freud said, glowering at his wife.

Oh, God, Minna thought. Why did she bring this up? She knew this was a sensitive subject. For the past ten years, Freud had held the title of *Privatdozent* at the University of Vienna—an unpaid lecturer in neurology—not professor. He had been nominated several times, but had been denied by the Ministry of Education and, unlike his peers, he had stubbornly refused to use political connections, known as *Protektion*, to help his promotion. As a result, year after year, he watched as his colleagues were promoted and he remained relegated to a junior position.

"He was on the list," Martha added. "With his seniority, he *should* have been next."

"That's right. Let's just regurgitate the whole story. I was passed over two years ago, passed over last year, and then, oh, yes, passed over again. Anything else you'd like to add, Martha?"

"As a matter of fact, yes," she went on, seemingly oblivious to Sigmund's growing anger. "Perhaps if you tried harder to be more cordial . . ." Martha said, refusing to let the subject die.

"Are you saying it's because of my lack of manners?"

"It's not what *I'm* saying."

"So *who* is saying it? Who would say such a thing?"

"People."

"Oh, *people*, is it?" he sneered, slamming down his fork and pushing his chair back from the table. "Which people? The *people* from the hospital? From the university? Or perhaps your little sewing circle?

"Is there nothing you can do?" Minna asked, trying in vain to neutralize the heated conversation.

"Of course there's something he might do. He might temper his conduct."

Minna shot Martha a look. Good God, doesn't she know when to stop? Even Oliver knew when to keep his mouth shut. The rest of the children were deadly quiet.

"Really, Martha. Extraordinary thing to say. Personalities have nothing to do with it. It's my theories they don't like. In fact, all my research is completely wasted on them. Sooner or later they'll have to recognize the scientific merit of my work. . . . But for now . . . who knows . . . they're all anti-Semitic anyway."

"There it is. You see, we mustn't blame ourselves, because *everyone's* anti-Semitic. That's his argument for everything," Martha said, turning to him. "There are things you could do to smooth your way. . . ."

"Such as . . . ?"

"You might . . . pay them a call . . . or send them flowers."

"This is what you're proposing? I'll be sure to do that, my dear. I'll send them *all* flowers. What a brilliant solution!" he said, erupting with angry laughter.

"You see," he added, turning to Minna as if they were the only two people in the room, "*that's* why I don't talk about my work with her."

A moment passed. Martha let out a long, melodramatic sigh, which Minna knew from childhood meant that her sister was resigned, but not defeated. Then she picked up a linen dishrag and small jug of boiling hot water that she always kept near her plate and began vigorously swabbing a bit of beef gravy that had dripped off Sophie's fork and onto the tablecloth. Minna watched in silence as Martha scrubbed the white linen. It was time to change the subject for it was clear this war would not be resolved.

"Martha," Minna asked, feigning a lighthearted air, "didn't you mention that Martin had written a poem?"

"Oh, yes," Martha said, setting down the cloth and rubbing her shoulder as if in pain. "Martin, why don't you read your poem now?"

Martin pulled a piece of paper from his pocket, rose ceremoniously from his seat, and faced Minna in what was obviously a rehearsed "welcome ceremony."

"It's called 'The Seduction of a Goose by a Fox,' " he recited.

"Let's see." Oliver smirked, snatching the paper from Martin's hand. "God! Your spelling is atrocious. How could you spell *beasts* wrong?"

Oliver sprang from his chair, as Martin bolted up after him, lunging frantically for the paper. The boys tore around the table until Oliver, equal parts thrilled and amused, crumpled the poem in a wad and threw it across the room. Minna noticed Martin's cheeks burning in humiliation. He and Oliver had always been at odds. When Ernst was around, Oliver kept to himself. Oliver, the brainy outcast, interested in math and abstract subjects. But now, with the buffer gone, he turned his attention to Martin, instinctively knowing just what drove his brother crazy.

"That's enough, boys! Stop it right now!" Martha said, standing up abruptly, holding her left arm, which had begun to shake and was now going limp. She dropped her spoon on the floor and grabbed her shoulder.

"What's wrong? What's happening?" Minna asked in alarm.

"It's just this disobedient arm."

"What are you talking about? When did this start?"

"Right after Anna was born. My arm sometimes stops working. I'm taking salicyl. Sigmund thinks it's some kind of writing paralysis, *Schreiblähmung.*"

"What's that?" Minna asked.

"It's a motor dysfunction, isn't it?" Martha asked, turning to Freud.

"Possibly . . ." he said, indifferently. "Sit down, boys!"

"And my teeth hurt, too."

"Oh, dear," Minna said, at a loss for words.

The boys hustled back to their chairs, shoving themselves into the table, Oliver smiling smugly. Freud opened his pocket watch and cleared his throat.

"I'm afraid I have to leave. I have a patient coming," he announced.

"What about the strudel?" Martha asked, still cradling her arm.

"Perhaps later."

He pulled out his chair and touched Minna lightly on the shoulder: "You're welcome to attend my lecture anytime."

"I'd be delighted," Minna answered, flattered by the invitation. And at that moment, she felt a twinge in her stomach that she could not explain.

5

. . .

All the Freud children had their peculiarities, and over the next week, Minna learned each and every one. Oliver was a kinetic tangle of energy; Martin, a chafe-cheeked troublemaker; Ernst struggled with his lisp, and little Sophie was a poor eater who couldn't sleep, even with her nightly concoction of castor oil and laudanum (an opium derivative that Martha seemed to use for every ailment). There was sibling rivalry, tantrums, and the occasional glimmer of gratitude.

At times, Minna found herself checking off a mental list of who was there and who was gone, and where the dickens were they if they weren't where they should have been, if, in fact, they should have been there? But then again, Martha was often surprisingly calm, even in situations where someone cracked his head open, jammed his finger in a door, or had a prodigious nosebleed.

Late one night, Sophie, barefoot and shivering, tiptoed through the darkened corridors to Minna's tiny bedroom. Minna hastily shoved a glass of gin and her cigarette case under the bed as Sophie approached.

"Therth's a big green monster in my room and whath's the monthly sickness, Aunt Minna?"

As Sophie crawled into bed next to her, Minna rubbed her back and read to her from *Alice's Abenteuer im Wunderland* about the caterpillar with the magic hookah. The child eventually nodded off, and the next morning, Minna took charge of Sophie's sleep habits, instituting story time in lieu of laudanum.

In contrast to the children, who were inescapable and everywhere, Freud was a ghostly presence. His contact with the children was minimal and he barely said "Good morning" or "Good evening" to anyone, including Minna. She would see him at dinner and, occasionally, at four o'clock tea. Other than that, he was solitary and self-absorbed, cloistered at the university, consulting with patients, or secluded in his study.

Minna had once read that children were either the center of one's life or they were not. And for Freud, most of the year, they were not. During the school year, the children saw little of him during the day, and most of the nights he stayed in his study, emerging only when they were asleep. Minna could understand this, given the importance and intensity of his work, but in the summer, on their vacations, he became the attentive father, taking them on hikes, mushroom hunts, and boating trips. He joked with them, telling them of his childhood, and read them stories from his favorite books. However, his behavior year-round toward Martha was unsettling. More often than not, his glances revealed his irritation, and Martha, in turn, would lapse into a kind of stylized discourse of her own, rife with nuance. It was a subtle version of survival of the fittest, talon and beak, two birds pecking away at each other and, although Minna hated to admit it, Martha usually started it.

One afternoon, Freud lingered in the parlor, reading his newspaper. He had removed his shoes and taken a tin of biscuits from the kitchen, which he dispatched with gusto, spilling crumbs all over the carpet. Then he lit a cigar and settled in his favorite chair, dumping the ashes into the upturned biscuit lid.

"So many ashes, Sigmund. And crumbs," Martha said, entering the room. "What happened to your patient?"

"Canceled," he said, not looking up.

"And your walk?"

Freud turned the page of his newspaper, ignoring her. Martha's shoulders stiffened as she glanced at the window.

"That new housekeeper left the window open. *Again.*"

"Don't close it. It's stifling in here," he said.

"Of course. I'll leave it open," she replied, as she walked to the window and shut it halfway. Then she fetched her workbasket from the stool near the fireplace, pulled up a chair near him, and began to embroider a small linen pillow.

"What are you reading?" she asked.

"The newspaper."

"Oh," she said, pausing a moment, waiting for him to elaborate.

It was obvious he was in one of his moods, giving her the distinct impression that her presence was superfluous. For want of something, anything, to say, she plowed on.

"Did you hear the Meyers are renting a villa in Florence for the entire month of August?"

He put down the paper for a moment in exasperation and relit his cigar.

"And then they're traveling to—what's that place in the Balkans? Quite exotic. Is it Marrakech? No. Help me out here, dear. What am I thinking of?" she asked.

She stood up and began dumping his cigar ashes in the dustbin.

"Constantinople?" he asked.

"No. That's not it," she answered, now grotesquely attentive, brushing away crumbs at his feet with her handkerchief. "In any event, they're always going somewhere. Last year they went to Calais. Or was it Biarritz? Are you going to your B'nai B'rith meeting this evening?"

"No."

"Gertrude told me you caused quite a stir at the last one. Her husband mentioned it. Something about your research? Is *that* why you're not going tonight?"

"I'm just buried here, in case you haven't noticed."

"Of course I've noticed. I live here, in case *you* haven't noticed. I just assumed they were offended by your research. Although I can't imagine why you'd *ever* discuss it with them. Oh, dear, what's that spot on the wall right behind the sofa?"

He put down his newspaper, regarding her incredulously.

"The spot behind the sofa," she repeated.

"What about it?"

"It's no use trying to get it out," she said. "I think an insect flew in from outside. . . ."

He took a deep breath and slowly let it out as she stared moodily at her needlework.

"And the room smells of horse manure."

He stood up, slamming the window shut as if it were the guillotine.

"Is that better?" he asked, his voice laden with reproof.

"Why, yes, my dear. Thank you," she replied with a spartan smile.

Minna couldn't tell when one of these scenes would start . . . but she knew there were many ways it could end. He could throw her off the bridge, he could stab her, he could cut out her tongue, or he could do what he always did, walk out the door and retreat to his study.

One Saturday, Minna awoke to a remarkable, springlike day which, after weeks of freezing rain, she found irresistible. The neighborhood was full of life. The windows were open in the apartment buildings across the street, and she could hear the sound of passing carriages, the muted gossip of servant girls standing on the pavement, and the whistle of a railway train in the distance. Inside, she heard the housemaids' endless click of dialogue as they stoked the stoves, brushed the grates, cleaned out the water closet, opened the shutters, and emptied the soot. Every nook and cranny of the house was attended to before breakfast.

Minna, as usual, decided to check on the baby first. Anna was sleeping in her bassinet, dressed in a milk-white nightgown edged with lace and ribbons. But shortly before dawn, her intermittent cries had turned to rage, and the wailing waxed and waned for what seemed like an eternity. Just as Minna was getting up to tend to her, she heard the nanny's tread in the hallway and a door open and close. Amazing how a baby's voice could sound harsh and soothing at the same time.

The nursery had the requisite whitewashed walls (a sterile environment to ward off infections), and it was sparsely furnished with a threadbare Chinese rug in the center of the room that looked as if it had been beaten to death. *Mrs. Beeton's Book of Household Management*, Martha's bible, suggested pounding the baby's carpet at least once a week, and under her supervision, this little bruised one was taken out daily.

Minna looked in on Martin next, the only Freud child with his own room. The boy, who was fighting a throat infection, was seated at his desk, smothered in two sweaters and a wool scarf and, when Minna appeared, he shoved a handful of toy soldiers into the drawer. Dirty clothes twisted inside out were strewn on the floor, books with injured spines piled up in a corner, biscuit wrappers and food-smeared dishes littered the bedside table. What a pigsty, Minna thought.

"How are you feeling?" Minna asked, carefully walking around a pair of ice skates with mud-crusted blades.

"I'm trying to study," he said pointedly, waiting for her to leave.

"I can see that," Minna said, reaching into the drawer and pulling out the toy soldiers. "French infantry. Very nice. History is *so* important."

"I agree," Martin said. His eyes were a bit bloodshot, but large and sympathetic.

"But not more important than arithmetic, which it seems you are failing."

"Who said?"

"Never mind."

"Who? Tell me," the child pressed. "I'm *not* failing."

"Good. That's good. Carry on, then," Minna said, picking up his math workbook from the floor and handing it to him. He reluctantly took the book, coughed like a dog, and retired to his bed.

"I'll bring you some fresh soup and those biscuits I see you like."

As he climbed into bed, Minna noticed the boy had raw

knuckles, scabby shins, and a faded black-and-blue mark on his neck. Always something with this child, she thought. A fight a week. She chose to ignore a small hole in the plaster wall, suspiciously shaped like a fist.

The oldest child, Mathilde, a ten-year-old mini-Martha, was lolling on one of Martha's best sofas in the parlor, her dirty boots resting on a velvet cushion. As Minna entered the room, she was being quizzed by the governess, Frau Schilling, an older woman with chronic allergies and a persistent wheeze who used purgatives and syrup of poppies with shocking regularity. The woman had arrived early today, a punishment for Mathilde's refusal to study the past week. All the Freud children were tutored at home, primarily due to Martha's fear of the spread of childhood diseases.

"When was the reign of Leopold the First?" the governess drilled, dabbing her watery eyes with a handkerchief.

"I don't know," Mathilde responded, bored to death and fiddling with the fringe on the pillow.

"From 1657 to 1705," said Frau Schilling, shuffling her papers with impatience. "And what year did he save Vienna from the Turkish menace?"

"I wouldn't exactly say he 'saved Vienna,'" Minna interrupted, pulling over a chair and casually pushing Mathilde's boots off the cushions. "I know they say Leopold was a great warrior, but the fact of the matter is, he was out of town when the bloody war took place and returned only when it was safe to do so."

Mathilde gazed levelly at Minna and planted her feet back on the cushions.

"So where was he?" Mathilde asked.

"In Linz."

"Doing what?"

"I don't know, maybe visiting his cousin, the count, or one of his several lady friends. Please take your boots off the cushions."

Mathilde unlaced her boots, threw them on the floor, and slammed her stockinged feet back on the cushions.

"What was the date of the Long War?" Frau Schilling frowned, focusing on the historic conflict and ignoring the one growing in front of her.

"Oh, the Long War, when the Ottomans took over Hungary . . ." Minna began.

"Excuse me, Fräulein Bernays. That's not the lesson. It's just the dates today."

"Yes, Tante Minna. It's just the dates today," Mathilde said, imitating the governess's congested, nasal tone.

Minna stood up calmly, picked up Mathilde's feet like two lead weights, and dropped them on the floor. Mathilde flushed with anger, pulling on her scratchy, high-necked collar, which dug into her neck like a claw.

Minna then launched into a detailed account of the invasion by the Turks in the fifteenth century and the grisly, barbaric wars that blighted Austria's medieval history, eventually leading to the long reign of the Hapsburgs and the founding of the Empire of Austria in 1804.

Mathilde sat sullen and silent, her mouth turned down at the edges in grim defiance. Right after Minna reenacted the Battle of Königgratz, which freed the duchies of Schleswig and Holstein, Mathilde stood up, threw a velvet cushion on the floor, and walked out, slamming the door behind her.

"I think that's all for today, Frau Shilling," Minna said.

"That child is obstinate and disrespectful and will never learn anything."

"Perhaps it's just a stage," Minna replied, feeling suddenly defensive and maternal despite the child's behavior. "She's at that age."

Minna made a mental note to talk to Martha about Mathilde, although she found the mediocrity of Frau Schilling's instruction almost as offensive as her cold, supercilious attitude. Everyone knew that girls of this age need warmth and attention, no matter how rebellious they happened to be.

The day carried on with the usual amount of errands and supervision of children. Sophie spent the afternoon with the speech therapist, and the boys were supposed to be studying, although they could get distracted at any given moment, according to their mood and inclinations. Today, it seemed that Oliver was the most disorganized of all. His brain was full of lurid tales of heathen barbarity when he was supposed to be studying civics, and he would suddenly erupt into descriptive streams of bloody slaughter that would make Minna want to laugh out loud. Then there was Martin. In addition to his fever, when she delivered his biscuits, she happened to notice that the third finger on his left hand was bent in a most disturbing manner. And when she tried to take a closer look, he hid it behind his back and ran away from her.

Martha, meanwhile, announced at mid-morning that she had a doctor's appointment—her intestinal colic was acting up and she felt bilious and out of sorts—which was perfect timing, since Minna had heard a slight scuffling behind the skirting board in the kitchen, but would rather die than tell Martha there might be a rat in the house. Her sister would quarantine the kitchen for God knows how long, and they'd be forced to listen to grisly tales of the Black Plague for the next two weeks. Minna would simply bait a few traps and throw them around, and that would be the end of it. But, then again, this wasn't *her* house.

When she first came to Berggasse 19, she believed her stay would be of a temporary nature. And every now and then, usually in the late afternoon, she would stop her household duties and consider her future, her mind circling her dead-end options, like a buzzard over a corpse.

She could swallow her pride, take the train to Hamburg, and live with her mother. Heaven forbid. She and her mother had, at best, a chilly relationship and she wouldn't want to be dependent on her now.

Or she could find yet another position as a governess or a lady's companion. This would most certainly lead to a dull, servile life with a brutal work schedule of seven days a week, with only a half day off on Sunday afternoon. But at least she could support herself.

It was at this point that her temples would begin to throb, and, fearing a vernal migraine, she would disappear silently into the kitchen and prepare a cup of tea, watching the leaves swirl around at the bottom of her cup.

Who else could she turn to? There was her brother, Eli, who had emigrated to New York. She could ask him to lend her passage to America, but starting over, in a new country with no husband and no friends, was a daunting proposition.

For Martha, there was no question of what Minna should do— settle for an aging bachelor or widower selected by the family. Wasn't there that man, Herr something or other, whom she had met last winter? Well dressed in a frock coat and smoking those gold-tipped cigarettes? Or the other one—the stodgy dry-goods merchant with a waxen pallor and heavy-veined hands. He was at least twenty years her senior, slow and stubborn, but rich. In any event, a marriage of convenience, in Minna's opinion, was simply no marriage at all. She had seen women settle for the family's choice—a "highly eligible," handpicked man. And one could argue that there was nothing wrong with living in a comfortable, well-furnished house with a hansom, two horses, a clothing allowance, and a man who paid for it all. It reminded Minna of her childhood friend, Elsie, a fragile, wary, and passive young woman, who purchased a pistol shortly after her arranged marriage. She methodically loaded it, hid it under her cloak, and hired a coach to take her to the train station, where she sat all day, contemplating the time of her demise. After much consideration, she instead went home, placed the loaded gun on her bedside table, and confided to Minna that she had warned her husband *never* to come near her again. And he didn't.

Perhaps if she had been more frugal over the years, less mercurial, she wouldn't be in this position. But for now, she would try not to lose heart and, in the meantime, stay here and help ease the burden of her sister's overwhelming life.

6

. . .

By three o'clock, Minna sat down halfway up the stairs. She felt frazzled by the day, an ache of exhaustion in her legs. She was desperate to get out of the house. Every sound she heard beckoned her—the staccato four-four beat of horses dragging their carriages, the belling of the trams, the muffled conversations of people strolling along the pavement. Finally Minna approached Frau Josefine and suggested she take the healthy children to the zoo. There was no entrance fee and the Imperial Menagerie had just been enlarged to include a bison den. The day maid could tend to Martin and Anna.

With that settled, Minna decided to take her walk. She powdered and pinked her neck and throat, sprinkled a few drops of rosewater on her wrist, buttoned up her gray duster coat, and skewered her plumed hat with long bonnet pins. She had planned to cross over to the Prater and then pay a visit to the public library, as she was longing to get a few more decent books, but as she walked through the vestibule, she heard Freud's distinctive voice.

"Is that you, Minna?"

"Yes, Sigmund. I'm going out. Do you need anything?"

"Not really," he said, "but I could use some air. I'll come with you."

"Of course," she answered, hesitating slightly, though she could not say why.

He grabbed his coat and hat and followed her out the front door, inhaling the fresh air as though it contained the essence of pomander. She had to admit that she felt a little awkward when he casually slipped his arm through hers, as if they were a couple taking a leisurely stroll. She moved away from him on the pretext of adjusting her hat, and thought it odd that she should suddenly feel uncomfortable with Sigmund.

Still, it was a radiantly gorgeous day, and she was glad to be outside. She never mentioned where she was going and he didn't ask. He led her briskly through a labyrinth of crowded, narrow side streets leading to the Ring, passing blocks of top-heavy, yellowed apartment buildings, shops with half-opened doors, and cafés where proprietors were wiping off tables and stacking chairs. Carts and carriages clogged the avenues, and one could just make out the romantic glow of the Gothic tower of St. Stephen's, the heart of the capital.

He picked up the pace as they got closer to the center of the city and at one point pulled a cigar from his waistcoat, clipping and lighting it. Then he steered her down a narrow passageway. Why couldn't he slow down, she thought. He was racing around the corners like a fugitive. A deep pink suffused her cheeks in her effort to keep up with him. And she had dressed far too heavily for the day. Normally she wore as many as nine or ten layers of clothes—knickers, corset, woolen stockings over cotton ones, cotton bodice, petticoat, camisole, blouse, skirt, coat. And her high-top boots, which were far too narrow and designed for women with no toes.

How could the man walk so fast and smoke so much? They ended up directly in front of the Greek-columned Houses of Parliament. She leaned over, unhooked the first few buttons of her boots, and quickly straightened up, ignoring a moment of vertigo, the heat, perhaps.

"See this?" he said, oblivious to her high color. "Vienna's version of the Acropolis—the model for the new hospital for the insane. What do you think?"

"Well, it's . . ."

"A complete travesty," he said, finishing her sentence.

He was referring to Am Steinhof, the hospital for mental and nervous patients that was being built a few miles outside of town and would take a decade to complete. He told her of the sixty buildings with patients segregated by illness—the curable, the incurable, the half quiet, the nervous, the violent, the syphilitic insane, and the criminal. In addition, he said, the plans called for electric trams, landscaped gardens, a piggery, stables, chapels, and, of course, a graveyard.

"The only thing modern about it is the architecture. The treatment is completely antiquated, just different types of confinement."

"Are your colleagues involved?"

"No . . . Some American named Briggs is running it," he said disparagingly. "Bottomless funds for mortar, and next to nothing for neurological research. The man cares only for the view."

He went on to explain that at this facility, as well as at others, once a patient was labeled a "chronic dement," anything could happen. Doctors would routinely remove whatever body part they assumed to be the cause of the illness—thyroid gland, teeth, tonsils, portions of the brain. They douched patients to treat depression, induced malarial fevers to help impaired mental function, or put the poor souls in a continuous bath that could last from one day to one week. In addition, they filled them with laudanum, barbiturates, bromides, and purgatives.

To Minna, his assessment sounded grim, but still an improvement over mid-century hospitals where patients were chained to walls and confined to cavelike rooms with small openings where the food was passed through. And she had even heard stories about "Sunday viewings," where the public would pay the guards a fee to view the "dements" in their natural habitat.

She told him that she did have some knowledge of current treatments. "My last employer, Baroness Wolff, was once treated with Erb's electrotherapy for depression. I watched as electrical currents were applied to different parts of her body. It was most unpleasant."

"Ah, the Battery Room."

"Why, yes, exactly," Minna said. She remembered the noxious odor of chlorodyne and alcohol as she peered through the open door into a room where bright brass disks of huge electric batteries glittered under a glass dome. Suspended from the walls were all kinds of queer apparatus, which were used to shock patients who were suffering from a morass of strange physical maladies. Minna thought it appalling, but settled herself in one of the chairs in the waiting area, sitting next to a woman whose son had just been readmitted after setting fire to his couch, claiming his father was hidden in it.

"I've complained many times about that protocol," he said. "I'm convinced that Erb's therapy doesn't help patients with nervous disorders, and that a partial recovery is the most that could be expected. How did your employer fare?"

"Not well, I'm afraid. She shot herself."

"Is that true?"

"No. Just wishful thinking," Minna said with a wry smile, as if they were sharing some private joke.

Freud looked at her, appraising her face, his eyes crinkling at the corners with unmistakable appreciation. Then he resumed in a serious tone.

"The fact is, electrotherapy and those other barbaric methods just don't work. When I studied in Paris with Dr. Charcot, hypnotism was the recommended cure, but I eventually found that it, too, was ineffective."

Minna remembered that Sigmund had gone to Paris around ten years earlier to study with the famous French neurologist.

"I always thought hypnotism was a bit far-fetched," she ventured. "But at least you got to live in Paris."

"Well, there *was* that," he said with a smile. "And in the beginning, hypnotism did seem to work. We put patients in a trance and got some encouraging results. But as time went on, the treatment left much to be desired. Not every patient could be hypnotized; some of them just weren't suggestible. I imagine you wouldn't be, either."

"Why would you say that?"

"Just a hunch. Maybe we'll try it sometime," he said lightly, as he placed his hand gently on the small of her back and guided her around a puddle. "In any event, even when the treatment *was* effective, the symptoms would usually reappear. It was disheartening, actually. The patients made so little progress. They still had nightmares, deafness, speech impediments, paralysis—a myriad of symptoms. But when I returned to Vienna, I discovered my most effective therapeutic tool was sitting right in front of me. All I needed to do was to get the patients to talk about themselves."

"Honestly, Sigmund, it sounds like such a simple way to get such astounding results."

"Yes. In theory, it's marvelously simple. In reality, a bit more complicated. But the crux of the matter is, my colleagues were dealing with hysterics from a neurological perspective and getting nowhere. I watched patients struggle with depression, delirium tremors, shifts of mood, phobias, and compulsions, and nothing we did seemed to help. But when I asked them to lie down on a couch and talk about their past—abusive fathers, distant mothers, childhood traumas, whatever drifted into their mind without censorship—all of their disturbing, even horrifying memories spewed forth. And then, by peeling off the layers, observing, interpreting, and guessing, one could discover what caused the symptoms. And by doing that, eradicate them."

"My God, Sigmund. It's cathartic, isn't it? It frees patients by encouraging them to talk about their past."

"Exactly. The couch is my laboratory."

"But if I may play the devil's advocate, for a moment?" she asked, holding up her index finger as he smiled indulgently. After all, this was why he liked her and she knew it.

"Why would anyone lie down with a complete stranger and tell him her most intimate thoughts, her inner secrets, even her perversions?"

"I'll tell you why. People who have been through years of horrendous pain will do anything if they think it will help. And once they start talking, they can't stop. Their memories overtake them, and they begin to realize what they've been suppressing all these years. There is meaning in the dark corners of human life and in that meaning lies hope."

She wanted him to go on. She wanted to ask him about his

patients. Specific examples. Specific results. But mostly she wanted to tell him that his discoveries were profound as well as humane. That if he was right, all treatment, as they now knew it, would be antiquated. That he could change history.

"It's so nice to have someone to talk to . . ." he said, looking at her intently, "someone who understands. My colleagues think I'm off on a quixotic mission. And so does Martha."

A flurry of women in crinoline hurried by, pushing them to the side, and the rattling of an omnibus, followed by a two-horse dray, drowned out the voices of the pedestrians around them. Minna looked up as he pulled another cigar from his pocket. He lit it, thoughtfully puffing, while he watched an aimless group of students loitering in the park across the street.

Her mind was reeling, but she was hesitant to say more. She leaned over self-consciously to fix her boot once again. It was now rubbing her ankle raw. She sat down on the nearby bench, trying to loosen the offending laces. He studied her as the afternoon light glowed softly on her hair.

"What are you looking at?" she asked, glancing up.

He held her gaze and smiled slightly.

"I'm looking at you."

7

. . .

A few days later, when the children were busy with the governess, Minna decided to attend Sigmund's lecture at the university. After all, he had invited her on the day she arrived, and
although he hadn't mentioned it since, she felt certain the offer had
been sincere.

The University of Vienna was just a fifteen-minute walk from
the apartment, and she could make it if she hurried. Minna crossed
the tree-lined Ringstrasse, rounding the corner at the Parliament
building, and continuing through the elite Rathaus quarter, with
its massive neo-Gothic public buildings. It was still unseasonably
warm, and by the time she reached the university, her dress was
damp with sweat and her hat slightly askew.

She wandered around the campus for a few minutes, searching
for the medical school. The imposing university buildings were
monumental in scale and purposely intimidating, she felt. Particularly the giant, overblown Greek mythological sculptures planted
here and there, glorifying this noble center of liberal learning. She
approached a few students to ask directions before finally finding
her way to the correct building. She struggled with the heavy door,

gathered her courage, and climbed the staircase to the lecture hall on the second floor. By the time she got there, Freud had already begun.

The room was filled to capacity, young men standing in the back, in the aisles, many of whom were wearing dark suits and yarmulkes. It was a well-known fact that the majority of medical students at this university were Jewish, as well as most of the doctors in Vienna. In fact, the emperor's personal physician was in Freud's B'nai B'rith group, as was the surgeon general of Austria.

Freud stood at the podium, his voice echoing through the chamber. He looked relaxed, even a bit amused. He did not have a powerful voice, nor did he project a particularly commanding image. And yet as he talked, he had this strange, monumental pull over her. She noted that he was wittier, more confident now, and he delivered his words with compelling force, like an evangelical at his Sunday sermon. Even at this early point in the lecture, the students had put down their pens, mesmerized as he entertained them with anecdotes and jokes that would most likely be circulated in the cafés afterward. In her eyes, he was magnificent.

"I'm reminded of a couple—I may have spoken of them before. Their marriage was tormented with a variety of conflicted feelings and misinterpreted signals . . . and, after weeks of talking to them, I thought we had something of a breakthrough." He paused melodramatically. "But *then* the wife said to her husband, 'When one of us dies, I'm going to Paris.' "

The students erupted in appreciative laughter as Minna scoured the hall, searching for a place to sit.

"But I digress. As we were discussing last week, neurosis is a frequent consequence of an abnormal sexual life, and in fact, I'm finding sexual repression to be the key to understanding neurotic illness and human behavior in general."

Some titters from the audience. Now he began to discuss the crux of his report titled *Studies in Hysteria*, concerning sexual repression and its effect on people.

"Gentlemen, I'm going to provoke you to astonishment. That is my goal."

He was so sure of himself, she thought, but his face was highly changeable and could shift abruptly, depending on his mood. One moment he was glaring at the students. The next, he was charming and animated, embracing his audience as if they were all sharing some intimate knowledge.

"We are all helplessly in thrall to traumatic memories from our past, and these memories are invariably of a sexual nature. Even our most impressive achievements are stained by the animality of our nature. That is our fate. And if you think this revelation that I alone have come up with is grim, you are correct. In effect, gentlemen, with the basics of this theory, I am bringing you the plague."

The students shifted in their chairs and a few of them smiled. At this point, they were used to Freud's hyperbole.

"We humans," he went on, "are infected with our past. The challenge for you, my good men, is to understand this revolutionary theory and to use it in the future to cure the many patients who are incorrectly diagnosed."

Minna smiled to herself at his grandiose certainty, a tone that had infused his letters to her over the years.

The late-afternoon sun filtered through the length of the tall, narrow windows, and Minna removed her heavy coat and gray leather gloves. She hadn't anticipated a full house. Not one empty seat. Trying to be unobtrusive, which wasn't easy, considering that medical schools were only for men, she balanced her coat in one arm and her purse in the other. She stood there, craning her neck to see if there were any available seats. A young man on her left noticed her and, after his initial surprise, stood politely, offering his chair. She thanked him and sat down, removing her large plumed hat (perhaps not the best millinery choice for that day). She didn't want to cause a stir by walking down the aisle. Even so, she could hear a few students whispering about "the woman in the class."

Freud went on to discuss the origin of his theory. "It all began," he told them, "with a patient named Anna O., the twenty-one-year-old daughter of a wealthy Viennese family, who had first seen my colleague Dr. Josef Breuer with unexplained paralysis of the right arm. Over the next few weeks, he found her symptoms multiplied. Persistent cough, numbness in the extremities, delirium, and even the inability to speak German, her native language. Dr. Breuer diagnosed her as 'hysterical' and treated her with hypnosis, but it was not effective."

It occurred to Minna that Sigmund spoke as he wrote in his letters: clearly, persuasively, and in great detail, and to her surprise, he never once looked down at a piece of paper.

"Anna had deeply tragic but beautiful fantasies and morbid daydreams," Freud recounted. "In one of them, a snake tried to attack her father, who in real life was ill and for whom she was caring. She tried to kill the snake but her right arm was useless. Her fingers turned into little snakes, and then the entire arm was paralyzed.

"And now I will tell you the breakthrough," he proclaimed, stepping down from the podium. He was clearly relishing the effect he was having on his audience. The room was dead silent, his low baritone reverberating off the wooden walls.

"Anna started talking about her dreams and her accompanying fears, in English, but you can't have everything," he said, waving a hand in the air as the students laughed. "But then her symptoms improved, almost disappeared. What accounted for the cure, you ask?

"I'll tell you," he said, growing more serious.

"Hysterical patients suffer from their memories. Memories of traumatic events that may even occur in infancy and, I repeat, are sexual in nature. But talking about them, or as Anna so charmingly called it, 'chimney sweeping,' helped chase away the demons."

Minna could imagine how this theory at first might seem preposterous—all neurosis originating from sexual causes. But now, listening to his reasoning, she was intrigued. He went on to analyze other cases and theories.

It was clear to Minna that Freud had honed his skills of communication, drawing heavily on literature, philosophy, science, sexuality, and the mystery of human relationships. He was far from the stereotypical handsome man, but when he spoke, his words and actions had a captivating quality, inducing excitement and racing pulses among the young men. Minna could see it in their eyes. The air was charged with creativity as he offered his audience fresh possibilities, new ways of thinking. He made them laugh and laugh again. They were drawn to his oddities, his contradictions, and . . . why didn't she just say it? To his greatness.

The air was beginning to feel close in this male sanctum. Minna pulled off her scarf. She glanced back at the podium as Freud smiled and nodded in her direction. She met his gaze and then nodded back. She wanted to freeze this unexpected, secret pleasure in her mind. The instant of eye contact was over in a flash, but it seemed to silence him momentarily. She wasn't sure how, in this large lecture hall filled with a sea of students, but the room suddenly became as intimate as dinner for two.

F reud's lecture went on for over two hours. He described disturbed patients who had come to him with traumatic stories of sexual fantasies, dreams, and guilt regarding illicit behavior. He talked about a young man who had had intercourse with a prostitute and was exhibiting bizarre paranoid symptoms. A young woman who had been molested by her father suffered hysteria and breakdowns. Others who were afflicted with paralysis of the limbs, nervous cough, headaches, inability to speak, terrifying hallucinations. A bewildering number of symptoms and psychological states resulting from sexual traumas. People who were so disturbed they had been given chloral hydrate, morphine, and chloroform to sleep or been hung by their limbs in metal cuffs and subjected to electrotherapy.

Afterward, Minna watched the students, many of whom looked young enough to be members of the Vienna Boys Choir, push forward and crowd around him, bombarding him with questions. Occasional bursts of male laughter reverberated through the hall and she moved slowly against the tide, making her way to the back door. She was almost there, her back to the podium, when somehow she felt he was looking at her.

"Fräulein Bernays," he called out, the sound of his voice suddenly silencing the din in the room. "Would you mind waiting a moment?"

She turned toward him and nodded. She had already put on her coat, hat, and gloves and was shifting, uncomfortably warm, from one boot to another as she stood near the door. He stepped down from the podium and lit a cigar, and the pungent odor of smoke drifted up to where she was standing. A few minutes later, he excused himself from the students still surrounding him and climbed the stairs to where she stood.

"I hope I didn't bore you . . ." he said, knowing full well that he hadn't.

She thought for a moment, wondering whether or not to offer an observation, but then, as usual, decided to forge ahead.

"You had your students' complete attention, and adoration, I might add, but when you stated that *all* hysteria was caused by sexual dysfunction, they seemed, well, rather, incredulous," she said.

His gaze became appraising. "No, my dear. That's not what I said at all. I said that the original *root* of hysteria would be sexual."

"I might have missed that."

"I find that hard to believe . . ." he said, a half smile playing on his lips.

"In any event, couldn't you argue that some cases of hysteria could be caused by, say, fear, death, or abandonment?"

"My reasoning is perfectly clear. . . ."

"Well, it might be confusing. . . ." she said, her words coming out with less force than she had planned. "For example, your patient, the twelve-year-old boy who wouldn't eat . . . that's very clear, he'd been molested. Certainly that cause and effect is easy. But others are more difficult. . . ."

"Difficult but not different."

"So there are no exceptions?" she asked.

"None that are noteworthy," he said, leaning in closer to her. "Some might say I have a doctrinaire stance."

"Some might."

"And they would be . . . ?" he asked, playfully.

"Unduly harsh, my dear . . ." she answered, flushing.

"That would be the correct answer."

"I thought so," she said, smiling, as she turned to leave.

"Just a moment," he said, staring at her curiously. She was expecting one additional point to bolster his argument, but instead he asked her whether she was available later that evening. She raised her eyebrows in momentary surprise and then remembered that this evening, as every Saturday evening after his lecture, Freud played in a regular tarock game with three of his colleagues from the hospital. But in an unusual turn of events, he said, one of his partners had taken ill at the last moment and sent his regrets. Evidently, it wasn't just an annoying cough, but a full-blown bronchial infection.

"Actually, my dear, it was Martha's idea. She reminded me how clever you were with cards, and might it not be easier to let you fill in."

Minna remembered the card games in the café when they were all students.

"That was so long ago. . . ."

"But I recall you annihilating us one time."

"Just once?"

"All right. More than once."

And so it was decided. Freud returned to a circle of waiting students and Minna headed home.

A few weeks before, she had been in utter turmoil, leading a solitary life with stolen pleasures. She had worked at so many houses, developing furtive habits of hiding food or gin, reading purloined books, and putting up with domestics who were constantly nipping at her heels. Now she was free, living with family. As she crossed the Ringstrasse, she felt a surge of optimism. If not a permanent solution, this was a welcome, much-needed hiatus.

8

. . .

The card game was always the same—almost a ritual. At precisely seven o'clock, Dr. Eduard Silverstein rang the bell and
was ushered into the parlor, where he clapped a fraternal arm
around Freud's shoulder and then headed straight toward the
refreshment table. He could always be relied on to make himself at
home in the cozy, domesticated room, and indeed he did, helping
himself to a large Sacher torte on a silver tray, spilling the crumbs
on the carpet.

"And how are you, Sigmund?" he asked as he sank deeply into
an armchair, stretched out his legs, and produced a slightly
squashed, pale brown Maria Mancini cigar from his waistcoat. He
stared at it in admiration, as if it were a woman.

"It's the genteel, slender body that I love," he said, with a handsome smile, not waiting for his host's reply. Then he lit up and
inhaled with exaggerated pleasure.

"Ah . . . moody, but pliable . . ." he added, flipping through one
of Freud's newspapers.

Freud nodded with good humor at his only bachelor colleague,
but professed loyalty to his stout, homely Trabuco. "It's less flighty,"

he volleyed, "less temperamental . . . with an even, reliable draw. You can keep the Marias of the world. . . . too much bother."

Dr. Ivan Skekel arrived next, removing his weather-beaten tweed coat and making the usual excuses for his tardiness—crowded omnibus, the "wife," his swollen ankles. He smoothed his square-shaped beard and straightened his woolen waistcoat over his sizable paunch, as he too headed for the refreshments and uncorked a bottle of wine. He was about to light up the third cigar, adding to the thickening cloud of smoke, when the door to the parlor swung open and Minna walked in.

She had changed into a white lace-trimmed blouse that was slightly open at the neck, her hair swept up in soft waves with a set of combs, and she was trailed by the scent of lavender-perfumed soap. For an instant, she hesitated, conscious of Freud's gaze roaming her face. Did he see it in her? she wondered. Her tense shoulders, her flushed cheeks, and the care with which she had applied her makeup?

He had noticeably transformed the moment she stepped into the room. His hard, bright eyes softened and his stiff demeanor relaxed. He had taken her hand, whispered a word of hello, and then given her another lingering glance. Minna wondered if this intimacy was merely her imagination but it gave her a peculiar sensation.

Earlier, when she was getting dressed, her sister had been all ambrosial sweetness, like a mother sending her daughter off to a ball. Why then did Minna feel as if she were doing something behind Martha's back? If there was nothing to hide, why did she feel guilty?

"Allow me to introduce my sister-in-law, Fräulein Minna Bernays," Freud said, rising from his chair, taking her hand in his, and ushering her into the room. "She'll be our fourth tonight. Eduard Silverstein and Ivan Skekel."

It was obvious to Minna that Sigmund had not discussed her joining the game, and his partners looked noticeably surprised. She calmly regarded the group with her hazel eyes and walked over to the sofa.

"Good evening, gentlemen."

"Delighted," Dr. Silverstein said, breaking the silence. He stood up, took her hand, and kissed it lightly. Then he poured a glass of wine from one of Martha's good crystal decanters on the sideboard and handed her a glass.

"How very kind," Minna murmured.

Minna knew very well who Eduard Silverstein was. Martha had mentioned him several times. He was on her list of eligible bachelors. The son of a successful doctor and an enthusiastic supporter of the arts, he took over the thriving family practice when his father retired. Minna thought he wore his hair a little too long to be stylish but, on the whole, he was handsome, with liquid brown eyes and a worldly air. And even though he seemed pleased to see her, he had to be wondering, along with Skekel, why Freud hadn't called one of their other colleagues who usually filled in when someone was indisposed.

Minna sipped the wine and settled herself on the sofa. She was still not quite at ease. Her feet felt prickly and ached from the day, the left boot pressing on her anklebone. She had left the children still awake, one of whom—was it Ernst? no, maybe Oliver—shouting something as she went downstairs.

"Are you up to this, my dear?" Freud asked solicitously, as he sat down next to her and lightly touched her on the shoulder. "Second thoughts?"

"Not at all," she said, and smiled, laying her hand on the sofa arm, which was covered with several of Martha's ubiquitous doilies.

They sat together while Skekel and Silverstein drifted over to the fireplace, finishing their conversation. They were talking about what everyone was talking about, the recent election of Karl Lueger, the new mayor of Vienna, who was known to be rabidly anti-Semitic.

"You know what this means, don't you?" Skekel said. "The liberals are losing ground. It's the Christian Social Party now, and they can't wait to take away our rights. It's like the Middle Ages."

"I wouldn't go around saying too much in public, old boy," Silverstein replied, draining his glass. "You might lose a few patients, as well as some of your imperial connections. Don't you agree, Fräulein Bernays?" he said, abruptly turning to her.

"Well, most certainly the emperor has no choice," Minna said, going on to discuss the disastrous ramifications of imperial support of Lueger, especially for the Jews.

"My sentiments exactly," Silverstein said, smiling at Minna. "My word, Sigmund. A beautiful, intelligent woman living in your house. What good fortune . . ."

"Let's play," Freud said, with sudden irritation.

Freud took the cards out of the pack and shuffled deftly. He glanced at Minna seemingly in annoyance, which left her slightly rattled. Then he cut the deck and dealt counterclockwise, sixteen cards to each player, carefully placing the six tarock cards face-down in the center.

As the bidding began, Minna found herself in a slightly awkward situation, trying to join the conversation with the men, darting from one subject to another, while making a respectable impression with her card-playing skills.

"I just canceled my subscription to *La Libre*," said Skekel, referring to the newspaper *La Libre Parole*, Lueger's political tool. "I couldn't endure any more of their fanatic ravings."

"I agree, I just read the *Neue*," Minna said, trying to keep her mind on the game. *Follow suit if you can.*

"I had a nephew," Skekel said, lowering his voice, "who changed his Jewish name to a Christian one . . . and then he went into the 'arts.' . . . Destroyed his mother."

If you can't follow suit, play a tarock.

"He can go to vespers twenty times a day, and they'll still call him a Jew," Freud added.

No tarock, so I can play any card.

The discussion carried on as Minna tried not to lead with a tarock until a tarock had been played or, heaven forbid, discard the wrong number of cards or, disaster, fail to beat the highest card. At one point, she thought, Perhaps I should just play the Fool. But then again, he never wins a trick. Finally, Silverstein got up to refill his glass, and the men decided to take a bit of a break.

"More wine, my dear?" Silverstein asked.

"Why, yes, thank you."

He walked over with the decanter and began to fill her glass.

"So when do you get a free day, Minna?" he asked. "Do they ever let you out of here?"

"She's not a domestic," Freud said, glaring at him. "She's my sister-in-law."

"Don't get so testy, Sigmund," Silverstein said, with an amused smile that was not returned.

There was an uncomfortable silence, and Silverstein wisely decided to change the subject. "I suppose you've read about Oscar Wilde?" he asked.

"How could one not? It's been in all the papers," Freud snapped back.

"He should have fled to France, but his mother advised him to stay and 'fight like a man,' " Silverstein said.

"That's what you get when you listen to your mother," Freud replied.

"He only has himself to blame, his behavior was reckless and indiscreet," Skekel added.

"And his play *The Importance of Being Earnest*, such a hit in America," Minna said.

"Well he's finished now . . . two years' hard labor, the maximum for gross indecency and sodomy—" said Freud.

"Gentlemen, I don't think this is an appropriate subject . . ." interrupted Skekel, nodding at Minna.

"I'm perfectly capable of discussing the Wilde case," Minna said, brushing off the man's patronizing, if well-meaning, concerns. "In my opinion, if he hadn't sued the Marquess of Queensberry for criminal libel, he wouldn't have been in this fix. A private prosecution at the height of his success. What a tragedy. And the salacious details of the poor man's life plastered all over the news."

"Bravo," Silverstein said, breaking into a proprietary grin.

"My dear, perhaps you don't understand . . ." Skekel explained patiently. "Mr. Wilde enjoyed the company of young . . . men. . . . These were *ho-mo-sexual* acts," he said, slowly enunciating each syllable of the word as if she were a complete idiot.

"I understand what the word *homosexual* means, Dr. Skekel," Minna said, clearly vexed. "In fact, some say homosexuality is just a passing phase. I hear university boys experiment with it all the time."

"Well, I went to university, and I can tell you we experimented with a lot of things, but we didn't do that. Maybe in the medical school . . ." Silverstein said, laughing and nodding at Freud.

"There's so much ignorance on the topic," Freud replied, ignoring Silverstein's attempts at humor. "My research has shown that homoerotic tendencies stem from a primitive oral phase, followed by an anal one and then a phallic one."

The word *phallic* hung in the air as everyone quieted down.

"Very interesting, but that wouldn't have helped poor Mr. Wilde in court," Minna said, without hesitation.

"Ah, but what if I could prove that *everyone* has these tendencies?" Freud said, looking at Silverstein.

"Sigmund!" said Skekel. "It is *highly* inappropriate to be discussing these things in mixed company."

"Nonsense. Minna wasn't put off by it . . . were you?" Freud asked.

"Not in the least."

"There. You see? Not in the least," he repeated, pleased.

"More wine, my dear?" Silverstein offered.

"Why, yes, thank you."

The game and the conversation went on into the night, with Skekel uncorking bottle after bottle of wine. At this point, Minna had lost count of how many glasses of alcohol she had consumed and watched with amusement as Skekel launched into an inebriated monologue on the state of the world.

"Things are going to hell here. . . . Every day, another demonstration in town, people shouting anti-Semitic rhetoric . . . and the monarchy—completely ineffective. God knows, the military can't deal with it. And it's spreading. Why, I read just the other day that we're a 'proving ground for destruction.' . . ."

"Don't believe everything you read, my man," said Silverstein, looking at Minna with an openly flirtatious smile. "Things aren't that catastrophic."

"Yes, they are. Even the suicide rate is up. . . ."

"Just a lot of bored aristocrats who amuse themselves by jumping off bridges," Silverstein said irreverently. Minna laughed, but didn't know why, as Silverstein stood up, squeezed her shoulder, ambled to the piano, and proceeded to pound out a dreadful but enthusiastic rendition of Müller's "The Fair Miller Maid."

"Gentlemen, it's late," Freud said, grimacing as he listened to the off-key notes. Skekel downed the last of his wine and slowly began to close the keyboard cover on Silverstein's fingers.

"Let's go, Eduard. I'll get a cab."

Silverstein swayed a bit as he stood up.

"Might I perhaps call on you sometime?" he asked as he kissed Minna's hand, lingering a bit too long. "It's a pleasure to find a woman who possesses such considerable knowledge of the world. . . . Magnificent," he added.

"How kind of you," she responded in a noncommittal way, as Freud escorted the two men out of the parlor and into the hallway. She could hear them arguing on the stairs and then Eduard's slurred voice.

"So she's forbidden fruit, is she?"

"You're drunk, Eduard. Go home."

Freud shut the front door a little too hard and then climbed back up the stairs.

"I wouldn't advise encouraging Eduard," he said, throwing a pillow aside and sitting down on the couch. He sulked as Minna gathered up the dirty glasses and bottles, and then he followed her into the kitchen.

"I wasn't encouraging him."

"One could interpret it that way."

"Are you asking me something or telling me something?"

"Both. In any event, I know him well. While an amusing companion for me, he's very much a ladies' man."

"I think my mother would like him," Minna said, teasing. "A nice Jewish doctor."

"Well, she didn't like me. And he couldn't cure a ham."

"Sigmund." Minna laughed. "I don't find him particularly appealing."

"Who *do* you find appealing?" he asked, following her back into the parlor.

"Ah, there's the question. Martha has been asking me that for years."

Minna fell silent and gathered up the last of the glasses, as a wave of fatigue hit her.

"Forget about those. Come here, my dear," he said, patting the space on the sofa next to him. She sat down, feeling the warmth of the smoldering logs and sharing one last glass of wine. He leaned back, stretched out his legs, and let out a sigh.

"Tired?" she asked.

"Exhausted. One of my patients isn't responding to treatment and another informed me that she isn't coming back—that talking to me was just 'too upsetting.'"

"And why is that?"

"Some of their perversions are extreme. And the reasons even more so. It might shock you."

"You know me better than that," she said.

He watched her press the wineglass to her lips and swirl the burgundy around her tongue, and he began to speak.

"I have a patient, a Russian aristocrat named Sergei . . . well, the name isn't important. He's extremely depressed, suicidal, a hypochondriac. Filled with obsessions, unable to function. He's also plagued with recurring nightmares—a pack of vicious wolves hovering outside his bedroom window, waiting to attack."

"How odd. Has he ever *actually* come into contact with wolves?"

"I don't think so. Although he's an artist and has drawn them with matted fur and bloody fangs. The sources of these compulsions are complex, but we've made tremendous progress with infantile neurosis. Just last week, near the end of our session, the man recalled his earliest sexual memories, and there it was . . . the presexual sexual shock. He confessed that when he was a child, he witnessed his parents having sex 'a tergo.' "

"'A tergo'?" Minna asked.

"You know. From behind."

Minna refused to look shocked. It was as if she were listening to tales of the supernatural peppered with incest, masturbation, sodomy, and so forth. He went on in such detail that, at one point, she thought he might be toying with her. She tried to keep her expression impassive, maintaining the fiction that her interests were purely scientific.

"Their genitals were in full view," he said quietly. "I'm confident that this exposure to his parents' lovemaking has affected his sexual appetites and made him voracious in a variety of erotic ways."

"For instance?"

"For instance, he has compulsive desires for women with large buttocks—preferably prostitutes and servant girls. He told me every time he sees his housemaid kneeling down, scrubbing the floor, he's instantly aroused. The image of her rear in the air is overwhelming to him and all he can think about is taking her right there."

"Does he?"

"Not that I know of . . . but debasement and humiliation seem to increase his desire. The world is filled with those who desire all sorts of things—fetishes, flagellation, sadism, even bondage."

"Why would anyone submit to that?"

He pressed in, his face close to hers. "There are many kinds of erotic tastes, my dear. For instance, if I were to slip satin ribbons around your wrists and ankles and tie them to the bedposts, then slowly make love to you while you lay naked, unable to move, allowing you to surrender to your darker, carnal urges. Even you, Minna, might find that erotic."

He stared at her, clearly pleased with himself.

He's definitely playing with me, she thought, flushing. This is maddening. But overriding that was a weird, tantalizing desire to hear more. The wild side of his intellect had always fascinated her.

"Could you light this for me?" she asked, pulling a cigarette from her pocket.

He struck a match and held it in front of her, watching her inhale deeply. She blew out a thin stream of smoke and then tried to engage him, one colleague to another.

"And your other patients?"

"There's a young woman, Dora," Freud continued, flicking the match just short of the fireplace. "She came to me complaining of a multitude of symptoms—fainting spells and suicidal depression. She had a nagging cough and sometimes couldn't even talk. After several sessions, I discovered that when she was fourteen, she used to mind the children of family friends. I'll call them the 'K's.' We all know them. But what she didn't reveal to her parents was that Herr K had been making sexual advances toward her for years. And when she finally *did* tell them, they accused her of making it all up."

"The poor girl."

"Yes. I got her to tell me everything. Herr K would ask her to sit on his lap, and then he would put his hand up her skirt and insert his fingers into her vagina, stimulating her into orgasm. She told me she could feel his erect penis against her thigh and that on numerous occasions he would ask her to stroke it. The problem was, although she vehemently refused to admit it, I think she actually *liked* the sexual arousal. When I pointed this out, she left my office in a rage."

Freud stared at Minna, waiting for her reaction.

"Well," Minna said, sitting back, trying to treat his explicit description in a purely professional manner, "I sympathize with your frustration. I do. But frankly, Sigmund, if I were fourteen and some older man was doing that to me, and then, years later, another older man told me that I secretly liked it, I might leave in a rage as well."

"You have to tell patients the truth or they'll never be cured. Men and women who can't eat, can't sleep, can't function. Some are in love with their sister's husband, some wish their baby brother dead. They desire forbidden things. Everyone does. We're all sick. And we need to talk about it."

"Isn't this just another form of confession?"

"Call it whatever you like. But it's not in the least religious or moralistic, it's about tolerance."

"Tolerance?"

"Yes, tolerance of ourselves."

"But, in the end, doesn't the mind go antagonizing on? I think Emerson said that."

"Sometimes even the Americans have insights."

The curtains were open a little, and over Freud's shoulder, Minna could see that the lights had gone out in the apartment across the street. She wondered what time it was. Surely well past midnight. She would regret this in the morning. She leaned her head against the chair and watched him walk to the fireplace and stir the embers. Assuming his full height, he turned back to her.

"She'll be back," he said, with a confident smile. "I know I'm right."

He reached for his wineglass and accidentally brushed her knee. Or was it an accident? Whatever it was, Minna felt a charge in her gut that was definitely unseemly. And the wine didn't help.

"It's getting late," she said, standing up, the flush of alcohol staining her cheeks.

Their eyes met for a moment and she wondered briefly when things had changed between them. She had expected when she came here that their relationship would remain as it had always been, uncomplicated and intellectual. But it was as if the Freud she had known for years had transformed into someone else. This felt like a new beginning. But *that* wasn't what she wanted. The thought that kept creeping into her mind was, would she have behaved this way in front of her sister? Would he?

9

. . .

"Minna, are you awake?" Martha called. "Come in here, dear, will you? Minna?"

Minna awoke with a dull roar behind her ears and dry, cakey lips. The space above her eyes ached and the light made it worse. She rolled over and sat up abruptly, increasing her discomfort. "I'm up. I'm up . . . I'm getting dressed."

She threw the sheets aside, and padded barefoot across the cold, buckled-wood floor. Narrow shafts of sunlight streamed through the cracks of the closed shutters and she could hear noises from the busy street below. She opened the window and a waft of clean, fresh air hit her face as she took a deep breath. My God, she thought, I haven't slept this late in years. Too much wine. She knew it before she went to bed last night. That had been the problem . . . too much wine for all of them. She would not do *that* again.

Normally Minna would put on a day costume, a crisp white blouse and tight-waisted skirt falling smoothly over the hips. But today she couldn't face the thought of hooking all those buttons on her blouse. She fumbled through her wardrobe and chose a simple blue serge dress with far less business. This will be fine, she thought.

The master bedroom was located directly next door, and last night Minna could hear Martha snoring through the walls as she undressed and got into bed. Right before she fell asleep, she was vaguely aware of heavy footsteps in the hall.

Minna found her sister sitting in bed, surrounded by her needle-work and two popular magazines, *La Vie Parisienne* and *Illustrated News*. Freud's side of the bed was smooth and cold, as if no one had been there all night. The shutters were closed, effecting an almost total absence of sunlight. As Minna stepped into the room she heard the downstairs door slam shut. He was leaving. At the same time, the insistent wail of an infant carried through the halls. Martha pulled the brass-handled bell rope by her bed, and a jingle traveled to the kitchen. A few moments later, Edna, the upstairs maid, could be heard outside the door.

"Yes, madam?" Edna asked, straightening Martha's bed linens and plumping the pillow on Freud's side of the bed. Edna was a large, raw-boned figure, about a head taller than most women, and she reminded Minna of Mrs. Squeers, a minor but memorable character in *Nicholas Nickleby*. Unlike Dickens's character, how-ever, Edna was not at all cruel. She was breathless from climbing the stairs and a bit out of sorts.

This morning she had already lit the fires, cleaned the grates, brought water to every room, awakened the children, and flushed the water closets.

"Does Nanny know the baby's crying?" Martha asked.

"Most certainly," Edna said, pushing a strand of hair under her white starched cap.

"And the other children?"

"Martin's throat still has the infection."

"Sophie and Oliver?"

"Their throats are now seedy, too."

"Well, keep them away from my husband."

As Minna listened, Martha proceeded to review methodically the children's activities and ailments, organizing and coordinating all the errands and tasks of the housemaids, nursemaid, governess, and cook. It made Minna's head spin. She was still not quite used to the constant mayhem and frantic rhythm of it all. Even though her duties in former households had been demanding, she had never dealt with six children before.

It was no wonder Freud retreated downstairs to his office. He spent most of his time there, a place strictly prohibited to the family. The geography enforced that edict. It was one floor down from the residence, but it might as well have been across town. When he was in his office, no one intruded.

Martha continued giving instructions to Edna, who suddenly began punching her thighs with both fists and then tilted her head back and grimaced.

"What's the problem, now?" Martha asked.

"It's my rheumatism acting up again."

"I thought it was lumbago?"

"It's both."

"Both. Of course. And the household knee?"

"That, too," she said, defiantly.

"So many ailments, Edna."

"Will that be all, madam?" she asked.

"Yes. And don't forget the plants. They need to be watered exactly at eleven."

Edna heaved a big sigh, then pointedly limped out of the room and shut the door. Martha looked pained, then drew her needlework out of the basket and began crocheting, resolutely jabbing the hook in and out. As if this house needed more doilies.

"Exactly eleven?" Minna asked.

"She always forgets."

"Then I'll do it."

"You shouldn't have to. That woman drives me mad. I swear, every week there's something else. One more ailment, I'm letting her go for good."

"No, you're not. She's been with you forever," Minna said, discounting her sister's annoyance with a wave.

"I'm just tired of all her woes. The debts. The husband who cheats. The ailing mother. The sister who lost her position. I spend all my time appeasing her, then I get angry and fire her. Then I feel guilty. It's just too much. Get me a damp cloth, will you?"

Listening to Martha was a stark reminder that in these times, women either kept servants or were one. In Minna's experience, wherever she worked, the world was divided into servants and masters, "us" and "them." Drifting within this rigid caste system were jobs such as governesses and ladies' companions. These women, like herself, were typically single and existed in a kind of social limbo. They were often upper middle class, but due to unfortunate circumstances regarding their family's fortunes or their marital status, they were forced to find a way to support themselves.

Minna learned the hard way that this existence was a domestic no-man's-land. The servants in the household often envied and disparaged her as having airs beyond her means. The fact of the matter was, she worked for a salary like any other domestic servant yet she was considered of a higher class. Her employers, while not treating her exactly like a servant, considered her a refugee from failed circumstances, thus not entitled to be treated as an equal.

But here it was different. After all, here she was family.

Minna picked up a linen towel next to the washbowl, dipped it in the lukewarm water, and handed it to Martha.

"Let's change the subject, shall we? Can we talk about Mathilde?" asked Minna.

"Why? Is she sick, too?"

"Sick of her studies. The child is completely uninterested. Although that governess makes history as boring as a dog's lunch."

"You could hire all the governesses from Vienna to Berlin and Mathilde still wouldn't be interested. Anyway, what does she need all that Latin and history for?"

"You're not saying she shouldn't be educated, are you? And, by the way, is she allowed to put her boots all over the furniture? The other day she—"

"Of course not," Martha interrupted. "My dear, I have a beastly headache. Didn't sleep a wink last night. Could you hand me my medicine? Top drawer on the right."

Minna picked up the cobalt-blue bottle of Mother Bailey's Quieting Syrup, one of the most popular laudanum pain relievers and, as she had learned in a former place of employment, as easy to obtain as salt. Anyone with a whit of a brain knew it was liquid opium, and it would cure whatever ailed you in a minute flat— hiccups, syphilis, bronchitis, a wretched existence. One of the governesses she knew downed it like gin every night after supper and then jabbered on until oblivion about her troubles. Minna wished Martha wouldn't use it, and it vexed her to no end that she was giving it to the children. You just had to look at the label on the bottle to see the insidious evil of it all. A Medici-like portrait of a mother dressed in flowing white gown and her cherub-faced baby. The woman wore an enigmatic smile as she held a syringe in her outstretched hand. It was as if she were about to administer a soothing, warm bottle of milk, and not poison.

"You should be careful with that," Minna said. "Why don't you take a bit of whiskey? It works just as well."

"Nonsense. You know that's not true. And, besides, *everyone* takes it," Martha snapped, placing the damp cloth back over her forehead.

Martha was right. Everyone *did* take it. Artists and literary lions from as far back as the turn of the century—Lord Byron, Keats, Edgar Allan Poe, Oscar Wilde, Sir Arthur Conan Doyle, and Elizabeth Barrett Browning. They all wrote of it. Some died from it. Even the altruist Florence Nightingale regaled on its soothing properties. Minna wasn't going to get Martha to dump it down the drain, but at least she could try to limit its use.

"But you shouldn't take it in the daytime."

"I told you, I didn't sleep a wink. Now hand it to me."

"All right. But I've stopped giving it to Sophie."

"Really. That child hasn't slept through the night for months."

"She doesn't need it anymore."

"Well, I do."

"What does Sigmund think?"

"Who knows? All he does is work . . . and he's so irritable."

Minna studied Martha's face as she took another dose. Her skin had the grayish tinge of an invalid, her hair lifeless and stuck to her scalp. Damn it to hell, she looks terrible, Minna thought. Why doesn't she care? Martha seemed twice as alive before all the children. Now everything she did seemed strenuous, too much effort. Sometimes she was all bustle and precision and other times it was almost as if someone had knocked the wind out of her and killed her, but she wasn't dead. Martha leaned her head back on the pillow and laughed dryly.

"I'd like to help him but he doesn't confide in me anymore. Walks around in foul moods. You've seen it."

"Not really, Martha. Have you tried talking to him?"

"Whenever I do, he gets annoyed. Also . . . his research. Truthfully, I can't abide it." Martha pulled the cloth off her forehead, leaned forward, and lowered her voice, "It all seems like pornography. . . ."

"In what sense?"

"In every sense," she replied, compressing her lips. "Everything's sexual. No one in polite society discusses these things. Sometimes I wish he were just an old-fashioned family practitioner. So much more dignified."

Minna thought back to the days of their childhood when her mother, like most women, pointedly avoided any discussions of sex or even reproduction, and how traumatized Martha was when she first got her menses. Her sister thought she was dying and ran downstairs screaming for their mother, who calmly told her it was the women's monthly "visitor," and proceeded to hand her a sanitary towel. "Throw it in the fire afterward," she had said. That was it. When it was Minna's turn, she didn't tell her mother at all.

Minna watched Martha's head lolling against the headboard, one arm limp against her chest.

"And some of his patients are so disturbed. I can barely stand to walk by them outside his office. Did you know one of them actually tried to kill himself right in our very home?"

"What?"

"Threw himself off the stairway. He wasn't successful. But caused quite a commotion, in any event."

"How inconvenient for you."

"I would say," Martha responded in a serious vein. Minna had assumed Martha would pick up on her sarcasm, but apparently not.

"But surely you can't deny the importance of his work," Minna said.

"You tell me. What of this new theory he claims might be central to everything? This Oedipus complex. I can't even bear to repeat it. Pure smut."

Minna's mind went back to an old letter of Freud's in which he touched on this concept but didn't explain it in depth. It was based on the Sophocles play *Oedipus the King* and the myth from which it was based. She knew the high points. An oracle warned Laius, king of Thebes, and his wife, Jocasta, that if they had a child, he would eventually murder his father and marry his mother. The couple, in fact, had a child, and left him to die on a mountaintop, but he was rescued and raised as a prince in a distant court.

When the child came of age, he was warned to avoid traveling to his birthplace. But one day he accidentally took the wrong road, met up with King Laius, and killed him, unaware that he was his father. He then made his way to Thebes to rescue the city from the Sphinx. Once there, he unknowingly married his mother, Jocasta, who bore him four children. From this ancient tale, Freud theorized that all boys lust after their mothers and resent their fathers. These feelings flood them with guilt, jealousy, and self-loathing.

"It's so upsetting," Martha said, absently massaging her forehead. "How does he come up with such bizarre notions? When I think about my own sons, it just makes my skin crawl."

"I don't know," Minna said, with a half smile. "It could explain some things. For instance, why do men marry women who look like their mother?"

"Are you intimating that I look like Amalia? That's not funny!" Martha said to Minna, who was now giggling.

"Oh, Martha, where's your sense of humor?"

"I have none right now. My head is bursting. Hand me the bottle, will you?"

Minna sat on the edge of the bed, picked up the fashion magazine *La Vie Parisienne*, and absently thumbed though the pages, all the while thinking of Martha's scathing assessment of her husband's research. During their courtship, she had shown at least a passing interest in Freud's work. At what point, Minna wondered, had it deteriorated into no interest and then not-so-veiled hostility?

She thought back, as she had so many times, to when Martha was engaged to Freud. And then the four-year-long engagement during which the couple hardly saw each other. Martha and Minna had moved with their widowed mother to a village outside Hamburg, while Freud stayed in Vienna, finishing his studies. As a medical student, living on loans, he was rarely able to visit. And he couldn't marry Martha in poverty. Out of the question! What would they do? Live in a garret, drink cheap red wine, and eat kugel for dinner every night? He was constantly beleaguered by his situation, calling himself "a poor young human being. . . . a scrounger and a *schnorrer*, tormented by burning wishes."

With the years of hardship and separation, it was no wonder that both Martha and Freud had built up illusions of what it would be like when they finally were together. He wooed her in his letters with a fierce, single-minded passion. She was his "Darling Angel,"

"Dearest Treasure," "Fair Mistress, Sweet Love," filled with radiance and goodness, and he was her prince, her "Blissful Lover, Sigmund."

Martha shared these letters with Minna, as well as with all her friends, who would marvel at Freud's ardent pursuit. On the rare occasion when he did come to visit, the two sisters would sit with him in the parlor, listening to stories about his university, "a great institution of higher learning, attracting students from all over the world," his professors "luminaries in their fields, scientists like Ernst von Brücke and Josef Breuer," his ranking "at the top of my class."

Martha was charming and sweet, sitting across from Freud with her hands folded neatly in her lap, but his achievements failed to capture her interest. Not that she wasn't happy for him. But Minna could tell, more often than not, that she would get antsy, feign enthusiasm, and then fuss with the cushions and twirl her hair. Then she'd stand up, leave the room, and return with a tray of coffee and strudel, or biscuits and hot tea, swooping in and out of their conversations, more than willing to have her sister *actually* listen to the preening young doctor.

A loud, slamming door and then the sound of feet running down the hall jolted Martha awake and pulled Minna reluctantly away from a fascinating article announcing the demise of the huge leg-o'-mutton sleeve.

"Mother! I can't bear to spend another night with Sophie!" Mathilde said, crashing into the room. "She's disgusting, her bed smells, and I think she's had another accident."

Martha raised her head from the pillow, considered her daughter a moment, and rubbed her eyes.

"My dear, there is nowhere else to stay," she pronounced.

"*Now* there's nowhere else to stay," Mathilde said, pointedly looking at Minna.

"Calm down, dear," Martha said, sinking back into the bed.

"Why don't you call Edna to clean up? Try to be patient with your sister," Minna added.

"'Try to be patient with your sister,'" Mathilde repeated in a singsong voice. "Easy for you to say. Why don't *you* try sleeping with her?" she snapped as she banged out the door.

"Minna, go after her and give her a piece of my mind," Martha murmured.

"She's just high-spirited," Minna said. "And I *did* take her room. I can understand her anger. Perhaps I'll take her with me the next time I go to the café. Get her an *Apfelstrudel*. What do you think?"

Martha lay motionless in the dark, airless room, nestled in a cocoon of down, one hand on her breastbone, the other clutching her now quiet crochet hook. Minna sat a few more minutes by Martha's bedside, watching her sister's face relax into a sweet, intoxicated half smile. Then she straightened the sheets, walked to the windows, and opened the heavy curtains a crack, letting in a few wisps of sunlight. She lingered there, gazing at the skyline. There would be no help from Martha today, she thought. She watched her sister rally for a final time and swallow another dose of the cinnamon-scented syrup, licking the spoon like a cat lapping up milk.

10

. . .

The outline of a crescent moon was still visible over the city's jumble of rooftops as Minna left Martha's bedside. She felt a mounting pressure to get things done before the midday meal, and wondered, just briefly, if Sigmund had a full calendar this morning. She knew he routinely consulted with patients in his office at around eight, right after his barber's daily visit, and rarely came back upstairs until dinner at one. Still, sometimes there were gaps in his schedule. Minna went back to her room to finish her toilette, rouge her cheeks, pin up her hair, and make the bed, then headed downstairs, where she encountered Edna, carrying a load of Sophie's soiled, wet bed linens.

"The washerwoman don't come till tomorrow. . . . I'll have to soak these in lime," she grumbled.

"Oh, Edna, I'm sorry. Please hang them outside. Otherwise they'll drip in the kitchen for days," said Minna.

"Someone should speak to the girl . . . such a nuisance!"

"No. No. Don't say a word. I'll talk to her."

Poor Sophie, Minna thought. It's not as if the child committed a cardinal sin. Perhaps I'll get her up a few times during the night, take her to the WC more often.

Minna proceeded down the hall and peeked into Sophie and Mathilde's empty room. Sophie's mattress had been stripped, and the air had the faint, urine-tinged odor of a dark alley. She opened the windows and then started downstairs. No time for coffee, it was already past eight. Martha usually did the marketing early and picked up her weekly bouquet of flowers before the stalls got too crowded, so Minna could manage only a few chores before she left, watering the limp, unhappy plants (alas, it wasn't eleven, but the plants didn't seem to mind), greeting the equally unhappy governess, and airing out the parlor, which reeked from a noxious mixture of last night's cigars and bratwurst. Everything smelled, Minna thought. Maybe it was her consumption of too much wine, she concluded once again.

It was a lovely, breezy November morning as Minna headed outside. As she reached the landing, Freud's waiting room door was ajar, and she could see him walking toward her through the tobacco fog. He had obviously caught sight of her as she was going down the stairs, and came to the door, smiling widely. She was still a bit confused about the night before but decided to act as if all was perfectly normal. He leaned against the wall, running his slender hand through his hair and looking for a moment like a man who had nothing better to do than to talk to the first person he happened to meet.

"My God, how can you smoke so early?" she said, waving her hand in front of her face. "Just the thought of it . . . Doesn't it ever make you ill?"

"No. Never. Unfortunately. Where are you going?"

"I'm off to run some errands. Martha isn't well."

"Come in. Just for a minute. I have something to show you."

She peeked into the empty waiting room and paused for a moment.

"Don't worry. I haven't a patient for another half hour. You'll appreciate this. Sit down."

She settled herself on the edge of a chair and watched him disappear into his study and then return carrying a small antiquity.

"It's my magical amulet," he said with pride. "The owner of this was supposedly endowed with supernatural powers." He went on to say that this particular "beauty" was from ancient Egypt. And then he held it up to the light so that she could see the sun glinting off the bronze.

"Magnificent, isn't it? My dealer moved heaven and earth to get it. Don't tell Martha. It cost a fortune," he said, gingerly handing it to her as if it were a jewel-encrusted Fabergé egg.

"It's beautiful. But what does this mean?" she asked, running her fingers over the invocations carved on the edges.

"This one depicts the lion-headed goddess Sekhmet, who had the power to destroy the enemies of the sun god. I actually have a dozen or so of these, all different, from Egypt, Rome, Etruria. Would you like to see them? No. Never mind, we don't have time. My favorite is the eye of Horus, son of Osiris, which heals as well as protects. They're all mythological—that's why I'm drawn to them. I've found that the mythological view of the world is nothing but psychology projected into the external world."

"As in *Oedipus*?" she said, standing up and handing the amulet back to him. "Martha was just telling me of your theory. . . ." Minna paused for a moment and decided not to mention that her sister found it obscene. "I remember you touched upon it years ago in your correspondence. I had no idea you were still working on it."

"Absolutely. It's become an integral part of my research.

Martha doesn't understand it at all. I'm sorry I ever mentioned it to her."

"You can't really blame her, Sigmund. This goes beyond anything one would mention in polite society."

"It doesn't bother you, obviously."

"No. Actually, I find it fascinating," Minna said. She could tell by his expression that her comment pleased him.

"Everyone thinks *Oedipus* is a tragedy of destiny," he went on, encouraged by her attention. "But it's much more than that. It represents the primal dream of mankind. From the day we're born, our first sexual impulse is toward our mother. And our first murderous wishes are against our father. The legend of King Oedipus is merely the fulfillment of our childhood wishes."

"Do you honestly think this is what Sophocles meant?"

"In a way. His play was about the vain attempts of mankind to escape their fate. But it can also be interpreted as a moral and intellectual question. His characters represent impulses that are suppressed but still found in our psyche. The fear and guilt from this situation could be the cause of *all* adult neurosis—a new universal law."

"Extraordinary," she said, understanding for the first time the importance of this theory. Her sister's reaction had been emotional and superficial.

"Being totally honest with oneself is never easy, but all little boys fall in love with their mothers and then become afraid of their fathers, fearing they will be punished or, even worse, castrated. The blinding of Oedipus is symbolic of the shock and disgust men feel when they realize they want their mother. . . ."

With Sigmund, nothing was what it seemed. He consistently

upended all that she had been taught. She had errands but she could stay here and listen to him for hours.

He stood there, his eyes fixed on hers, surveying her face in a most personal way. She suddenly felt uncomfortable and worried he might touch her or take her hand, and was relieved when instead she heard footsteps behind her as a patient approached.

"I should go, Sigmund. This has been so . . ."

"Illuminating, I hope."

"Yes. Illuminating," she said as she walked briskly out the door.

The street sweepers had finished their work and the pavement was brushed clean for the moment, free of horse manure, brown leaves, and trash thrown from uncivilized wretches in passing vehicles. She glided along the cobblestones, with the kind of speed reserved for a young girl. She hardly heard the heavy, labored sound of hooves until they were just behind her. She hastily stepped out of the way and narrowly missed the spray of birdseed flung from a child in the open carriage. All the exhaustion she had suffered at the baroness's house was gone. She thought back to Sigmund's soft smiles, their conversation. She had been dead these past few years. Feeling a wave of warmth, she cast off her jacket and swung it over her arm.

She walked past a stand of immense chestnut trees, then crossed the Ringstrasse, passing grand residences, gated courtyards, bronze fountains sporting dancing nymphs, and attractive shops built into the remnants of the ancient city wall.

A breeze lifted the curls off her neck and, after she picked up Martha's flowers, she made an impulsive decision to cut through the Prader, passing a crowd of pedestrians, all milling around and clutching hot chocolate, pastries, and parcels tied up in string. The park was alive with activity—street vendors hawking hot rolls and live rabbits in cages, and farther down the crowded footpaths there were mime artists, students handing out flyers, pipers, fire-eaters, and puppeteers. And then the ladies, swanning through the lanes with high-necked costumes and extravagant hats trimmed with feathers, hummingbirds, beetles, and butterflies. But Minna wasn't inclined to admire them. She kept thinking about him.

Why, Minna, the flowers are beautiful," Martha said. Then she sat down at the dining room table, ignoring the brief ruckus between Oliver and Martin regarding who had left the marbles on the steps and where were they now.

"How much?" Freud asked, raising an eyebrow in the general direction of the vase.

"Yes, how much?" Martin echoed.

Martha scowled at Martin and gave no reply.

"We don't need flowers every day," Freud said sourly. "You could *perhaps* be more frugal."

Martha's cheeks tinged red as her husband went on about the rising cost of beef, candles, pastries, and the children's medical expenses.

"And *you* could *perhaps* consume chicken instead of beef," Martha interrupted, her voice raised by an octave. "In addition, you could *perhaps* skip the antiquities dealers and the cigar store."

"All I'm saying is that you might find a way to cut our expenses."

"I *do* cut our expenses and you still find a way to buy your antiquities. There's always extra money, isn't there, if you look for it."

Minna sat quietly, consumed with guilt about the damn

flowers. She felt like stomping on them. In fact, she was a bit appalled at the whole conversation. Her mother had always considered the discussion of money vulgar. She never talked about it, even though their life revolved around it. And if it was discussed, it was only in reference to other poor souls "in unfortunate circumstances." But Minna was finding that in this house, money was an open topic of discussion. And Sigmund was not the same man as this afternoon or even last night. He was dour and impatient. As opposed to charismatic and romantic . . . no . . . not romantic, why did she even think of that? Scholarly was what she was thinking.

"Tante Minna, when's your birthday?" asked Oliver out of the blue. Thank goodness for Oliver, unpredictable, eccentric little Oliver. His off-the-wall conversation stoppers were most endearing to her now.

"June eighteenth."

"So you're a Gemini?"

"I suppose so. When did you learn the signs?" asked Minna.

"Oh, I know all about them. Astrological planets, dwarf planets, asteroids, lunar nodes . . . Frau Steinholt told me."

Freud sighed heavily upon hearing the name of a former governess whom they had dismissed several months before.

"You don't believe these things, do you, Oliver?" he asked.

"You know, Sigmund," Martha interjected, "astrology has become quite popular. One of my friends has recently consulted with a well-known astrologer in Munich. The Bavarian aristocracy is quite taken with her."

"Well, she must be an authority, then," he answered wryly.

"Exactly. Quite extraordinary," Martha chattered on, oblivious to the slight. "It seemed she prophesied my friend would die of crayfish poisoning, so now she's being very careful with her food intake."

"Does it make sense, Martha," he asked slowly, his voice haughty and contemptuous, "that so detailed an event as falling ill from crayfish poisoning could be inferred from the date of someone's birth?"

"I understand she's quite accurate," Martha answered, digging in her heels.

"Is that credible? Predicting someone's future based on the day they were born? These people are nothing more than Gypsy fortune-tellers."

Martha, silenced, began mashing her cabbage into mush. She hadn't touched the oxtail soup, waved away the beef, and now, God help her, it looked as though her arm was going limp.

"Did you know, Sigmund," Minna smoothly interjected, "that in the sixteenth century, Galileo and Nostradamus were both practicing astrologists? And that astrology is one of the most ancient philosophies—even Plato used it. I must admit it took a downturn when Galileo used a telescope, but even so—" She broke off, eyeing Martha. "In those days it was impossible to tell the difference between astrology and astronomy."

"In those days, perhaps. But that was hundreds of years ago," he said.

"No one knows for certain about this," Minna said. "You can't be certain. Astrology has had many famous followers. Augustus, Constantine, popes, military heroes . . . even doctors."

"I'm not one of them."

"Well, Martha has a point . . . . "

"Oh, never mind. . . It's of no consequence. . . ." said Martha as she gingerly pushed her plate aside.

"That's for certain," said Freud.

"Wait a minute," Minna said. "Martha is not alone here. I for one have followed the teachings of the modern French poet Jean Louis from Kragenhof, who happened to be obsessed with astrology. In fact, it was the cornerstone of his literary career. In his famous exit discourse, *Discours de la Sortie*, he confirmed that it was the purest of sciences, the only way to understand the secrets of time and the soul."

"The secrets of time and the soul?" Freud repeated, tilting back in his chair and studying her. He crossed his legs and, for the first time, looked as if he might actually linger at the table. It bothered Minna that he looked so impeccably put together, his suit pressed, his shirt starched, and his beard neatly trimmed, while her sister looked so disheveled. Martha had changed from her dressing gown to a day costume, but it looked as though she hadn't bothered to brush her hair or fix her face.

"Yes. Using both birth and transitional charts," Minna said.

"I'm vaguely familiar with Jean Louis," he said, with a small smile. "Wasn't he the one who committed suicide in a charming little hotel in Marseille?"

"Why, yes, I think he did."

"And remind me of his style?"

Minna paused for an instant, searching her memory. "Well, he's generally categorized as a disciple of Racine and Descartes," she said, beaming.

"Descartes and Racine," Martha echoed, more confident now that Minna had taken up her cause.

"Ah, yes," he said, his eyes bearing down on Minna, as if she thought he were born yesterday.

He excused himself, stood up, and, as he passed Minna, casually leaned over so close that she could smell the musky aroma of wine and cigar on his breath.

"Perhaps next time," he whispered, "you might give your imaginary poet a name more original than the French hairdresser down the street."

Minna did not react until he was out of the room, at which point, she released a sheepish smile to no one in particular.

11

. . .

That evening after supper, Minna was in her bathroom unpinning her hair when she heard Martha rapping lightly on her door.

"Can I come in?" Martha asked, opening the door, not waiting for a response. She was dressed in her nightgown and clasping an overfilled glass of bicarbonate of soda, which she could hardly hold steady. One slight nudge and it would spill all over.

"Is something wrong?" Minna asked, noticing a distinct frown line between her sister's eyes.

"I'm not feeling well and I'm dizzy. Would you mind taking Sigmund his evening tray? It's all prepared—sitting on the kitchen counter near the cupboard."

"Oh, Martha. Can't the maid do it? I don't want to go down there now," she said, tired and desperate for a break.

"She's left early—some family emergency. Or so she says. Frankly, I think the children just wore her out. And she always detested working on weekends. Anyway, you're still dressed and I'm not. Just walk in there and leave it by his desk. It'll take you five minutes."

Minna sighed as Martha left. She walked into the bathroom and stared at her red-rimmed eyes and tried to calm her uncivilized tangle of curls. Martha *would* ask her to go down there on a night when she was exhausted and looked like hell.

The first thing that hit her as she entered the stairwell to his office was the smell. The hall reeked of sour, stale cigars, and as usual smoke hovered in the air like a noxious cloud. She tentatively knocked on his door, balancing the tray in one hand.

"Come in," he called out in a low smoker's voice.

Minna opened the door and peered into the room. Freud was sitting at his desk, staring at an open notebook. A lit cigar burned in an ashtray and there was an open bottle of wine nearby. He was in rolled-up shirtsleeves, his jacket flung over the chair, and his hair rumpled as if he had just awakened from a restless night. She thought briefly that he looked so much more attractive this way than all buttoned up in his impeccable suits. She could see his bare arms up to the elbow and the creases at his neck where his shirt was unbuttoned. The sight of him like this slightly unnerved her as she wedged the tray between two piles of books on a table near his desk.

"Oh, it's you," he said, looking up at her. "Where's the maid?"

"She went home. Martha asked me to bring down your supper. I hope I'm not disturbing you."

He looked at her a moment and then leaned back in his chair.

"You have your hair down. . . ." he said, staring at her, almost studying her. She pushed her hair back and smiled modestly, a bit flustered that he even noticed.

"I was about to go to bed when Martha asked me to deliver this. Didn't have time to . . . freshen up. . . ."

She stood there, feeling slightly awkward. She knew that no one went to Freud's office uninvited. . . . She wished Martha had done this instead.

"Sit down," he said, taking the tray from her. He set it on his desk, hastily pushing aside a pile of papers and inadvertently toppling a few of the many ancient figurines lined up like a little army.

Minna looked for an empty chair. She would sit for a few minutes and then leave.

There were figurines everywhere, on shelves, tables, the floor, in a set of glass cases, and jumbled together willy-nilly on every other available surface. Also, here and there, were several ashtrays overflowing with snubbed-out butts. Minna knew he was a collector, but she had no idea of the extent of his passion. And then there were the bookshelves. Walls of them filled with hundreds of books.

"'*Video meliora, proboque, deteriora sequor,*'" he said. "'I see the better way and approve it; I follow the worse.' Publius Ovidius Naso."

A smile of recognition appeared on her face as she settled herself down and smoothed her hair. "You mean Ovid."

"He was referring to cigars, of course," he joked, blowing out a stream of smoke, which brought tears to her eyes. "Poor bastard. Banished for poetry, a crime worse than murder. But then again, he married three times before the age of thirty. Have to admire that."

Minna couldn't help herself, she laughed.

"Love, poetry, and adultery. You've got to give the man credit. Olympian urges."

He relit his cigar, inhaling in short, rat-a-tat puffs, and then coughed loudly, rolling into a bronchial spasm.

"My God, Sigmund. Why don't you stop?"

"I've tried a dozen times . . . but it's impossible to concentrate without it. The longest I've ever lasted was seven months. I was unable to work. Completely incapacitated. Barraged by arrhythmia and depression."

"A disaster . . ."

"Exactly," he answered, coming up next to her. "But when I use coca, the urge for tobacco is diminished. Magical drug. Five hundredths of a centigram of cocainum muriaticum in a one percent solution. The perfect dose. A few minutes after taking it, I feel confident, almost euphoric."

"I remember your paper on the subject."

"You read it?"

"Of course I read it. You sent it to me."

"Oh, yes, I remember."

"No, you don't, but I remember you were quite convincing that it was useful for all sorts of things, digestive disorders, hunger, fatigue . . ."

"As well as alcohol and morphine addiction . . ."

"But wait a minute, aren't you just substituting one drug for another?"

"Not at all . . . There are no physical aftereffects from coca . . . and, used in moderation, it's quite effective."

"Martha tells me it makes her nervous and uncomfortable."

"What doesn't? And why would you listen to her anyway? She took it *once*. In fact," he said, "it's just the opposite. One feels deliriously calm and content and, at the same time, charged with this marvelous kind of energy. I can work all night. Why do you always wear your hair up when it looks so lovely down? Would you like to try some?" he asked, his face turned toward her, his intelligent eyes softening slightly.

Minna's mind was racing. She was instinctively aware that he was looking at her differently, and her first thought was that she should leave. Absolutely. She was here merely to deliver the tray. But while a person's first thoughts are generally reasonable, they are not always the most persuasive. And to be honest, she was curious about this coca. She could stand to be a little more content. And who couldn't use a little more energy? So she nodded yes, as he reverently plucked a small blue bottle out of his drawer, opened it, dabbed some solution on his fingertips, and rubbed it inside his nostril.

"Just paint your nose like so," he said, passing her the viscous, opalescent mixture, which had a strong medicinal smell.

She carried the bottle to the window and looked into an odd-shaped mirror hanging there. As she carefully applied the solution, she caught a fleeting glimpse of him standing near his desk, watching her.

"Oh, it burns."

"Only for a moment."

"And there's this bitter taste running down my throat," she said. Her windpipe itched, as if she were about to cough.

"You need to paint a little more, perhaps on the other side," he suggested helpfully. She gravely did as instructed, almost sitting on a winged Eos statue placed on a chair near the desk.

"I feel nothing," she said, handing him back the bottle, "except my throat, which burns like fire. And my temples ache. I don't see why you think . . ."

"Yes?"

Minna ran the tip of her tongue over the smooth enamel of her two front teeth. She was overcome by an urge to get up and move about, so she rose from the chair and walked across the room. She stumbled and experienced that out-of-control sensation one gets from missing a bottom step. The normality of things started to shift. This was *not* nothing.

"My gums are numb and so is my tongue."

He smiled and puffed on his cigar. And then she felt it. The rush, or more like a surge in her being, which grew stronger, gaining power, consuming her in one perfect, magnificent single moment. She felt invincible and complete. Blissfully calm. In fact, she felt inexplicably better than she ever had before, yet also deeply focused and energetic. There was a sudden, sharp sensation in her sinuses and she put her fingers to her temples. He explained that it was the cocaine lighting up the limbic system and flowing through the ventral striatum, midbrain, amygdala, orbitofrontal cortex, and prefrontal cortex. All she could comprehend from his dense, medical words was that the coca was cascading through her brain, leaving pure pleasure in its wake.

And then the magic was gone.

"It's over," she said. ". . . I think."

"Sometimes," he replied, "I repeatedly paint the nose, which might be excessive, but I have a lot of work tonight and it won't harm you." He stubbed out his cigar, applied another dose, then walked over to Minna and handed her back the bottle. This time it burned white hot, as if someone had poured alcohol directly on an open wound. She momentarily panicked and pinched the bridge of her nose.

"I'm afraid . . ."

"Don't be . . ." he said, putting his arm around her.

As the pain from the drug subsided, the numbness in her mouth returned, invading her teeth, gums, and upper lip, traveling down her throat and making it difficult to swallow. The surge came even faster this time. The warmth flowing down her thighs, charging streams of heat in her cheeks, her lips, her shoulders, her brow. One moment she was solid, flat, and planted to the earth. The next, everything was lifted. She threw her head back against his shoulder almost in prayer.

"God, how long does this last?"

"It's a moderate dose . . . it'll fade away eventually," he said, his voice all port and velvet, his eyes hooded. She moved away from him and watched as he painted his nose yet again and picked up a small Egyptian statuette from his desk and stroked it gently.

"Isis, sister-wife of Osiris. Funny," he said, fingering it in his palm, then folding his hand around it. Then he rearranged the grouping of antiquities on the shelf behind him. He noticed her watching him with curiosity.

"It started as a hobby, you see. But the addiction soon seized me. Now, I suppose, one could say that collecting these antiquities is a form of love. It directs my surplus libido at something inanimate."

Surplus libido? Minna thought as she stared at the ancient objects and envisioned one of them, a gorgon-like phallic female alive with writhing snakes, coming to life, pulling herself off the shelf, and walking around the room, unleashing seething passions of sex.

"In any event," he went on, oblivious to her coca fantasies, "it relates to my work, you see. I like to think of myself as an archaeologist of the mind."

He walked over to one of the bookshelves and pulled out a heavy leather volume.

"Have you read this?" he asked, handing her a book entitled

History of Greek Culture by Jacob Burckhardt. "I'm consumed by it. Primitive myths and religions. Keeps me up until three in the morning."

She watched in silence as he selected a fresh cigar from his cedar humidor, clipped off the tip, lit the end, and rotated it slowly. He began talking and talking, smoking and smoking, swooping in and out of topics, then he stopped abruptly.

"How are you feeling?"

"I'm feeling lovely. . . . Somehow light . . . warm . . ."

"Content?"

"Why, yes . . ."

"Phenomenal, isn't it? So many uses . . . I give it to my patients for depression, melancholy, and . . ." he added, almost as an afterthought, "it's also a powerful aphrodisiac. Sometimes, not always, it has a stimulating effect on the genitalia."

Minna nervously fiddled with her hair. She felt heady, filled with self-absorption, and, come to think of it, desire.

"I'm curious," he said, watching her graceful profile. "You never tried this with Ignaz?"

"Of course not. He never even suggested it."

"He should have. Might have made him more interesting."

"Ignaz *was* interesting."

"Oh. *Very* interesting. When he wasn't discussing the nuances of Sanskrit, he just sat there half-dead."

"That's unfair. Admit it. You never liked him."

"Absolutely not true. What makes you say that?"

"Don't you remember your letter?"

"What letter?" he asked innocently.

"Your so-called condolence letter when Ignaz died, the one in which you told me that I was better off without him and that I should break off all relations with his family and burn all his correspondence?" she said, taking a swig of his drink.

He was silent for a moment.

"Oh. That letter."

He thoughtfully took another cigar from his humidor and began, once again, the whole ritual of cutting, rolling, lighting. Minna watched, waiting for some further response. He finally drew on the cigar.

"In any event," he said, exhaling luxuriously, "you and Ignaz were effectively estranged."

"Ignaz said this to you?"

"He didn't have to. It was obvious to everyone that the relationship had cooled. That you had cooled."

"I was *madly* in love with him."

"Madly?"

"Madly, passionately, completely," she said, now weirdly craving to touch the man standing across from her. Horrified, she crossed the room and stood as far away from him as possible. She could feel her skin burning under her blouse.

He watched her and then thought for a minute. "Wine, my dear?" he asked, his eyes bright and trained right on her.

Minna nodded yes and then took a handkerchief from the pocket of her skirt and dabbed her running nose. A thin sheen of sweat appeared on her face, and she noticed her heart was beating faster than usual. She had no idea that coca could do this to her. She must get a hold of herself.

She ventured over to the bookshelves and brushed her hand across the thick leather volumes, an abundance of riches that suddenly overwhelmed her with joy. She felt as if she could take any book from the wall and read all night and into the morning and into the next day and the next. Her eyes flew from shelf to shelf as she tried to register all the titles. One would think there would be mostly medical journals, but instead the library was filled with books on archaeology, history, art, religion, and philosophy.

Bursting from the shelves were strange and fabulous tales, fantasies, myths, plays, legends, and novels. Shakespeare, Goethe, Twain, Milton, Homer. Tragic heroes abounded. Hamlet, Macbeth, Dr. Faustus, Oedipus Rex. Detective stories, adventure stories, stories that dealt with the unknown continents of the human soul. The books were in German, English, French, Italian, and Spanish, the languages she knew he spoke fluently.

"If I owned your library, I'd assemble and reassemble the books for days. I'd alphabetize them by subject matter. . . ."

"I have."

"Well, then, by author . . . or both. I'd have a separate section for all these rogue volumes, the ones too tall for the shelves."

She turned around and noticed he was staring at her.

"By the way, do you still have that Thomas Carlyle I lent you? Years ago, when you were engaged? Remember?" she asked.

"Vaguely . . ."

"Never mind, it's just that over the years I've had to get rid of most of my books. . . ."

"Let me give you one. . . ." he offered, walking toward her.

"How sweet of you, but I couldn't possibly. Did it ever cross your mind, Sigmund, that you don't need friends with all these books around?"

"You don't?" he answered, looking amused.

"Not at all. In fact, if I had all these books, I wouldn't even have the impulse to actually read them. I'd just stare at them and think about how clever I was."

"You *are* clever, my dear," he said, gently pushing wisps of hair back from her face, his fingers resting on her neck. She was momentarily unnerved by his touch. She could explain away everything else about the way she felt when he was near her—his voice, his eyes, the way he looked at her when he thought she wasn't noticing. But the feeling of his warm skin on hers was different. There was no escaping the raw physicality of it. A flush of desire swept through her and she brushed his hand away, trying to dispel the afterglow. Good God. She hoped this was the coca.

She crossed to another bookshelf, pulling out a well-worn brown leather-bound volume. Freud poured her a glass of wine and glanced at the book she was holding.

"Plato's transcription of Socrates. He forced people to confront themselves, like I do. The Latin for this is *elenchus*—an inquiry or cross-examination. But I've noticed my patients only ask questions they already know the answers to. That's where Socrates and I part ways."

"You're parting ways with the great Socrates?"

"One can question giants. One can question anyone. It's the only way to get answers. And everyone wants answers. Everyone except, of course, my wife," he said, fidgeting irritably with a paperweight on his desk. His brow was creased with annoyance, bristling at just the thought of her. "She's an example of a person who doesn't seek answers because she has no questions. How can that be, I ask you? How can anyone have no questions? Except concerning our children, of course. Well, even then, she has no questions. If they're sick, she calls the doctor. And they're always sick. I can never recall a time when one of them wasn't sick. They get throat infections, scarlet fever, German measles, mumps, whooping cough. Everything available except smallpox and the plague.

Mark Twain said his home had 'a heart and soul and eyes to see us with . . . peace and grace and benediction.' What can that be like?"

He spoke in quick frenetic bursts, with the intensity of a revved-up adolescent, as his conversation grew more and more elliptical.

She watched in silence as he turned the glowing cigar in his mouth. Supper sat in its tray, untouched. Congealed herring salad, small squares of pumpernickel with butter, cheese, and German sausage.

"The *elenchus* of things. Asking questions. It makes people happier, maybe more virtuous. That's why Socrates chose death rather than give up his questions. Not that I'm suggesting that for Martha." He smiled wryly, painting a bit more coca in his nose. "You see, I take coca and Martha takes opium. She has her reasons and I have mine. I take it for work and she takes it for everything. I don't get involved in her logic and she doesn't get involved in mine."

He stopped abruptly, looked at her, and seemed undecided as to whether to proceed.

"You see what we have here?" he said softly, his voice catching for a second. "I am alone in a house full of people."

Something about this frank revelation made her want to look away. She was uncomfortable witnessing his sudden confession. It occurred to Minna that all etiquette had been dispensed with and she was hearing things she'd rather not. But the smoke smelled sweet, almost nostalgic. And the wine was spectacular. She was about to say something important, perhaps in defense of her sister, but then completely lost her train of thought, her mind floating off into space.

"The Delphic oracle, 'Know thyself,' that's what Socrates

believed," he continued. "Did you know he was the first to insist that dreams didn't come from the gods? Brought philosophy down from the heavens, his greatest achievement."

This is what he's like when he's lecturing, Minna thought. Head thrust forward, eyes so dark and luminous they seemed almost theatrical. She inspected an Etruscan antiquity, a carving of a sphinx, half lion, half woman. Then spoke with a bravado that surprised her.

"You know," she said, "Socrates was an artist and a stonecutter. That's what he was. But some people believe there was *no* Socrates at all. Perhaps Plato just invented him to suit his own philosophy. After all, there's no actual record of him giving lectures, teaching, or even writing books. So as Plato's puppet, he simply asked questions. Granted, they were deep questions about ethics and virtue. But what's the proof he ever existed?"

He gave her an exploring gaze and for a moment she felt it. An imperceptible shift in the air. As if they understood each other. As if they were experiencing a significant moment, a realization that what was occurring here was important. As if something had been settled. Or maybe it was the coca.

"What's the proof he didn't?" he asked. "More wine?"

"Maybe Plato took liberties," she said, holding out her glass. "Thank you. My mouth is so dry. He was a dramatist, you know."

"Well, it doesn't matter to me whether Socrates existed or not. It isn't important, is it? He's an idealized being, like God. I don't talk to Him, either. I don't ask Him for pointless favors. Martha does that. She's the religious one in the family. I do, however, celebrate Christmas. And Easter."

He flashed a diabolical smile and Minna thought about her family's strict Orthodox upbringing and their grandfather, the old rabbi from Mainz, who'd have been outraged if he hadn't died suddenly from apoplexy.

"How can you celebrate these holidays?" she asked, taking a gulp of wine. "You're a Jew."

"Do you think I'll be punished? Struck down in my prime?"

"Are you a godless man, Sigmund?" she teased.

" 'I can understand murder but not piety.' Arthur Schnitzler," he quoted, with an irreverent laugh.

"Scandalous playwright."

"Of course, that's part of his appeal. You know that most of his work is autobiographical." Freud drew on his cigar with a heightened sense of appreciation. "Ahh, it feels good to smoke again. Don't know how I ever gave it up. Nothing warm between my lips for seven months."

"Autobiographical?" Minna reacted. "His male characters are so cold. They change mistresses every week."

"He has that reputation . . . even famously counts his orgasms," he added, carefully gauging her reaction. "Writes them down in a journal."

"Really?" she said, her curiosity overriding her sense of impropriety.

"Yes. I've heard the count is over five hundred so far this year. Sex has much the same place in his life as cigars have in mine."

"Five hundred. Is that possible?"

"Oh, it's possible."

"And you have knowledge of this?"

"Not personal of course, but clinical."

"Of course," Minna said, now feeling slightly dizzy and uncomfortable.

"You see . . . Martha and I have been living in abstinence," he said, "so you can understand why I've taken up smoking again."

Minna tried to keep her face expressionless as she watched him take one last elegant drag and slowly exhale. She felt a sudden chill in the air and even the coca couldn't mask her surprise at this revelation. The whole scenario was fraught with inexplicable peril, and all at once she felt afraid. She fixed her gaze at the far end of the room and politely concluded the conversation with the feeble excuse that she was exhausted. Head aflame, she stumbled out of his office.

Through all her years of knowing him, this is what she learned that night. He was an unhappy man. And unhappy men are dangerous.

12

. . .

Minna was having that dream again. Someone was sleeping beside her, his chest pressed against her back, his arm draped gently over her hip. She could hear the slow, steady rhythm of his breathing as he intertwined his legs with hers and cradled his head in the crook of her neck. He inched closer, the heat of his body permeating her bedclothes and engulfing her in a low burn of desire.

But the feeling was brief. A sense of unease came over her, a moment of inexplicable anxiety, and then she saw him. It was Ignaz. The effect was vivid and immediate. There was a sudden constriction in her chest, a tinge of pain as she pressed her hand upon her heart. She slowly reached for him, her hand striking nothing but space and darkness.

She awoke with a start. Gradually, she grew accustomed to the dark. Her temples ached and her nose was congested. Last night, she remembered climbing the stairs, barely able to unbutton her boots and pull her clothes off before she collapsed on the bed, dead to the world. She was exhausted, but afraid to go back to sleep, her thoughts wandering from lucid awareness to the gray of dreams, a confusion of events, past and present, all mixed together in some unintelligible way. Over the years, she had had this night-mare before, and it always left her unnerved and vulnerable. Sometimes she had the urge to lock all the doors and windows, as if someone was lurking in the darkness. Other nights, she just lay there, longing for the light. She hadn't mentioned this to Sigmund, of course. What *did* she mention to him? It was all a blur.

She got up, took off her drenched flannel chemise, and opened the small window in her room. Her hair was matted with sweat, and the muscles in her lower back had stiffened up. She put on her dressing gown, draped a shawl over her shoulders, and looked out toward the canal. The day, a pink smear above the Vienna sky, had barely begun. Directly to the north, a succession of cross streets glowed, as if each still held the dawn, and the street lanterns gave off a halo of feeble orange light. It was bitter cold and the unusually warm air had disappeared. Patches of ice had begun to form over the breadth of the Danube. In another month, the river would be frozen solid until spring.

Minna stood like a sentry, wondering why she was still dream-ing about Ignaz nine years after his death. Perhaps it was her dis-cussion with Sigmund the night before. Or perhaps it was guilt. She had not visited Ignaz, even at the end, when he was dying of the white plague. When he first discovered he had tuberculosis and had to drop out of the university, he adopted an air of noble melan-choly, writing her letters filled with snatches of poetry or philoso-phy stolen from Immanuel Kant or Joseph Butler. But then he turned angry and resentful and dashed off terse letters from the sanitarium telling her not to visit. So she stayed home. She should have gone to him. Sigmund had said that they were estranged, but that wasn't true. Ignaz just wasn't himself. Who, after all, wants to die alone?

Minna rubbed her hands together and watched her breath transform into opaque puffs of vapor. Her feet and hands were growing numb with cold, and her throat tasted bitter. She lit the coal fire, reached under her bed, grabbed her bottle of gin, gargled, then spit into the basin. She was desperate for a bath. And even though Martha didn't like her bathing too early—the gas geyser heating the water was noisy, not to mention combustible; occasionally it exploded. She filled the tub anyway and slipped into the warm water.

As she sank in, she batted away the little voices rattling on in her head, dissecting the implications and consequences of her behavior the night before. She had always held herself up as someone with high standards and an inbred sense of propriety. And yet she couldn't help feeling that what had happened last night was, at the very least, inappropriate, at the most, dishonorable. Was she a muse or a Judas? Was she capable of such a thing? Guilt—the unwanted emotion—engulfed her like a toxic hangover.

There was a sudden compulsion to go over every detail, from the moment she stepped inside his office until she stumbled out several hours later. First of all, did she set the supper tray down on his desk, or did he take it from her? Then, did she sit down on her own or did he invite her to stay? When did he first offer her the coca? And why didn't she just say no?

Furthermore, after she painted the coca, did he offer her the second dose or did she somehow imply she wanted more? And who brought up the subject of Martha? He had. Of this she was certain. But then he had gone on to malign her. Why hadn't Minna rushed to her sister's defense? For shame. It must have been the coca. The whole scenario was completely out of character. She wasn't the sort of person who would tarry in a gentleman's private sanctum, engage in intimate conversation, and share coca with him at the drop of a hat. Even if it was medicinal.

Although it wasn't what she *did* that was bothering her, it was what she was *thinking*. And what she was thinking was that Sigmund had been far too engaging. And she had been far too conspicuous in her appreciation of him.

At this point, she heard familiar, heavy footsteps in the hall, and they seemed to stop in front of her door. She held her breath and waited. Would he *dare* come in? The bathwater had obviously awakened him. Her bedroom door was closed but the bathroom door was open. She dunked her head into the water and waited for the footsteps to recede down the hall.

This morning Minna would not take pains with her appearance. Normally she would wear a light-colored day dress, but today she deliberately put on a dark wool ensemble, shapeless and severe, the one she used to wear when she accompanied her prior employer to the rectory. No salved lips, no pinked cheeks. As she passed the mirror, she noticed dark, bruiselike circles under her eyes, and for the rest of the day, she refused to look at herself.

Before Minna could leave the room, Martha appeared at her door looking frazzled, as if it were the end of the day and not the beginning. Her hair was pulled tightly back from her head, and little beads of sweat were forming on her forehead. Her blouse puffed out over the top of her skirt, which was already wrinkled.

"Are you ready?" Martha asked.

Minna had forgotten that this was her day to take the children to the park.

"Almost," Minna said, jamming combs in her hair. "I was just—"

"Well, hurry up. I think I'll join you. Sigmund won't be home for dinner. He's *consumed* with work at the university. By the way, thank you for delivering his tray last night. I couldn't bear the thought of dragging myself downstairs one more time."

It was at that moment that Minna felt she should tell Martha about the night before. To dismiss the night's events would be a deceit. Completely out of the realm of possibility. But what if she *was* making too much of it? At the lecture, Freud's demeanor was so similar to the way he acted last night. He had been charming and humorous one moment, intense and dramatic the next—his literary references, his humor—all there, carrying himself with unflinching confidence and energy.

A man who could explain the soul so profoundly. Perhaps none of it last night was for her benefit alone. Perhaps it was just Freud being Freud.

She decided to casually mention that she had lingered in Sigmund's office after she delivered the tray.

"I hadn't realized what an extensive library he had, how many valuable artifacts piled up in a heap—well, not in a heap, God no—but certainly displayed on every conceivable surface. . . ." Minna paused, as if she had suddenly forgotten what she was going to say and then was conscious of a chalky dryness to her mouth.

"In any event, I'm afraid I overstayed my welcome. In the future, I'll certainly be more considerate of his time, in case he happens to mention my absence of tact in this matter."

Minna knew she was not being truthful. She grew conscious of this fact in the middle of explaining it away. She also knew that Sigmund was not likely to complain about her presence. Another wave of guilt struck her.

"Don't be silly. Sigi works late, and has no difficulty expressing a desire for privacy. Anyway, he enjoys an audience," Martha said, neglecting to add that she herself hadn't spent time in his office in years.

Minna heard children's voices shouting down the hall and was glad to have the conversation at an end.

"Mama, do I *have* to go?" Mathilde said in her typical obstinate way.

"You know the answer to that. The fresh air and exercise are good for you. Where are the boys?" Martha asked, as Ernst gleefully burst into the room.

"Mama, Mama, come look! Martin and Oliver are having a big fight!"

By the time Martha and Minna arrived on the scene, the two boys were on each other like a pack of dachshunds, their canines cutting through earlobes, tufts of hair flying, nail marks on stomachs and necks. Martin had Oliver pinned on the floor and was finishing him off with one more blow while Ernst was egging them both on.

"Boys! Stop it right now! Martin, get up!"

"I hate him!" Oliver cried, through a swollen lip, his nose dripping blood.

"It's all *his* fault. He started it," Martin said.

"Martin, go to your room. You could have poked his eye out."

"But, Mama . . ."

"Not another word."

"This isn't fair. He's a liar!" Martin said, skulking off to his room.

"And you, too," Martha said to Ernst, who was flushed with excitement.

Minna marveled at Martha's ability to be nervous and irritated about so many minor things, yet cool as a cucumber when it came to her children. They could tear each other's hearts out in front of her, and her demeanor would be almost pathologically calm. And this instance was no different. After the assault, Martha calmly announced that she was canceling the outing and then disappeared into the kitchen to consult with the cook. Meanwhile, Minna took Oliver, sobbing and dripping blood, to the bathroom.

"Christ almighty," she whispered under her breath. She had been in this household long enough to understand one constant in Martha's life—the children fought all the time, about everything. She dipped a washcloth into a basin and began gently dabbing Oliver's wounds. The cut on his lip was bigger than it seemed.

"Does this hurt, sweetheart?"

"Yes," he said, bursting into tears. As she held him in her arms, stroking his head, she wondered how a pack of children could be so sweet one moment and so uncivilized the next.

And why was it that Sigmund was never around when the children were behaving badly? His *Studies in Hysteria* could be the household diary.

Later that afternoon, after the bloodshed, Minna thought she heard Freud's voice calling her from the kitchen, so she quickly walked into the living room. There she stood pressed into the corner, waiting for him to leave. A little while later, when she heard his low voice again in the hallway, she took the long route to her bedroom, out the back door, through the garden, around the house to the front door, and up the stairs to her room. She knew this behavior was silly. She was acting like a foolish schoolgirl. But even a short exchange after last night would be awkward and embarrassing. And, come to think of it, why was he home so early? He never showed up at this hour. It didn't much matter. She preferred not to see him just now, especially when the house was so quiet. Martha had fled the scene to the Karnter Strasse to do some shopping, and the boys, who were usually underfoot, were still banished to their rooms. Minna assumed Mathilde and Sophie were with the governess.

She closed the door to her room and tried to read but it was hard to concentrate. She was restless and distracted, so she decided to take a walk, always a soothing diversion. But before she could get halfway down the stairs, she heard Sophie's distressed little voice on the landing.

"Tante Minna! Where are you going? I want to come. . . ."

"Sophie dear, you still have your lessons. I won't be long."

"No, no. Don't leave," Sophie sobbed, rushing down the stairs and sitting on Minna's feet. "It'th not fair. We were thuppothed to go to the park. Oliver and Martin ruined everything and Mathilde ith being horridly mean. Why can't I go with you? Pleathe?"

"Good heavens, Sophie. You're so dramatic," Minna soothed, sitting down on the step and pulling Sophie onto her lap.

Sophie nodded and wiped her nose. Then she curled herself up in Minna's lap and let out a sigh.

"I'll tell you what. Why don't we go in the parlor and have a sweet, and then you can go back to your schoolwork," Minna said.

Sophie's face brightened as they stood up and walked downstairs. Meanwhile, the child broke into a stream of gibberish, most of which Minna couldn't quite understand. Sophie's lisp got progressively worse the more excited she became. And her speech lessons didn't seem to be working in the least. They stopped off in the kitchen, where Minna put a few precious leftover dinner sweets on a plate, and carried them to the parlor.

"Tante Minna? Whoth's older? You or Mama?" Sophie asked, seating herself on the sofa next to Minna and wolfing down the cake. Children from large families, like packs of dogs, learn early to consume unexpected treats as fast as possible, or suffer the consequences. Someone else could snatch it before they could say "mine."

"Your mother's older. Why?"

"I just wondered. I told Mathilde you were much younger becauthe you're prettier, but Mathilde thaid you have a long face and you're not really that young. Do you want the lath one?"

"No, you can have it."

"Do you have a huthsband?" Sophie pressed, wiping her mouth and licking her hands.

"Here, use my handkerchief, you're all sticky now. No. No husband. How about you?"

"I'm too little," she said, smiling.

"I'm teasing."

"Well, when you *do* get married, will you sthill live with us?"

"I certainly hope so," said Freud, walking into the room.

"Papa, we have cake!" Sophie said, jumping up.

"How lovely, but there's none left, my princess," he said, picking up the child and giving her a hug.

Minna leaned back and watched him with his daughter. She had spent the better part of the day deftly avoiding him, which was silly. Naturally, she was bound to run into him sooner or later. They both lived in the same house, for heaven's sake. So why did she feel so uncomfortable?

Ingesting coca with this man was definitely a lapse in judgment, but the more troubling issue was the fear that she was becoming infatuated with him. If that was the case, this was an unacceptable state of affairs. Nevertheless, and despite her misgivings, she registered everything about him at once as he walked in—the tinge of color in his face, his affectionate glance in her direction, the gentle embrace he gave his daughter.

Sophie disengaged herself from his arms and began skipping around the room. The shrill voice of the governess could be heard upstairs, calling her in frustration.

"Go on now," Freud said in an authoritative tone. Sophie reluctantly walked out the door and banged up the stairs.

"I should go, too," Minna said, rising from the sofa. "I was about to take a walk. . . ."

"If you don't mind, I'll join you."

"No patients this afternoon?" she asked.

"Canceled," he said.

How odd, Minna thought. He doesn't seem the least bit concerned about our conduct last night. In fact, as they ventured out into the streets, he acted as if nothing had happened. Perhaps nothing did, she thought.

But she knew it was a lie.

13

. . .

It was twilight, with a perfect quality to the air, and gaslights flickered on the corners where heavy-booted policemen were beginning their night shifts. They walked down a narrow side street, past a row of art dealers and a cigar shop, where he ducked in, walking directly to the back to consult with the owner. She waited up front, surrounded by glazed walnut cabinets, inhaling extravagant, husky aromas of complex notes. The whole place evoked a kind of exotic adventure with names like Monte Cristo, Quintero, and La Gloria Cubana carefully typed on white parchment and displayed in brass plates on the door of each cabinet. Sigmund considered several different brands, selected one, and rolled it gently between his fingers as though it were a fine piece of silk.

"H. Upmann, produced in Cuba by a German banker. It's delicious," he said, lightly pressing the cigar to her nose. It was sweet and dry with a dark, mahogany-colored wrapper.

"Heavenly," she whispered, in mock reverence. There was a hush in the room, almost churchlike. Men and their cigars, she thought. And their wine. And their women . . .

They were almost home when he suggested they stop for a drink.

Minna could see Café Central up ahead and a few waiters loitering outside. She should have been back hours ago.

"It's getting late," she said, with a tentative smile.

"It's not that late and I'm parched. . . ."

"I don't know . . . it's been so long . . . the children . . ."

He stared at her, dangling his offer in the air.

"Really, Sigmund, I can't stay."

"Well, if you were *going* to stay, what would you have?"

She smiled, giving in. "A glass of wine. Half hour at the most."

The place was dimly lit, with bentwood chairs leaning against bare tables. A few stragglers were still sitting around, nursing their drinks, immersed in early-evening conversation but, other than that, the café was empty. If this were four o'clock, there wouldn't be a seat to be found. The turned-down gaslights hissed softly as they walked to a table toward the back. Minna settled in her chair, unbuttoned her jacket, and straightened her blouse. He sat opposite her, called over the waiter, and ordered a bottle of Barolo. She listened to him tell her how much he loved this café, how it was a refuge from his demanding schedule. How weary he was at the end of the day. And even before. Then he abruptly changed course.

"So tell me candidly, my dear. Are you happy here with us?" he asked.

"Why, of course. Why wouldn't I be? Everything's wonderful."

"Everything? That's remarkable, Minna."

"Well, of course, not everything."

He looked at her and said nothing. He was a man who used silence to his advantage. She peeled off her gloves and then fussed with her napkin while he continued looking at her. He noticed that her neck was longer than her sister's and her lips were glossy and unlined. She glanced up at him, her cheeks still shining with color from the walk.

"Sometimes I worry that I'm a burden to this household," she said, dabbing her forehead with her handkerchief.

"You're far from that. I hope we've conveyed that to you."

"And my future. I can't impose on you forever."

"It's no imposition. I don't understand your—"

"It's not that difficult to understand," she said, interrupting him. "I'm without a job, funds, penniless, impoverished, destitute," she said wryly.

"Insolvent?" he added helpfully, with a hint of a smile.

"Exactly." She laughed.

"Joking aside, Minna, you know you always have a home with us."

"That's extremely kind but I can't stay here indefinitely."

"Why not?" he asked, casting his eye over a group of students who were about to sit down next to them and then thought better of it.

"Surely you don't have to ask. It's keeping me up at night."

"What is?"

"My future."

"Your future is keeping you up at night?"

"Well, not only my future," she said, pausing. "If you must know, I've been having these strange dreams, *Nachtmahre*. Highly disturbing."

"In what way?"

"Are you analyzing me?"

"Of course not. Do you remember anything about them?"

"Oh, they're nonsense, mostly," she said, taking a sip of wine.

"Do you dream of missing a train?" he asked.

"No."

"Do you dream of flying through the air or falling off a cliff?"

"No."

"Do you dream of standing naked in front of strangers with no embarrassment whatsoever?"

"No. Do you?"

"It's a common dream, Minna."

"How long have you been having it?" she asked, smiling.

He laughed and then became serious.

"Tell me."

"Well," she said in a low tone, leaning forward slightly, "I see myself as an old spinster, living alone in a dreary pension with lots of mangy cats. You're allergic, as I recall? Anyhow, the place smells like mackerel and no one ever comes to call."

He gave her a withering look. "Don't humor me," he said.

"I doubt that I could," she said, draining half her glass of wine. "All right, if you *must* know, sometimes I see Ignaz beside me in bed. He's dead. And he looks terrible, ghoulish. He scares me."

"Your beloved Ignaz?" he asked, poker-faced.

"I don't know why I'm even telling you this. It's ridiculous."

"It's not ridiculous. Not at all. In fact, I've been working on a way to interpret dreams."

"Interpret them? I thought they came from problems with one's internal organs or indigestion or some such thing."

"Most doctors will tell you that, but they're idiots. It's astonishing that, in spite of thousands of years of effort, the scientific understanding of dreams is still so backward. We're not much better off than the ancients."

He went on to say that in prescientific times, the classic philosophers believed that dreams were connected to the world of superhuman beings—revelations from gods and demons. And they could foretell the future—a life of good fortune or tragedy.

"Even now," he said, "the majority of doctors and scientists will argue that dreams are merely a reaction to some external disturbance, like a flickering light from a candle, rain, thunder, or a lumpy mattress. The most educated men of our century still think dreams are caused by sensory stimuli when that's only a minor factor. It's all so unsophisticated. They believe the mind is somehow cut off in dreams. When in fact, the mind is *everything*."

"So if dreams don't come from rain and thunder, and they don't come from indigestion, where *do* they come from?"

"Ah," he said, smiling and clearly relishing the question. He gently tapped her on the side of the head. "They come from you. They're derived from your own experiences. *Internal* sensory, not external. And *I'm* the first person to say this.

"Dreams have meaning."

He searched her face for a reaction, to see if she appreciated his stunning discovery. The image of him at that moment, in magnificent self-confidence, his dark eyes shining, stayed with her long afterward. She took a sip of the very good wine and then said, "So tell me what my dream about Ignaz means."

"It's not that simple. It's disguised, maybe something from your childhood."

"I'm not sure what you're talking about, Sigmund."

"A dream borrows from many places, its fragments from another day, another time . . . strange images of an aunt, a cousin . . . a fiancé."

"I don't usually remember my dreams, but when I do, they all seem like nonsense."

"Seemingly. Past loves smiling on the couch beside you, asking after your health and then brandishing a weapon . . . or perhaps a sexual encounter with someone entirely unsuitable. More wine?"

"Yes, please. Go on."

"My patients' dreams are anything and everything, mixed up from their past and present. Sometimes their stories are completely absurd, and yet, when you understand their lives, it makes perfect sense."

"For example?"

"For example," he repeated, "one woman came to me with dreams of her sister in a coffin, an aunt whose jaw dropped off in front of her, and people pelting her with dead animals."

"It makes mine seem rather tame . . ."

"Ghoulish fiancés aren't that tame," he said, as he continued on about a forty-year-old widow who had been severely traumatized when her wealthy, older husband dropped dead in front of her while reading a newspaper. His family blamed her for the death, and she was beset by feelings of guilt and shame, which was why, he said, she was plagued by these dreams. And then there was the English governess who was hired by a wealthy widower. She was secretly in love with him but the feelings were not reciprocated. She was eventually fired, but losing the connection to the children caused her to dream about burned pudding. Another young woman kept having nightmares of men with angry faces attacking her, and would wake up with shortness of breath and a crushing feeling of strangulation. After meeting with her several times, he said, he found that her nightmares started when she discovered her sister was having intercourse with her uncle.

He stopped for a moment, carefully unwrapping his new H. Upmann. He clipped the end, wet it with his tongue, and then lit it.

"The reasons for these dreams are hidden," he said, "but after examination, it all becomes clear. Dreams are simply symptoms, messages to ourselves conveying what's wrong. An allegory for our innermost thoughts, wishes, and beliefs. For instance, another patient dreamed that she kept trying to insert a candle into a candlestick but the candle was broken and wouldn't stand erect. So this meant—"

"Let me guess . . ." Minna interrupted, trying not to smile.

"Of course," he said, "the symbolism is quite transparent."

"Have you discussed this with your colleagues?"

"Many times. No one takes it seriously. They call my work fairy tales and foolishness. As Virgil said, '*Flectere si nequeo superos, Acheronta movebo.*' 'If I cannot bend the higher powers, I will move the infernal regions.'"

There was a silence.

"Sigmund, would you happen to have a cigarette?"

He put down his cigar, motioned to a waiter lounging in the corner, and asked him for a smoke. The man handed him one from a pack in his waistcoat. Sigmund lit it and then offered it to Minna.

"So you'll unlock the mystery of my dreams?" she asked, inhaling deeply and leaning back in her chair.

He smiled at her. And then his smile changed into something different.

"I will indeed unlock the mystery of your dreams. And you, my dear."

She looked at him and felt a surge of something close to happiness. Something she hadn't felt for years.

"We should leave," she said reluctantly.

"Just one more drink."

"I can't. Not for another moment. And I stayed far too late last night."

"Do you want to talk about it?"

"No, I don't," she said, standing up.

"I didn't think so," he said, throwing some kronen on the table and helping her on with her coat.

There is a moment just short of touching, a slight gesture of the hand, perhaps, an angle of the head or the way two bodies move in tandem that gives a couple the look of intimacy. If someone had been passing Minna and Freud, as they walked out the door of the café, he would have noticed it: Minna, her face moist and flushed, her dark coppery bun slipping out of its confinement, and Sigmund, his hand grazing the small of her back, leading her toward the door.

14

. . .

When Freud and Minna arrived back at the apartment, they were met by the silver-haired night maid, who opened the door at the fourth pull of the bell. The gas lamps in the hall were already lit, and by the sound of the clattering dishes and children running around upstairs, it was obvious they had missed supper.

"Sigi?" Martha called out from the top of the stairs, looking down on the couple. Freud nodded with a forced smile as he helped Minna take off her coat.

"Didn't you hear the bell? We've been standing out there for some time," he said in annoyance. "Is that maid hard of hearing?"

"Not at all," Martha said, climbing down the marble stairway. "We were just sitting with the children. Would you like your supper now?"

"Thank you, but I'm not hungry." He nodded slightly at Minna and then walked past Martha toward his office. She gave him a perfunctory kiss on the cheek, which he barely acknowledged as he disappeared into his study.

"Where have you been?" Martha said, cradling her bad arm. "You've been gone three hours. I had to feed the children myself." The air smelled of boiled beef, vinegar, and tension.

"I'm sorry, I lost track of time," Minna said, taken aback by Martha's anger. "I ran into Sigmund and accompanied him on a few errands."

"Well, you've missed supper, but I can have Cook put together a plate for you."

"Thank you," Minna said, irritated. After all, she wasn't a child.

"The beef might be a bit tough. Our butcher was ill and his assistant cut it with the grain even after I told him how I liked it. Now it's falling into stringy threads, which couldn't in any way be called tender . . . *and* it's been cooking for so long. Perhaps you'd like something else?"

There was a long silence as the question hung in the air, Martha holding her ground and Minna deciding how to respond.

"I'm sure it'll be fine," Minna replied.

"All right, dear," Martha said, "but the cherry dumplings have gone cold. Would you like Cook to reheat them also? Although, on second thought, she might have left for the evening."

"It's fine, Martha. Never mind. I'm tired, anyway."

"All right, then," Martha replied, as she fiddled with the key on the gaslight, turning the wick down, lifting off the globe, and blowing on the flame.

"They smell less if you blow them out," she said. "By the way, in the future, suppertime is not a good hour to disappear. Unless of course, Sigmund needs you."

Her sister's tone was strained, her inflection brittle. How unpleasant she was, Minna thought to herself. Getting so upset because she was a few hours late, when heaven knows she had been working nonstop since she'd arrived. The two sisters stood opposite each other, their countenances so similar. The evening light played on the surfaces of the freshly polished wood as Minna was suddenly seized by a wave of guilt. The problem was not merely that Minna had been at a café drinking with Martha's husband while her sister stayed home to care for the children. The more explosive issue was that Minna's feelings toward Sigmund were not altogether innocent. There was no excuse for it and she knew it. She went back to her room in uncomfortable silence. As though they'd had an argument and both decided not to mention the real reason.

She opened the door to her room to find Sophie sitting cross-legged on her bed, with a book of folktales on her lap.

"Mama thaid you'd read me this before I go to sthleep," she said.

"Oh, Sophie dear, it's so late," Minna said.

What she'd really like to do is have a bit of gin, take a bath, and crawl into bed. However, one look at the child's disappointed face and Minna pulled Sophie on her lap and began to read.

It was the story of Franz, a little country mouse who lived in a little country house with red-checked curtains, two mouse-sized armchairs, and a cozy fireplace. He wore a red beret and glasses, and was filled with joy as he had just stolen a plate of strawberries and tartlets from a nearby farmhouse and delivered it to his three good-natured mouse siblings and adorable, round, furry parents, the sort of characters that populate children's literature, but not, alas, their real lives. The stories were sweet and rambling, and as Sophie cuddled into her, both Minna and the child fell fast asleep.

. . .

The next morning, Minna awoke early and deposited Sophie back in her room, taking care not to wake Mathilde. She was desperate for coffee and bread, as she had had no supper the night before, but the thought of running into Sigmund kept her in her room until the appointed breakfast hour. This morning, as she had done since she arrived, she got the children up, fed them breakfast, and helped organize their schedules. Martha was perfectly pleasant and there seemed to be no residual annoyance from the night before.

"How did you sleep, my dear?" Martha asked.

"Just fine, thank you. And you?"

"Like a baby. I was so exhausted I could barely move. Fell asleep the moment my head touched the pillow. Sigmund, on the other hand, was up most of the night working in his study. I just don't know what to do with that man."

Martha put on her hat and coat and left for the butcher. She told Minna she was planning to complain about last night's meat, and then afterward she would stop at the dressmaker's. Minna wanted to tell her that she might consider another dress pattern rather than the dowdy, outmoded one she always used, but decided against it. She was straightening the parlor when she heard loud voices coming from the foyer.

Minna peeked out the door and saw Dr. Josef Breuer, Freud's closest colleague and mentor, standing in the vestibule below. Fourteen years older than him, he had the appearance and demeanor of a kindly uncle. The cadence of his speech was impressively slow, like that of a scholar, in contrast to Freud's sharp retorts, infused with unapologetic disappointment and anger.

"Try as I might, I can't agree with your conclusions. My case studies just don't support them," Breuer said.

"Then your case studies are wrong," Freud replied, scowling at his former mentor.

"You're taking this too personally, Sigmund."

"How am I supposed to take it?"

"I'm not saying I disagree with everything. But your findings are a grave overvaluation of sexuality. You've gone too far."

"You think I've gone too far! I haven't gone far enough!" Freud said, his fury filling the air with tension.

Minna assumed they were arguing over Freud's *Studies in Hysteria*. The lecture that she had attended had been defensive at the end, and he had told her that his conclusions concerning hysteria were being challenged by other scientists.

"You're my most brilliant student. Your theories are inspired, but you must compromise . . . make some changes. . . ."

"There is no compromise with the truth," Freud fumed, his voice rising as he waved a bunch of papers in the air.

"I'm simply suggesting that you need further findings before presenting this to the council. These men are strong willed, like you," Breuer said, smiling, trying to appease him. "If you continue in this vein, they'll cut you off."

"Let them."

"Sigmund. You know I support you. I send you patients. When you've been short of funds, I've tried to help. But I'm telling you, by doing this, you're isolating yourself."

"Good day, Josef," Freud said, his face red with indignation, as he walked the man to the door.

"Can we discuss this another time?"

"I don't see the point," Freud said.

Minna watched as Breuer carefully placed his hat on his head, straightened his tie, and left as Freud stormed back into his office, slamming the door. She ventured down the stairs and knocked on the door to his study.

"What!" he barked.

"It's me," Minna said, hesitantly opening the door.

"Come in! Did you hear that? Doling out praise as he tries to destroy me."

He was sitting in his desk chair, shoulders hunched, puffing on a cigar with that hot-under-the-collar look.

"He thinks just because I owe him money, he can tell me what to do," he said, flicking his ashes on the floor and kicking them aside.

"I'm not sure that's fair. It didn't sound like—"

"Fair! You tell me what's fair. I work day and night, I'm on the verge of a major breakthrough, and he harasses me with his picky objections," he said bitterly. "And what good has he done? I'm not even a professor. Year after year he stands by watching others get promoted over me. Still a *Privatdozent* after all this time."

"You can't deny the man cares for you."

"Don't defend him. You have no idea. I hope his practice is obliterated, in ruins. See how *he* likes it when someone wreaks havoc on his work."

Minna was suddenly reminded of Martin after Oliver teased him about his poetry.

"I hate you," Martin had said, his face turning red, his veins sticking out of his neck. "I will hate you until the day you die. I hope everything you do turns to filth."

"You look tired, my dear," Minna said, observing Freud's puffy eyes. "Martha tells me you didn't sleep at all last night."

"I was revising part of my theory," he said, putting his research together in a packet and handing it to her. "And for what, I might ask?"

"What's this?" she asked, taking the folder.

"Worthless pieces of paper, if you listen to Breuer. Read it and decide for yourself. I'll be gone next week, but we can discuss it when I return."

"Why, of course," she said, thrilled, clutching the folder under her arm.

M inna stayed up half the night looking over the notes. She was well aware that Freud had flung this thing into her arms, almost on a whim, after banishing his mentor, Breuer, from his study. Nevertheless, she was flattered. At first she thought it might be just a summary of what she had heard in the lecture. But from what she could glean from a preliminary reading, he had added more case studies and more proof of his discovery.

For the next week, Minna's days were filled with family activities, errands, and outings. But after the children were asleep and the house was finally still, she sat on her bed and took out his report, sifting through it as if it were buried treasure.

I decided to start from the assumption that my patients knew everything that was of any significance to their treatment and that it was only a question of getting them to communicate it . . . penetrating into deeper layers of memory, using all the weapons in the therapeutic armory, forcing our way in, overcoming resistances all the time, like a surgical intervention akin to the opening up of a cavity filled with pus. . . .

She stayed up writing notes on the side, compulsively filling an empty journal with her thoughts. Her neck strain came on about the third night and she borrowed a writing desk from downstairs. She wished she had electric lights in her bedroom. It would be much easier than reading by candlelight. It was a difficult and slow process to digest it all, but this solitary activity gave her a window into how Freud's mind worked. She could hear his disembodied voice in the report and she longed to discuss it with him, but he was still away at a congress in Berlin.

Through it all, she began to form her own opinions of his work. She could see why Breuer had some objections . . . why he disagreed with the proposition that every neurotic symptom had a sexual origin. Weren't fear, injury and disease, the loss of a family member, bankruptcy pivotal? Couldn't these misfortunes also cause neurosis and hysteria? For instance, she had been devastated by Ignaz's death. She still had nightmares about it. But the cause of her discomfort wasn't sexual. Ignaz died of the white plague. She felt guilty she didn't visit him, but what, one might ask, is sexual about that?

Also, she noticed that almost all of Sigmund's case studies were women—upper-middle-class women and very unhappy ones at that. She thought about her mother, who used to eat gobs of strudel at tea or retire to her room for days on end when she was "not herself." Everyone always knew when Emmeline was upset, which was most of the time after their father had died. Now, according to this report, Sigmund would argue that her mother's behavior was driven by guilt over some secret form of sexual deviance and that she needed to be prodded and pushed to talk about her feelings. This process would eventually make her feel better and, supposedly, she wouldn't continue to torture the rest of the family with her bitterness and frustrations. This sounded highly doubtful to Minna. In Minna's experience, the more her mother focused on her problems, the more she bedeviled those around her. In fact, in Minna's opinion, the less she talked, the better. Perhaps she might be better off not thinking about her mother at all.

When Minna finally reached the last line of the report, she smiled. It was so typical of Freud's unbridled sense of entitlement.

"We shall, in the end, conquer every resistance by emphasizing the unshakable nature of our convictions. . . ."

Like one of his heroes, Julius Caesar, Minna thought. If he couldn't tolerate criticism from his mentor, Breuer, he certainly wouldn't welcome it from her. She could still safely give him her reaction and perhaps just touch on her reservations, but she would have to be extremely careful.

She looked out the window and saw the light breaking through the thick rain clouds that had gathered during the night. It was still quiet in the house except for the wind rattling the windows and the metal radiator hissing away, sounding like an old man half asleep. The heating system was antiquated and erratic, as were most things in this apartment. Her eyes ached and she felt as if she'd been drugged.

By eight a.m., the rain was coming down in hard, steady sheets. The governess had not appeared, and lessons would not resume until tomorrow. The children were naturally at loose ends, their routine upset, their outings canceled.

Minna tried to organize a few activities, starting with reading time. All the children were told to choose a book from their bookshelves. And as they settled in their rooms, Minna tried her best to pull herself together but, she had to admit, she was beginning to look as disheveled as Martha. Her hair, limp and tangled, was knotted carelessly at the nape of her neck, and she had on one of her least attractive shirts and skirts.

She was in the kitchen, filling Anna's bottle, when she heard a high-pitched scream from the girls' room. She ran upstairs to discover Martin, sitting in his pajamas, reading a copy of *Der Struwwelpeter* to Sophie. It was a wildly popular children's book, written by a Frankfurt physician, that ostensibly read like a fairy tale. But it was actually a collection of nightmarish stories, cautionary tales of what happened to children who disobeyed their parents. Minna had read this book to a few of her older charges when it was first published. She didn't think it was the most suitable book for children, but then neither was *Kinder und Hausmärchen* by the Brothers Grimm.

There was the story of little Daumenlutscher, who was warned by his mother not to suck his thumb and ended up having his digits lopped off by giant scissors. Then there was Kaspar, who wouldn't eat his soup. He wasted away and died. And don't forget poor Pauline, a little girl who played with matches and then burned to death.

Martin was reading these stories slowly with a quirk of a smile, relishing four-year-old Sophie's reaction.

"I don't want thith book!" she cried, pulling the book out of Martin's hands and throwing it on the floor.

"Martin, what on earth are you doing?" Minna asked. "Why don't you choose another book?"

"She likes this one," he said, with the expressionless stare of a child feigning innocence.

"I highly doubt that."

"Tell her, Sophie," Martin pushed. "You *asked* me to read it."

"Did not . . ." She sniffed.

"Martin, why don't you go get dressed?" Minna asked.

"No."

"You're *not* sitting in your pajamas all day."

"Why not? Mama does it."

"Only when she's under the weather."

"Well, *I'm* under the weather," he said, grinning at her with a row of pointy white teeth, his hair curled up into two little horns behind his ears. It was at this point that Martha poked her head in the room.

"What's going on?" Martha asked.

"Tante Minna's making me get dressed and I'm not not feeling well. *At all.*"

"The boy *does* look flushed," Martha said. "I think he's getting sick. Are you getting sick, dear?"

Martin faked a dry, rattling cough. ". . . And my throat hurts something terrible."

"I knew it! Go to bed," said Martha.

Martin banged out the door, flashing Minna a small, triumphant smile. My Lord, Minna thought, if he didn't drive you crazy, you had to admire him. But why did her sister have to interfere in something so trivial?

"You undercut my authority, Martha."

"But the child *is* sick."

Minna held her tongue, but this was one of those times when Martha's peevish behavior made her want to poke her with a parasol.

15

. . .

The next morning was a clear, sparkling Saturday. Ernst was at speech therapy and the girls had gone with their mother to the Tandelmarkt, so Minna decided to take Martin and Oliver skating on the iced-over lake. It seemed that Martin had made a "most remarkable recovery" overnight and, once on the way, he and his brother ran ahead, leaping across puddles and swinging on overhanging branches with unmitigated glee.

When Minna thought back to what happened next, she had to admit that she had heard a faint chorus of hoarse, high-pitched voices coming from somewhere, before the boys even laced on their skates. Perhaps at that moment she should have sensed the impending danger, been forewarned, and steered the boys away from the scene. But no instinctual alarms rang out in her brain as she settled herself on the sandy shore, and then sat there, immobile, as a gang of four or five older boys burst out of the bushes and swarmed around Martin and Oliver, hurling insults and brandishing rocks and sticks. Even a deer knows when a hunter has his scent.

"Dirty Jew," one oversized, snub-nosed adolescent barked as he knocked Oliver down and pummeled him in the face and chest. Another boy pushed Martin to the ground and the two went at it with alarming ferocity, fists and boots flying, blood spraying in the air. Minna's shouts echoed across the lake as she ran over and tried to yank the assailants off them. Then it was over as fast as it had begun. The bullies retreated into the woods as more and more people crowded the scene, and someone called for the police.

Minna knelt down and wrapped her arms around Oliver's thin, shivering shoulders, then wiped his swollen eye and held her handkerchief to the cut on his forehead, his blood smearing the front of her blouse.

"What hurts?" she asked.

"Everything," Oliver moaned.

"And look what they did," Martin said, hobbling over to her. "They broke my skate."

"But you chased them away, brave boy," she said, with a pained smile.

As they trudged back to the apartment, the boys were mostly silent. At one point, she tried to console them, but her words sounded empty. She knew very well that incidents like this were happening all over Vienna. What could she say?

When they walked in the door, Freud was standing in the vestibule, still wearing his traveling clothes, having just returned from his congress with Dr. Wilhelm Fliess, a young doctor from Berlin who specialized in ear, nose, and throat ailments. The boys were near tears as they told their father what happened.

"Papa, they hurt us," Oliver cried, one eye closed and swollen. "They were hitting us for no reason."

"There were at least ten of them," Martin said, lying, averting his eyes, "but I chased them off."

"No, you didn't," Oliver said, and then began sobbing.

He took stock of their bruised faces, broken skates, and torn clothing, clapped a paternal arm around them, and then sent them upstairs to wash their wounds.

"We'll get you new skates," he called after them, attempting to sound cheerful. But he wasn't. Not in the least. As soon as the boys were out of earshot, he turned on Minna.

"They're always fighting down by the lake. I don't know why you took them there in the first place."

"Sigmund, that's not true. We go there all the time—"

"This isn't the first time I've heard of this sort of thing," he said, cutting her off. "You have to be more careful."

"It all happened so fast," Minna said, taken aback by the rebuke. "I'm sorry."

Sigmund listened in silence as Minna went on to tell him what had happened, how they were ambushed, and what was said, but at a certain point, she knew he wasn't listening. He was shifting back and forth on his feet, looking out at the street, trying to control his mounting anger. She could see little beads of sweat on his forehead as he took a handkerchief from his pocket and wiped his brow.

"I'm relying on you to take care of them," he said, as if his patience had been put to a severe test.

"Of course," she replied. "I'm as upset as you are."

"I'm glad to hear that," he said, as he looked her in the eye for the first time that day.

Minna was puzzled by his curt manner. It seemed as if his irritation was based on more than simply the children's harrowing experience. He was treating her like an irresponsible governess. Nothing more. Perhaps he was overtired by the trip and it was all just a misunderstanding on her part. She struggled to maintain her composure and then ventured a hand on his arm. The gesture was clearly misguided—he lowered his head and moved away from her. The serious lines on his face, between his nose and mouth, grew deeper and his dark eyes looked unfamiliar. Just what had happened when he was away? And could it have anything to do with her?

Sigmund spent the rest of the day ensconced in his study, not even coming out to join the family for dinner. Minna had wanted to discuss her notes with him upon his return, but the fight at the lake had obviously affected him and she had no choice but to wait. Upon reflection, she decided to put aside the nagging image of his cool demeanor, attributing it to exhaustion and nothing more.

When she finally ventured downstairs to his study the next day, the door was open. He was standing with his back to her, looking out into the dark courtyard and puffing on his cigar. She hesitated a moment, then knocked lightly on the heavy wooden door-jamb. In the dimness of the room, she noticed the desk was strewn with a messy pile of papers that had not been there the day before.

"How was your trip?" she asked, attempting to sound nonchalant.

A long moment elapsed before he answered. There was something in the air that was amiss, and she had a feeling of discomfort. There was nothing in his stature to reveal this, but she felt it, nevertheless. She waited uneasily for him to turn around, and when he finally did, his expression was absolutely blank.

"Most productive," he said, nodding at her politely, but she noted that he did not ask her to sit down. He picked up a large file from the table next to him and placed it on his desk, sat stiffly in his chair, and began thumbing through the documents.

"If you don't mind, I must review these. . . . I'm presenting a paper tomorrow."

"Well, then, I won't disturb you," Minna said, still standing at the door. She turned to leave, but then, against her better judgment said, "I read your report and jotted down some notes. Anytime you'd like to discuss it, I'm ready."

"Actually, I went over the report with my colleague Dr. Fliess, in Berlin. We examined everything in great detail and, I must say, he was extremely helpful," he said, not looking up from his papers.

"Oh," Minna said, deflated, as she handed him the report.

"Thank you," he replied, glancing up briefly. She watched as he casually flipped the report onto a pile of files stacked on the floor behind him.

"My notes are attached." She paused as he picked up an antiquity that had fallen off the side of his desk.

"Duly noted . . ." he said, examining it with concern. "I think there's a chip. See there on the left side? That wasn't there before. . . ."

He handed her his Egyptian goddess Isis, sister-wife of Osiris, one of his favorites, which he often brought to the dinner table, to Martha's chagrin.

"Look at the headdress, by the horn. That's *definitely* a chip. . . ."

"It might be," she said, sighing imperceptibly. "When do you think we can discuss the paper? To be frank, I've spent a good deal of time on it."

He stopped and gave her an odd look. She detected an aloofness in his bearing as he cleared his throat and addressed her in an offhand manner.

"That's very nice of you, dear, but you needn't have done that. How are the boys?"

Minna flushed and blinked her eyes as a sharp pang of reality hit her in the gut. He was *not* interested in her opinion and he was *not* going to read her notes. In fact, he never had any intention of reading her notes. Oh, maybe momentarily, when he first handed them to her, and he was outraged at Breuer's remarks, but then it obviously left his mind completely.

"They're fine. So you *don't* want to read my notes?" She couldn't help herself.

"No offense intended, but I think my colleague Dr. Fliess has given me all the help I need."

"Has he?" she asked, bending over and picking up her notes off the pile. "Well, then, I'm sure he's touched on the possibility that perhaps not *all hysteria* is sexual in origin?"

"He had no such criticism."

"What if someone were upset over the death of a child?"

"Well, that could be—"

"Or they lost all their money?"

"That also—"

"Or they didn't like their lying, philandering husband?"

"Now, Minna, I can tell that you're perhaps—"

"Or they were stuck in a house under the thumb of . . ." She stopped herself. He rose to his feet so they were standing almost eye to eye.

"In any event, I can think of many reasons to be hysterical," Minna said, turning abruptly and walking out the door.

He watched her leave. Then he sat back in his chair and stared at the open door. He just couldn't, for the life of him, figure out what the woman wanted.

16

. . .

She was such a fool. Why had she taken the time to pore over his report, to delve into his world of demented humans with horrifying dreams, to force herself to understand the meaning of sexual neurosis and hysteria and phallic symbols, like flagpoles and trees hovering everywhere, when he obviously didn't have the slightest inclination to listen to a word she had to say? Perhaps he had *never* taken her seriously. Even that night in his study, with talk of Aristotle and Sophocles, she had merely amused him. Have another dab of coke, my dear. Oh, yes, paint it on and sniff it up and then I'll discuss with you some problems in my life that are nobody's business, and I'll never regret it for a moment and you will, likewise, never regret it unless, of course, it ruins your life. To hell with him! She could tell she was working herself up into a frenzy and she tried to calm down.

Now it was three a.m. Minna forced herself to think of something else so she could get to sleep. Maybe she would venture into Sophie's room, get her up for the umpteenth time, and take her to the WC. Or maybe she'd go downstairs to the kitchen and fix a cup of tea. No. She couldn't risk running into him if he happened to be working late—which he often was. Even after all this, in her insomniac opinion, she imagined he was still interested in her. Then again, maybe not. Perhaps he was indifferent yesterday because he *was* indifferent. But hadn't he made her privy to his most private thoughts? Even volunteered the information that he and Martha were "living in abstinence." You'd think these things would be out-of-bounds, but to Sigmund *nothing* seemed out-of-bounds. Not even his problematic marriage to her sister. Who, by the way, would prefer he were some society doctor specializing in rheumatism or gout.

Marriage, to Minna's mind, never quite worked out the way it seemed. The passionate side of marriage, that ineffable image of bliss, subsided; the intensity dissolved and an almost mechanical lack of interest set in. So the husband focused on work and the wife ran the household, an arrangement almost preordained to cure even the most romantic nature. In Minna's eyes, most women, including her sister, envisioned a relationship that would last for all eternity, but it inevitably became tyrannically conventional and boring, a dull beast.

It wasn't until dinnertime the next day that Minna saw him again. She was determined not to repeat her petulant behavior in the study. When she thought about it, there was something so demeaning about the entire episode. And what was she doing anyway? He wasn't a suitor who had snubbed her. He was her sister's husband. Somehow, in the midst of her laborious, critical dissection of his work, she had forgotten this glaring fact. It was a dangerous thing to forget, and she was pained that she had done so in such a selfish manner. She had initially convinced herself that reading his notes would give her an occasion to delve deeper into his mind, that it would be a point of departure for discussion. And she loved these discussions—lived for them. But being attracted to his mind had led her to foreign territory where she didn't belong.

As Sigmund passed her in the parlor, he approached with a conciliatory gesture, touching her lightly on the arm.

"Minna, my dear. I was hoping to talk to you. I was thinking about it. I'd be happy to look at your notes."

"Oh, that's not necessary," she said, smiling at him as if yesterday's incident had never happened. "Not at all. In any event, I'm not sure where they are. I might have thrown them in the dustbin."

"You're still angry."

"Why would I be angry? You must be terribly tired. I'm sure the trip was exhausting," she said, entering the dining room. "Would you like a glass of wine? Would you mind getting Dr. Freud a glass of wine?" she asked the kitchen maid.

"Oliver, dear," she called to the boy. "Come tell your father about our little outing to the cemeteries while he was away."

Oliver, who was just entering the room with the rest of the family, was only too happy to comply in his fastidious, detailed way, reveling in the minutiae of Mozart's grave, comparing it to other composers' final resting spots in Vienna.

"Mozart died at Rauhensteingasse 8 in 1791. He was buried in a pauper's grave just outside the city, then exhumed in 1855 and relocated to St. Marx Cemetery. Beethoven died in 1827. His memorial is much grander. I liked that the best, next to Schubert's, who died in 1828. They're both at Zentralfriedhof."

Minna listened attentively, but at some point noticed Sigmund pulling a cigar from his jacket and rummaging through his pockets.

"Poor Mozart," Minna said as she stood up, walked to the side table, and picked up a matchbox—"a true musical genius, but spent his final years in poverty, borrowing money from his friends, interred in a common grave. Pathetic, really."

She struck a match and held it in front of Freud's face. "Light?"

"Why, thank you," he said, backing up from the flame, which was held just a little too close to his nose.

"And then there was Baron Ernst von Feuchtersleben, a philosopher best known for . . ."

"That's enough, Oliver," Freud said, impatiently.

"Bravo, Oliver, quite informative!" Minna shot back.

"Minna, I'd be happy to read . . ." Freud persisted.

"Not necessary," Minna insisted. "It's such a bore, isn't it, going over and over one's thoughts. What else shall we talk about? The new play at the Hofoper? Martha, what shall we talk about?"

Martha stared in silence at her sister, wondering what had gotten into her.

"Martha?"

"Well, Frau Simon just joined our sewing group. You should join us. We're doing the most marvelous crochet work. You'd love it."

Freud was quiet for the rest of the dinner as the two sisters chatted on about nothing. Just before the cheese course, he excused himself and disappeared downstairs.

Late the following morning, Minna decided to accept Dr. Silverstein's request to call. The timing was fortuitous; Martha had been campaigning for him, and now Minna was ready to accept.

She sat in the drawing room, feeling like an aging ingénue, wearing a rose-colored day dress that nicely complemented her skin tone. Eduard was seated next to her in an armchair by the window. Her first impression of him at the tarock game had been correct. He was nice looking, with thick eyebrows and dark eyes. He had high cheekbones and a patrician nose—the face of an aristocrat—and he was taller than Sigmund, broad shouldered with a strong jaw. He was dressed faultlessly, in a suit that looked as if it had come from a London tailor, but still he didn't look British. And when he first arrived, he presented her with a box of chocolates. A nice gesture, she thought. She would give them to the children.

The two of them had the house to themselves for the moment. The children were at the Prater, Martha was at the *Gartenmarkt,* and Sigmund at the university. She offered Eduard a glass of wine from an open bottle on the tea trolley and took one for herself.

"And you now live here permanently, I understand?"

"Well, not permanently. No. Not at all," Minna said. "I'm helping her at the moment with the children. As you know, she just had her sixth child. And things can be a bit chaotic, as you can well imagine. . . ."

"How fortunate for them," he replied tactfully. "I'm sure your sister would like to keep you here forever."

"It's kind of you to say that, but I'm thinking of traveling abroad next year." Heaven forbid he should think of her as the spinster sister with nowhere to go.

They talked of politics, art, and the latest theater. It was obvious he was up-to-date on the current state of affairs and that he read the better periodicals. What was it then that was lacking here? It was clear that he had no passion for medicine. He had inherited the practice and he was not shy about admitting that "it paid the bills."

He was on the board of the Kunsthistorisches Museum in

Vienna and he happened to own a few small works by Klimt. He traveled extensively, visited galleries in Paris and the south of France, and talked in a cultivated voice of the new influence of the young avant-garde German artists who were scandalizing the establishment with their vivid portraits of prostitutes and naked young girls. But his discussions of art always seemed to veer off to the "exclusive" opening events and gallery parties—who was there, the social side of things, and not the art itself.

He moved from the art scene to the world of racing, confessing that his other interest was horses. He could tell which stallion was breeding with what mare on every horse farm in the country. As he unhurriedly crossed his legs and leaned in toward her, he was struck by her composure, the unusual quality of her beauty, and the shape of her ankles, which he had not noticed before. She had more knowledge than most women her age. But then again, what *was* her age? He didn't dare ask.

"So, my dear Minna. Have you ever been to Mayerling?"

"Mayerling," she repeated. "Isn't that near the crown prince's hunting lodge?"

"Not too far. I have a small house on the lake across from the village."

"Were you there when the prince killed himself?"

"Fortunately, no. I was traveling."

"What was that . . . five or six years ago?" she asked.

"Six years ago January. The palace initially said it was heart failure, but the local police chief, the one who found him, told my gatekeeper that the prince shot his mistress first, then sat around drinking for several hours before shooting himself."

"How tragic."

"Quite. I used to see them in the Prater, holding hands and kissing. She was so young. They looked as though they didn't have a care in the world. The gossip here was that the emperor demanded his son end the relationship, even though they all detested his wife."

"Poor Rudolf. Perhaps he should have shot *her*."

Eduard laughed. "Would have been better for the empire, that's for certain." He looked around the room. "Hard to imagine doing that when you own everything, have everything. They've now converted the hunting lodge to a convent. Can you imagine?"

"Nuns and guns . . . how picturesque," she said, sipping her wine.

"The Carmelites seem to enjoy it."

"How long have you owned your house?"

"Been in my family for years. Directly on the lake."

The more he talked about his retreat, the more she grew oddly disinterested. Any woman, especially any woman in her position, would be enthralled. He was clearly courting her, but she couldn't stop herself from wondering whether she might have left the door to the pantry open or whether or not they had enough bread for supper tonight or if she was supposed to stop at the bakery this morning.

Minna was about to offer Eduard some tea and cakes when she heard the front door close and recognizable footsteps on the stairs. Then Sigmund walked through the door, bundled in his woolen topcoat, greeting her in mock surprise. Why was he back? This was no coincidence. He *must* have known she was entertaining today. It was all Martha could talk about.

"Hello, Eduard," he said in an unquestionably cool voice. He stood there, his chest out, his back straight, as though held up by a string.

"Sigmund," Eduard said, nodding politely in his direction. The two men appraised each other for a moment in silence. Since he arrived home, Sigmund's affect toward her had been so distant, his tone so flat and brusque, as to be almost disorienting. And now here he was, protecting his turf, like a dog with a ruff of fur raised at the neck.

"I hope I'm not disturbing you."

"Not at all," Eduard said, shifting uncomfortably in his chair. He took out a silver engraved case from his jacket, plucked out a cigarette, and lit it. It smelled aromatic and expensive.

"That's good. I have an appointment . . . but perhaps I'll visit for a few minutes. . . ." Freud said, dropping onto the sofa next to Minna.

He rummaged through his pocket, pulled out his watch, glanced at the time, and then settled back on the sofa, tapping out a rhythm on the floor with his heavy black shoe. It was obvious he meant to stay.

The tension made the air feel close and stifling. Minna rose to her feet, yanked back the thick damask curtains, and opened the window. The afternoon light was fading, the streets were getting busier, and she could hear passing omnibuses, pedestrians, and horses and carriages clattering across the cobblestones. The children would be home soon. Why was he doing this? The nerve. Watching Sigmund stick a cigar between his lips and suck on it, she made a spur-of-the-moment decision.

"Eduard, I thought we might go to the café. I'd love a cup of coffee or . . . a beer, perhaps," Minna said as she walked to the door and pulled her coat off the rack.

Eduard looked at her quizzically, and then nodded agreeably.

"Of course, I'd be delighted."

Freud stood, a flash of surprise crossing his face.

"A pleasure, Sigmund," Eduard said, his hand lightly resting on Minna's back. And with that, the two of them walked out the door, leaving Sigmund standing alone, feet planted firmly on the carpet, a captain abandoned by a mutinous crew. He watched them hail a cab, as he clipped the end of another cigar and threw it into the fire.

Perhaps it was the wine, but on the ride back from the café with Eduard, Minna couldn't stop thinking about Sigmund. Why did she look at this eligible man sitting next to her and feel nothing? When he talked, she imagined his words dissolving into puffs of smoke—filaments of gray vapor floating up to the ceiling. Nothing he said was even slightly worth repeating, much less remembering. Obviously, many women would hang on his every word. He had good breeding and good manners, but she was suffocated by his courtliness.

And yet there was another reason she was loath to admit. Sometimes the heart is drawn to not only the light. Sometimes it's drawn to dark ambiguities of character and brooding silences. And an acute understanding of some shared concept or secret. The issue of appropriateness is beside the point.

Minna flushed as the circumstances of her situation became clear.

"Are you unwell?" Eduard asked, looking at her with concern. "Driver, slow down."

"I'm quite well."

"I'm glad," he said, taking her gloved hand in his.

Sadly, she was not even remotely moved by his advances. She thought back to how grateful she had been when she first moved in with her sister. But now what had seemed a godsend—Vienna, the house, the children—had suddenly become the opposite.

She must leave this house. There was nothing to recommend staying but the perversity of desire, which did not subside with time. Initially, she had wrestled with the possibility that the desire didn't exist, or if it did, her sense of common decency would help her resist. But the heat of unreason burned in her brain.

Her behavior went against everything she had been taught, everything she had learned. The conventions of the day would not protect her. To the outsider, she was the helpful sister, the caring aunt, but behind the facade lay the undeniable truth. Desire. How was it possible to find such a thing floating beneath this space?

And what of the actual circumstances of her relationship with Sigmund? He was clear in his intentions, of that she was certain. So the decision was hers. And anything but leaving would be disastrous. This was not a harmless flirtation.

She climbed the stairs to her room. Thank goodness no one was around. How could she possibly pretend that everything was normal when the fact was, she wanted her sister's husband.

She tried to sleep but her conscience kept her awake. She deserved to toss and sweat and suffer. She deserved her building migraine. Her stiff neck. The shooting pains radiating down her arm and across her heart.

She could hear Martha through the walls, sleeping peacefully, snoring away. A clear conscience. The sleep of the righteous. Minna got up, wrapped her shawl around her shoulders, and sat down at her writing desk.

Vienna, January 1896

My Dearest Sister,

It is now three in the morning and I'm trembling as I write this letter. I believe you must know what I'm about to say, but if by chance you don't, I beg your forgiveness.

I've decided to leave this household. I pray you will in time allow me back into your heart.

It has come to this. We are both in love with the same man. I don't know how I could have allowed myself this irretrievable moral lapse, and all I can do is tell you that I never meant to cause you pain.

Can you, my dear sister, ever forgive me?

Minna couldn't bear to sign it. She placed the letter by her bedside, intending to give it to Martha the next morning, but when she awoke, she crumpled it in a ball and threw it in the fire. Perhaps, she wondered, even as she was writing it, she never intended to deliver it.

17

. . .

"I'd like to visit Mother for a few days."

Martha was sitting at her dressing table, arranging her hair clips and combs in stacked wooden cigar boxes that she had covered with velvet and brocade. But even Martha's handiwork couldn't disguise the strong smell of tobacco.

She regarded Minna with suspicion. Her sister would not voluntarily visit their mother. Their relationship was fraught with "little miseries," as she liked to describe her life with Emmeline. As a teenager, Minna had often told Martha that once she left Hamburg, she was *never* coming back, a youthful exaggeration, but one Martha believed was heartfelt.

"What's wrong?" she asked.

"Nothing's wrong. I'd simply like to go home. I haven't seen Mother since last summer."

Martha looked at her skeptically, and then launched into a litany of blame.

This was all her husband's fault for behaving as if they were headed for the poorhouse, and continually complaining about their money woes in front of Minna and the children.

"That isn't the reason," Minna said. "I'd just like a few days away."

"Is it the children? I know Mathilde's a bit difficult . . . and Sophie clinging to you night and day. Has Martin been acting up again?"

"It's not the children. I adore them. If you really want to know, I haven't been feeling well. I'm afraid I'm getting a cold . . . or the flu. Or maybe something worse. I just need the rest."

"Oh, dear, I thought you looked a bit feverish yesterday. I hope you didn't act sickly around Eduard. You didn't complain about your health, did you? Men don't like that."

"For heaven's sake, Martha. I did *not* complain about my health. And if I did, he probably would have been quite sympathetic."

"Well, perhaps a few days away would be good. We don't need another disease spreading through the house."

"I'd like to leave this evening," Minna said, knowing that Sigmund would be with patients until nine.

"Very well," Martha said. "There's a night train to Hamburg. I'll see if it's still on the schedule."

How peculiar, Minna thought. Escape for her had never been *to* Hamburg but *away* from there. Hamburg had barely entered her thoughts the last time she had a crisis in her life, and it wouldn't now if she had anywhere else to go. But a person has to be *somewhere*, and her options seemed to be shrinking down to a succession of impossible choices.

Later that evening, she heard the clattering of a carriage roll up as the clock on the marble mantelpiece struck six. The past few hours had been an endless whirl of packing and preparing. Martha had given Minna more than enough kronen to cover her expenses, and now the deed was done. The children tumbled obediently out of their rooms and bid their farewells. Ernst and Oliver gave her exuberant hugs, almost knocking her down. Martin, at first pretending that he didn't care, pressed a small folded note into her hand.

"Read it later," he said, blushing in front of his brothers.

"Why, thank you, my dear," Minna said, kissing his forehead and putting the message into her satchel.

It was then that Minna noticed Sophie standing alone near the stairway.

"When are you coming back, Tante Minna?" Sophie asked softly.

"I'm not sure, my little sunshine."

"But who will put me to sthweep?" Sophie shyly lisped, averting Minna's gaze, studying the wax on the floorboards. Minna leaned down, feeling the warmth of the child's arms around her neck.

"You can go to sleep by yourself now. You're a big girl. And if you wake up in the middle of the night, light your candle and write me a letter," Minna said, weighed down by a decision that she now found heartbreaking.

As soon as Minna walked out the door, she felt an air of dreary melancholy. Hamburg. She could not stay there long. But what then? Another home to settle in. Another mistress to serve. She climbed into the carriage, leaned against the seat, fighting back despair. As the cabman flicked the whip across the rump of the reluctant horse, she opened Martin's note and read the words. *Dear Tante Minna, I hope you feel better. Love, Martin.* Another wave of sadness as she reckoned with her personal loss of the children—and of Sigmund. Things happen to people when they're not where they belong. And she didn't belong here. They weren't *her* children. And, Lord knows, he wasn't her husband. And that was the point.

. . .

Minna arrived at Vienna's Westbahnhof at seven in the evening, and briefly sat down on a wooden bench in the waiting area. She was in her traveling outfit, a dark blue dress trimmed with bands of pale cream. She studied the timetable and noticed her train was delayed. She watched the flow of people on the way to the platform—harried mothers and their fidgety children, shopgirls, clerks, merchants, a wizened street vendor with a sack over his shoulder. Off to the side, near an officer of the guard, was a bridal party with aristocratic young women dressed all in white—velvet capes and ermine-trimmed skirts. They were seeing off a smiling, sweet-faced bride and her groom, who were proceeding slowly through the crush to their waiting train.

She listened as the stationmaster's whistle barely penetrated the noise of the crowd and then asked the porter when the train would arrive. He shrugged his shoulders. She should have known. This station had a reputation for never running any of its trains on time. Botched connections were a fact of life. So she settled in, pulling a book from her satchel and feeling strange, even slightly indecent, as if she were running away from home and had no business being here. But where else would she wish to be? Perhaps on a guided European tour, of which she'd blithely blathered on to Eduard. A side trip to Venice with its black canals. Excursions to trattorias, churches, villas, and the beach. She wanted a change, she had said to him. But it wasn't a change of scenery or pace—she wanted a change of heart.

The wait was intolerably long and boring, and the people who had been crowding the platforms slowly disappeared as trains arrived and departed. In the soft evening light, the building looked like a cathedral with its marble floors, huge arched windows, and wooden benches. Indeed, it felt like a spiritual no-man's-land for the lost and wayward.

She could hear the muted sounds of bells and train horns giving signals as she pictured the details of her departure: Sophie's warm hands, the children's good-byes, Martha's chatter. She didn't want to think about the gravity of the situation she had escaped.

By ten, there was still no train, and a porter told her that it had been canceled altogether and there wasn't another one to Hamburg until the next morning. He directed her to a pension across the street where, he said, passengers usually stayed when their trains did not appear.

By the time Minna walked down the street to the small pension, a blanket of dark clouds had raced across the sky from the north, and the oncoming storm was beginning to break. Flashes of lightning illuminated the front of the small rooming house, and there was a glow of flickering lights behind the heavy curtains of the entry that faced the train station.

A beggar approached Minna from the shadows, his hand out. "Please, Fräulein, help an old man in need." The rain, a slight drizzle at first, had now become a full-fledged downpour. She put down her valise, reached into her pocket, and gave the man a krone, then climbed the stairs and entered the modest foyer.

Minna registered in the worn leather book and took the last bedchamber available. It had a slanted, beamed ceiling, green wainscoting, and a small fireplace in the corner across from the high bay window that overlooked the street.

She entered the room and flung her coat and hat on the oak chair near the simple brass bed, which took up most of the room.

She noticed it was covered with crisp white sheets and layers of blankets. Unusually clean, she thought, for this type of pension, but still she pulled back the covers to make sure there were no bugs. Then she lit the candle on the mantel, took her nightclothes and dressing gown out of her valise, and undressed. She retrieved a small silver flask from her pocketbook, put the bottle to her lips, and sipped the cool liquid.

She fell into bed, but sleep eluded her. All she could think of was that she was going back to Wandsbek, the litttle town near Hamburg where her mother lived. She pictured herself in her childhood bedroom, closed off from the world of Vienna, doing her mother's bidding. The thought of it, the dread of it, worked through her brain like a slow bullet. She tried to read something, anything to divert her attention, when she heard someone knocking on the door. She put on her dressing gown and opened the door a crack. Sigmund was standing there in his dark woolen overcoat, soaked and dripping.

18

...

When he first approached her, she backed against the wall, as if he were an intruder.

"Sigmund . . ." Minna said. Her mind was racing and she pulled her dressing gown tighter around her. "How did you find me?"

"It wasn't hard. This is the only inn near the station."

"I don't think—"

"I'm not interested in playing games," he said, cutting her off. "What do you want, Minna?"

"It's perfectly obvious what I want. I want to go home."

"I highly doubt that. Say what you mean."

"I'm not one of your patients."

"And I'm not your doctor," he said, moving closer to her. "Do you want me to leave?"

"No," she whispered.

"Good," he said, taking off his wet coat and then his waistcoat as she stood there watching him. The floorboards creaked under his feet as he turned away from her and stood at the window, removing his sopping shoes and socks. She was still in her robe, her arms bare below the elbow, and she nervously rubbed her hands together, then bolted the door and slid the chain. A fine film of sweat covered her chest.

"Come here by the window, I want to look at you," he said.

She didn't answer, didn't move, so he went to her, smoothed a lock of hair behind her ears, and ran his hand down her face and neck. Then he carefully slipped off her robe and put his arms around her waist.

It felt as if they had decided to do this from the moment they met, even though neither of them would have arranged it. She couldn't get away with calling it fate. That would be too easy.

The first kiss was extravagant—the sudden luxury of it all frightening and unexpected. She was giving in so quickly it was astounding. She paused for a moment and struggled to remember who she was . . . but the outside world was falling away.

"Lie down," he whispered, and pushed her toward the bed.

He took her face in his hands and she couldn't think. She felt a little mad.

"Sigmund," she said. Her voice sounded thin to her and unrecognizable.

There was tobacco taste on his mouth as he seemed to inhale her, pulling off his tie and pushing his shirt aside. He pressed his mouth on her neck and then caressed her shoulder with his lips, starting off gently and with such tenderness that she was taken aback. He pushed their bodies together with a slow, deliberate rhythm. The desire started low down and then spread through her limbs at a frightening pace.

They made their way through the carnal hours, breathing in and out. She never wanted him to stop. It was as if she were suspended in time with no history, morally weightless.

Afterward, it was strange. He lay on his back with his hands behind his head, studying her. They hardly talked. Maybe because nothing they could say would make it right. She didn't weep as most women do when it's their first time. And they made no declarations. Still, she was in love with him. Of that, there was no doubt. And now, look what they'd done.

"What's the matter?" he asked.

She turned her head away from him, ready to get up.

"Come on now, don't be like that. After all this, don't push me away."

"I have no choice."

"Meaning what?"

"Meaning you can't rewrite history."

"We don't need to," he said.

"You'll have to go now," she said, standing up abruptly and retrieving her robe. She felt something inside her snap.

"Are you coming home, then?"

"No, I'm leaving. Tomorrow."

"You'll come back to me," he said, with confidence.

"Impossible," she replied. But he kissed her and smiled knowingly as she responded to his touch.

In the morning she attempted to be casual when checking out of the inn. She just wanted to look like an ordinary woman, walking to the station to meet her train. But it was no use. It was as if she was wearing an evening costume when everyone else was in day clothes. From the moment she stepped out of the room, she refused to indulge her emotions, managing to hide her feelings of transgression. She would be on that train no matter what.

She walked through the main concourse to the platform where the train was waiting, its black, brutish hulk shooting off plumes of steam in the frosty air. No more, she thought. Not ever. The whole thing was unforgivable. But at the same time, she knew she would die if she never saw him again.

In the distant tunnel, she could see the rail workers, dressed in heavy woolen jackets and battered leather work boots, navigating the crisscrossed tracks. She tried to keep her balance as the platform began to tremble and another steam engine rolled past, the movement of the coupling rods on the wheels rhythmically rotating and straightening like the flying shuttle of a mammoth loom. A hunched-over porter passed her, heaving a large luggage van burdened with leather trunks, valises, and boxes tied with rope as the passengers streamed onto the platform.

She felt thoroughly drained as she settled down and eyed the anemic young woman seated across from her. The train hissed and shuddered and rolled into motion.

Minna stared out the smeared, dirty windowpanes as she watched the city retreat behind her. She closed her eyes and rested her head against the wooden seat. What was he doing right now? Was he thinking about her thinking about him?

She went through the details over and over again. What he did to her and what he said. What she did to him. She could hear horns from the trains signaling as they streaked through the gray fields of snow.

The monotonous motion of the train and the lack of rest the night before were slowly lulling her to sleep. After a long, drawn-out whistle she noticed the woman across from her snoring softly.

Like a death in the family, everything in her life was now divided into before and after. She never decided in any conventional way that this would be the day or that would be the day of such an impossible entanglement, but, indeed, that day had arrived and there was an irreversible blotch on her moral fiber. Life before felt fleeting and unimportant. And life after, a looming catastrophe that consumed her with dread.

Not just an affair with a married man. It was an unseemly, unpalatable betrayal. The black sheep of the family was blacker than black. The very image of destruction and decay. How could her feelings for him be wildly passionate one moment and then, in an instant, switch to the dark, barbarous world of sin and remorse? She thought of those demented women she had seen on street corners, dressed in rags and babbling in demonic tongues—a bit morbid, but still, was this her justified fate? Try as she might, she couldn't excuse her own perceived abnormalities. No mere mortal could express her mounting emotional distress as she made her way home to her mother.

And yet rationalizations crept in to halo a sinner's head. She had tried to escape, but he had appeared last night in a storm. And she couldn't resist him. Something was shifting profoundly in the way she thought about herself. It was foul and an outrage, her complete undoing, but still she wanted him.

The moment she let him in the door, she was thrillingly lost, shedding her innocence and inhibitions in a rush of erotic fury. The sedate sister-in-law, sinfully luscious as forbidden fruit. The sex was vivid, demanding, deranged, and endlessly self-indulgent. She should shoot herself, throw herself over a bridge, be branded, flogged, or stoned.

Outwardly, she thought, if nothing ever happens to me again, I will accept my life, which will pass calmly and uneventfully. Like a novice, passing though the convent doors for the first time, she would willingly give up everything because she had tasted it all. But inwardly, she would forever live with a memory that constantly mortified her, an incestuous assault on her family that must never be exposed.

19

. . .

As the train approached Hamburg, Minna could see the river Elbe, now covered with ice, and the sweeping skyline marked by the familiar spires of St. Nicholas, St. Michaelis, and St. Peter's. But she wasn't inclined to admire the view. After all, despite the thousands of bridges and canals crisscrossing the city, this certainly wasn't Venice. And this time of year was particularly harsh and forbidding. The temperatures were close to freezing and the winds, blowing from the North Sea to the west and the Baltic to the east, cut right through to the bone, no matter how many layers of clothing one wore.

She gathered her belongings, put on her coat, and stepped off the train. The platform was lined with a thin sheet of ice and she could already smell the smoke from the factories that lined the southern shores of the river. A few years before, the city had been gripped with the worst cholera epidemic in Europe. Luckily, her mother had been traveling at the time, but the death toll was staggering.

She took a cab from the train station to the rural outskirts of the city, where the roads were increasingly treacherous and difficult to pass. At one point, the driver got stuck in a patch of cracked black ice and had to dig them out of a deep rut.

"This will cost you extra," he said in his Low German dialect.

"Just carry on," she replied, her breath trailing visible puffs of steam. Normally she would have argued with him but now it seemed hardly worth the effort.

They arrived at her mother's house, Hamburger Strasse 38, in the late afternoon. It was a modest, two-story redbrick with a gabled roof and a large yard. Minna climbed the steps and knocked lightly on the front door, but there was no answer, so she walked around the house past some overgrown shrubbery to the service door and let herself in. Her mother never locked that door, one of her lifelong peculiarities. At one point, Minna had asked why she insisted on leaving it open.

"Then, if I'm locked out, I can always get in the back door," her mother had replied matter-of-factly.

Minna entered through a narrow corridor that led to the kitchen. The hearth was cold, and there was a single plate on the unpainted wooden table with a half-eaten piece of streusel and a pot of tea that had gone cold. Her mother was probably out shopping. There had been no time to get word to her that she had decided to come home.

Everything about this place seemed austere to Minna, drab and frugal except the smell of pine, which she always associated with home. She walked up the stairs in silence, demoralized, and entered her old bedroom. There was the carpet she had always hated, a threadbare mess of indeterminate color with stains still there from her childhood. It seemed her mother had taken over the room. Well-worn shawls and sweaters hung from pegs by the door, and a sewing kit was open on the small table near the bed, with swatches of fabric lined up in a row. All Minna's childhood things had vanished, even her books, stored in the attic, probably. Feeling suddenly fatigued with a slight sense of panic, Minna sat down on the neatly made iron bed and glanced around the room, dazed, as if she had just awakened from a dream.

She leaned back, closed her eyes, and tried not to think about what her body felt like when he was holding her. She wanted his arms around her, his legs wrapped around hers. She felt empty and ashamed.

It was the strangest thing. It didn't occur to her at the time, but he seemed not to care about the consequences or anything else but their desire. It was reckless and wrong . . . and it must never happen again.

Minna thought back to the days when she was fourteen and just beginning to be noticed by men. In her mother's eyes, there were two kinds of women: prostitutes, who reveled in obscene pleasures of the flesh, or chaste, passive wives and daughters unencumbered by sexual feelings of any kind. It was a common sensibility, one that blithely categorized sensual women as mistresses or whores. As opposed to loyal wives who dutifully engaged in sex in order to procreate or satisfy their men. Wives like Martha.

It was getting dark now and Minna dreaded hearing her mother's footsteps. She should have been home by now. She pulled the blankets around her and started to doze off. She didn't notice her mother standing in the shadows by the door.

"Martha? Is that you?" she asked.

"No, Mother, it's Minna," she said, as she looked up with a weary smile. Minna felt like an intruder, not a child who had grown up here.

Emmeline took off her heavy woolen coat and hat and stood in the doorway, peering at her daughter. She was dressed all in black, as usual. Ever since Minna's father had died, her mother preferred the black of mourning, even though she was years past the required time for bereavement. The color did not suit her. The severity of it made her skin look sallow and the sharp angles of her face more pronounced. She had also accepted the Orthodox Jewish tradition of shaving her head upon marriage and had worn wigs ever since . . . even after being widowed. Minna thought that the moment her father died, Emmeline had aged twenty years and stayed there. And now, with her coarse gray hairpiece pulled back in a bun and her skin hanging loosely on her once-pleasing profile, one might guess she was over seventy when, in fact, she was in her mid-fifties. She had become what she previously emulated—an old lady.

"Minna! My goodness, this *is* a surprise. How long have you been here?" she asked.

"A few hours . . . I came for a visit."

"Nonsense. You never visit."

"Of course I do."

"When was the last time?"

"Mother, surely you don't want to argue when I've just arrived."

"And you never write, either," Emmeline added petulantly.

"Is it warm in here? I'm so warm . . ." Minna said. Lack of sleep and tension from the night before were taking their toll.

"What's the matter? Is something wrong?" Emmeline asked, putting her ice-cold hand on Minna's forehead. "You look pale."

"It's nothing. I'm feeling fatigued, that's all, and Martha suggested I visit you."

"That's odd, you're never fatigued, but I shouldn't doubt it in that household. So much for Martha to do. I wish you would have let me know, though. I'm expecting Uncle Elias and Aunt Mary for supper, and now I don't believe I have enough."

"I'm not hungry," Minna lied. Her stomach had been growling since she arrived in Hamburg, and she sorely regretted refusing breakfast on the train.

"Well, certainly, you don't have to eat, but I don't want it to appear as if I haven't enough."

Good God, Minna thought, looking outside at the dismal darkness. She *actually* wants me to go to the market.

"And you know your uncle. He has such a huge appetite. Eats enough for the two of them."

"Would you like me to go out and get something?" Minna offered weakly.

"Heavens, no. I wouldn't ask you that, don't give it another thought. Although the table might look sparse . . ."

Minna collected herself, sat up, and smoothed her hair. A thick, impotent feeling swept over her. She knew that one of her mother's biggest fears, even in front of her own brother, was looking as though they couldn't afford an ordinary meal.

"What would you like, Mother?" she asked, pulling her boots out from under the bed.

"Just another challah . . ." Emmeline answered immediately. "And as long as you're there . . . you might as well stop at the cheese shop and get some Gouda . . . go to the cheese monger on Hasselbrook."

"It's so much farther. . . ."

"He's single. Do you need money?"

"No, I have enough," Minna said. She'd rather die than ask her mother for one krone. She leaned over and hooked the long row of buttons on her boots, left foot, right foot. And then put on her coat and hat. Her mother was being unreasonable and Minna knew it.

But she would go anyway. No one could accuse her of not being accommodating. She followed her mother downstairs, grabbing an apple from a bowl as she walked through the kitchen.

"Hurry, dear. The shopkeepers are closing. I'll make you a nice dinner," Emmeline called out warmly.

This was Emmeline's signal to her daughter that she should now be grateful. Minna couldn't bear it. Martha, on the other hand, would have been dutiful and appreciative. "Oh, thank you, Mother," she would have said. I'll be damned, Minna thought, remembering her stormy adolescence.

The realization that she would be here for a while was disheartening. She'd been a governess and lady's companion for the past ten years, and what did she have to show for it? There was a moment of panic that her life was no longer under her control. But she must try not to be resentful. Whatever their past relationship had been, Minna's fall from grace had nothing to do with her mother.

20

. . .

The table was set and the Sabbath candles ready to be lit when Minna returned home. She was out of breath from rushing to the baker before he closed, and then to the cheese shop, and the sense of urgency about it all made her head ache. She was about to sit down and take off her muddy boots when she realized her aunt and uncle had already arrived and were sitting in the parlor.

"Put the parcels in the kitchen and come join us," Emmeline said in a silvery tone.

Minna obeyed, scuffing off her boots on a mat near the door and hastily shoving the last bit of a puff pastry into her mouth. She hadn't eaten since the night before and couldn't resist. She licked the cream off her fingers and entered the parlor.

"Isn't it wonderful, Elias—my Minna has come home to visit," Emmeline said, stretching out her arms, leaning over, and drawing up a chair near her own.

While Minna was out, it seemed as if the considerate, sweet Emmeline had suddenly appeared. This was the public face of her mother. Only the very immediate family members, including Sigmund, who made no secret of his intense dislike for his mother-in-law, had to deal with the other Emmeline—the exacting, aggressive one.

"Minna, my dear," said Uncle Elias. "What a surprise! You look so beautiful. I wish I'd known. Elsa would have loved to see you. Did you know she's expecting? Hard to believe. Her little terrier is so jealous, all he does is whine and jump in my lap. Dogs seem to have a sixth sense about this, don't you think?"

"You know Minna's been caring for Martha's children, don't you?" Emmeline broke in.

"Oh, yes. And how are Martha and the *Kinder*? What a lot of grandchildren our Emmy ended up with, in spite of herself. Eh, Emmy?" he asked, smiling broadly at Minna and leaning back in his chair.

"Time to eat," Emmeline said, taking Minna's hand and motioning them to follow. The smell of roast chicken with liver stuffing permeated the dining room. There were also colossal slabs of bright red beets, and sweet-and-sour green beans drenched in butter nestled next to chunky sour-cream potatoes. Minna covered the challah with a white linen cloth. As they gathered around the dining table, Uncle Elias put on his yarmulke, while Emmeline placed a small black lace veil over her head and lit the Sabbath candles.

"*Barukh atah Adonai Elohaynu melekh ha-olam, asher kidishanu b'mitzvotav v'tzivanu l'hadlik ner shel Shabbat.*"

Minna listened to the familiar words and began to recite the prayer with her mother, as she and Martha had done every Friday night of their childhood. Sigmund, of course, had put an end to all that. He considered all religions "patently infantile and foreign to reality," and she had heard him often refer to Emmeline's Orthodox beliefs as a "crazy piety." Especially since he felt she offered up only petitionary prayers, asking God for this or that, rather than prayers of gratitude. Emmeline in turn resented him because he refused to allow her daughter to observe the Sabbath at all or even recite prayers at the dinner table.

But the animosity between them went far deeper than that. He blamed Emmeline for "abducting" Martha to Hamburg when they were first courting, believing it was a deliberate scheme to separate them. In her eyes, he was an impoverished student with an uncertain future, a poor match for her precious Martha. It was no secret that Emmeline had declared war on Sigmund, and indeed she may have won the initial battle, but he proved a tough opponent, and in the end, victory was his.

The blessing over the bread had just finished, and now Minna's uncle was looking at her with interest.

"And when are you going back, my dear?" he asked kindly.

"I haven't decided, I might stay awhile," Minna answered, noticing her mother examining her face from across the table.

"What are your plans, then?" he asked.

"I'm not sure. I was thinking of seeking employment in Hamburg."

"Oh. This could be quite fortuitous," chimed in Aunt Mary. "Perhaps you'd like to help Elsa with the new baby. They were just about to interview for the post."

Minna felt like saying, Not as long as I've a breath left in my body, but restrained herself. The thought of working for her young cousin, whom she used to care for, was far too humiliating.

"I've actually been offered a post in the city, but if it doesn't work out, I'll certainly let you know," Minna lied easily, avoiding eye contact with her mother.

"I just thought of something," continued Aunt Mary. "Remember that man someone introduced to Elsa, the one she didn't like? Why don't we find out if he's still available for Minna?"

It was perfectly acceptable and even considered polite for women to drink five to six glasses of wine at a formal Sabbath dinner. And Minna felt she needed every glass. In fact, the alcohol filled her with a renewed but unfounded state of calm, effectively easing her anxiety for a time.

Later that night, as she and her mother washed the dishes, Minna carefully avoided questions regarding her hasty departure from Martha's house and what exactly *was* this new position. When her answers were too obtuse, her mother changed the subject.

"Such good news about Elsa," Emmeline said as she wiped the last platter. "She was such a lovely-looking child. The prettiest of all the cousins."

Emmeline placed the plate on the upper shelf of the cupboard, closed the glass doors to the cabinet, and turned to her daughter.

"Are you eating enough, dear?"

"Of course I am."

"You're looking far too thin. Only young girls can stay this thin. It affects your face, you know."

"Do you think I look old?"

"What I think is that you might perhaps attract a man if you seemed a bit softer. It makes one more approachable."

"I don't want to attract a man." Even as she said it, the hypocrisy of that remark was not lost on Minna.

"Well, if you want to have children *of your own* . . . you can't just blithely go along year after year without a man. Women who do that . . . well, there's a kind of sadness about them. You remember our neighbor, poor Fräulein Hessler? That's how everyone referred to her. I can't remember anyone saying her name without the word 'poor' in front of it. And now you're nearly twenty-seven . . ."

"Twenty-nine . . ."

"Twenty-nine, my goodness. Time marches on," Emmeline said, wiping the last of the dishes and handing it to Minna. "You know, tomorrow we could visit Rabbi Selig. He always has such good advice. And he's known the family for so long. Then we could crochet, and I could show you my new yarn. You might take up needlework again."

"Good night, Mother," Minna said, her stomach churning. "It's been a long day. I think I'll go to bed."

"Good night, dear."

Minna walked up the stairs, thinking that she hadn't been home for even twenty-four hours and she had to get out. Things always slid back to the way they were. Homesickness, she thought . . . one affliction she had *never* suffered from. Living here would be like being buried alive. She would waste no time and look for a position immediately. She unpacked her bag, filled the iron tub with warm water, and sank into it. Orthodox Jewish law forbade bathing on the Sabbath, but her mother rarely enforced that edict with her daughters. Thank goodness, because Minna needed its therapeutic solace that night. Later on, as she lay in bed reading, there was a light knock on the door.

"I brought you some water," Emmeline said, placing a pitcher with a chipped spout next to her bed.

"Thank you," Minna said, feeling helpless at her resentment. After all, her mother *was* trying.

Minna listened to her trudge back down the stairs, lock the front door, then walk back up the stairs into her bedroom across the hall. I'm twenty-nine years old. My mother didn't need to remind me, Minna thought, gazing around the bedroom. Everything looked the same, but shabbier. The floral wallpaper was yellowed and peeling off in the corners, and the dresser drawers were scratched, with half of the knobs missing. This wasn't what she had dreamed of when she was a child. But then again, she never had those domestic dreams that captured other young girls. She had somehow always known that motherhood was not her fate.

She rolled over and tried to sleep, but she couldn't stop the sudden rush of remorse. It was a stranger who lay in that man's arms. It wasn't her. She couldn't erase those memories but she would try. She would *not* let them affect her future. Up until then, she had led a respectable life. She would find a new position in another town and would build a life where nothing remarkable ever happened again. She turned on her side, pulled the blankets up around her chin. Then she heard a rustling noise outside and remembered that the back door was unlocked. Was it a possum? A rat? Or maybe something bigger . . . ?

"Oh, hell!" she said as she threw off the covers and ran downstairs and slid the bolt.

As she crawled back into bed, she wondered, just for a moment, if he was thinking of her.

21

. . .

The next morning, Minna slipped out of the house early and headed for the café at the edge of town. Gusts of icy wind from the night before had quieted down, but the breeze was still strong enough to ruffle the curbside litter and blow her hat off her head. She intended to consult the local newspaper for employment positions, but as she looked around at the barren landscape and sullen little houses, she suspected she'd have to widen her search. Everything here had that bitter aftertaste of being left behind.

When she reached the café, she grabbed the newspaper on her way in and sat at a table in the back. Then she fished in her pocket for some kronen and pulled out a small piece of paper. What was this? The script was unmistakable. It was from him.

Thursday, February 2. 4 o'clock. Hotel Vier Jahreszeiten, Hamburg

That was the day after tomorrow. Impossible, she thought. She considered throwing the note in the rubbish and pretending she never saw it. It would be so easy. It's what she *should* do. But instead, she folded it up, put it back into her pocket, and tried to proceed with her day. I'll deal with it later, she told herself, treating it like an enormous bill that one couldn't possibly afford to pay. But, in truth, Sigmund's message weighed on her body like a brick. When had he put it in her coat? Why hadn't he just told her he'd be in Hamburg? Perhaps he had a conference, although the timing was suspicious.

She ordered a coffee, propped her head on her hands, and tried to concentrate on the ads, circling a few promising ones. Guilt—an exercise in self-indulgence. That's what Sigmund would say. "You don't need to suffer it unless you choose to." Nonsense. Guilt was not a choice. No one would choose to feel as if her life had deteriorated into a morass of longing and pain. There was no part of her that was unaware of the danger in seeing him again . . . but, in the end, she knew that she would meet him.

On Thursday, Minna took a train back to Hamburg and walked a few blocks to a pub located slightly below street level. It was cold, dark, and cavernous, like purgatory, a perfect place to wait. She took off her hat, ordered a coffee, and warmed her hands on the cup.

She pulled a pocket mirror from her handbag and appraised her face. Her eyes were slightly rimmed in red and her lips were dry. She smeared a bit of tinted salve on her lips and then noticed one cheek was more pinked than the other. Thankfully, her mother hadn't noticed the rouge. In her opinion, makeup was only for prostitutes and actresses.

She thought about her mother chattering away this morning, happy because she assumed Minna had all but obtained a prestigious position with the Kassel family, a fact that Minna had grossly exaggerated. What was simply Minna's response to an advertisement in the local newspaper, had now, thanks to her duplicity, become a certainty. Well, she was positive the Kassels would at least ask for her credentials when they received her letter of inquiry.

"You know the Kassel family *is* one of the oldest in Frankfurt . . . and well known here as well. How did you say they'd heard about you? The baroness? She must have offered quite a ringing endorsement for them to arrange to see you so soon."

Minna was deep in thought when the waiter asked her if she would like another coffee.

"No, thank you . . . but I will have a whiskey," she said, with a strained smile.

The waiter hesitated a moment—this was an attractive, seemingly refined woman, drinking alone in the middle of the day. Not his usual customer. He set down a shot glass beside her coffee cup and filled it to the top, then leaned against the back of the bar and watched her drain the glass. She felt the long, slow slide of the liquor flow through her system.

"Another?" he asked, in a tone that Minna didn't quite like.

"No, thank you," she said, motioning for the check. Then she paid the bill and left.

The wind from the sea had started up again; it smelled of salt and brine and whipped her coat open as she walked down the street. She considered her route and then cut through the St. Pauli neighborhood, the global capital of louche, its Reeperbahn one of Europe's most notorious red-light districts. She and Martha would always walk well away from it when they were girls, warned by Emmeline that it was a sordid place where seamen came to spend their kronen. But it was the most direct route to the hotel, so what the hell? And, besides, in the daylight, Grosse Freiheit's bars and cabarets were boarded up, the Teutonic whores and their clientele hungover or dead asleep. No danger for her here.

She passed several bars, then avoided a pile of debris, and crossed over to a more refined area where the town burghers had recently undertaken a beautification project. By the time she reached the hotel, it was past three. She had managed to stall for nearly three hours.

She hesitated for a moment in front of the heavy iron door to the fashionable hotel, then pulled it open and walked in. For a few moments, the glare from the sun was intense and blinding, the way it is just before it gives up and sinks into the dusk. And then she saw him. He was standing in the lobby with his back toward her, silhouetted in the fading light.

It was extraordinary, she thought, how familiar he was to her now. His hair, his stance, the way he held his head . . . there was something distinctive about him, even from behind. He turned to her.

"I wasn't sure you'd come."

"You knew I would," she said, putting her gloved hand in his.

It was not yet dark, an ungodly time for a man and woman to be in bed. She had entered a new world, a secret world, she thought, where you don't go to the place you're going, and you disappear once you get there. And, when you return, you pretend that nothing happened. Anonymity is everything. You can't risk direct looks, simple exchanges are often transparent, and the mundane is transformed into the hypnotic. There is mutual agreement about what is safe and what is not, a certain modicum of polite behavior upon meeting, and then that wash of relief as you finally fall together behind closed doors and ignite into flames.

They stood next to each other in the back of the wood-paneled elevator, nerves tingling, staring straight ahead at the wrought-iron door, pretending that they weren't together. The old elevator operator glanced back.

"Floor, sir?"

"Seven, please."

"And you, Fräulein?"

"Seven," she said, not looking at Freud.

The man didn't blink as he closed the door and pushed the lever sideways. She heard the cranking of the gears as she saw the elegant lobby fall away beneath her. Sigmund had checked in earlier. It was all so carefully planned and beautifully executed. Pitch perfect. And here they were. Two strangers in an elevator.

As soon as they were alone in the room, he pressed himself against her, and a wave of desire hit her as he pulled off her coat and then her blouse. She could see by his expression he felt the same way.

"Have you missed me?" he asked.

"What's wrong with you? How can you ask me that?"

One would have to be made of stone, she thought, to turn away from these feelings. She felt almost inhuman, wicked and exhilarated. It was a delicious depravity.

Afterward, he leaned across her body, opened the bedside table drawer, and took out a pack of cigarettes. For the first time, she noticed a champagne bottle in a silver ice bucket and two glasses on the dresser.

"Here, my love," he said tenderly. "I brought these for you."

She took a cigarette from the box, sat up in bed, and leaned her head against the headboard. He lit it for her. She inhaled once or twice, then rolled out of bed, snubbed it out on the windowsill, and reached for her clothes.

"Where are you going?" he asked. "I have the whole evening."

"I have to get back. Mother will worry."

"Pity. Let her wait."

"She'll wonder where I am."

"Only if it inconveniences her supper. Let's talk."

"Are you going to tell me how modern we are, how deliciously unrespectable? Or are you going to try to cure me of 'us'?"

"Impossible. There is no cure," he said, kissing her, tasting the smoke on her mouth. "Come back to bed."

Later, before she left him, she glanced around the room—the white towels like puddles on the bathroom floor, the sheets askew, empty crystal flutes by the bed. She thought of tangled arms and legs, wet and slick. The light slipped through the draped window, like a secret message under the door. He called her to him. She bent over and kissed him lightly on the mouth. He pulled a strand of her hair back from her face and stared at her, silent, thoughtful.

"What are you thinking?" she asked.

"I'm wondering when I can see you again."

"Don't spoil it."

"Aren't you thinking the same thing?"

"No."

"Liar."

"I'm counting the hours. Is that what you want to hear?" she said.

"I want to hear the truth."

"The truth is that it's hopeless."

"Nothing is hopeless."

22

. . .

Before she boarded the train home, Minna stopped at the Apotheke near the hotel. The ritual of prophylactic douches after sexual intercourse had not been foremost on her mind, chiefly because after their first encounter, she had resolutely decided never to see him again. Not that she couldn't have conceived the first time. What was she thinking? She wasn't. But now she must be smart and take precautions like any married woman or prostitute on the block. The safest thing, of course, would have been to jump out of bed and perform the ritual right there in the hotel bathroom. But for whatever reason, she didn't have the potion or the apparatus. She entered the small establishment, passing walls of apothecary cabinets with neatly labeled drawers. She was matter-of-fact in her tone with the chemist, and so was he as he handed her a uterine syringe and a premixed solution of water and carbolic acid.

Before she even greeted her mother, she rushed upstairs to the bathroom and performed the necessary procedure. Then she hid the syringe in her valise and later stuffed it in the dustbin. She would not need it again.

"So? Did you get the position?" Emmeline asked.

"I think so," Minna answered.

"Well, they certainly took their time with the interview. You've been gone for hours."

Minna spent the better part of the evening plagued by a foreboding she feared might be the end of her. And she spent the better part of the night wide awake, staring into the darkness. At one point she got up and walked into the bathroom. I am a monster, Minna thought as she gazed at her cold, hard reflection in the mirror. She couldn't stop thinking about the sex. Being with this man yet again was like plunging into a pool of quicksilver. Deadly poison and yet a godsend.

She should have been embarrassed by her ardor. She should have been more demure. She had clung to his body for hours, their faces glistening like glass. Right before she left, she confessed that her encounter with him had been shockingly thrilling. He told her that these drives were instinctive and basic, for women as well as for men, and sexual satisfaction was the key to emotional happiness.

So why wasn't she happy? Somehow she felt they had touched each other everywhere and nowhere.

Shortly after she finally fell asleep, she was up again, agitated, edgy, listening to the clock ticking on her mantel, a restless neighbor's dog howling pitifully down the street, and, every hour on the hour, the faint, mournful echoes of the church bells of St. Michaelis. If Minna were Catholic, she would go to confession, gain absolution, and go on with her life. Why did that sound more appealing than doing penance in front of her old rabbi in one of the three daily prayer services at her mother's synagogue? Perhaps the Catholics knew what they were doing when they invented the confessional booth that shielded one's secrets from judgmental eyes. At one point, she got up and drank a glass of water, but her mouth was still dry. She was chilled and then inexplicably hot and fretful. How could something so basic and peaceful as sleep be such torture?

She had read of women who openly turned away from the confines of Victorian conduct, women who talked of the pleasures of eros, women now hidden behind burning cheeks and migraine headaches. But who would be willing to stand in the fire to feed this hungry beast?

Still, if she were to throw herself on the mercy of the court, forced to take an oath of honesty, she would have to admit that it was not without regret that she left him there without any hint of future assignations. But there was no other choice.

Luckily, the next day, a message arrived from the Kassel sisters, offering her a provisional position as a lady's companion at their home, depending upon their mutual satisfaction and compatibility.

When Minna finally bid her mother good-bye, she felt an unexpected tug of sadness. There was little show of emotion on both sides, and she knew, as she always did, that her mother was relieved to get back to her solitary life. This was a staunch and upright woman who had been hit by a series of bitter losses and who could never forget decades of major and minor slights from neighbors, relatives, close friends, and even her own daughters. Somehow she always forgave Martha, but not Minna.

Being home reminded Minna that as a young woman she had chosen a different life for herself, but it never seemed to work out the way she had envisioned. Shadowing her wherever she went was the issue of what to do next, never being settled, never getting anything quite right. Leaving her mother's house should mean that she would be happier someplace else. But the reality was, she was leaving for a life of servitude and self-denial. A life that was considered refined, yet for her, a misfortune. Misery in opulent surroundings.

The house of Kassel was an old-line family in Frankfurt, and the spinster sisters, Bella and Louisa, were the end of the dynasty. They lived in an elegant, neoclassic manor in the Sachsenhausen district, with three floors, four reception rooms, eight bedrooms, and four baths. It was a handsome, white-painted structure with rectangular multipaned windows capped with elaborate decorative moldings. The overall impression of the structure was of simplicity, proportion, and balance—a philosophy the sisters had discarded long ago. Everything about the place was tasteless but exuberant.

Minna's accommodations were on the top floor, overlooking the hedges and formal back gardens. After her luggage was deposited on the landing, she was summoned to a reception room, where she found herself in the middle of an overstuffed feminine nest, crowded with a hodgepodge of ornate furnishings. The room was old, grand, and freezing. The walls were a startling ruby red, the windows draped with fringed swags layered over heavy side panels. And she had never seen so much bric-a-brac in one room— photographs, watercolors, statuettes, books, vases, two Turkish helmets used as flowerpots, rococo-gilded mirrors, and a profusion of jade and rose quartz figurines. In addition, most of the artwork consisted of badly rendered imitations of past masters, the kind of things found in pawnshops.

Decor such as this was not uncommon, Minna thought. Her prior employer, the baroness, was the victim of a similar, barely inhabitable craze. In fact, to Minna's mind, many people of wealth blithely bastardized whatever jumble of styles they fancied in an homage to the nobility of the past.

Minna found the two sisters propped up by fringed pillows on the burled walnut sofa. Louisa, the oldest, was about four foot ten with a pale, severe face and a nervous twitch. She placed a cold, limp hand in Minna's as she looked at her with nearsighted deprecation.

"Sit down, Fräulein," she said, motioning to a chair in the corner. No hint of a smile.

Minna reluctantly shrugged out of her coat, but kept it over her shoulders as she sat down next to a cinquecento side table, her knees trembling from the cold. Don't these women believe in heat? she thought. The woman examined Minna over the top of her spectacles as she lectured her about expectations and conduct (continually referring to herself as "we," meaning herself and her sister) and admonished her that under no circumstances would they tolerate mediums, communists, vegetarians, or vulgar Venetians. And, oh, yes. No alcoholic beverages were permitted by the staff, enforcement carried out by daily inspections.

The younger sister, Bella, who was heavily made up, had inherited the same sharp nose and chin, but in contrast to her birdlike sister, was doughy and overweight. In addition, Minna found that she had a habit of repeating whatever her sister said, as if it had just occurred to her, or, alternatively, finishing her sentences. Bella let Louisa conduct the initial interview without raising her eyes from her needlework. The needles crossed and crossed, clicked and clicked, up and down, again and again. Thank God, at some point, she stopped the infernal clatter and joined in the conversation.

"Sunday lunch we receive our guests."

"Respected officials and bankers."

"One should never associate with people below one's rank."

"We detest social climbers and charitable women."

"They tend to be so cloying."

"We have card games on alternate days."

"And we both sing and play the piano."

"Also on alternate days."

"Fridays, we have our parlor games."

"Usually with our most faithful and genial friend, Julian."

"*Cher, trop cher* Julian."

After listening to their silly discourse for over an hour, Minna still had no idea what her duties entailed. But she was told to go to her room, settle in, and begin work in the morning. She assumed she was hired, and that the sisters had looked at the list of references she had sent them, which had included the baroness's name. Fortunately, however, they did not ask to see the baroness's actual letter of reference, which, of course, was nonexistent.

Minna climbed the stairs to her room, changed out of her simple gray traveling outfit, and put on her robe. She felt unadorned and thoroughly plain. When she glanced at her reflection, she noticed that her hair was weasel brown, her skin dull and lifeless. It was almost as if she had made it her mission to disappear from herself and create a different Minna in a different world, a moral, proper world where people believed in honor, self-denial, and fidelity.

She lay in bed, facing yet another restless night. Even in this fortress of a house, she could hear leaves rustle under the onslaught of heavy winds. Thunder rolled in the distance and she felt that familiar pang of melancholy. Another home to settle into, another set of rules and perverse restrictions. The job had nothing to recommend it, but she hoped that her discomfort and dismay would subside with time. After all, she had managed to escape her mother's house and find a place to stay while she tried to decide what to do with her life.

And what was that exactly?

Another blast of wind hit the roof. Minna prayed she could keep her mind tranquil until morning. She would *not* see him again.

She finally nodded off and was plagued by disturbing dreams. She was abandoned, locked in a vacant house, and no one noticed she was missing. She awoke at five a.m. with a filthy cold, the wind still howling outside, and now she was agonizing over the fact that she had managed to betray the only person who cared about her. She sat up and pushed away such monumental thoughts. It was far easier to complain about physical ailments, and her back did ache and her head throbbed. She got dressed, went down to the kitchen to make some tea, and stood in front of the enormous blackened hearth, which had not yet been lit. She pulled her shawl tighter around her and wondered if there were rules about this, but she was so cold she didn't care. She lit the fire before the scullery maid arrived and sat there warming herself, awaiting the sisters' instructions. As the hours passed, she looked around at cabinets brimming with dishes and serving platters and glasses of all sizes and shapes. She noticed copper pots hung from the ceiling and an entire wall of spices, which infused the air with exotic smells from India, China, and other far-off lands. These women must entertain quite a bit, she thought. But who in the world would want to come here?

She waited there, dozing off and on, until eleven, when the sisters rang for her. She went up to the parlor to find them on the sofa, preparing to go upstairs for a nap. She soon discovered that sleeping was the sisters' foremost pastime and most constant complaint. Daily discussions would revolve around the lack of sleep the night before, how many hours they *did* manage to sleep, and at what time they would go to their rooms during the day to "reflect," which meant a nap. Minna was instructed to dispense pills, medical prescriptions, and pepsin, as well as figure out how much infusion from the pharmacy bag was just the right amount for a satisfactory night's sleep. The sisters would talk about sleep from morning to well into the night, and they were always suffering from a state of "inertia," an affliction they attributed to lack of sleep rather than their unwillingness to leave the house. Throughout the day, Louisa would talk softly to herself in an undertone, even as she was nodding off, usually on the parlor sofa. Bella would soon follow, her needlework a clump of mangled yarn in her lap.

Minna found that her daily duties were nothing unusual— getting the sisters up in the morning, and running errands in the afternoon while the sisters were resting. They never accompanied her anywhere, fearing it would tire them. This proved fortuitous, for some days she could slip away for a short time, go to a local pub, and drink a beer or two before she had to return.

On Friday, as she arrived home from an errand, Louisa informed her that a letter had arrived in the morning post and the maid had taken it up to her room. The moment she saw the envelope, she knew it wasn't from him.

Vienna, February 22, 1896

My dearest Minna,

    I can't tell you how shocked and disappointed I was when I heard you left Mother's house last week and took a position in Frankfurt. I received her postcard yesterday, which informed me of your new address, and, I must say, you might have told me of your plans, especially since the children and I have missed you so much and we were expecting you to return within the month.

Sophie was particularly sad to hear you're not coming home. She has reverted to her old sleep patterns and is distraught much of the night. Sigmund seems to think you're intent on earning an income and that you possibly felt you were a burden on our household. But I can assure you, from my perspective, it is quite the opposite.

We all belong together. Please reconsider your decision, and if you must, make your stay in Frankfurt a temporary affair. I can only beg you so much, my dear sister, and then hope you will decide in our favor.

It occurred to me that Mother may have influenced you to take this position with the Kassel sisters, and that it was under her advice that you agreed to do so. If that's the case, then I can only remind you that, as Sigmund says, she often pays little attention to our happiness. Although he can be rather severe with her, as you well know.

By the way, this morning as I was returning from the florist, I bumped right into Eduard, who apparently had finished his rounds at the hospital. He walked with me a bit and we chatted away amiably, catching up on the gossip. Did you know his Thoroughbred will be racing this summer in Dresden? He also told me he had just come back from Florence, and raved about some wonderful ceiling frescoes at the Uffizi. When he inquired after you and I informed him of your new position, he seemed a bit taken aback.

"Why Frankfurt of all places?" he asked.

"That I cannot answer," I responded. Because I couldn't.

But what an attractive man! With exquisite manners. He asked for your new employer's address, hoping it wasn't too presumptuous and that he hadn't overestimated your enthusiasm. I assured him that you would welcome a note from him, which, I assume, will arrive shortly.

What more shall I write? The children's schedule is hectic. Anna is teething, Martin and Ernst have tonsillitis, and Edna is sick, if you can believe her. God give me strength. Sigmund has been ensconced in his study as usual, but he did come out briefly last night to play the children's favorite travel game with them, One Hundred Journeys Through Europe. He sends you his best.

I'm enclosing Sophie's letter to you. She asks for you every day. I cling to the hope that you will reconsider your decision and join us soon.

Your loving sister,
Martha

Minna was overcome with emotion by Martha's innocent appeal for her to return home. She had managed to get through the past week by resolving not to repeat her transgressions and to get herself thoroughly away from Sigmund. But deep inside, there had been an unrelenting desire to see him again. But no more. The burning question rolled in once again, like a tidal wave. How could she have done this to her sister? The Seventh Commandment seemed to be a law that was broken indiscriminately. How often had she heard that "this one" or "that one" was having an affair. It was almost an epidemic. But Minna's unique set of circumstances trumped this national phenomenon. *Blut ist dicker als Wasser.*

23

...

A few days later, while Minna was struggling with her response to Martha, a short note from Eduard did indeed arrive.

Vienna, 26 Feb, 1896

Dear Minna,

Your sister, Martha, kindly gave me your address. How fortuitous that you are in Frankfurt. I happen to be traveling there next month for the annual Thoroughbred sales at the Frankfurter Rennklub in Niederrad, just a few kilometers south of the city. The track is modeled after the one in Paris, turrets, towers, so forth, and there's a marvelous restaurant nearby. Perhaps you could join me.

My dear Minna, perhaps I hadn't paid enough attention to your wanderlust when we were last together. I admire your adventurous spirit and look forward to seeing you again.

Yours truly,

Eduard

She tossed the postcard in her drawer, where it disappeared into a pile of papers, and reflected on Martha's ringing endorsement of the man. Her sister was right. Eduard was a brilliant prospect for someone. But considering where her thoughts were at the moment, she couldn't possibly respond.

When she finally went downstairs, she found the sisters in the reception room, reading a hand-delivered message from their close friend, Julian Barnett, a decorative arts consultant. He had been abroad for some time, but was arriving home that very afternoon. In celebration of his return, they decided to throw an impromptu dinner the next evening, "à huit heures sonnantes."

The cook, kitchen staff, and housemaids were given their instructions; the hearths scrubbed; furniture dusted and oiled; and Minna was sent to buy candles, flowers, crystallized fruits, pickled nuts, bottles of champagne, and savory forcemeats. At least there would be heat in the house—and alcohol.

The next night, the guest of honor arrived at the stroke of eight, walking into a house that was warm, illuminated, and filled with white roses, the very vision of abundance. Minna had been told by the sisters (more than once) that Julian had an impeccable eye, so they had instructed the staff to hide the ratty shawls and coverlets that were always left like abused pets on the sofas.

"*Cher* Julian. How we missed you!" the sisters said in unison.

"My two most delicious patrons," he replied in a soft, reedy voice, handing his silk top hat, silver-tipped cane, and woolen cloak to the footman and then casting a languid eye at Minna, who stood in the hallway. He beamed at the two doting women and elaborately pressed their hands to his lips.

Minna appraised the tall, rail-like man. He had a pale, ghostly pallor; high cheekbones; and immaculate, slicked-back hair. His hands were soft and round, like a woman's, with a large sapphire ring on his left pinky. They crossed the threshold into the reception room and sat amid the dense bric-a-brac and musty bowls of potpourri.

"As usual, your home is lovely," he said, looking around the room. "You both have the most impeccable taste." Ah, yes, if you like mortuaries, Minna thought.

The last-minute party was a small affair with twelve guests, most of whom seemed to know one another and were a mix of public officials, pretty young socialites, and two rather forbidding academics. They were the kind of people one really didn't like, but who came in handy at dinner parties. Minna marveled at the sisters' ability to draw such a crowd, even if they *did* trade endless anecdotes about their ancient Continental adventures and the latest lurid scandals.

"It reminds me of the World's Fair in Chicago," said Professor Wertheim, a distant cousin of the Kassels.

"I read that President Cleveland pushed a button and a hundred thousand lights went up in the fairgrounds," responded Herr Bahr, a former minister of parliament who arrived with a raven-haired young woman, later described by Bella as a *"jeune femme fatale."*

"It's true. . . . I'm converting my whole house."

"How was your holiday?"

"Wonderful. Don't you long to be in Paris?"

"I hear the city is filled with Americans."

"Avoid them like the plague."

"Speaking of the plague . . . have you heard about this Dreyfus fellow? Poor man, the news gets worse from Paris every day," said Wertheim. It seemed he had "inside information" about the Dreyfus Affair, a scandalous bit of news that had spread like a pox all over Europe. Some of his more progressive friends were making a public display of support for the Jewish artillery officer, Captain Alfred Dreyfus, who was convicted by the French government of treason, spying for Germany.

"A civilized nation, and look how they behave, degrading him in public, ripping off his medals," Frau Wertheim added, watching her husband gulp down several portions of Gruyère and ham from a silver tray. "Poor soul, chained to his bed on Devil's Island, kept sane apparently by reading Tolstoy and Shakespeare."

Minna quashed the urge to add her opinion, which was that the whole affair was a complete miscarriage of justice. The evidence was obviously forged. After all, he was the only Jew on the general's staff . . . so there you have it.

After the party, Minna retired upstairs to her room and paced the floor like a caged animal. She toyed with the notion of stealing down the back stairs to the now empty parlor to pinch a glass of wine, but the place was so damn cold (the fire had long gone out) that she decided against it. Now she had to focus on the problem at hand. How was she to answer Martha? She must stop procrastinating. She hoped the sisters would sleep through until morning. She had found they were like fitful infants, rarely sleeping through the night, bothering her for a hot water bottle, a cup of tea, an extra blanket or pillow that had to be fetched from the attic, or, worse, instructions to go outside and stop the neighbor's "infernal" dog from barking. The thought of another knock on her door at two a.m. was simply unbearable.

She lit the candle on her small writing desk, pulled out a piece of paper from her valise, and began writing tentatively, scratching

KAREN MACK AND JENNIFER KAUFMAN

out the first of many drafts. She jumped from subject to subject—from accounts of how lonely she was, how confused she felt, to confessions of how much she missed the children, their idiosyncrasies, their squabbling, their increasing hold over her.

"You must dissuade the nanny from putting Sophie back on laudanum. . . . Perhaps you can look in on her a few times during the night. . . . Has Oliver completed his test for the gymnasium yet? . . . How are the boys feeling? . . . Please check Martin's room and make sure it's not too cold."

She struggled on into the night, looking at all the crumpled, discarded notes on the floor around her chair. Crossed-out lines, insincere passages, subjects of no interest. Hour after hour passed. The candle dripped down to nothing as she wrapped her shawl around her and then put her coat on over everything, searching for just the right thing to say. Eventually, she gave up and wrote her sister a short, breezy note . . . ordinary, yet shadowed by deception.

She wrote that she was obligated to her new post and could not, in good conscience (how ironic), abandon her elderly employers. As to Martha's personal appeals, she acknowledged, as expected, that, indeed, she missed the children terribly and looked forward to the holidays when the family could all be together. To Sophie, she enclosed a note and promised to send her Reverend Charles Kingsley's *Water-Babies*, a book she thought all the children would enjoy.

Regarding her position, she gave Martha little snippets of this and that. There was no mention of the real circumstances, which had become oppressive.

Minna did add that while she was flattered by Eduard's interest, she didn't think there was a future between them because she just didn't feel "that way" about the man.

She wrestled with the question of whether to send regards back to Sigmund. But, first of all, it was so hypocritical it was almost criminal. And, second of all, he hadn't written to her, not one post-card, and why was that? He was perfectly capable of writing, that she knew. He was, in fact, a compulsive letter writer with all sorts of rules, such as one must answer correspondence within twenty-four hours. The problem was that her motives and desires were so complicated and confused at this point, even she didn't know what she wanted. Of one thing she was still certain—she must distance herself from this entanglement. She decided not to mention Sigmund at all.

In the end, Minna looked at her letter and wondered how she had gotten to this point. She was gripped by that primal human sentiment of the what-ifs. What if she could go back in time? Could she have tried a little harder to resist temptation? Perhaps. But it was of no consequence anymore. For she knew that she was now incapable of stopping herself from wanting him.

24

. . .

Dear Minna,

I was so happy to finally hear from you, dear sister, but for the life of me, I still don't understand why you are there, and you make no mention of when or if you're coming home. I fear that somehow I might be at fault, or that there is some other reason you can't confide in me. I try to comfort myself with the notion that you are, as always, my independent-thinking sister and that your venturing off has nothing to do with us. Am I correct in this assumption? Or could you possibly still be angry with me for contradicting you in front of the children? In retrospect, I shouldn't have interfered in such a trivial matter.

In any event, I won't bother you further about this. You know what's best—except, perhaps, when it comes to the matters of the heart, which brings me back to Eduard. He'll not be around for long. I was at the Sterns' the other night and their daughter (conspicuous creature) was practically flinging herself at him.

She sat right next to him on the sofa, laughing too loud at his jokes, leaning in so close she was almost on top of him, and then staring at him with a silly, vapid smile. Finally, he rose to get a drink and I followed him to the bar, where I brought up your name and deliberately monopolized his attention until dinner was called. If I could give you an added incentive to come home, he seemed eager to hear about you. If fate cannot intervene, then I must.

At this point in your life, Minna, perhaps you're too old for romance or flirtation, or whatever expectations you have floating in your mind. Try to be practical for once and think about your future. You mustn't wait until the bloom is off the rose. Time is not on your side.

I hope you can read this spindly handwriting, as my arm paralysis, although better, makes for unruly correspondence. The children are keeping me quite busy. Little Anna is doing wonderfully, guzzling Gartner's whole milk, the picture of health. Mathilde, however, is struggling with a light case of scarlet fever. We've isolated her in her room, and so far none of the others have caught it, thank God.

I'm exhausted, as we just returned from dinner at my mother-in-law's. As usual, Sigmund was late and, as usual, Amalia was completely frantic until he arrived. She knows he's always late, and yet she spends every minute until his arrival barely acknowledging the children, grim-jawed, darting back and forth from the door to the landing to the front steps. And Sigmund's father just sits there in his big chair, silent. Honestly, I don't know how he stands it. And when her "Golden Sigi" finally did arrive, Amalia told him that he looked pale and thinner than usual.

"Are his meals adequate?" she asked, turning to me and implying that it was somehow my fault. Then she made a rude remark about my weight.

No one married to Sigmund could ever live up to her expectations. God forbid she should notice my arm problems or the fact that several of the children were home ill. I did tell her that Sigmund's practice was growing. At least that made her happy—a rare occurrence. By the way, I read him your last letter and he was pleased that things were going so well.

In any event, my dear, everything here is quite monotonous without you. Do send us more information in your next letter so I can ease my mind about your absence.

Your loving sister,

Martha

Frankfurt, March 15, 1896

Dear Martha,

I just read your letter and must tell you that our petty disagreements over the children had nothing to do with my decision to take this post. I would never leave over such a trifle. I just felt that I had to make a life for myself and not impose on your family any longer.

I am saddened to learn that your arm is continuing to plague you. My employers speak of a new pill called aspirin, made by the Bayer company here in Germany . . . it's supposed to be better

*than laudanum for the treatment of pain. You might ask
Sigmund if he can get some for you.*

*It sounds like Sunday dinners haven't changed. And what of
poor Jakob? Sigmund's father always seemed so put upon, like a
rat in a trap, waiting for the next barb. Amalia has to be aware
that her indelicate remarks make everyone uncomfortable, but
she doesn't seem to care, nor should you. She is a silly old woman,
and you know as well as I that even Sigmund can't bear to be
near her.*

*I appreciate your concern regarding Eduard and my future
prospects (which you seem to think are dwindling). Despite your
admonitions, I can't enter into a relationship or a marriage
simply because the timing is right. You urge me to disregard
sentiment for the sake of a good match. I still require, as I always
have, some feelings of a romantic nature.*

Love to the children.

Yours,

Minna

Minna posted the letter and began her duties at ten. What had
started out as a routine position a few weeks earlier had become
brutalizing and demeaning. The sisters now requested she stand
outside their bedroom doors each morning awaiting their call, and
her duties had expanded to include bathing the women, a job ordi-
narily handled by the ladies' maid, who had quit unexpectedly the
week before.

Today she entered the dark, airless room where sister Bella lay
like a leviathan, breathing heavily. Minna opened the curtains, lit

the gas lamps, pulled down the bedcovers, and helped the heaving woman out of bed. Supporting her by the arm, she shuffled together with her to the water closet and stood listening to complaints concerning blocked urination. Afterward, she took hold of the lady's hand, steered her away from the puddles on the floor (which the upstairs maid continually complained about), and bathed her girth in a white enameled cast-iron bathtub that was encased in mahogany, like a large coffin.

Minna had suggested that Bella use the shower ring, which fit nicely over her neck, but Bella insisted on submerging herself in the tub, requiring Minna to haul her out, which put a terrible strain on Minna's back and gave her a most unwelcome and graphic view of the woman's naked body.

After the bath, Minna opened a wooden cabinet, which was supplied with an apothecary of remedies, purifiers, lozenges, oils, extracts, and various mixtures of opium powder, tinctures, sedatives, plasters, and soap. She waited while Bella selected the day's medications: White Pine Cough Balsam with a hint of morphine, brown sarsaparilla syrup for purifying the blood and skin, Dr. Claris' Family Liniment in an amethyst-colored bottle, Old Dr. Jessup's Kidney Pills. Bella also swallowed her favorite draft for headaches and lethargy, which contained an alarming amount of mercury and lead.

Then there were the cosmetics. In her youth, Bella had spent time in France, where beauty salons were beginning to make their appearance and cosmetics were eagerly used and readily available. She believed the ancient Roman adage that "a woman without paint is like food without salt." As a result, Bella used lip reddeners made from mercuric sulfide, eye shadow from lead, and face whitener from zinc oxide.

But she drew the line at belladonna, the juice of the deadly nightshade, which some of her peers used to rinse their eyes in the hopes of obtaining that bright-eyed, youthful look. There had been a few incidents of temporary blindness. She did, however, sometimes sleep with her face wrapped in thin strips of raw beef, which was supposed to have antiaging properties.

Minna then brushed Bella's long, tangled gray hair and began to dress her.

Today's morning costume was a day dress with bright blue and heliotrope stripes, which required a heavy, boned corset with flexible steel wires in front. In addition, as was common for problematic figures, and in order for the waist to fit, Minna needed to wrap a band of leather around the whole thing, squashing and flattening any protruding rolls of flesh. It took Minna over thirty minutes to tightly lace the corset and wrap the leather band, breaking most of her nails in the process.

After Minna deposited Bella at the breakfast table, she awoke Louisa and started the whole process all over again. By eleven, Minna was desperate to rest, if only for a moment, but that was impossible. Her duties after breakfast included stopping at the pharmacy, greengrocer, butcher, and baker, picking up chocolates, flowers, and the sisters' favorite—*Blutwurst*.

When she returned from all this, she was required to sit in the parlor and act cheerful and interested in whatever feather-headed drivel the sisters chose to discuss. This afternoon, they were talking about purchasing additional pieces of furniture and ornamentation at an auction in the suburbs. Julian suggested two end tables and a chinoiserie lamp with matching urns. Lord knows, thought Minna, where in the cluttered, tasteless reception room they were going to squeeze them in.

"What do you think, Minna?" Bella asked. "Should we add some Bohemian glass? I so adore Bohemian glass. The real thing, of course."

"Imitations are so vulgar," Louisa added.

What to say about Bohemian glass? How to tell them, in a nice way, they had enough garbage in this house for ten villas. How to tell them that this house was already vulgar so they needn't worry about imitations? How to tell them that her head ached, and that she would quit this dreadful job in an instant if she could.

They were interrupted by the day maid, who handed Louisa an envelope on a silver tray. A smile broke out on her face as she read the handwritten card.

"It's from Julian. He's invited us to a house party at his villa next month!"

"I imagine the Olbriches will be there. . . ."

"And the Bahrs . . . Goodness gracious, he's *even* included you, Minna."

"How lovely," said Bella.

"Yes. How lovely. He's always so polite, even inviting the staff," said Louisa, pointedly looking at Minna.

Truth be known, Minna would rather stay home than spend a weekend listening to the sisters' high-pitched voices, which reminded her of two hummingbirds flapping their wings at frantic speeds and going nowhere. In fact, when *was* the last time she had had a decent conversation? And then she remembered. The last time was with him, of course.

25

. . .

Over the next few weeks, the sisters were in a tizzy, preparing for the weekend trip, and Minna was working twenty-hour days. Late one afternoon, she noticed a letter sitting on her dresser. This time it *was* his writing.

Vienna, March 25, 1896

My dearest Minna,

It's late at night and I can't sleep. In fact, I haven't slept well since you rushed out of that hotel room in Hamburg, as if you'd seen a ghost. You must know I have no intention of letting you stay in Frankfurt forever, and that I must see you again.

I'm longing for a few uninterrupted days with you but I'll settle for a night in Frankfurt. I have colleagues there and I can create a reason to visit anytime you can arrange to get away. Despite your behavior, I know you will see me and that your protestations of "never" and "impossible" should not be taken to

heart. Especially if I come bearing gifts, perhaps cigarettes
or a bottle of gin? Ah, if only it were that easy . . .

I infer from your note to Martha that you've settled in your post
for the moment, and have achieved your goal of abandoning me
to this infernal state of loneliness and privation. And, yes, it is
your doing, along with the shallow mercies of my research, that
fill the evening hours and give me monstrous headaches. Even the
coca, damn you, doesn't alleviate the pain.

I am now sitting at my desk, staring at Athena, who has
become my favorite antiquity. She rests on the table next to the
window, beautiful and lifelike. I'm beginning to understand why
the ancient Greeks used to chain their statues to prevent them
from fleeing. I, like the ancient Greeks, do not want to let you go.

When can I see you again?

Yours,

Sigmund

Minna folded the letter and carried it around in her pocket for the next several days, reading and rereading it. But she didn't need the letter to keep him relentlessly present in her mind. He was all she could think about.

The question was, How far was she willing to go? Could she be pushed once more into something so destructive? No. Never again. Her affair with Freud was over. She would not continue these moments of madness. She still felt stained by her disloyalty even as she missed his touch. After all, there were boundaries in *her* world, if not in his.

How should she answer? She decided not to write to him at all. What would be the point? She would only lie to him, tell him that she couldn't get away or claim that she didn't want to see him. No, it was better to hope that silence would dissuade him, and distance her.

Vienna, April 1, 1896

Dear Minna,

For God's sake, send me a note! You're either very busy or you're deluding yourself into thinking that you can run away from all this. You wonder how I am? You haven't asked, but I will tell you. Thoroughly miserable, like a dog. Depression, fatigue, unable to work.

I assume that you want to conceal the true state of affairs between us. That is noble of you. But I beg you not to do it in this way. Martha and the children are planning to go to Reichenau soon for a short trip. I am supposed to meet them two weeks later. If I don't hear from you by then, I will come to you uninvited, if I must.

Yours,

Sigmund

Frankfurt, April 15, 1896

Dear Sigmund,

I will get straight to the point. Your letter scared me to death! Are you mad? You can't arrive here unannounced and spoil everything. We will not see each other again!

I am happy, no, thrilled, with my new position and I have no intention of jeopardizing this life that I have built.

I'm sorry that you're uncomfortable, but I feel you must be exaggerating your symptoms for my sake.

Yours,

Minna

P.S. You could still send me the bottle of gin.

Over the next few days, the Kassel household staff spent much of the time preparing for the weekend visit to Julian's villa, while the sisters hovered over them like two skittish hens. Bella constantly voiced reservations over whether the whole trip was too much for them, and her nervous chatter threw Louisa into fits of anger. They had the dubious distinction of not having been in a hotel, train station, or café for years, and Minna kept wondering if, after all the packing of faded sables, yellowing blouses, and woolen suits (smelling distinctly of camphor) they might cancel at the last minute.

The night before they were to leave, Minna didn't get to her room until almost midnight. After dinner, the sisters requested that she review their medical requirements for the trip, telling her to go through both of their medicine cabinets and carefully pack all the medications, writing down the scheduled times and dosages for each one. Minna reluctantly agreed, but the boredom of the task tempted her to dump all the medications into the dustbin. It did occur to her, at half past eleven that night, that she could kill them both with just a slight discrepancy in dosage. The threat of an official inquisition into foul play was the only thing that held her back.

When she finally reached her room, another letter was waiting.

Vienna, April 30, 1896

My dearest Minna,

I have closed the door to my study and shut all the windows so I can sit calmly at my desk and deal with your mulish refusals to see me. I have laid bare my feelings for you, and now all I can do is appeal to you as a desolate and lonely man who is suffering in every aspect of his life.

You know that my colleagues are still refusing to acknowledge my work. I began my career with the best of intentions—a love of research and of medicine. But I am beset by the unimaginative Neanderthals of the medical establishment who are intent on ruining me. My misfortune is that I can't compromise and proceed with false flattery, even though Martha never stops reminding me that this is what is keeping me from rising in the ranks of the university.

My "social failing" in her mind is compounded by my views on sexuality, which, as you know, she finds repugnant and embarrassing. She is not interested in discussing my work with me. Never even a whit of intellectual passion about what I do. In her mind, if she runs the household well, that is her sole obligation. In the past, when I've tried to explain to her that a man has other needs, she has turned her back on me. Now we are pulling in different directions. We are less sympathetic with each other on almost every subject.

So I turn to you, Minna, for solace. You've always understood me.

By the way, I would like to point out that, contrary to your condescending inference that I am suffering hypochondriacal

symptoms, the doctor just left, and I have a severe case of the
most violent arrhythmia and some dyspnea.

Yours lovingly,

Sigmund

P.S. What brand of gin do you prefer?

Minna folded the letter and put it with the others in the drawer. Honestly! Couldn't the esteemed doctor come up with something better than "my wife doesn't understand me"? Minna had often been accused of stubbornness and independence. But such characteristics were not always detrimental. For now, she would rely on them to save her soul, if that was even possible at this point. An errant thought crossed her mind, an old history lesson she had learned as a child. Beware of Turks at your door threatening Christendom. Just as in the siege of Vienna in the sixteenth century, one party would finally win, but a heavy toll would be exacted from both sides.

26

. . .

On the morning of departure, the sisters chatted with excitement as the maid and footman heaped a pile of shawls and luggage in the front hallway. Julian arrived right on time, oozing charm, and smiled gaily as the sisters emerged from the house, followed by Minna.

"We're profoundly grateful to you, my dear Julian, for inviting us," Louisa said.

"Profoundly," Bella echoed. They were dressed in matching gray serge coats, hats, and black leather gloves, an endeavor for Bella, whose gloves had to be pulled in a glove stretcher in order to accommodate her thick, meaty fingers.

"My pleasure," Julian answered.

It was agreed that they would all travel together in the sisters' extra-wide coach.

Minna's long skirt rustled in the breeze as Julian ushered her into the carriage, graciously taking her hand and briefly brushing his lips across the top of her glove. She settled herself on the seat, balancing her purse and a book on her lap.

Julian's family villa was fifty kilometers from Frankfurt, built by his father after his Grand Tour of Italy in the mid-sixties. Julian, the only heir, had inherited the estate more than a decade ago, following the untimely death of both parents.

They drove for several hours through the frost-covered countryside, past churches, villages, and ancient ruins, and maneuvering through the narrow streets of medieval towns. The imposing *villa rustica* sat at the front of a wooded hillside at the edge of town, surrounded by a thick grove of unusual firs and fruit trees. The group passed a kennel, housing packs of hounds for hunting fox and quail, but the half-timbered stables were overgrown with weeds and empty.

When the carriage finally arrived at the house, Julian climbed out and rang the bell, waiting several minutes and ringing again, until a butler, who was hastily pulling on his suspenders, squinted at Julian through a crack in the door and then slowly opened it. Minna assumed that Julian's visits to the villa were probably irregular, especially at this time of year, and he obviously hadn't notified the staff of his plans.

The butler placed wooden steps beside the coach door and helped the sisters out of the carriage, ordering the drivers to unload the baggage. As Minna walked through the grand entry, she noticed that although the villa was large and rambling, it was also in disrepair—the paint was chipped and bubbled on the outside walls, the doors needed fresh varnish, and various windowpanes were cracked or missing altogether, having been boarded up rather than replaced. Furthermore, fir trees in front of the public rooms were so thick that there was no light or view. And, walking by the kitchen, Minna noticed what looked like feral cats congregating near the side door. For all his pretensions, it looked as if Julian needed more from the sisters than just their "good taste."

While the group gathered in the parlor for late tea, Minna proceeded directly upstairs to supervise the unpacking of the sisters' belongings.

She came down several hours later to help the sisters retire to their rooms to rest before the evening festivities. As they reached the landing, Bella, breathing heavily and complaining of pains shooting down her arm, put her arm around Minna, leaned in, and in a sweet, cocktail-scented voice said, "Who would have thought Julian's home would be such a ruin. I can't imagine what my sister sees in him."

Minna looked at her, taken aback. She'd assumed they were both enamored of the man.

"Don't look so surprised. I humor him for Louisa's sake. Honestly, do you really think we need all those silly cachepots from Aix-en-Provence?"

Minna looked at Bella's chalky skin and the dark circles under her eyes and felt chastened. There was a depth to the old bat that she hadn't anticipated.

After Minna put the sisters down for their nap, she retired to her room. She tried to nap as well, but the green malachite clock ticking loudly on the dresser was keeping her awake. She drew back the drapes, wrenched open the window, and placed it outside on the ledge. She hoped it wouldn't fall into the foliage. She lit a Turkish cigarette she had hidden in her baggage and lay awake a bit longer, looking out at the brooding grayness of the countryside.

She awoke to a knocking on her door. It was Louisa, in a dressing gown and bedroom slippers, saying it was time to get dressed for dinner.

"Could you please wake Bella?" she asked. "I've knocked several times but she's sleeping like the dead."

Minna put on a robe, walked down the hall, and lightly tapped on Bella's door. No answer. She thought she heard a noise, opened the door slightly, and peered inside. One of the mangy cats had found its way in and was scratching on the quilt near Bella's head.

"Shoo!" Minna whispered, batting the air as the creature leapt past her and flew into the hall. Something made her turn to look back at Bella. Maybe it was the absence of any noise whatsoever, not even the light snoring Minna sometimes heard from her room. Bella's head was turned to the side and resting on the pillow, her hair hanging limply, covering her face. Minna bent down and gently swept aside a tangled strand of gray. She had only to look at her for an instant and she knew. Bella was dead as a doornail.

I t was customary for undertakers to send two mutes to stand outside the mourner's home, as sentries. Why mutes? Minna had asked her mother at a funeral years before. Because, she was told, they were thought to be appropriately solemn and silent and, in addition, positions for the handicapped were limited, poor devils.

The day of Bella's funeral, these two grim-faced fellows were standing guard, dressed in shabby, long black morning coats, soiled crepe cummerbunds, and ill-fitting top hats. Only invited guests were allowed access to the bereaved family's home. The buffet and drinks were for mourners only. Those who happened to notice the wreath of black crepe hung on the door and sought entry for mere curiosity's sake would be immediately turned away.

The sisters' household had been in turmoil since their tragic return. Everything was focused on arranging the elaborate funeral to the point of obsession. The first few days included visits to mourning warehouses, stationers, and dressmakers for appropriate mourning attire, which Louisa ordered for her entire staff.

Louisa, who had been inseparable from her sister since birth, was inconsolable. She sat in the drawing room, alone at the end of the sofa, her needlework untouched on her lap, her thoughts drifting, no one knew where. She didn't talk, she didn't eat. The only movement Louisa made was to retire to her bedroom periodically for more medication.

Minna's duties during the visitation period consisted mostly of sitting in the parlor next to Bella's corpse, which had turned an unhappy color of puce, even with the bowls of salt strategically placed on the body to slow decomposition. Specially selected strong-scented flowers did little to mask the smell of rotting flesh.

The stream of visitors, mostly widows and distant aunts and cousins who quickly gave Louisa their condolences, took in the dismal sight of Bella's body ("Doesn't she look lovely?") and hastily left. This was not a home where anyone wanted to spend a moment longer than was required.

After the funeral and the requisite visitation period, Louisa informed Minna that they would be required to sit inside the darkened home for the next six months. It didn't take long for the first rush of visitors after Bella's death to drastically drop off, and now practically no one came to call. But what was worse, if anything could be worse, it seemed Louisa was slowly losing her hold on reality. One would expect some changes in behavior from the bereaved, but no one could address the problem of Louisa's constant and glazed conversations with her deceased sister, Bella.

Minna knew she should be offering charity and understanding but, truthfully, she was not capable of dealing with the situation any longer. Sometime over the next few weeks she gave notice and contacted a private registry to find a position as either a governess or a lady's companion.

But then she broadened her search to include positions such as a clerk, secretary, or bookkeeper, new fields for women in which she could earn her keep and not be forced to live in someone else's home. The more she thought about it, the more she liked it.

One afternoon, when Minna was so bored she was contemplating reading one of Bella's silver spoon novels, she heard a carriage pull up to the front of the house. The sound of horses' hooves on the cobblestones, harnesses jingling, and then low voices came from the street. She looked out the window and saw Sigmund alight from the cab, holding a valise. He hesitated for just a moment, checking the number of the house. A midafternoon glow of light illuminated his profile as he removed his hat, smoothed down his hair, and headed toward the front door.

Minna watched him and her heart sank. She wanted to rush upstairs to get her bearings, but it was too late. With a mixture of fear and elation, she opened the door.

"Don't look so disappointed," he said brightly, leaning in to kiss her on the cheek.

"Disappointed? I'm stunned," she replied, flustered. "What are you doing here?"

"Cheerful place . . ." he said, ignoring her discomfort, glancing into the musty parlor. The pungent smell of old rugs and dead flowers was overwhelming.

"We're still in mourning."

"I can see that," he said as he walked toward her, refusing to keep his distance. She was struck by how unchanged he was—his neat, official appearance, his polished shoes, and his crisp linen shirt. And the presumption that he would be welcome. Before she could even think, he backed her into a corner and kissed her on the neck. She shrank back against the wall.

"You shouldn't have come," she said.

"But aren't you glad I did," he replied with a confident smile, unfazed by her tepid reaction.

"You might have written, informed me that . . ." she said, in a strained whisper.

"I did. I specifically told you that I would come."

She met his gaze and resented how she still felt about him. She wanted him to stay and she wanted him to leave.

"Let's take a walk, Minna. Go to a café and talk. Unless you'd like to visit with me here."

"It's not a good time. . . ."

"So what would you suggest? I've traveled halfway across the country to see you. You could meet me later if you'd like, or come with me now and have a coffee."

He took her hand in his, and for one merciful moment they didn't say a word.

"Just a drink," she said, disengaging her hand, trying to recover her equilibrium.

She left him standing in the hall, coat and hat back on, as she briskly climbed the stairs to her room, washed her face, and ran a comb through her hair. Then, without stopping to see who might spot her, she walked out with him into the fresh cool air.

Outside on the streets, they walked together toward the river and, at one point, he gently put his hand on her back and steered her around a group of street hawkers. She breathed in deeply as they entered a tavern, and she followed him to a table facing the water.

They settled in and he ordered a bottle of wine and then a plate of fruit, cheeses, and bread. Polite conversation followed, with the two of them exchanging bits of news. Minna spoke in half sentences about Bella dying; the long, drawn-out mourning period; and Louisa's flight from reality. He nodded sympathetically as he filled her glass several more times and talked on about the continued obstructions by the Psychiatric Board in Vienna and his frustration with their failure to endorse his research.

She stared beyond him at certain times, feeling as if she were in a whirlwind of sound that would blow itself out at some point, even though the place was still half empty. She kept drinking, but her lips felt parched, her mouth dry from the strain of sitting across from him.

"So then, my darling. Have you had enough of Frankfurt?"

"I'm not staying on with the Kassels, if that's what you mean. I actually have several options for a position."

"Doing what?"

"It depends. I might find salaried employment in a new field."

"Such as . . ."

"Working in an office or a school or . . ." She stopped and lowered her eyes as an idea occurred to her. "Perhaps selling hats." The thought amused her in a dark sort of way, and then she wondered how many glasses of wine she had consumed.

"A shopgirl?" he laughed, not sure whether or not she was serious. "That's ridiculous. Completely inappropriate."

"I shouldn't think you're the one to talk about what's appropriate. Why *not* sell ladies' hats?" she said. "Fancy ones, from Paris.

The very latest. You know, the ones with ribbons and feathers and dead butterflies."

He looked at her skeptically as she pressed on.

"Hats make women happy. I've never seen an unhappy woman leave a hat shop. Which is more than you can say about *your* patients." She smiled inwardly, waiting for his reaction.

"My dear, I think sitting in that room with the corpse has affected your judgment."

Freud leaned back in his chair, lit a cigar, and appraised the situation. He had *that* look. The look someone gets when he's about to ask a question he's been holding back for hours. Let him show his cards, Minna thought.

"Have you ever been to Maloja this time of year?" he asked suddenly.

"Maloja?"

"It's a resort in Switzerland. In the Alps. Come with me."

"I can't. . . ."

"It's just a few days. I'm not asking for much."

"Oh, yes, my dear, you are," she said, looking at him over the rim of her wineglass. She reached awkwardly for her purse. His proposal made her feel light-headed and vulnerable. She should have known all along this was the plan. It seemed so clear now, in retrospect. She met his gaze and then turned away.

"How could I live with myself?" she asked, her voice tightening. "The guilt . . . My God, Sigmund."

"Morals and God don't come into it—"

"I've heard that lecture," she interrupted. "Guilt is simply self-imposed punishment thrust on us by civilization. Isn't that what you said? You can justify everything, can't you?"

"Sexual needs are rights, and no one should be expected to live without gratifying them," he said, putting down his cigar.

"So it's simply a philosophical and academic question."

"If you want to look at it that way. It's the truth. Guilt is imposed by society to stop us from loving who we want to love. Don't you want to be with me?" he asked, his eyes softening.

"That has nothing to do with it."

"Come with me. Do you know what the *Kohlröserl* flowers smell like in the final stages of bloom? So strong and sweet," he said, "and the hillsides are filled with them. Wild purples and reds."

She rifled nervously through her purse, stalling.

"Light this for me, will you?" she asked, handing him a cigarette.

He took a match from his pocket and lit her cigarette. As she inhaled, he noticed that her hands were shaking. She leaned her head back and blew a shot of smoke into the air. He reached across the table and gently moved a strand of hair from her face and stroked her cheek lightly. She could feel his fingers on her skin and pushed his hand away.

"I keep thinking about you," he said, "about the way we—"

"Don't romance me," she said, cutting him off. "It doesn't become you. And I don't want to hear about flowers and the hillsides. Stop talking."

"All right. I'll stop talking," he said, not the least bit deterred. He waved to the waiter for the check, the way a businessman would when he wants to close the deal. "Finish your drink. You're coming with me."

"I don't know. I just don't know," she said, shifting in her seat. He took her hand and squeezed it. He could see her wavering.

"Stoicism has its benefits, but it's never been known to be amusing."

"You mustn't be clever now," she said. "I haven't any energy left for banter."

"I won't banter," he said, moving closer to her.

"You're not going to give up," she said, stating the obvious.

"No."

"Even if I walked out of here."

"Even if you walked out," he repeated, his breath warm on her face.

"And I won't be able to resist," she said, her heart pounding against her breastbone.

"Poor Minna," he said.

She knew what he meant. That overpowering feeling she always got when she was near him had taken over and there was no decision to be made other than the one she was making. When she got back to the house, she gathered her belongings, stuffed her letters and books in her valise, and banished all traces of the waxen, wrinkled faces sitting in the living room. Her final thought, as she met him at the rail station, was Seneca's line "Let the wickedness escape . . . for every guilty person is his own hangman." She would go with him.

27

. . .

They walked down the platform at the Central Bahnhof, headed for the first-class coach. Departure time to Switzerland was in less than thirty minutes, but teams of workers were still huddled on the rails, hosing down cars, examining wheels, and pouring oil on the wheel boxes. In spite of her misgivings, Minna felt a surge of energy and excitement.

The crush of carriage-class passengers fell behind, and still she and Freud walked on, past sleeping cars and club cars, chair cars and dining cars, until they reached the spot where dignitaries, wealthy families, and state officials were transported to their elite quarters. Electric lights burned like beacons through the large, curtained windows, and she could see stewards, maids, and waiters clad in white jackets moving back and forth between the cars.

Minna gathered up her skirts and boarded the train, then maneuvered through the narrow aisle to the private compartment Freud had obviously reserved in advance. She quashed the somewhat disturbing thought that he had assumed all along that she would go with him.

The porter arrived with their luggage, and Minna caught her

breath as he unlocked the door. The room was spacious—palatial, even—with black walnut woodwork, gold-framed windows, polished brass fixtures, and a large picture window with elaborate, draped curtains. The banquette sofa, which converted to a bed, was upholstered in lush, bordello-red brocade, as was the chair by the private bathroom. She never dreamed that a train could be this luxurious.

"Sigmund . . . this is so . . . grand," she said. "I feel like we're eloping."

As if in response, the car jolted backward with a screech and lumbered forward past the platform. She turned her face away from his and glanced out the window, restraining the urge to call it off. And for what? A rescue? Too late for that. They were entering the land of make-believe, of sweet beginnings. This was the bright side of love, their world transformed with a brilliant false light.

"Do you remember . . . ?" he asked. "When was that? Eight, ten years ago? When you came to visit? I was working late, Martha was upstairs with the children, and you wanted to go to the Prater to see the carnival. I needed fresh air so I went with you. A gust of wind came up, your hat flew off, your hair came unpinned and blew all over the place. We chased after the hat . . . and I finally caught it . . . we were laughing as I put it back on your head. I remember, you were so excited, you threw your arms around my neck, and for the first time I felt your body next to mine."

She remembered the carnival and the embrace, but assumed it meant nothing to him.

"It was all I could do not to kiss you," he said, leaning forward, sliding his arms around her waist, and kissing her full on the mouth. He stroked her hair, shoulders, and back. "You knew that. You had to have known that."

"I didn't. I thought you were interested in my mind."

"You were naive."

"I'm not naive now."

She smiled, pushed him away, and slowly stood up, pulling the shade down and locking the cabinet door. She wanted him and nothing else mattered. She unbuttoned her high-collared white silk blouse, letting it drop on the floor, and took off her plain summer skirt. Then she stepped out of her petticoat and began to slowly unlace the pale dove-gray bones of her corset.

"Don't," he said, pulling her toward him, "leave it on."

Afterward, she turned toward him, her head propped on her hands, and she saw his strong, sharp profile in the fading afternoon light. Lying there beside him, listening to the soothing sounds of the train and his sighs of desire, she was filled with a mixture of enormous relief and a lovely languor. The evening still stretched ahead of them, and she knew it was nearly time for supper, but the luxury of lying there with him, her curved body nestled in his arms, was liberating.

"What are you thinking?" she asked.

"I'm thinking," he whispered in her ear, "what would have happened if I'd met you first."

The dining car was a study in opulence. The ceiling was covered with painted frescoes, and Minna's feet sank into the deep-piled burgundy carpet. Each table was strategically placed next to a picture window and was set with crisp white linens, fine china, and heavy silver cutlery. The head steward greeted them, addressing Herr Doktor Freud by name. Before leaving their compartment, Minna put on her gloves. It wouldn't do for anyone to see the absence of a wedding ring.

They were seated at one of the front tables and immediately served champagne from a silver bucket, and oddly shaped canapés dolloped with caviar. It was all so formal and elegant, and with the formality came a momentary calm. She picked up the menu and read it silently as the train rumbled over a bridge, causing the dishes to rattle on the table.

The steward now cast his attention on an elderly couple making their entrance. The man wore a gray Inverness cape over his shoulders and a dark, soft hat, and carried a walking stick, which he used to steady himself as the train continued to lurch. His wife was wrapped in fur and seemed hardly to notice as her husband handed a wad of bills to the steward. The man then lit a cigar, turning it in his fingers as he picked up the menu.

"Darling, put that beastly thing down. You know it's bad for your heart," his wife scolded. He looked at her in silence, then crushed it on the gold-rimmed, china bread plate, grinding it several more times than necessary.

"We're off to the mountains. For his health. Our physician tells him he shouldn't smoke, but he never listens. Nasty habit."

The husband was now reading the menu, clearly uninterested in carrying on a conversation with either his wife or the strangers at the next table.

"Are you from Frankfurt?" the wife asked.

"Vienna," replied Freud, not introducing himself or Minna.

"I thought so. You can always tell passengers from Vienna. You look familiar. Are you friends with the Gunthers? Wilber and Elise?" she asked, glancing at her husband, who was finishing off his fourth canapé. "No more of that, dear," she admonished him, and then, turning back to Minna and Sigmund, said, "His weight, you know."

Her husband wiped his mouth with a napkin, threw it on the table, and stood up.

"I'm going to the WC."

"The Gunthers?" she repeated to Minna, resuming her conversation as though nothing had happened. "Do you know them?"

Minna stiffened. She had heard that name somewhere. Friends of Martha's, perhaps? No, maybe not. Then again, she couldn't be sure. She glanced at Sigmund to see if the name resonated with him, but he showed no sign of recognition and seemed unconcerned. Strange that it never occurred to her that they might bump into someone they knew. She felt a tickle in her throat and the urge for a drink.

"Don't know them," said Freud. "Pardon me, madame. We're going to have to change tables. I'm planning to smoke through the entire meal."

"Oh. I didn't mean for you . . ." the woman said, then paused, flushing with embarrassment at the slight. She looked down at her napkin as Freud and Minna stood up and moved to the other end of the dining car.

They ordered three courses, starting off with a clear beef *Rindsuppe* and moving on to a medley of game slices and fresh crepes filled with spinach and cheese. Minna ate little and drank a recommended white Riesling while Sigmund switched to beer. He talked about a few referrals (a man crippled with seizures, a suicidal woman) and then, in a much more spirited tone, described his new antique acquisition—a pre-Columbian plate, which Minna feared might eventually be used as an ashtray.

At a certain point, the conversation turned to the children and their various ailments, activities, and outings. Minna felt a sudden tug in her chest and stopped herself from flooding him with questions. Was Sophie sleeping? Mathilde studying? Martin staying out of trouble? But she said nothing about the children because that would inevitably lead to questions about Martha, and she was not ready to discuss her sister or her own transgressions.

At the end of the meal, he rummaged through his jacket pockets for another cigar, lit it, leaned back, and rubbed his temples.

"You look tired," she said.

"I'm working myself to the bone, if you want to know."

"Of course, I want to know."

"I've been in Berlin, meeting with Fliess. I've told you about him. Quite brilliant. And unlike Breuer he hasn't the least doubt about my theories."

"I hear things have gotten worse with the association . . ." she said, hesitating to mention that Martha was the one who told her.

"I'm simply ignoring their criticisms. *Especially* Breuer's. He disagrees with me on almost every front. Purposely robs me of all credibility. He just won't believe that the anxiety of my neurotic patients has to do with sexuality."

"So nothing's changed . . ."

"Nothing."

"What can you do?"

"I have to find cures. That's what I have to do," he said, opening and pouring both of them a glass of champagne.

"But on a good note, I've had a crucial turn with my dream book. I'm now analyzing my own dreams, finding that they reveal an enormous amount about one's childhood. This information can be key in determining why we think the way we do, why we feel guilty or jealous or competitive. As they say, the elucidations and clues are flowing."

"You're analyzing your own dreams?" she asked.

"Yes. And you're the only one I've told . . . outside of Dr. Fliess, who is becoming as indispensable to my emotional life as you are."

Minna leaned back and looked at him. Her mind was spinning and the room was getting warm. *Indispensable.* If she was being truthful to herself, she would have to admit it was what she'd always wanted.

"The more I dig, the more I find that I'm discovering the roots of my fears and desires. The intellectual beauty of this work is . . ." A half smile played on his lips as their knees touched.

She felt the rhythmic swaying of the train, and watched the expression in his eyes, the movement of his hands and lips when he talked. She was tired, too much wine and too little sleep, but the thought that they were here together after all these months comforted her. The monotony and grime of her former life were gone. She reached across the table and gently took his hand.

"My dear, you're quite ruining my critical faculties. I can't think with you sitting so close . . . after so long . . ."

He motioned to the waiter for the check, picked up the bottle of champagne, and led Minna back to their cabin. On the way back, she had to cling to a brass railing as the train lurched sideways around a bend and Sigmund reached over to steady her. They opened the door to their compartment to find that it had been transformed while they were gone. The banquette was made into a bed with crisp white linens. Next to the bed was a small silver vase with one red rose.

Sigmund methodically hung his jacket on the hook, locked the door, and slid the curtain closed. Then he opened his travel valise and took out the small blue vial of liquid coca. He motioned for her to come near and repeated the ritual she now knew, dabbing a drop of coca in one nostril, then the other. He handed her the bottle.

"I decided I wasn't going to do this again. . . ."

"It's good for you. Not at all addictive. Unlike alcohol and morphine. Go ahead now."

She rubbed it inside her nose, sat down in the chair, and waited. And then it hit her—the strange, sudden exhilaration, the feeling of lightness. No more fatigue, just a general sense of euphoria.

"Divine," she said, leaning her head against the cushion.

He smiled at her indulgently and then his eyes narrowed slightly.

"Have you heard from Eduard?"

"Excuse me?"

"Eduard. You remember Eduard, don't you?" he asked, dabbing more coca into each nostril.

"Why on earth bring this up now? And the answer is yes."

"That's nice."

"You don't mind?"

"No. I've told you what I think of him."

"Did you?"

"He's a rogue. And a liar."

"Sigmund, my dear, this is beneath you," she said, not even trying to hide her amusement. "Let's talk about something else."

"Such as?"

She looked at him, her eyes softening, the coca flushing through her system. She bent over and whispered in his ear.

"You'll think of something. . . ."

He slipped his hand inside her blouse and gently caressed her breast.

"Let's start with your mouth; it's soft and expressive, and I like the taste of gin when you think I haven't noticed. I like the fact that you have a man's brain and the way you blink when you get angry and the fact that you can't embroider. I like the way you stand tall and straight and the way you fidget when you're bored. I like the way you look in a dress and the way your collarbone juts out of your chest."

Then he slipped his hands under her skirt and he began caressing the inside of her thighs. "I like your thick auburn hair and the way you try to hold it back with your combs but it keeps falling down. I like your skin, the way it feels when I touch it. Your beautiful eyes and your thick brows . . . your laughter and your fists pounding on my back. I like the way you smell and taste. That little spot on the corner of your mouth that you lick with your tongue. I like the way you cry out when we make love. I like when you're naked."

She was drifting far away now. Thousands and thousands of miles. She could hardly hear his voice. She forgot who she was. She forgot who he was. And that was the beauty of it all.

28

. . .

The train wound its way through the night, descending from the high plains of Germany to deep folded valleys and thick black forests. It jolted to a halt at several little villages as they crossed over the Swiss border, and just before midnight, it stopped dead on the tracks for no apparent reason. Minna opened the cabin window, and looked out into the darkness. The air outside had gotten colder, thinner, more foreign, almost forbidding in a way she couldn't explain. She closed the window and curled up next to him.

In the morning, at the bleary-eyed hour of five, they changed trains and boarded the local Rhaetian Railway headed for the upper Engadine Valley. No dining car, no first-class cabins, and, alas, no champagne or hot water. This was a small, tired model left over from the thirties, and it huffed and heaved through the rocky landscape, letting out protracted, almost painful whistles at every curve or tunnel entrance.

Minna and Freud sat opposite each other in a wooden-benched compartment, their coats swinging on hooks and their valuables sliding back and forth on ledges above the window. He looked out the window for a while, then reached for his briefcase. He shuffled through it and then pulled out a pile of papers. They traveled through obscure medieval towns while he worked and she read a German translation of *Hamlet* by Schlegel and Tieck that Sigmund had brought along for his dream research.

As he handed her the slim volume, he told her he was now convinced that Shakespeare was a fraud and Edward de Vere, the 17th Earl of Oxford, was the true author of the great bard's works. Then he fired off a litany of reasons, starting with the fact that only a nobleman could have written with such familiarity about the intricacies of the royal court and ending with the argument that Shakespeare left no correspondence, no original literary manuscripts, or any other evidence that he was the author.

"This is all very colorful, Sigmund," she said, amused, "but it still sounds highly improbable."

"I'm sure I'm right. Even Mark Twain agrees with me."

"Well then it *must* be true, if Mark Twain believes it," she said, laughing.

They were quiet for a while as the train began its steep ascent into the rocky slopes of the Bergell region. At one point, he looked up from his research and rubbed his eyes.

"Difficult?" she asked.

"Immensely," he said.

"Tell me."

He spoke calmly and methodically, and she never took her eyes from his. He told her about the new theories he had discovered while in the midst of his self-analysis for his dream book.

He began by saying that man was *not* the rational creature one would think, that "we're all roiling cauldrons of conflicting desires we can barely keep in check."

"What about Kant and Spinoza and their theories of the rational man?" she asked.

"That was hundreds of years ago," he said, dismissing her. "And it was philosophical, not scientific."

"Well, if you're going to toss out the great thinkers of the Western world, then you'll have to elaborate."

"Gladly," he said, leaning back and crossing his arms with self-importance.

He explained to her that there were three parts of a man's psyche—the id, the ego, and the superego—all of them constantly at war with one another. The id represented man's savage passion—the ego, his reason. Think of the image of a horse and rider, he said. The ego was the rider, the id, the horse. It was the rider's job to rein in the superior strength of the horse and keep it from succumbing to society's temptations.

He then described the third part of man's psyche, the superego, which, he believed, was the most stunning of his scientific discoveries. According to his theory, the superego could be compared to the conscience, but, as he hastened to point out, it was more complicated than that. The superego was an unconscious, highly critical judge that condemned, rewarded, or punished man's unacceptable id impulses.

"I'm not sure I understand, Sigmund," she interrupted. "How does this all work? Who's fighting who?"

He paused for a moment, his gaze trained brightly on her.

"Well, for example, if a man is wildly attracted to a woman, it's the passion of his id that seeks expression. However, should civilized rules somehow deem this passion sinful, then the ego fights back, repressing the id. But the superego could also join the fray and exert harsh self-judgment. Even to the point of trying to put a stop to this overwhelming attraction. However, one would be doing oneself more harm than good by trying to keep all these elements in check. There would be no inner peace."

"So what you're saying is," she said, with a certain wry humor, "to be happy, one must let these drives have their say."

"Exactly, my dear."

As usual, Minna thought. Happiness, in Freud's world, was all about sex.

The hours went by. They slept and read, put their coats back on, complained to the porters about the cold, and braced themselves on the bench, as the train climbed up the steep side of the valley and then leveled out to the Wetterhorn mountain range. There were stunning views wherever one looked, and he talked of their destination in Maloja, the hidden lakes, waterfalls, high alpine pastures, and air that made one light-headed.

Later on, she rested her head gently on his shoulder and clasped her gloved hand over his. She could not remember when she had felt happier. And the farther the train traveled to this cold, unearthly place, the more elated she felt. She was free, in the way that prisoners are free when they make a run for it. And although, deep down, she knew this divine interlude was fleeting, the specter of her fate did not alter her mood. In the glare of the afternoon light, she shielded her eyes and tried to ignore the fact that she was doing absolutely the wrong thing.

29

. . .

The platform at the Maloja stop was deserted when Minna and Freud stepped off the train in the late afternoon. No one was in sight, except a young girl clad in a theatrical version of the local dirndl, standing in front of her souvenir cart, her grizzled mountain dog dozing next to her.

Freud impatiently paced the platform, searching for a cab, while Minna wandered over to the young girl and looked at postcards featuring soaring glaciers and close-ups of edelweiss and trout.

They had apparently just missed a party of officers from the local garrison, who had commandeered all the hansom cabs for an arriving member of the imperial family and his entourage. The stationmaster told her that the royals were staying at the same hotel, the Hotel Schweizerhaus, and when she looked surprised, he informed her that they always came this time of year for "our fresh air and the restorative waters of the mountain springs." Other transportation, he said, would be available in a few minutes.

Minna settled herself on a crudely fashioned wooden bench and breathed in the crisp, clean air floating off the mountains, the husky aroma of pine mixed with wildflowers. Just before they boarded the next cab, she noticed Freud cross the platform to the souvenir cart, where he bought a postcard and slipped it into his pocket.

After seven they arrived at their destination, an elegant alpine resort, high above the tree line, surrounded by gardens and manicured paths. The sun, which sometimes stayed out until ten at night, was hidden behind clouds moving in from the glacial regions. The temperature was plunging and a light flurry of snow dusted the windows, but the grand Art Nouveau lobby was warm and glowing with exquisite chandeliers and luscious, inviting sofas. A group of bejeweled women in evening gowns lounged in leather club chairs, speaking snippets of French and German, and Minna could hear the sound of violins floating in from the dining room. One red-haired beauty in a gold silk wrap was wearing a small tiara, discreetly nestled in a clump of curls, and she handed a waiter an empty goblet as he walked by, signaling him to refill it.

Minna let out a soft, delighted laugh. She smiled at Freud and he squeezed her hand in response.

"Does this meet with your approval?" he asked.

"It's a shame you couldn't find us a nice hotel," she teased, looking around the room.

The bellman brought in their bags, while a butler offered them refreshments and directed them to the reception desk. There she stood beside him, suddenly self-conscious, her nerves tingling in her fingertips as she stared down at the beech-wood parquet floors. She heard him give his name to the chilly desk manager, emphasizing the fact that he had reserved a deluxe mountain-view room.

Then, briefly raising her eyes, she watched in silence as he signed the worn, leather-bound registry.

Dr. Sigm. Freud u Frau.

He led her by the arm into the elevator and down the hall, her skirt softly sweeping the highly polished floor, which smelled faintly of beeswax. He turned the large brass key in the lock and opened the door. The room was lovely. There was a wide balcony with a view of the mountains, a high vaulted ceiling, patterned wallpaper, a fireplace, two plump armchairs, and a chandelier lit by electric lights. And then there was the bed. It was carved white-lacquered wood with a canopy of elaborately draped trousseau lace, like a wedding veil. On either side, there were matching bed tables, and in the corner of the room, a writing desk laden with silver trays of cheese, chocolates, and, in a silver bucket of ice, a bottle of champagne. From the moment Freud had signed the hotel ledger, she was no longer who she was, or she was someone other than herself. But this place made duplicity easy to forget.

Minna chided herself about her next thought. Here she was on the honeymoon she would never have, with a man who would never be her husband. No sense thinking about reality—it ruined everything. She did, however, think briefly about the romance novels she read as a girl, and the heroine at the end of the book who would triumphantly declare, "And then, kind reader, I married him."

The first thing he did was uncork the bottle of champagne and pour them both a glass. He drank it down like a beer, winced from the bubbles, and then opened his valise and took out his vial of liquid coca. He motioned for her to come near.

"Again?" she asked.

"It's an aphrodisiac."

"And all this isn't?" she said, glancing around the room.

He gave her an indulgent smile as he dabbed a drop of coca in each of her nostrils and repeated the dose on himself. And once again for both of them. He watched her get up and walk to the balcony, open the door, and step out. He followed her, shivering in the mountain air, and wrapped his arms around her. Faint strains of a romantic Viennese waltz floated up from the dining room. She felt that first, now familiar rush.

"It's freezing," he said, rubbing her shoulders. "Let's go back inside."

Minna followed him, standing a moment in front of the fire; then she flicked off the lights and lit a candle by the bed. He handed her the bottle of coca again, which she dabbed inside her nostrils. She sniffed deeply, rubbed her temples, and sneezed a few times.

She thought back to her situation a few days before. The hopelessness. Despondency. And now, with the coca coursing through her system, she felt only jubilation. She wasn't sure whether it was solely the coca or the expensive room. But everything was undeniably more romantic, more thrilling than anyplace she had ever been. A cheap rooming house had its charms but . . .

She plumped the pillows on the bed and was about to lie down when she noticed a large brown spot at the hem of her skirt. What was this? Some kind of dirt? Minna felt herself sweating. Her clothes were so heavy and cumbersome, covered with soot from the train. She felt like a pile of unwashed laundry.

"Would you like some supper?"

"I'm not in the least bit hungry. How can you ask that?" she said, wandering into the bathroom.

He heard the water running. "Minna? Minna, what are you doing?"

"I can't hear you over the bathwater. . . ."

"Are you taking a bath?"

"Not yet . . ."

There was a shelf above the tub, laden with expensive bath salts, powders, collections of soap, and thick Turkish towels embroidered with a gold *S*. She inhaled the sweet smell of lavender and rose as she waited for the tub to fill. She didn't notice him standing by the door, watching her as she poured in the salts and oils, peeled off all her clothes, and climbed into the bath, her heavy locks of hair unraveling on her wet back.

Dear Lord, she thought as she immersed herself in the warm water, cleanse me from my sins.

Later, as the two of them lay in each other's arms, she asked, "I wonder what life would have been like if we were married?"

"I know what life would have been like."

"Tell me."

"Do you want the truth?"

"Of course."

"I wrote an essay on this once."

"I don't recall."

"It was called Civilized Sexual Morality et cetera, et cetera, with the emphasis on the 'Civilized.'"

"And you concluded?"

"A satisfying sexual relationship in marriage lasts only a few years. After a while, the wife is weighed down by her domestic duties, the children, the household, et cetera, and the passion disappears. In addition, contraceptive methods cripple desire . . . and can even cause disease. . . ."

Minna raised her eyebrows in annoyance. It was obvious Sigmund was using his marriage to her sister as the universal example, and she didn't want to listen to this any longer. Not now.

"My conclusion was that spiritual disillusionment and bodily deprivation doom most marriages, and the husband is left with only dim memories of the way it once was. Furthermore—"

"Stop, Sigmund! Enough! It wasn't an academic question."

"What did you want me to say?"

"Something different . . . something complimentary. Tell me that you'd worship me," she said.

He smiled as he looked at her lying next to him, her skin warm and glowing from the bath.

"I'd worship you," he teased, running his hand down her back. "I'd walk through fire for you. I'd climb—"

"All right." She laughed. "That's enough. Never mind."

Afterward, as she sank into the pillows, she heard the loud, lurid call of a snow finch rattling on and on.

30

. . .

The next few days they spent touring the area, walking around the lake, and lingering over quiet meals in charming inns, where the soft light reflected the midsummer snow. She imagined what it must be like to live in a place like this, with its barrage of fragrant flowers in the summer and pines fringed with ice in the winter. A place where she could shut out the world. A place where they could be together.

They would fall into a routine every night. She would take off her clothes and slip into bed next to him, enveloped in the cocoon-like comforter. At first, he would talk at an intoxicating pitch, with all his energy and concentration directed toward her. Everything he said had sparkle and brilliance, as if he were presenting her with an extravagant gift of jewels. His intellect was like a drug, intense and erotic, and she couldn't keep her hands off him. And afterward, when they were spent, she rested her head on his shoulder, entwined her legs around him, and thought, with peculiar gloom, that he was the only person she had ever loved.

He told her stories of his childhood. Hours and hours of talking. She had heard bits and pieces from Martha over the years, but he retold it now, as the fire burned low and he gently stroked her cheek. He told her how he was the chosen one, the favorite—his five sisters and their parents shared three bedrooms while Sigmund had his own spacious, light-filled room and gas lamps instead of candles. About his baby brother, Julian, who died of an intestinal infection when he was eight months old. Although Sigmund was only two at the time, he remembered wishing his brother would die so he could regain his mother's attention. He felt "dethroned and despoiled" and even fantasized about killing him. Then blamed himself when his wishes magically came true.

About his father. How as a young boy, Sigmund was enthralled by the heroic lives of famous warriors. How his relationship with his father, Jakob, a traveling dry-goods salesman, was tenuous, based on years of disappointment due to the man's lack of backbone, success, or ambition. He told her that one of his father's more colorful blunders was investing in South African ostrich feathers just as women's fashions changed and the demand collapsed. He then compared Jakob to Dickens's character from *David Copperfield*, Micawber, the hopeless optimist who famously repeated, "Something will turn up." He said it was because of his father's shortcomings that he began his obsession with Alexander the Great, Hannibal, and Garibaldi.

And then there was the story. Everyone in the family knew the story, but he told it to her again with as much emotion as if it had happened yesterday. When Sigmund was a child in Moravia, he looked forward to his Sunday strolls with his father. They would get dressed in their finest apparel, Jakob wearing his best woolen coat and fur hat, and walk together down the main street of town. His father would amuse him with tales of life on the road. One Sunday, in the middle of their walk, a young thug came up behind them, knocked Jakob's cap into the mud, and taunted, "Jew, get off the pavement." Sigmund was humiliated when his father calmly bent over, picked up the muddy cap, and continued on, like a beaten dog, without a word in response. This seemed less than heroic to a boy who was as engrossed as he was in the stories of Hannibal and, in particular, the tale of Hannibal's father, who made his son swear at an altar he would take vengeance on the Romans.

"I couldn't forgive him," Sigmund said, his voice wavering. "I tried. But I couldn't."

During these intimate confessions, she tried to memorize everything about him, to pretend she belonged to him. She told herself that they weren't like other people. An ironic statement she knew wasn't true.

She wanted the days to stretch out before them, but she couldn't help feeling that time was accelerating. Time. It was not on her side. Wasn't that what her sister had said to her? Or maybe it was her mother.

One evening, she lit a cigarette, stood out on their balcony, and watched as clouds gathered over the mountains. The air was getting cooler, and she could just make out the fog-enshrouded lake across the grassy pasture. The patches of snow on the rocky slope glistened, and there were outlines of black pines everywhere she looked. Just a few more days and then . . . what? Where was she to go after this? Certainly not Vienna. And not Hamburg. Not anywhere. If she had the power, she would begin anew, like a Mary Shelley character, except she would not be a hideous, disfigured monster but a beautiful young girl, pleasant and uncomplicated, and she would live a pleasant, uncomplicated life. She took another drag of her cigarette and tried to remember the last time she hadn't felt anxious about her life. Maybe last night in his arms.

That night at dinner, they sat at a table next to large picture windows overlooking the beautiful Engadine Valley, a stone's throw from the Italian border. Freud was in an excellent humor as they dined on sole in wine sauce and *galantine de veau*, drinking a different wine with each course.

Near the end of the meal, Minna happened to look up and was taken aback as a couple she thought she recognized entered the dining room. She felt a sudden lurch in her stomach and let out a short gasp.

"What's the matter?" he asked.

"I think I know that woman."

"Which woman?"

"The one over there. I can't point. The one with blond hair, wearing a blue evening gown. Change seats with me," she said, feeling suddenly trapped.

"This is ridiculous. Calm down. Even if it *is* her, there's no problem. It's not unusual for relatives to travel together."

"Just move," she hissed.

Minna stood up to switch seats with Freud and stole another glance at the woman. Maybe it *wasn't* her, she thought. The hair was curlier and combed up high over the forehead, the nose broader, the eyes too close together. And the woman she knew wouldn't wear hoop earrings like a pirate. She squashed the urge to rush out of the room.

"Would you like to go back upstairs, my dear?" Freud asked, unruffled.

She nodded.

Minna felt a wash of relief as they slipped away unnoticed

through the lobby, with its brocade settees and watery paintings of alpine sunsets, and climbed the stairs to their room. Safe, Minna thought.

She disappeared into the bathroom to get ready for bed. She splashed her face, combed her hair, and smeared some glycerin on her lips. When she came out, Sigmund was sitting at the writing desk, smoking his cigar. The postcard that he had purchased at the train station was in front of him. She walked to the desk and looked over his shoulder. She had only to read the first two lines:

Dear Martha,

    I hope you and the little ones are doing well. I've taken lodgings at a modest pension.

"I'm almost finished," he said, smiling up at her—"just a few more lines. . . ."

So here it was. Right in front of her in black and white. Freud cheerfully writing postcards to her sister while she looked on. Not that she ever fooled herself that moments like this wouldn't occur.

"This doesn't bother you?" she asked.

"What?"

"Writing to Martha while I'm standing here . . ."

"Not in the least . . ."

She looked at him skeptically.

"Minna dear," he said patiently, "I've explained this to you before. Martha and I are living in abstinence, she has no interest in my career or my personal pleasures, and while I sometimes feel sorry for all her troubles, I don't feel guilty in the least, and neither should you."

The devil's rationale, Minna thought. She listened without

further comment, but her calm expression felt pasted on and stiff. His position on guilt left her cold. "Self-imposed" or not . . . it was there. Maybe he could get rid of it, like a reptile shedding its skin, but warm-blooded human beings have a much harder time. The only thing she *could* agree with was his theory that guilt created a morass of hysterical symptoms and made people very unhappy.

She listened to the sounds in the hall outside the door. The chambermaids were ending their evening room service, couples were coming up from dinner. She heard the bell-like laugh of a woman with a friend whose rush of conversation had something to do with her house in Prague and an upcoming party. Everyone here was eventually going home. What a simple concept, which somehow always eluded her.

31

. . .

On their last morning, Minna agreed to a ride on a funicular near an ice glacier called Eiskapelle. Freud had insisted on booking it despite Minna's tepid response, the problem being that, for Minna, all ice glaciers looked alike. This particular tramlike vehicle was pulled by cable from the base of the mountain, 3,200 meters up the steep granite wall, landing at a rickety viewing terrace on top.

The cabin was hot and crowded with loud, fidgety tourists who had flocked to Switzerland from all over the German lowlands. Many of them wore traditional Bavarian costumes and posed in little groups for photographs before embarking. Minna had on a jacket, a flowing, ankle-length skirt, a long-sleeved blouse with a stiff collar gripping her neck, and far too many layers underneath. Freud wore a shirt with the sleeves rolled up, knickerbockers, and a green wool hat, which Minna thought didn't suit him at all. He carried a knapsack filled to the point of bursting with bread, sausage, and cheese, whose ripe smell mingled with the odors already emanating at close quarters.

She stood against the wall of the cabin, cradling a thick black beer in her hand, which was warm and unsatisfying. The windows were opened halfway, but no breeze flowed through, only the heat of the valley floor. She tried to ignore the little beads of sweat dripping down her back. A young boy in boots, high, thick stockings, and lederhosen leaned against her as the funicular began its steep ascent, smearing his sticky pastry on the side of her skirt.

The tram rocked and swayed precariously, passing copses of spear-shaped trees, which gradually thinned out toward the top. A local guide, whom Minna had seen working as a porter, began to give a short history of the area, but no one was listening. When they finally reached the platform, the temperature had dropped significantly, and the tourists, wrapping their coats around themselves, flowed out onto a serpentine pathway that led to the glacier ice cap.

Freud marched around the rocky terrain in an excellent humor, seemingly oblivious to the fact that this was their last day. It was perplexing, this nonchalance about their departure. Minna, however, could think of nothing else, and she had a hard time focusing on his enumerations of the prehistoric granite shelves: "the Piz Palu, the Piz Bernina, the Piz Trovat . . ."

She closed her eyes in irritation. Who could concentrate on geology at such a time? After a few more steps, she pretended to be affected by the altitude and told Freud she was taking the next tram down. She'd had her fill of the cold, barren landscape, which seemed only to increase her fears about the future. They agreed to meet in two hours at the tourist café at the bottom of the mountain.

All the way down, Minna struggled not to weep. Normally she restrained the impulse and, in fact, disliked it when other women cried in public. It made her uncomfortable to watch their bottom lips tremble, their jaws clench, and tears well up in their eyes.

Weeping women always seemed so . . . well, unstable. One minute they were fine, and the next, waterworks. She had always prided herself on her ability to be stoic in the face of problems. But now her resistance was crumbling.

No, she thought, staring out into the void. She would not leap into that precipice. She would divert herself, think of something else, like Baudelaire's poems, or the succession of the Hapsburg monarchs. Or she could try to switch around the numbers from the Jewish to the Christian calendar so that she'd be slightly younger. Yes, that would work. Her eyes were dry as a bone.

When Freud finally appeared at the café, Minna was ready to deal with the inevitable. They could no longer defer the discussion. He sat next to her in the booth, ordered a beer, loosened his boots, and smiled with anticipation. She knew what would come next. He was about to run down, God help her, more specifics about the ice caps. Oliver would be riveted, but she wasn't. How could he be so oblivious?

"After you left, we—"

"Sigmund," she said cutting him off, "I need to make arrangements to return to Hamburg."

No sense "beating around the bush." A governess once told her that this expression originated with laborers hired to hunt wild boar. They would beat the bushes to avoid direct contact with the savage beast. She had done that long enough.

"What do you mean, Hamburg? You're coming home with me." He seemed genuinely puzzled.

"I couldn't possibly. How could I live under the same roof as my sister?"

"It worked perfectly well before. You were an enormous help to her. She desperately wants you home."

"She wouldn't if she knew about us. . . . For God's sake, we're talking about basic morality here, not housekeeping."

"I can tell you're getting upset. Try to be rational. . . ."

"You can't just pretend we're a normal family. Or young lovers somewhere meeting under a bridge."

"Minna, my dearest. The prospect of your leaving me again is unthinkable. I can't live without you. If I could afford it, I'd get you an apartment—maybe something with a view of the Prater."

She looked at him, incredulous.

"We can't do this."

"Of course, we can," he said.

"Don't act as if I'm simply being puritanical. This is far beyond the bounds of decent human behavior."

"Oh, morality again, is it?" he said irritably, waving away the waiter who had arrived with his beer. "We're not sinning against 'God's law,' if that's what you think."

"Of course not, because for you there *is* no God. But for those of us who still believe, the morality of our actions matters."

"Just another form of self-flagellation. Self-created hysteria and punishment. Not for me."

"No. Not for you. The rules never apply to you."

"I know you're upset. Struggling, trying to do the right thing. Many people have these feelings. We're all erupting with primitive sexual desires that we can hardly control. . . ."

Minna rolled her eyes and shook her head. Here it comes again, she thought. His theories turned on her when all else failed.

"But these feelings we have toward each other are inevitable and powerful," he said, "and by denying them, you're traumatizing both of us. You have to acknowledge that these forces exist and respect their power and authority ... or else they can turn into something nasty. . . ."

"If you start talking to me about urges and drives and repression, I swear, I'll scream. You can't simply conjure up scientific arguments to justify us," she said, her voice rising with anger, although she knew it was impossible to separate the man from his theories.

"I wish I could give you some assurance that this would all turn out well."

"You can't," she said, "because it's not possible. You have *no* idea how this will all end."

"Yes, I do. You'll be living in my house and you'll be—"

"Not your wife."

He was quiet for a moment.

"No. Not my wife," he said gently, almost apologetically.

They sat there a few minutes, neither one of them wanting to move. She sighed and looked at him.

"Did you ever worry that I would find a husband?"

"You had many prospects, Minna," he said, his eyes softening. "You never wanted a husband." He paused. "Did you?"

"If I had wanted one, I'd be married by now," she said in a hushed tone.

She thought to herself. No. She had never wanted a husband. She had often wondered why, and it suddenly occurred to her. She had always wanted him.

32

. . .

As they packed to leave, Minna wondered what Martha knew about their whereabouts. Had there been some sort of negotiation? Did they talk about her desperate situation, her pathetic life? Was she the unwanted relative, the charity case? What *exactly* had he told Martha? she asked.

"Everything," he said. Martha knew that Freud had a conference in Frankfurt and would spend a few days in Switzerland before returning. It was decided that if he could talk Minna into accompanying him, he would bring her to Switzerland (although there was no mention of a grand hotel) and then home afterward. No one would question the arrangement. And Martha would never find out the truth. Ironic he should say this, Minna thought, when he had written in one of his papers that "even when lips are silent . . . betrayal forces its way through every pore."

She was suddenly beset by another round of doubts. How could she face her sister, knowing what she had done? And done again. Her mother had always promoted the biblical tenets that if you aggrieve someone, your conscience will torture you until you seek forgiveness. But how could Minna seek forgiveness while living in that house and yearning for her sister's husband?

Sometimes she felt as if the past events were beyond her control. Passion—the emotion that sent her sinking into her bed, wondering if she could ever regain her footing. An emotion that allowed her to forget everyone.

Most people would consult clergy, seeking solutions to their moral dilemmas. But Minna knew very well what the solution was. She was just unable to carry it out.

Culpa. The Latin word for guilt.

Mea culpa. My fault. A beloved aunt and sister makes room for a woman who sins.

Passion. From the Latin word *patior,* which means to suffer.

She continued in this chaotic whirl, but in the end it was fairly simple—she wasn't ready to give him up. She was too far gone to stop. She now knew that there was another state of being. It was a feeling that invaded every cell of her body, a force that changed her from a rational being into one who was decidedly not. Desire—it was a kind of insanity.

It was evening by the time the two travelers arrived at Berggasse 19, and the weather had turned ugly. A summer storm had blown in and sheets of rain hammered down on the two-horse carriage, a ferocious wind ramming the wheels against the muddy curb. The coachman, bareheaded, wrestled with the sopping reins as the horses stamped and spooked each other, their hides steaming with mud and sweat. Minna emerged, clutching her useless crepe parasol, and sloshed through mounds of muck that piled up in front of the apartment. Freud hastily followed, head bowed in protective mode.

Martha and the children were standing in the doorway, huddled against yet another blast of rain. When the pair finally reached her, Martha pulled Minna toward her as if rescuing a drowning victim and embraced her. She looked relieved to see her sister, and if she noticed anything out of the ordinary, she did not reveal it.

"I've been so lonely without you, my sister," Martha said, pushing back the stray, wet strands of hair that had fallen across her sister's forehead. "This is your home for as long as you wish. Would you mind taking your boots off before you come in?"

Minna could not help but think that this scene was much like the first time she had arrived at the Freud residence. With one exception. Today she had arrived home on the arm of her brother-in-law. She searched Martha's pale, drawn face for some sign of hesitation or doubt, but there was none, just a weariness beneath her welcome.

The children were delighted to greet them and, for once, all of them were healthy at the same time. Sophie took Minna's hand, claiming her in a possessive way and imploring her to come upstairs to see her new dollhouse. The boys surrounded their father, pelting him with questions: "Did you collect mushrooms?" "Swim in the lake?" "Go fishing?" and then there was Oliver's stream of detailed inquiries concerning the height and flow of the glaciers.

"Come in, my dears," Martha said, as she kissed Freud lightly on the cheek. He smiled at her, greeted the children, and seemed perfectly comfortable with the whole arrangement.

"Sigi, my dear. I thought we'd have a cup of tea and you could tell us about your trip."

"I'm sorry. I can't possibly right now. I've lost an extraordinary amount of time these past few weeks and I have to work," he said as he headed for his study.

"Of course," Martha said flatly. "Ernst, Oliver, Martin. Someone help Tante Minna upstairs with her valise."

The boys argued among themselves for a moment; then Oliver grabbed the bag and headed upstairs. Minna found her room exactly as she had left it, the wardrobe still holding her dresses. She sat down on the bed and took off her clothes, leaving them for dead in a heap on the floor. She stood before the mirror, pulled out her combs, and brushed her damp, wavy hair before selecting a fresh outfit from her suitcase.

Edna, the housemaid, helped her unpack, all the while chirping merrily like a jaybird.

"It's so nice to see Frau Freud up and dressed. She's been feeling so poorly lately. Her nerves and all. Truth to tell, she's barely been able to handle the children these last few months. And the doctor never comes out of his study. I'm so glad you've come home. Sophie was in tears after you left. You were sorely missed, I can tell you that. . . ."

There was a light knock on the door as Martha came into the room. Minna glanced at the dark circles ringing her sister's eyes, and noticed a slight strain in her voice.

"Are you unwell?" Minna asked, wondering fleetingly if Martha suspected anything.

"I didn't get a wink of sleep last night, and when I was finally on the verge, Sophie walked in my room and burst into tears. I swear that child cries at the slightest provocation."

"It's the nightmares. I find that if I read to her, it gets her mind off it."

"No wonder she adores you. I haven't the strength to read a book at three in the morning," Martha said, squeezing her sister's hand. "In any event, you must be tired from your holiday. Tell me all about it."

Minna examined Martha's face. There was nothing to reveal anything other than polite interest. But Martha was talking in a tone that Minna knew so well. The tone she used when she was saying one thing but conveying another. Sometimes she wished her sister would just come right out and tell her what she was thinking. Throw a tantrum, scream, get angry. Sometimes Minna would have liked to know what was really going on in her brain. This, however, was not one of those times.

"Well, Switzerland was lovely. We had much free time . . . we discussed his research . . . and I'll admit that some of it is so complicated, it tried his patience explaining it to me."

"But you eventually understood it?"

"Oh, yes. He's found that neurotic behavior can be directly attributed to—"

"I'd much rather hear what else you did. Did you go hiking? Swimming? Mushroom hunting?"

"Well, just a bit of hiking . . . and we went up a funicular . . ."

"Dreadful contraption! I hated every moment of it when we went once. But then, if I never go to Switzerland again, it would be good riddance. And what did you do at night?" Martha asked, tidying up Minna's scattered clothes.

"At night? Well, there's really nothing to do up there," Minna said, now clasping her hands tightly together.

"They had a nice dining room, as I recall."

"Yes. But I wasn't in the mood for the music."

"Music? At that place? They didn't have music . . ."

"I think it was just a visiting musician. Nothing fancy," Minna said, rattled. "In any event, I was tired from the journey and just wanted to rest."

"My sentiments exactly. Travel is tedious and difficult. In fact, if I had my way, I'd no longer travel at all. Except for an occasional visit to Mother and our annual holiday with the children."

"But surely you don't want to spend your entire life in Vienna. There are so many places to see."

"Let Sigmund tour the world—Rome, Paris, New York, Athens. Let him go wherever he wants with whomever he wants. Lord knows, he doesn't want to go with me."

"I'm sure that's not true—"

"Did you ever get a letter from Eduard?" Martha broke in, abruptly changing the subject.

"Yes, I did," Minna said.

"And how did you respond?"

"I didn't."

"That seems rather rude. How unlike you."

"I didn't want to encourage the man."

Martha paused, as if deciding whether or not to continue. Then she exhaled heavily.

"*Oh, Minna*, who else do you think is going to come along at this point?"

There was that stubborn angle to her chin that Minna knew from years of experience meant she was just getting started. She never gave up once she had her teeth into something. This was the prelude to her "you're your own worst enemy" lecture.

"Lord knows, I've said this often enough, and it's not my place to keep harping, but sometimes you're your own worst—"

A shriek from the parlor interrupted Martha. Then a crash.

"Mother! Martin just broke your good vase and he's bleeding," Mathilde shouted in her usual annoyed tone.

"I'm coming! Get a cloth from the kitchen! I swear, Minna, I'm at the end of my rope."

Martha and Minna hurried down the hall, passing Sigmund, who was striding in the opposite direction.

"It's such a coincidence," Martha said. "The minute something happens with the children, he's nowhere in sight, or racing out of here."

"Perhaps he's otherwise occupied," Minna replied.

"He's *always* otherwise occupied."

It was not lost on Minna that he had, indeed, been "otherwise occupied" these last few days. With her. But momentarily she felt a strange lack of guilt, which stayed with her as she helped Martha clean up the mess and patch up Martin's hand. The thought of settling for a pale imitation of Freud was unthinkable now. And she would do whatever was necessary to be near him.

33

. . .

Vienna was sweltering. August arrived with a vengeance, and for the first time in years, the Freud family did not escape the oppressive heat for their mountain retreat in Altaussee. To the children's bitter disappointment, their father had contacted the landlord of the cottage they rented in Obertressen, near the lake, and canceled their reservation. Throughout the month, Martin, Oliver, and Sophie had a succession of illnesses that they then passed on to Martha. In addition, Freud was still wrestling with the final chapters of his dream book, and his publisher, Franz Deuticke, was eager to see it. Deuticke owned a small scientific publishing house in Vienna and had initially sounded surprised at the subject matter, but no more so than with *Studies in Hysteria*, which he had also published.

So the family stayed in town, and as the summer days wore on, they were often confined to the house. Most days it was too hot to walk, and all errands were accomplished before noon. Sudden thunderstorms offered little relief, and in the evenings the air was still, heavy with humidity.

"In America, they have electric fans," Oliver offered.

"That would be the *only* reason to go there," his father shot back.

When Minna and Freud first returned from Switzerland, both of them had agreed that the affair could not exist at Berggasse 19. But that didn't stop them from meeting at the small pension near the train station on an odd afternoon, or carrying on their late-night discussions in his study. Whenever he'd ring for her, after supper, when the children were in bed, she'd change into a muslin summer dress, fill a pitcher with cold beer or lemonade, and walk downstairs to see him. She'd bring along her silk fan in the pocket of her skirt and sometimes apply a cold, damp cloth to the back of his neck as they talked softly into the night about his work—his dream theories, his patients, his self-analysis, and always, the sexual basis of neurotic behavior. Eventually the heat would get to both of them.

"I can't go on. It's like an oven in here. And my shoulders are aching," he said, smoking so much she could hardly breathe.

"Would you like a bucket of ice? I could run upstairs. Or would you like me to rub your neck?"

"No, no," he said, standing up and snubbing out his cigar. "It's suffocating. I'm done for the night. Close the window, will you?"

"Of course." She paused. "Good night, then."

"Yes. Good night, dear."

During this period, Freud's research was all-consuming and he became increasingly obsessed as the weeks went by. Night after night, he stayed in his steaming office, the windows open, nursing a sweaty pitcher of beer as he read through pages of case studies, scratching out copious notes on the margins.

His only diversion was a short trip to Munich for a conference with Dr. Fliess. He had become even closer to Fliess since his split with Dr. Breuer, and Freud spoke of Fliess's theories almost reverentially, even though Minna found them all wildly far-fetched.

To begin with, the doctor believed that nearly every major disease and symptom in the human body was caused by the nose. Physical maladies from migraines to heart ailments, stomach pains, and joint disorders could all be related back to the runny mucous membranes of the olfactory organs. But Fliess went even further, theorizing that the nose was also responsible for sexual disorders.

Minna wasn't exactly clear on how the good doctor from Berlin made this leap from a sinus infection to frigidity or bisexuality, but Freud seemed fascinated, even bewitched, by such absurdities.

When Minna heard about Fliess's preoccupation with the nose, she made a few wry comments comparing Fliess to Cyrano de Bergerac. Freud was not amused, so she kept the Pinocchio joke to herself.

Since Minna's return, she had taken over almost complete supervision of the children. They kept her busy from morning until night, all of them underfoot and each one restless and bored. She and Martha had always shared the duties in the household equally, but now Martha delegated more responsibilities to her sister.

"It's only fair. I worked so hard while you were in Frankfurt," she said more than once, as if Minna had been on a four-month vacation.

Ever since they were girls, Martha had been vigilant about a strict division of labor and rewards. Everything with her sister had to be exactly equal. If they shared a piece of cake, she insisted that one cut it and the other choose. If Martha ran an errand for their mother, she'd tell Minna, "Next time, it's your turn." She always kept score, in precise terms, of who did what and when, sulking when things didn't come out even. Minna was hoping that her sister had grown out of this childish form of sibling rivalry, but it seemed that Martha still viewed her world as tit for tat, quid pro quo.

One morning, when there was a slight breeze and the temperature edged down a few notches, Minna decided they couldn't, in good conscience, keep the children cooped up one more minute. The house was oppressive and Martha's instructions made it worse. Windows and drapes were routinely closed against the harsh sunlight during the day, and then only opened again at dusk. In addition, there were no hot meals. Martha "couldn't tolerate a fire in the kitchen."

Despite Minna's pleas, Martha specifically told her that she didn't want the children roaming around the streets.

"It's too hot, too dusty, and there are reports of random looting downtown. You *must* have heard about it. Florence Skekel told me they were targeting Jewish shopkeepers. 'Semitic polluters,' that's what they call us. Can you imagine?"

"I've heard Florence is an alarmist."

"From who?"

"Her husband, when we played cards."

"He doesn't understand her."

Later that afternoon, after Minna had been run ragged all day, Martha finally relented, allowing the children outside.

"Take them to the Prater," she said, waving one hand in the air, as if she were shooing away gnats. And upon hearing a loud crash added, "As soon as possible!"

But at this point Minna was dead tired. "Martha, let's do it tomorrow. It's been a hectic day and I don't have the energy."

"Really, Minna. It's not *that* much trouble. Why are you so tired?

You certainly had enough rest. Lord knows I've dealt with this household by myself all these months you were gone. Are you ill?"

"No, I'm not ill. But I'm exhausted and it's just too late to go now."

"Perhaps you're tired because you've been visiting Sigmund in his study until all hours, although it's good Sigi has someone to talk to . . ."

There was a pause as the two sisters looked at each other. Then Minna slowly turned and headed for the kitchen.

"I'll have a cup of coffee and then take them."

Minna slunk back into the kitchen. She felt perverse around Martha, even pathetic. She was now in the position where she had to lie to her sister about the most basic things and then wonder, constantly, if her words sounded plausible. She had a bad taste in her mouth, felt squeamish even, as if there were something rotten in the room that reeked but she had to ignore. Before she left the house for Hamburg, she was conflicted, even anguished by her desire. She convinced herself that the attraction she felt for Sigmund was something that had befallen her rather than something she had instigated. But now that she was reestablished in the household, there were moments when her stomach turned as Martha and she talked about the marketing, the children, the everyday occurrences. And then afterward, she was surprised at how she could act so cool, and indifferent, as if this brazen violation were not happening.

Minna sipped her coffee in the kitchen, leaning against the sideboard and wilted by the heat. What if she were a family friend or a neighbor, and had fallen in love with Sigmund? Would that be easier? Yes, easier, she thought. It would be an affair, and wives get over affairs, but this was different—more sinful. At least she still had the decency to be disgusted by her behavior. She smiled to herself at the ridiculous reasoning of this statement.

But along with everything else, she was frightened. Not just for herself any longer, but for all of them. It was as if she were waiting for that moment when Martha would suddenly turn and accuse her. But that moment had not come. Sometimes she almost wished it would happen so that she would be released from the torture of her shallow, shameless self.

34

. . .

These days, she was always the one waiting.

What's taking him so long? she thought as she paced the floor. He was over an hour late this time.

The pension seemed dingier in the daylight. There was a stain on the quilt at the end of the bed. The wallpaper was peeling in spots, and the floorboards were buckled and scratched. Didn't there used to be a carpet here? She could hear a couple in the next room arguing. And then a door slam. She leaned out the window and caught sight of him entering the hotel.

He came into the room and sat down on the bed next to her, unlacing his shoes. Then he apologized for being late as one does when he is in no way sorry.

A few months ago, he would have been early. A few months ago, she reminded herself, she would not have been here at all.

It was getting increasingly difficult to arrange these meetings because of his schedule. This time, there was little more than a moment's notice.

"I couldn't get a cab. I had to walk blocks until I found one," he said.

She began fidgeting with her blouse, trying to unbutton the line of tiny buttons. He touched her cheek, pushed her blouse off her shoulders. His lips quickly kissed her stomach. Then he stripped off her clothes and pulled her to him. From the first touch of his fingers, she still felt the thrill. It didn't take much.

Once they'd done it on the floor. And once in the bathtub. She liked to bring a bottle in her purse and have several drinks before he arrived. Usually he was able to stay awhile afterward, but today he drew away from her and began fumbling for his pants.

"I have to go."

"So soon? You just got here."

"I have a patient waiting . . ." he said, in the same tone he used with Martha when he wanted to get out of the room. She watched him get dressed, poured herself another drink, then called his name as he walked out the door. He turned back to look at her with an impassive expression.

"Never mind," she said.

Later, when she went back to the house and resumed her life, a listlessness of spirit would overwhelm her. It wasn't only the fact that she felt a diminished affection on Sigmund's part. But also, the fear of getting caught was beginning to blunt the afterglow of desire.

Sometimes Martha would look at her oddly and say, "Are you all right?" The question would inevitably set off a rush of despair in her gut and she'd scream inside with rage, No! I'm not all right.

. . .

Sometime over the next week, a formal envelope arrived, embossed in gold leaf and addressed to Dr. Freud and Frau. The Freuds were invited by Herr Zelinsky and his wife to the opening of the opera and a dinner party afterward in their splendid apartment in the elite Reichsratsstrasse district.

Minna eyed the invitation with more than passing interest as she and Martha sat down in the parlor and sorted through the mail. Gustav Mahler had just been named director of the Hofoper and was currently the most celebrated figure in Vienna. The opera house itself was recently finished in the grand Imperial style with painted, domed ceilings and Doric columns. And, most important, everyone agreed it had excellent acoustics.

"Oh, it's *Don Giovanni*," said Minna, her voice rising in excitement.

"At least Sigmund won't be bored. Last year it was *Norma*, and he fell asleep."

"What a thrill to watch Mahler."

"Not for me. He's been *such* a disappointment."

"Disappointment?"

"That whole distasteful conversion business. Now he's a *Catholic*? If you ask me, it won't help him in the least. He *still* won't be invited to the palace. Once a Jew, always a Jew."

"He had to convert, you know that, or he'd never have been given the appointment."

"In any event," she said, with a dismissive wave of her hand, "his mother must be rolling over in her grave."

"Martha, if you don't care that much about the performance,

I'd be happy to go in your place," Minna ventured, as if the thought had just occurred to her.

"You mean accompany Sigmund instead of me?" Martha shot back.

"Only if you didn't want to go," Minna responded, backtracking.

"What gave you that impression? Of course I want to go. It's *the* event of the season."

"Well, perhaps I'll just buy a ticket." Minna said, perversely pushing the issue.

"On opening night? It'll be a fortune. And anyway, who'd watch the children?"

Minna stared at her sister without comment and then walked out of the room before she said something she'd regret. Martha's reaction was troubling. Minna knew for a fact that her sister was not a devotee of the opera. And Martha knew for a fact that Minna loved it. Was this simply a case of her sister being insensitive—a blatant disregard for her feelings? Or was Martha suspicious of Minna's motives? For the hundredth time since she arrived back at the house, she wondered, Did her sister *know*? Were there fire clouds under Martha's irritable demeanor? Possibly not. Especially when she later popped her head into Minna's room and graciously offered to give Minna her opera ticket next time.

"We can take turns," Martha said, diplomatically. "But you know how I adore the opening."

Thank God, Minna thought. It's not about Sigmund. It's about the party.

On the night of the event, Martha selected a crimson silk evening gown with velvet epaulets and a gored skirt that looked like a half-opened umbrella, black satin boots, and a French jet bracelet borrowed from their mother. Minna walked in as Martha was gathering up her wool capelet and Empire fan. Sophie was fluttering about, telling her mother she looked like a princess, and Mathilde was her usual critical self.

"Mama, that capelet doesn't match. Take your fur instead," Mathilde insisted. "And you shouldn't be wearing a gold bracelet with silver buckles. Don't mix your metals."

"Martha, Sigmund's waiting for you," Minna interrupted.

"Let him wait. It's the opera. We're not catching a train," Martha said, unhurriedly pinking her cheeks and taking one last look at her profile.

Sigmund was smoking and pacing in the parlor. He was carefully groomed in a formal white waistcoat, top hat, black cravat, and patent leather shoes, and he kept pulling his watch out of his fob pocket, muttering to himself about the hired carriage waiting outside.

"It's about time. We're half an hour late," he said, annoyed. "And we still have to pick up the Bernheims, who live in the opposite direction. I don't know why you offered to get them in the first place."

"*Goodness*. You *could* say something nice about the way I look, Sigmund. I'm wearing your favorite dress. A woman needs a compliment now and then, doesn't she, Minna?"

"Absolutely," Minna said. "Sigmund, tell Martha how lovely she looks."

Freud rubbed the back of his neck in exasperation and then stubbed out his cigar. He shot Minna a look of helplessness and resignation.

"You look lovely, my dear," he said, in a tone Minna found to be thoroughly unconvincing. Still, it was apparently enough for his wife.

"Now, Minna," Martha said, "it's getting late. Don't let Sophie talk you into those bedtime stories. She must go to sleep without all the nonsense. And tell Nanny to change the baby before putting her down. She didn't last time, and it was a mess. Oh, dear, my opera glasses," she said, rushing out of the room.

Minna walked over to Sigmund and brushed an imaginary piece of lint off his shoulder.

"And would you like me to do anything for *you*, Sigmund, while you're out?" Minna whispered. "Perhaps shine your shoes?"

"Stop it. That's not funny."

"I wasn't trying to be funny."

It was odd to think that in other circumstances, Minna would be happy for her sister. But right now, she detested her. As if this painful incident were all Martha's fault. Sometimes she couldn't even stand herself.

Minna took Sophie's hand in hers and escorted the tired four-year-old upstairs. Mathilde was playing cards with the boys in the parlor and there were faint cries from the nursery, where Nanny was feeding the baby. Sophie's room was strewn with baskets of toys and knickknacks, and all the furniture from the dollhouse was spread out on the rug like a miniature fire sale. Minna felt a headache coming on, the kind that throbs behind the ears and makes the eyes water. She decided to ignore the mess. She was tired and blue. What did she expect when she came back to this house? That he wouldn't go out with his wife? Here she was, feeling sorry for herself because she was left behind at the ball. But the fact of the matter was, she wasn't Cinderella, she was the evil stepsister.

She changed the child into her stiff white nightgown, washed her face and hands, and tucked her into bed. Then she blew out the candle on the dresser and pulled the covers up to her neck. But as

Minna bent over to kiss her good night, Sophie put her soft arms around Minna and pulled her down toward her.

"Don't go," she whispered.

"But, Sophie dear, I'm so tired. I have to go back to my room."

"Don't go," she whispered again, her brow creased with worry. "Can't you sthay with me, Tante Minna? I'm sthcared."

Minna could feel the child's sweet, warm breath on her cheek. She relit the candle and sat down on the side of the bed. She would often read Sophie stories until she fell asleep. Her favorites were Catherine Sinclair's tales about giants and fairies and elves, especially the fairy Do-nothing. She relit the candle next to the bed.

"I'll tell you a story about a beautiful fairy," said Minna, "whose cheeks were rouged to the very eyes, her teeth set in gold, and her hair of a most brilliant purple."

The next morning, Martha slept late. Minna heard Sigmund leave for the university at his usual early hour, but Martha didn't stir until after eleven. She came down to the parlor in her dressing gown, nursing her cup of coffee and looking for Minna.

"How was the opera?" Minna asked halfheartedly.

"Well," Martha said, eager to share the events of the evening, "our seats were right behind the royal boxes, and you wouldn't believe the furs—sable, ermine, chinchilla . . . all paws and heads and tails. *Tout* Vienna was there."

"How nice."

"Then the royals made a grand entrance, their entourage sat right in front of us. They never stopped talking, you know, through the entire performance. Sigmund was so annoyed. I had to keep him from saying something. By the way, you remember the

Rosenthals, don't you? They brought their daughter, who even in her lace décolletage, looked just like her father, poor thing. I heard she was in love with an Italian but couldn't marry him because he's a Christian. In fact, the father went on a hunger strike until the girl signed a document that she would never see the boy again."

"And the music?"

"Marvelous. That new tenor from Frankfurt was a sensation—standing ovations at the end of each aria. And, of course, Lilli Lehmann was perfection. She's returning to the Met, I hear. Anyway, I'm simply exhausted. The performance lasted until after midnight, and we didn't get to the Zelinskys until one. Sigi was so hungry by then, he stuffed himself. Everyone thought he hadn't eaten for days."

Minna strained to keep her face from falling as her sister went on and on, describing the gowns, the opulent furnishings, and how much Sigmund had enjoyed himself. It crossed her mind, briefly, that perhaps Martha was doing this on purpose. And it was working. Minna was totally deflated. But the fact was, if she was to continue this duplicitous arrangement, she was just going to have to swallow her resentment, her pride, and learn to live with the fact that Martha was, and always would be, the wife.

35

. . .

Where *was* he?

Minna stood by the open window of the pension, breathing in the hot air. September had brought some relief, but today was brutal. She could feel the sweat evaporating on her skin, and her palms were wet and sticky. She had even left the door ajar, hoping a breeze would flow through the room. But nothing helped. She heard that some of the better hotels had electric fans on the ceiling and machines that blew air over a bucket of ice. The rich always managed to stay cool.

When they first returned from Switzerland, Minna sat in her room most nights, awaiting Freud's call like a courtesan, eager for one of their late-night discussions. But in the past month, he had summoned her to his study only once, and Minna found herself alone, just like today, waiting for him. But even worse, the last few weeks when he passed her in the hall, there was just a slight change of expression. It seemed as if he purposely wasn't looking over at her. Perhaps he was just being careful, or was distracted by his work, she thought. She still expected him to seek her out after his long hours in the study, to give her a sign, a look, anything that would bring back the sensation of his touch. But he was oddly absent and sometimes, even with six children and Martha in the house, the place seemed deserted.

Minna couldn't imagine what was taking him so long to get here. The pension was just a few minutes' walk from the university. She stared at the door a little longer. Then she slowly stood up, gathered her belongings, and walked down the claustrophobic stairway to the lobby. She fumbled in her purse for some kronen. . . . Oh, no. Not enough to pay for the room.

The proprietor's small office was just inside the entrance, and Minna approached the young girl sitting behind the desk. She was wrapped in a shawl, even in this heat, and her head was buried in a magazine.

"I won't be needing the room any longer," Minna began, her voice strained. "May I send you payment in the morning?"

There was an exasperated sigh.

"We require payment upon checkout," the girl said, without looking up. It was apparent she had said these exact words many times before.

"I was only here two hours," Minna said brusquely, placing a few kronen on the desk and walking out the door. Let her get off her rump and try to stop me, she thought. What a little guttersnipe.

She paused on the street for a moment, checking to make sure she had everything, her purse, coat, and hat. Yes, she had all her belongings, thank God, because she certainly didn't want to go back in *there*.

It was now almost rush hour, and she crossed the street and

dodged the traffic. The circuitous streets around the train station were unknown to her, filled with factory workers holding lunch boxes, and businessmen in dark suits and hats. A swarm of commuters heading home.

Minna walked on, the cobblestones burning and sticky underfoot, her blouse drenched in sweat. Her skirts and petticoat got heavier and damper. How *could* he have forgotten? Hadn't they arranged this last week? Or was it two weeks before? She couldn't remember. Perhaps she should have reminded him this morning. But when? With Martha in the same room, hovering over him? Lately, it had been so hard to catch him alone. When *was* the last time they had had an actual conversation?

The other morning, she had innocently come upon him in the hall and given him a cheerful good day. He responded, in an irritated tone, that his barber was ill and had sent an inept replacement who shaved him horribly, leaving his Adam's apple all "bristly and cutting me under the nose." Not one word of affection.

Minna fumed just thinking about it. She walked to the corner and absently stepped off the curb. There was a shout and the sound of wooden carriage wheels grinding against cobblestones.

"My God, woman! *Watch out!*"

The carriage driver yanked his mares away from her, his curses ringing through the air. Minna leapt back on the curb as the horses streaked by, so close she could touch the sweat streaming down their flanks. Goose bumps covered her arms and neck.

"I didn't even see him," she said to a woman standing nearby. Minna shook her head, now furious at Freud for almost getting her killed. Then she hurried to the next omnibus stop and waited for the ride. She had just enough change to get home.

She arrived at the house before supper. Even before she reached the study, she heard the sound of deep male voices. The door was open, giving Minna an unobstructed view from the hallway. Sigmund was holding a glass of wine in one hand and a cigar in the other. The bastard. Across from him on the couch, staring out through the semi-dark haze of smoke, sat the young doctor from Berlin, Wilhelm Fliess.

Fliess was dark-haired with narrowed brown eyes and a meticulous mustache. Minna had already decided that she disliked the man and his bizarre theories, and it didn't help that Freud was now posting letters to him almost every day. He had once told her that he saw Fliess as a fellow scientific pioneer, someone willing to risk it all for the sake of discovery. But the fact of the matter was, when one is enamored, one is willing to believe anything.

Minna stood silently in the doorway, waiting for a smile from Freud's lips, a wave, or something resembling an apology. She saw the two men look at each other with affection and felt a pull of disappointment in her stomach. It was dispiriting to watch him give Fliess the same all-encompassing focus he had previously bestowed on her. How could he do this? Perhaps they were in the middle of a serious scientific discussion, and he couldn't get away.

But wait. She watched Freud set down his glass of wine and his cigar. He held the familiar blue vial in his hand. A cocainization of his left nostril. And then his right. He handed the vial to Fliess and looked up, turning his face in her direction. He looked infuriatingly indifferent.

"Minna. My dear friend Wilhelm is visiting," he said, not noticing the bright anger in her cheeks.

"Apparently," she said, with a stiff smile.

"Fräulein," Fliess said, kissing her hand, "so nice to see you again. I was just telling Sigmund of my latest findings. . . ."

"I should like to hear it," Minna said, sitting down uninvited.

"And I should like to tell you. I know Sigmund values your opinion," Fliess said. "If you start with the theory that both women *and* men have monthly cycles and that these are intimately connected to planetary movements . . . then, take your birthday, multiply it by a factor of five, add the days of your menstrual cycle and, voilà, a diagnosis and prediction of future health issues."

Minna thought that this lunatic's numerology made astrology seem like an orthodox science. She nodded as if all this made perfect sense.

"Impressive," she said, thinking, Yes, impressive *for a quack*. What a pretentious ass, and here was Sigmund fussing all over him.

Fliess stayed for supper and then a late snack. At midnight, he followed Freud back into his study, where they were ensconced until dawn.

The next day, Fliess arrived before noon, and the two men launched, yet again, into feverish discourse, Freud sweeping him into his study as if he were a visiting head of state. He returned the following day, and the days after, arriving early in the morning, loitering in the parlor, trailing the scent of his Maria Mancini cigars and lilac shaving cream, thumbing through newspapers, helping himself to tinned biscuits and candied fruits from the pantry. He'd become a fixture in the household, exchanging little pleasantries with the help. Minna found herself standing behind corners and doors, straining to hear what they were saying, registering a cool expression when she happened to run into them.

They discussed Plato, Dante, Stendhal's musings on passion

(even bringing up the indelicate fact that the man dropped dead of syphilis on the streets of Paris).

"*'Vitae summa brevis spem nos vetat inchoare longam.'* Horace, first book of *Odes*, number four," recited Fliess at dinner one day, while all the Freud children sat there unnoticed and completely bored.

" 'Life's brief total forbids us cling too long off hope,' " translated Freud, "But don't you feel the earlier parts of the book merit equal adoration? *'Quodsi me lyricis vatibus inseres, sublimi feriam sidera vertice.'* "

Minna had heard enough. She went upstairs and walked to the dresser, where her books were piled up in a messy heap. Ah, there it was, the copy of Homer she had borrowed from Sigmund last month. Childish game, tossing around quotes in Latin. She could toss quotes, if she wanted to. She threw the book on the floor. There! She had tossed quotes.

Oh, dear. She picked up Homer and placed him back on the dresser. It wasn't *his* fault.

A nd so it went. One day she found Fliess in the parlor, snacking on Sacher torte and holding up his coffee cup to Minna, blithely signaling a refill.

A few days later, she was awakened by a violent downpour. A constant stream of water dripped, dripped, dripped on the floor near her bed, the sound of it amplifying as she placed a lead saucepan under the leak. She opened the wooden shutters, thinking the world looked oppressive—the skies, the trees, the river, all blending together in a dense blur of gray.

She dressed mechanically and walked downstairs to supervise the children's breakfast, getting as far as the parlor. And there was

Fliess, sitting like Goldilocks in Freud's chair, reading his news-paper and drinking coffee from a delicate cup and saucer belonging to Martha's "good china," a set that no one used.

How odd to be jealous of a man. Just looking at Fliess made her sick. His beady little eyes, his Neanderthal forehead, and bushy tangled beard. His eyebrows joined in the middle. And his voice. How annoying and ironically nasal. Physician, heal thyself!

She watched him take a sip of the coffee, sloshing the dark liq-uid into the saucer, then abstractedly placing the cup directly onto the antique side table. Before she could stop herself, she grabbed the cup and wiped off the table with her skirt.

"You'll leave a ring," she said, her voice tightening. Then she heard a noise behind her and saw Freud standing in the doorway, his eyes dark and remote.

"You can wipe up later," he said brusquely, not even using her name.

She was about to respond, but his expression had narrowed and hardened, so she plunked the cup back into the wet saucer and walked out of the room without saying a word.

How dare he treat her like a fussy housekeeper. She went back upstairs to nurse her depleted spirits, but a creeping feeling of dread rose from her stomach and filled her head. To her astonish-ment, tears welled up in her eyes.

36

. . .

The next Sunday, like every other Sunday, Freud's family gathered for an obligatory dinner at his parents' apartment. At the appointed hour of noon, Minna, Martha, and the children climbed into the crowded omnibus, cramming together in the last two rows of the bus. It was a rainy morning, the weather had dramatically changed overnight, and the horses jog-trotted through the cobbled streets, snorting off jets of steam.

It was Minna's humble opinion that omnibus conductors were foremost in the ranks of thievery, extorting as much money as they could from their passengers. Before the rates were fixed, there were numerous squabbles on the corner as to how much the cads would charge from point A to point B. But finally the council set the rates, which made omnibus travel much more pleasant.

Minna straightened her shawl and smoothed the front of her dress. The windows were beginning to fog and smear as a heavy, damp closeness hovered in the air. The children were in their Sunday best, hunched up, rubbing their eyes and sullenly staring out the grease-streaked windows.

"I'm suffocating!" Martin said, as he leaned over and pulled down the glass-paneled window.

"No. Thut it," Sophie lisped. "I'm cold."

Oliver leaned over to close the window, just as a splash of muddy puddle water from a massive two-horse brewer's dray hit the bus and sprayed brown droplets down the front of Oliver's immaculate sailor suit.

"Now look what you've done!" Martha said.

"Not my fault," Martin shouted.

"Just sit there and be quiet," Martha scolded, dabbing at her face with a handkerchief.

"Why do I always get blamed?"

"Because you do stupid things," said Oliver, as Minna, who had a bilious headache, tried to change the subject. She was still angry at the way Sigmund had treated her the previous afternoon, but she had no choice but to come today. At any rate, she didn't have the energy to start a scene with Martha about wanting to stay home. The children did enough of that as it was.

"If you all look to your immediate right you can make out the spires of St. Stephen's," Minna said, even though no one was listening.

"Couldn't we arrive just once at your grandparents' without a battle?" Martha sighed.

"Why do we even have to go?" Mathilde whined. "Father doesn't like it, either."

"Of course your father likes it."

"No, he doesn't."

"Yes, he does."

"Then why isn't he here?"

"Because he's meeting with Dr. Fliess," Martha said. "Now, no more discussion."

The conductor suddenly veered off the wide expanse of the Ring, crossing the invisible boundary from the Sixth District to Leopoldstadt, the traditional Jewish section. Once an overcrowded ghetto, it was now a modest to middling neighborhood where Sigmund's parents still lived in a slightly run-down but genteel apartment. The abrupt jog of the horses threw the group back into their seats and stilled the simmering argument. When they finally neared the building, Minna signaled the driver to stop. Amalia was standing in the doorway, as usual, waiting for Sigmund.

Of all Amalia's seven children, Freud was the obvious favorite. As Sigmund had told Minna in Switzerland, he knew he was privileged, even as a young child, and the household was organized accordingly. Any conflicts within the family were resolved unequivocally in Sigmund's favor. Amalia treated him as gifted, as a prince, as someone who would bring the family great fame and fortune, and not one member of the family disputed Sigmund's preferential treatment.

Minna stepped from the omnibus, clasping the hem of her dress and pulling it over the tops of her high black boots. Wisps of hair fluttered from her hat, and her skirt billowed with the brusque wind. The children silently scrambled out after her and dutifully greeted their grandmother, who barely acknowledged them. Martha gave her mother-in-law a kiss on the cheek.

"Hello, dears," Amalia said, impatiently lifting her beaky chin, her dark eyes searching for her son. "Where's Sigi?"

"I'm sorry, Mother. He's in a conference and won't be able to join us."

Martha gave Minna a knowing look as Amalia turned her back

on all of them, bit her thin lower lip, and climbed purposely back up the stairs. She's impossible, Minna thought.

When they entered the parlor, Jakob, Freud's father, was sitting in his armchair reading a newspaper, puffing on his pipe. He smiled, rose from his chair, clapping an arm around each of the children. He was a tall, good-looking man, and Minna was fond of him, even though she knew Sigmund found him an embarrassment.

But the children adored him. He pulled out a cigar box filled with cards he had bought from street hawkers and let the children choose from a variety of pictures—frog jockeys riding enormous rats, cat princesses at a ball, elves playing ring a ring o' roses. In addition, he had postcards picturing the emperor flying above the clouds like a winged deity, his puffy white hair and rosy skin making him look like a strawberry ice, topped with whipped cream.

"Let's all sit down, shall we?" Jakob said, ignoring Amalia's irritation about Sigmund's absence. The dinner table, set for ten, was layered like a woman's petticoat, with a white undercloth, a runner down the center, and several lace overlays. The smell of sauerbraten, *Zwiebelkuchen*, and *Blatten mit Kraut* brought the children to the table. But the combination of odors made Minna queasy.

"I hired this new girl—maddeningly pathetic," Amalia said, sitting up ramrod straight, sipping her soup. "She can't cook or clean. I've a good mind to get rid of her tonight. Although, heaven knows, we don't have the money to hire anyone better."

Minna and Martha shifted uncomfortably in their seats as Amalia casually insulted Jakob in front of the children.

"Even with all his crazy schemes—stockpiling this or that—we used to at least have enough for decent help, but now he just sits around borrowing money and—"

"I have some exciting news," Martha interrupted.

"News?" said Amalia.

"Sigmund was nominated for *ausserordentlicher Professor*!"

Minna laid down her fork. "He was? When? Why didn't he tell me?"

"I'm sure he assumed *I* would tell you, my dear," Martha said, looking at her sister with the slightest hint of a smile. Minna, at a loss for words, poured herself another glass of wine and nibbled weakly at her dinner. When dessert was served, she pushed away the cream-filled torte.

"Aren't you going to eat your sweet?" Martha asked.

"You have it," Minna said, sliding the plate toward her sister.

"Well, it's a shame to waste it," Martha said, forking the creamy lumps into her mouth.

When they returned home, Minna went directly to her room, exhausted and baffled. How could he not have told her? Something so momentous, so important to him. She lay down on the bed, sinking her head into the pillow. She needed to rest. When she awoke, it was dark and she realized she had slept for hours. At one point, the maid stuck her head in the room and Minna vaguely remembered telling her, "Go away! I'm sick." After that she was left alone.

When she was finally able to drag herself out of bed, she filled the tub and sank into the warm water, thinking that this was the arsenic hour downstairs, the time when the children required the most attention. They were tired and cranky, needing help with their studies, then baths and supper—sniping at each other, vying for her attention, and then scrambling to the table, hungry as little piglets. She dried herself slowly by the fire, then climbed back into bed. She couldn't help it. She wasn't leaving her room.

Sigmund had been so aloof and dismissive these past few weeks it had been torturous. How strange to get the silent treatment from the self-proclaimed king of the talking cure. Several times she had swallowed her pride and tried to approach him, but he was impersonal and often closed himself up for days at a time either with Fliess or alone. She rationalized that he was under a lot of pressure with his dream book deadline. He was now working on it full-time, and it was all entangled with his self-analysis, the Oedipus complex, and his theories on the id, ego, and superego.

But even so, the distress of his cold shoulder was constant. She woke up with it and carried it around with her even when she was busy with the children. It took away her appetite and her ability to appreciate anything. Sometimes she would feel it throbbing in her neck and traveling down her arm. Other times, she clenched her teeth so hard she gave herself a migraine. Even reading was no respite. It could be her imagination, but more often than not, she worried that perhaps he was tiring of her.

The only relief was to deaden the brain with gin. What the hell, Martha was addicted to laudanum and Sigmund was addicted to nicotine and cocaine.

She put on her nightdress, opened the windows, and inhaled the fresh air. The sky had turned from silvery lilac to a darker shade of purple and then black. She pulled the bottle of gin from under her bed and poured herself a large shot and then another . . . and another until she felt something stir inside her akin to a small firestorm. What was she doing, sitting around waiting for him to summon her? What happened to her backbone and resolve? Did he think she would take this sort of treatment forever? No one in her right mind would put up with this behavior. She thought about it for a moment. Well, then, if he wasn't so inclined to talk to her, she would talk to him.

She threw on her robe, thought better of it, changed into a skirt and blouse, and combed her hair. Then she rinsed out her mouth—her breath still reeked of booze. Just thinking about the confrontation filled her with exhilaration. She marched out the door and down the stairs.

The door to Freud's study was ajar, and Minna entered without knocking. She found him at his desk, his elbow leaning on a pile of papers. The usual haze of smoke clouded the air and the ashtrays were spilling over with snubbed-out cigars.

He looked up, startled.

"Minna?" His face was flushed and sweating and he had deep, puffy circles around his eyes. She hesitated.

"Are you unwell?"

"I'm afraid I have a problem with a patient. . . ." he said. There was a pause as he looked up at her. "I think Wilhelm has caused serious injury."

"What happened?" She wasn't surprised that that lunatic Fliess had finally made a grave error.

The patient's name was Emma Eckstein. Minna knew that she was the daughter of a socially prominent family in Vienna. Freud told her that the young woman had originally come to him seeking help for mild depression and stomach ailments. He diagnosed her as having symptoms related to mild hysteria, and then consulted with Fliess. The complications arose when Fliess determined that all her suffering was nasal related, and he proceeded to perform a long and disfiguring operation that removed a chunk of her nose.

"I blame myself for allowing him to operate on her. After

Wilhelm went back to Berlin, the young woman's family contacted me, concerned that she was still in severe discomfort. By the time I examined her, pus and blood were oozing through the binding and there was a putrid smell emanating from the infected wound. I was fearful rot had set in."

"Good God," Minna said, somehow taking perverse pleasure, not in the girl's pain, but in Fliess's ineptitude.

"I immediately called in a specialist. He took one look at the girl and reopened the incision. And do you know what he found?"

"What?" Minna asked, leaning in toward him.

"Long threads in her nasal cavity from a wad of gauze that had been left inside the wound. The surgeon told me it was a dirty business to clean up the bloody mess and that Wilhelm had gone against all orthodox practice—he might have killed her."

"I'm so sorry," Minna said, relishing Fliess's comeuppance. The man was a moron, and Sigmund had to see it.

"What a disaster. I'm even having nightmares about the poor girl. Sit down, I want you to hear this," he said, his formal, impersonal demeanor gone.

Minna obeyed, sitting down at the end of the sofa, her eyes fixed on his face. She had been teetering on the edge of his life, and now she was his confidante once again.

"In my dream, I'm at a party in a large hall. One of the guests is a woman named Irma, who is obviously Emma. I take her aside to scold her for not following my medical advice. She argues that she's still in pain and it's more severe than ever, and I worry that perhaps I overlooked something. At that point, I examine her throat and it's covered in grayish scabs. Many of my colleagues are at the party, including Breuer and the children's pediatrician, Oskar Rie, who, it turns out, had actually given the young woman a dirty injection of trimethylamine. In my dream, the only one of my friends who is helpful is Dr. Fliess, and he assures me that it's not my fault."

Minna didn't say anything at first. It was obvious Sigmund was trying to vindicate his beloved Fliess and reassure himself that neither he nor Fliess had done anything wrong. But his insistence that Fliess was not at fault, even in a dream, bewildered her.

"I think this is all Wilhelm's fault," Minna argued. "And, frankly, I can't understand why you don't see it. The man left gauze in the wound and then sewed it up."

"That's not entirely fair," Sigmund countered. "I should have never urged Wilhelm to perform the operation here in Vienna, where he couldn't follow up."

Minna didn't feel like arguing. Sooner or later, Sigmund would see that Fliess was incompetent. She continued to watch him pace the room and listened as he analyzed his dream. It was clear the whole experience had shocked him. In view of all of this, her complaints seemed unimportant at the moment. And, in any event, here he was, taking her back into his confidence, and wasn't that what she wanted, after all?

37

...

Minna slept well that night. The Fliess fiasco had been a blessing in disguise. Or so she thought. Now that the man's reputation was tarnished, Minna assumed that she would return to her former position of prominence as Freud's friend, lover . . . even his muse.

In fact, the opposite occurred. In the next few weeks, Freud returned to his brusque manner and brutal schedule. He brushed silently by her in the hallway and made no effort to come home for meals or engage in any conversation. But the worst was, except for discouraging glances, he had stopped looking at her.

Somewhere, in the midst of all this, it was slowly dawning on Minna that the more upset she got about her banishment, the more cheerful Martha became. In fact, Martha went about her duties and social schedule with a kind of renewed energy, bright-eyed, independent, and, oddly, optimistic. Martha had changed into the "happy" wife, and now Minna found herself suddenly recast as the one who must somehow carry on.

"Minna, dear. It's such a gorgeous day. I think I'll go down to the Tandelmarkt and stop at the florist afterward. The mums are so lovely this time of year, don't you think?" Martha said, flitting about the room.

"They're quite expensive," Minna said, not so subtly reminding her of Sigmund's feelings about wasting money on flowers.

"Heavens. Stop worrying. Things aren't that desperate. Would you mind running to the butcher for me? I had him put aside a nice rump roast for the *Rindfleisch*, and while you're out, pick up the cheeses and the bread."

Minna hardly relished the thought of more errands, but she resolutely grabbed a stray shawl from the front closet and left. She didn't bother with her hair or her face. It was just the market. She made the rounds of the various merchants, thinking that it was nice to get out, but she didn't seem to have much energy.

On the way home, her mood lifted with the clouds, and she noticed that the church spires in the distance were haloed in brilliant light. She decided to prolong the walk, despite her heavy load of marketing, and ventured down a path through the Prater leading to her neighborhood. It was then that she spotted Sigmund, strolling with a fashionably dressed woman, wrapped in an ermine cape and carrying a silk parasol. The couple was deep in conversation, heads bowed, and at one point, she lightly brushed a leaf from his shoulder and rested her hand there for a moment.

Minna stopped, watching in fascination, as she heard him chuckle at something his companion said. The woman trilled back an inaudible reply. They advanced slowly, while Minna struggled to keep her composure. Then she adjusted the packages in her arms and cast a backward glance to see if there was anywhere she could escape where she wouldn't be noticed.

"Why, Minna," he said, spotting her, his voice chilly yet cordial. "I see you've done the shopping."

There was an uncomfortable pause as he waited for Minna to say something, but she could think of nothing as she stood frozen on the path. His companion smiled brightly, and Minna noticed with dismay her beautifully flushed cheeks, high forehead, voluptuous figure, and perfect white teeth. Her hair was immaculately groomed, Grecian style, with soft curls framing her face. She was not young, but still striking.

"Are you with the Freud household, my dear?" she asked.

"Yes," Minna said, straightening her thin woolen shawl as she waited for Sigmund to introduce them, but he did not. She stood there awkwardly, like a girl with no names on her dance card.

"Lovely day, isn't it?" the woman added.

Minna nodded, her hands nervously clutching her purchases, trying not to stumble into some kind of low comedy exit.

"We'll see you at home, then," Sigmund said as he took the woman's arm and they proceeded in the opposite direction.

Who *was* she? Minna thought, as she did her best to keep walking, her head held high. But by the time she reached the apartment, she was shaking with indignation. Once again, he had treated her like the help. As if no introductions were necessary. Who the devil was she?

The house was quiet when Minna returned. The children were with their governess and Martin was in school, so Minna decided to put the groceries in the kitchen and then go back out. She went upstairs to quickly address her frazzled appearance, dabbing her face with a bit of powder and combing her hair. Of one thing she was certain: she didn't want to be here when Sigmund and *that woman* returned.

She didn't quite make it. As she walked back into the vestibule, she sensed the distinct aroma of expensive perfume mixed with cigar smoke. She couldn't help herself . . . she followed the scent down to the study.

Minna stood in the doorway, holding her coat and hat. The woman was seated on the couch, and the maid was serving her from Martha's well-polished silver tea service. Sigmund was standing in front of her, holding his newest antiquity. When was the last time anyone had visited him in his study at this hour? And she had *never* seen him take tea.

"It's my magical amulet. The ancient Egyptians believed the owner of this was supposedly endowed with supernatural powers," he said, holding it up to the light so that she could see the sun glinting off the bronze.

What does he do—rehearse this? Minna thought. It's exactly the same thing he told her. But without the tea and sugared biscuits.

The woman was tilting her head back, gazing up at him, holding the cup delicately to her lips, obviously captivated. Her skirt was intricately ruched and pleated, and her gloves edged with pearls. Minna hadn't noticed the details before, all of which added up to an aristocratic presence.

"Magnificent, isn't it? My dealer moved heaven and earth to get it."

Minna could stand it no more. Feigning innocence, she stepped into the room under a pretext she had not yet invented. Sigmund looked over at her with what could only be called a pained expression.

"We meet again," Minna said, ignoring his reaction. "I'm Minna Bernays. Martha's sister."

Frau Andreas-Salomé regarded Minna with large sympathetic eyes, visibly surprised.

"Forgive me. I didn't realize you were family."

There was an awkward moment as Minna waited for Sigmund to say something, but he stood there, his eyes fixed on hers, in no way welcoming. The woman broke the stalemate.

"I'm Lou Andreas-Salomé," she said, moving over slightly on the couch. "Won't you join us? Sigmund was just showing me his collection."

"I've seen it before," Minna said coolly. "In any event, thank you, but I'm on my way out."

What did she expect? At least a semblance of cordiality from him? Of course, she did.

She went out the door, weighed down by the revelation: There was another woman in his life, and it wasn't her sister.

As she headed down the bright, airy Ringstrasse, passing grand residences with gated courtyards, she wiped her forehead and felt her pulse oddly racing. Perhaps she was a bit faint from the sun. Or maybe it was anger. Or the humiliation of it all. She desperately needed sleep, and her eyes were stinging. She had sat up the night before with Sophie, who had contracted a mild case of the stomach flu, and now she herself had an uneasiness of the stomach, even though she was hungry. She could have caught Sophie's bug. In addition, she was precariously close to crying. Definitely not in her character.

Minna sought refuge, entering the nearest café, sitting down at a small marble table, and fanning her cold, clammy skin with her hat. She took off her woolen jacket and hung it on the back of her chair and then loosened the waistband of her skirt, unbuttoning a few of the tightest top buttons. She ordered her favorite coffee, a rich Turkish brew topped with sugar and sweet whipped cream, as she nibbled on some bread and cheese, trying to quiet her growling, churning stomach.

The café was crowded with lunchtime shoppers, military officers in their brightly colored uniforms, and students absorbed in a wide variety of newspapers. In one corner, three young men and a pretty girl were huddled together, tilting back on their beech-wood chairs. They whiled away the day, drinking, smoking, seemingly unscathed by life's complications. The young girl, who had been listening to the others, suddenly burst into laughter, her eyes and cheeks glowing. Minna settled herself at her table, dabbing the back of her damp neck with her napkin, and tried to think, but she felt out of context, helpless.

Without warning, the offending odors of the sweet, syrupy, strong Viennese coffee mixed with cigarette smoke overwhelmed her with disgust. Her windpipe and larynx constricted like a noose as a wave of nausea swept over her, and she fought the urge to retch. She clutched the side of the table and closed her eyes. She rested there a moment and then slowly got up. She had to talk to Sigmund.

38

. . .

When Minna arrived back at the apartment, Sigmund was not in his study, and Martha was arranging the mums in a vase in the hallway.

"Where's Sigmund?"

"He's out with Frau Andreas-Salomé. Have you met her?"

"Yes."

"Beautiful woman. Poet, I understand. She's taken a real interest in Sigmund's work. Attended several of his lectures. This could be very good for us. She's wealthy and well connected. The gossip is, four men were in love with her at the same time. *And* not just any men—Klimt, Rilke, Nietzsche, and another one, who actually committed suicide when she left him."

"How fortunate for her."

"Indeed," Martha said, missing the sarcasm, "to have a man love you that much . . ."

Minna felt overtired, weary, like a child on the verge of tears.

"How long has he been seeing her?" she asked faintly.

"Seeing her? That's a strange way of putting it. How should I know? Really, Minna. I don't concern myself with that kind of thing. Do you think I should have gotten the pink ones? They had pink mums today."

"Will he be home for dinner?"

"I'm sure he will, because he's leaving tomorrow for a conference in Göttingen. . . . Frau Andreas-Salomé arranged it."

"Oh."

"Get some rest, my dear. You look like death. . . ."

Minna turned to go upstairs, then paused.

"How do you do it?" she said, her back to Martha, gripping the railing. It was so quiet she could hear her own breathing. A trickle of sweat dripped behind her ears.

"Do what, dear?"

Minna slowly forced herself to face her sister.

"How do you stand it when he goes from one person to the next, giving them his full attention, and ignoring everyone else? It's maddening, don't you think? It makes you wonder where his real affections lie and. . . ."

"No, it doesn't. I don't worry about that. Not anymore. Let him have his little flings."

"Flings?"

"Well, yes, not really. The important thing is, it's never serious. He likes someone who stimulates his mind. They never last. I don't worry in the least about this woman, and you shouldn't, either."

"But, Martha . . ."

"Minna, think about Herr Dr. Breuer. And then Herr Dr. Fliess and several in between. He worshipped these men, and now he won't even mention their names. He's like a petulant child in that way. Don't you see? He hates this one and that one. He adores that one and then this one. Men. Women. Ancient warriors. Merciful heavens!" Martha said with a gentle laugh. "I can't keep up with all of it, honestly. I have enough trouble with the children."

Minna could not respond. Perhaps Martha didn't realize that she and Sigmund were lovers, but she certainly wasn't oblivious to the fact that Minna was just one more person who "stimulated his mind." And that this attachment would eventually pass, just like the others. How ironic, she thought. The one person who could finally confirm her worst fears about Sigmund was Martha.

39

. . .

Minna climbed the stairs, storming inwardly, hardly able to conceal her humiliation. She started toward her bedroom but then stopped in front of Martha's open door. She hesitated, then went directly for the shelf where Martha kept her indispensable books. She found what she was looking for next to a German translation of *Mrs. Beeton's Everyday Cookery and Housekeeping Book*.

HINTS TO MOTHERS FOR THE MANAGEMENT OF HEALTH DURING THE PERIOD OF PREGNANCY AND IN THE LYING-IN ROOM (1877)

by Thomas Bull and Robert W. Parker

There are certain signs which a female is taught to regard as essential evidences of pregnancy; and it is supposed by most, if not by all women, that their presence is absolutely necessary to the existence of this state.

1. Ceasing to be unwell—the first symptom of pregnancy is the omission of the regular monthly return, which, in

female phraseology, would be described as "ceasing to be unwell."

2. Morning sickness—soon after conception the stomach often becomes affected with what is called "morning sickness." On first awakening the woman feels as usual; but, on rising from her bed, qualmishness begins; and perhaps, whilst in the act of dressing, retching takes place.

3. Shooting pains, enlargement of, and other changes in the breast—when two months of pregnancy have been completed, an uneasy sensation of throbbing and stretching fullness is experienced, accompanied with tingling about the middle of the breast, centering in the nipple. The nipple becomes more prominent. . . .

Minna had read enough. There was no need to consult a doctor. The signs were all there. She put the book down on her bedside table, leaned back against the pillows, and wiped her hot, sweaty palms against the cool sheets. *Hints to Mothers* was the bible for every "young married woman," but it was of no further use to her.

She closed her eyes and fell into a fitful sleep. Supper came and went, and when she woke up, it was past ten. She stared into the cold darkness of her bedroom, sat up, and wrapped her shawl around herself. How could she have allowed this to happen? She pushed aside a wave of sadness so overwhelming that acknowledging it would destroy her. One thing was certain. Sigmund must know right away. There was no sense in waiting. None at all.

Minna opened her wardrobe, reached into the back, and pulled out a bottle of gin. She poured a large glass and gulped the burning liquid down like medicine.

The urgency of her situation was apparent. She would tell him tonight.

It was past midnight when Minna heard the front door open and Sigmund's heavy steps on the landing. She'd been half dozing, but the creaking door abruptly brought her back to life. She jumped out of bed, put on her dressing gown, and grabbed the burning candle from the dresser. The house was quiet, except for the sounds of his walking into the parlor and then back to the landing. She stood there, waiting and listening, stiff with tension. Could he have been with that woman all this time? His foot was on the stairs. If she was ever going to talk to him, it had to be now.

"Sigmund," she said, leaning over the banister and peering down at him.

He took a step up and saw her, the light from the candle playing on her face. "Minna—you're still awake?"

"I need to talk to you."

"Now? It's late and you're in your robe. Can't it wait until I get back from my trip?"

"No. It can't," she said, her cheeks two pinpoints of anger.

"Why don't we go down to my consulting room," he said. He rubbed his eyes irritably, yawned, and slowly took off his coat and hat. He looked resigned, or was he simply cornered?

In the past few hours, Minna had rehearsed what she would say, how she would unleash her anger and hurt. But when they finally sat down across from each other, that piercing gaze, which had always intimidated his students, gave her pause.

"I'm listening. Is there a problem?" He fished for a cigar in his pocket and came up empty.

"I understand you're going to Göttingen."

"Yes."

"For how long?"

"I'm not sure, the usual, ten days or so. Is *that* what this discussion is about?"

"When were you going to tell me?" she pressed, trying to control her tightly wound nerves. He looked at her, confused.

"I wasn't aware I had to share my schedule with you."

"You're right. Why would you share *anything* with me? We've barely exchanged two words this past month."

"Of course we have. This is absurd."

"Am I imagining it, then?"

"I'm sorry if you feel slighted, but you, of all people, should understand how I work. It's sometimes necessary to blot out everyone."

"Well, not *everyone*," she said, thinking enough was enough. His weak, pathetic attempts to justify his behavior made her want to scream. "How long have you known Frau Andreas-Salomé? Is she traveling with you? I notice you didn't bother to introduce me."

"Minna, you're being foolish."

"Well, I'm a foolish girl. You're the prime example of that. Why didn't you meet me at the pension?"

"I won't try to explain. . . ."

"I doubt that you could."

"This is ridiculous. I need to get some sleep."

"Well, that's too bad, because *I* need a little dose of your talking cure."

He let out an exasperated sigh.

"This is *not* the time. . . ."

"But it *is* the place. . . . Shall I lie down on the couch?"

"What's wrong with you?"

"Almost everything." There was a moment of silence as she stretched out on the couch, adjusting her robe around her legs. "Oh, this is most comfortable," she said sarcastically, snuggling into the large velvet pillows. "Where shall I begin? Perhaps I'll start with a question. Or is that your bit? Never mind. Why did you talk me into coming back to Vienna with you?"

"I assumed it was a mutual decision," he shot back.

"As mutual as 'I can't live without you' can be. But why quibble?"

"I don't understand. What do you want?"

"What do I want? Isn't that your specialty?" She broke out in a sharp laugh. "You don't have the slightest idea what I want, do you?"

"Would you mind lowering your voice, Minna."

"Is this better?" she whispered. "Let's be honest. I've changed my whole life for you. And for what?"

"You're upset," he said, scrutinizing her pale, fatigued face.

"Brilliant diagnosis. Your talking cure quite works."

"I can't fathom why you're doing this. . . ."

"You can't? You study women who are upset. You want to know why they're upset? I'll save you years of research. They're upset because men like you tell lies to women like me who are stupid enough to believe them."

"Will you please calm down?" he said, standing over her. "I don't want to talk about this anymore."

"I'll bet you don't," she said. She sat up and adjusted her robe. Her shoulders stiffened as she stared at him in fury. "Well, let's change the subject. Let's talk about your work. Something scientific . . . and calm. Didn't you write—where was that? Oh, yes, *The Psychology of Love*—didn't you write that an obstacle is required in order to heighten the libido? That passion and marriage can't coexist?"

"Good God, Minna . . ."

"Didn't you write that?" she asked, seething.

"I did but . . ."

"So that's what I was? The 'obstacle' to heighten your libido?"

"You're hysterical."

"I'm not hysterical. To you, *every* woman who has a problem is hysterical."

"Well, I think you are."

"You're wrong, Dr. Freud," Minna said defiantly, staring him right in the eye. "I'm not hysterical. I'm pregnant."

He took a step back and closed his eyes in disbelief.

"Are you sure?" he asked.

"Yes, I'm sure. You're aware of basic biology, aren't you? Of course you are. *You're* the one who thinks condoms are psychologically harmful—producing anxiety and depression. However, you were talking about their effects on *men*, when in reality, it's the *woman* who ends up with the anxiety—*severe anxiety*—when she discovers she's pregnant."

She pushed aside the perverse urge to sweep all the antiquities off his table and shatter them on the floor. To pull the books out of the bookcases. What was the matter with her? Without so much as a hint of her silent tantrum, she stared at him, unblinking. This time he made no effort to answer her back.

"My dear, I'm so sorry," he said gently, sitting down and putting his arms around her. The impatient look had vanished from his face as he pulled her toward him. She felt his touch for the first time in weeks, and it all came back to her, that slow burn that swept over her each time he was near. She knew what she wanted. She wanted the passion back. And this thought made her even angrier. She didn't want his pity. It was degrading even to contemplate that he would now feel an obligation toward her. The magnitude of what they had done seemed lost on him. It was astounding. The situation was so monstrous that she could not share it with another living soul.

"I'm not sure what you want of me anymore," she said, pulling away from his touch.

"I want what I've always wanted. My feelings for you haven't changed."

She listened as he discussed the future with pragmatic cool, like watching water turn to ice.

He told her he had a colleague who "handled these kinds of things discreetly in Meran." The procedure could be arranged in a matter of days, with little difficulty.

Afterward, she could stay at a private spa nearby, a place where people went when a "change of air" was suggested, as opposed to more isolated, hospital-like sanitariums that accommodated tubercular patients who arrived and, often, never left.

She remembered once at an afternoon tea hearing whispered discussions about a woman's unwanted pregnancy. It was said that there were plenty of inexpensive abortifacients available to induce abortion, many of which were advertised in the newspapers as methods to "regulate menstruation" for "women's salvation." They mentioned purgatives, oxytocics, iron sulfite, iron chlorides, em-menagogues, the root of worm fern called "prostitute root," and an old German folk remedy, an abortifacient tea that consisted of marjoram, thyme, parsley, and lavender. Of course, they said that "fashionable" women of Vienna who were "in trouble" generally had operations at private hospitals, and that the cost was upward of five thousand guldens.

How would he afford it, she thought. But then realized that was his problem.

"I'm afraid you'll need to stay for a while afterward."

She nodded, but as she looked at him, she felt that something between them was ruined. She couldn't speak anymore. She was finally done talking.

Sigmund had initially offered to accompany Minna all the way to Meran, but she decided it would be easier for all of them if she went by herself on the night train. She needed time alone, she told him. What she didn't tell him was that she hadn't decided whether or not she would actually go through with the procedure, or even stay for more than a fortnight at the sanitarium.

He should know that it was not in her nature to slink quietly away and take care of things to his satisfaction. She would make up her own mind in her own time. And at the moment, her mind was conflicted. She was, in fact, floundering, beset by the agonies of indecision. Sigmund's deliberate efforts to arrange things did not assuage her fears, not in the slightest. One thing was certain. She would not allow him to decide her fate. She was aware that most women in her "condition" wouldn't feel this way, but she could not change her personality. Even when it fell short of other people's expectations.

He had paid for a first-class compartment with a sleeping cot, and, for a while, she stared out the window at the blur of scenery, the sky hanging low and gray. Eventually the world of Vienna fell away. At several points, the train stopped at small villages to refill its water and fuel tanks, but even when the ride was smooth, the wheels gliding back and forth on the rails, she sat there rigidly, staring off into the black night. She fired off questions to herself like a grand inquisitor. Why didn't you leave him when you had the chance? Where was your loyalty? She thought about her sister and once again felt the pain, the burden of betrayal. "Guilt upon the conscience," the scholar Bishop Robert South once wrote, "like rust upon iron . . . eats out the very heart and substance of the metal."

40

. . .

Minna arrived at the Meran train station on a gloomy Tuesday morning. A man in livery who said he was from the Neue Meran Sanitarium introduced himself and asked for her baggage ticket. He collected her valise and escorted her to the carriage. Minna watched the rooftops of the village retreat as they climbed a narrow, mountainous road bounded on one side by dark, high rocks.

"How long are you staying?" he asked in a guttural accent.

"A few weeks," she answered. In reality, she had no idea.

The therapeutic air, for all its ballyhooed magical powers, was damp and frigid, and she took an immediate dislike to the building as they pulled up to the entrance. She had seen structures of this type before, of the Viennese school led by rebellious "Die Jungen" architects. The unadorned, blocklike modern building, a combination of brick and concrete, was supposed to be sophisticated, avant-garde. But all it conveyed to her was cold isolation. Degenerate moderns.

She thought back to her conversation with Martha shortly before she left. Sigmund had told her sister that she had contracted a case of pulmonary apicitis and needed to stay at the sanitarium for a few weeks or, perhaps, even a few months. Martha immediately entered Minna's room, a worried look on her face.

"How could you get such a thing? You have no history of it."

"I'm not sure."

"In any event, my friend went to Meran for her lung ailment and came back thoroughly renewed. It's not a punishment, far from it. More like a holiday."

A holiday, Minna thought. She wished it were true.

After she checked in, the young female attendant took one look at Minna's pale face and held her arm as she escorted her to the assigned room on the third floor, its balcony overlooking the property. The place had bright white walls and practical furniture, a simple metal bed, an iron table, a wooden wardrobe, and, outside, a lounge chair on the balcony, with a folded woolen blanket on the end. The perfect place to disappear.

"Your procedure isn't scheduled until Friday, but Dr. Schumann will see you tomorrow. If you need us, just ring the bell near your bed," the girl offered, knowing well enough not to ask any personal questions concerning family, husband, and children.

Minna glanced at her small overnight bag filled with books, toiletries, nightclothes, and a few simple skirts and blouses. She thought about unpacking, but then lit a cigarette and went out on the balcony.

She exhaled a thread of smoke as she stood overlooking the enormous grounds. A woman was singing in the next room. And someone coughed a few rooms down. She thought about the procedure that would end her pregnancy in a few days' time, then collapsed on the bed and fell asleep fully clothed.

She did not emerge from her room until several hours later. She walked through the lobby into the elegant dining room and was seated between two women near the end of a long banquet table covered with a starched, white damask cloth. An attendant hovered nearby as Minna ordered clear bouillon and broiled chicken, followed by a plate of cheese.

"My dear. So lovely to meet you. Is this your first visit?" The fashionably dressed young woman laughed and took a sip of wine as if she were mingling at a cocktail party. "Ah, then we'll have to become friends instantly. You're the only person even close to my age. What are you? Twenty-seven, twenty-eight?"

Her wavy, blond hair was coiffed in a large, elaborate chignon and her organdy dress had a collar that was faced with "white Tibetan goat," a fact she confided to Minna as if they were already good friends. She introduced herself as Lady Justine Brenner, but Minna was skeptical about the "lady" part.

The exuberant display was in stark contrast to the rest of the other, frail-looking guests, quietly filing in from the veranda and talking softly among themselves about their symptoms, how the weather affected their symptoms, and what various treatments had been prescribed for their symptoms.

"I must take these shoes off. My feet are rubbed raw. So where would you think these were made?" Justine asked in a breathy voice, lifting one high-heeled patent boot, which peeked out from under a lilac silk petticoat.

She didn't wait for Minna to reply.

"Paris? Wrong. They're from New York. All the best shoes come from New York. These are trimmed in swans' down. My Felix buys me every color. That's part of his great charm," she said as she carefully sipped her wine. "Although right now I'm extremely cross with him. He and his wife have gone to America and left me here all alone. Devilish man. But he did send me perfume from Berlin." She smiled, revealing a hint of a dimple on the left side.

Minna nodded charitably, hardly knowing how to respond. Frankly, she wished the woman would be quiet. Just because they were around the same age didn't mean they had anything in common.

An older woman, a Frau Bergen, on the other side of Minna, nodded in Justine's direction.

"She acts like she just arrived from high season at Mayerling instead of a month of electrotherapy," she said, throwing out this tidbit like birdseed.

Minna put down her spoon and gave the woman a puzzled look.

"Everyone knows," she whispered. "Her married lover checked her in after she 'accidentally' drank an entire bottle of laudanum."

The room suddenly grew dim and Minna felt the color run from her cheeks. Sweat pooled under her arms and across her chest. Who were these people? She watched the room spin through a sickening red and green haze. Closing her eyes made it feel worse. This is what going mad must feel like, she thought.

"My poor dear. Are you ill? You look quite pale. Can I accompany you back to your room? Here, take my arm," Justine said.

Minna stood up, painfully aware that the other guests were staring at her. She gratefully grasped Justine's arm and allowed herself to be led out of the dining room through the glass doors at the back.

They walked slowly through the lobby, past the game room and private consulting rooms, the purple haze of twilight refracting through the windows. Several attendants, leaning against the wall, whispered to each other as Minna passed in front of them. She heard the word "pregnant" hang in the air as they crossed over and ascended the white stone stairs.

41

...

I t's impossible to keep this rosy countenance," Justine said, stepping out of the pool, as an attendant wrapped her plush, voluptuous body in a thick Turkish towel. "Believe me, I've tried. But for
the moment, isn't it transforming?"

Justine and Minna were "taking the waters" at Meran. Justine
was explaining away her suicide attempt as a "slight miscalculation
in dosage," and Minna was attempting to forget about her upcoming procedure.

Minna sank into the warm water, half closed her eyes, and let
herself float on top of the submerged marble bench. Miraculously,
the pressure released from her temples—sacraments from the
water gods. She lowered her head, the water covering her ears as
Justine's voice faded away. All she could hear were soft waves lapping against the side of the bath and the whooshing of blood as it
coursed through her aorta. It was all so effortless, like drifting off
into a warm daydream.

Minna glanced around the room at the other female bathers,
reclining in languid poses on benches and basking in the liquid light. They reminded her of the odalisques so favored by

contemporary artists such as Cézanne, Gauguin, and Matisse. She remembered one work in particular by a young German named Kirchner who scandalously painted nude bathers at a beach on the Baltic Sea. It was said that the artist would go on outings with his mistresses to these secluded spots and paint them as they picnicked and sunbathed.

"Paradise, isn't it?" Justine said blissfully.

She would have the world believe she was perfectly happy being a mistress, living in an elegant pied-à-terre off the Ringstrasse and owning all the fine dresses and shoes she desired. She "relished" her independent existence. And, no, she said, she didn't have the obsession to get married, like other women her age.

Minna climbed out of the bath and sat down on a marble bench next to Justine. A few of the older women drying themselves across the room gaped at Justine as she threw off her towel and draped herself on a lounge. One of them inhaled sharply as if she were a spectator at a beheading.

"Let them stare. . . ." Justine whispered. "Old cows."

"They're probably jealous."

"Probably not. One of them actually tried to lecture me on the Sixth Commandment. . . ."

"Maybe the Seventh? I think the Sixth has something to do with murder."

"Doesn't matter. God knows, none of them has ever done anything even the least bit adventurous. I have no illusions as to what they think of me," she said, grinning.

"You must try the pine-needle baths in town," she added, rolling over on her stomach, propping her chin up with her hands. "Dreadful greenish color, but smells delicious. All the country people do it. We should go. It'll be our little outing. . . ."

"We're allowed to leave the premises?"

"My dear, we're not in captivity," she teased. "Just in disgrace."

"So you've heard about me, then," Minna said, flushing.

"Of course. This place is a hotbed of gossip. Really, what else is there to do here? No wonder they have this absurd nine o'clock bedtime."

For a moment, Minna wished she were a bit more like Justine, at least the side of Justine she was seeing now—a free spirit who didn't seem to care what society thought of her. Minna was just over thirty, the age when some would say she was too old, and others would say she was at her most beautiful. Especially now, lush with child, her skin glistening in the dampness. And yet, there was a sadness clinging to her that grew inside her along with the baby she was carrying. And for maybe the first time, she wondered what it would be like to hold her own child in her arms.

It was a day that couldn't make up its mind, a lovely morning and then a gray afternoon as a spate of vile weather descended on the valley. Justine and Minna, having had enough of the deserted veranda, decided to take a walk. Dressed in almost identical black skirts, cloaks, and dark bonnets, they made their way along a dirt path fringed with pine trees, the wind whipping at their backs. In the eerie, misty light, they looked like two witches flying through the air.

"Cheery spot," Justine said, her voice straining in the wind. "Oh, dear, here comes that dreadful woman, Frau Bergen. What should I tell her?"

"Tell her we're looking for Heathcliff."

Justine started laughing.

"You've read it, then," Minna asked.

"Don't be so surprised. Mistresses read. We have to fill those empty days with something. Come with me . . . hurry."

She grabbed Minna's arm and dragged her off the path through a clump of straggling hedges. The sanitarium loomed behind them as they ran through a stand of trees to a clearing and collapsed breathless on a small bench.

Maybe it was Justine's offhand laugh. Or the fact that they were huddled together, the two of them against the world. Or maybe it was Justine's unflinching dignity and composure after all she'd been through. But something made Minna decide to confide in her, first telling about the affair, even revealing that it was with her brother-in-law, and then about his cooling off when they returned home from Switzerland.

"At first, I tried to persuade myself that a love affair, like marriage, couldn't be maintained at the same level of passion. But then I realized—"

"You realized that you were superfluous to him. He went on with his life as if nothing had happened. And you were left living with a ghost."

Minna was relieved at Justine's lack of shock throughout the whole galvanic confession, which helped temper Minna's shame and self-pity.

"And when he learned you were pregnant, he reacted like any other married man," Justine said, moving closer and hooking her arm into Minna's. "How could you expect anything else?"

"I thought he was different. He's a scientist, you see. I thought that he knew what women wanted, what they needed. But his theories about women and their emotions are completely misguided."

"I've found that most men's obsession with sex has to do with them not getting enough at home. But a baby. That changes every-thing. It's inconvenient, embarrassing . . . expensive—"

"But not impossible," Minna interrupted.

"Well, my dear, it depends on your definition of impossible."

"What I mean is, some women *do* have children out of wedlock."

"Yes, an occupational hazard, but I wouldn't recommend it."

"I want to keep this child," Minna confessed, and hearing her-self say it made it clear. Justine looked at her with sympathy.

"And what would you do? Where would you go?"

"I don't know."

"You wouldn't go back to your family, then?"

"No. I couldn't do that. I'd find someplace else. Someplace where people wouldn't judge us. Where we could live quietly and I could raise the child in peace."

"No place like that exists. But if you happen to find it, I'll go with you," Justine said.

She turned to Minna, her eyes serious. "He promised to marry me, you know. I didn't think he'd ever go through with it, of course, but it was nice hearing him say it."

After dinner that night, Minna thought about her options. She decided to stay at the sanitarium a few more days, then make arrangements to move to America. She could live with her brother and his wife until the child was born, and then she'd figure some-thing out. Sigmund would object, of course. He'd have a thousand reasons why she shouldn't do this. But she wouldn't listen to any of them. No. This was the best solution. No one would be hurt this way.

On her way back to her room, she stopped at the front desk to leave a message for the doctor, telling him she was canceling the procedure on Friday. As she walked away, the receptionist called her back, handing her a letter that had been delivered in the day's post.

Vienna, November 1896

My dearest Minna,

I was on my way to visit you when my father fell mortally ill, and of course I couldn't leave. Please understand, if I could tear myself away, I would. I'd travel there and bring you home, but that's impossible now. The old man's illness came on suddenly— meningeal hemorrhages, soporous attacks with unexplained fever, hyperesthesia, and spasms. He's been tormented mercilessly, and I can do little but sit by and watch him die.

As you know, in the past few months, I've been consumed by my research, working myself to the bone and facing incredibly bleak moments. I've never experienced such a high degree of preoccupation, and I worry, will anything ever come of it? My book is still not developed enough for publication, but I press on.

My dear Minna, how difficult this whole business must be for you. I'm sorry if I haven't been as attentive as I might. All my thoughts at the moment are filled with self-reproach. I'm losing my father. I don't want to lose you, too.

At any rate, my darling Minna, I hope you'll agree that you can't go anywhere else—your future is here with us. I'll always take care of you. What else can I say?

I've talked to Martha about arranging your return, and you should hear from her as soon as she has worked out all the

*details. She has been as worried as I about you and is eager
to have you home. I kiss you, my dear sweetheart, and I'm
impatient to see you. Be well.*

Yours,

Sigm.

Sigmund's letter threw Minna into a state of confusion. Here
were the words she'd been longing to hear ever since they'd returned
from Switzerland. Now he wanted her back. He was, it seemed, in a
weakened state, distraught about his father and in need of a sympathetic ear. And he was struggling with his work, as always. She wondered if he would be writing this if he had any idea that she had
canceled the procedure. But she already knew the answer.

42

...

Minna was lying undressed on the examining table, covered with a single white sheet. Early that morning, she had received a message from the doctor suggesting she have a prenatal examination before she checked out, since her medical services were fully paid. She was more tired than she could remember, feeling limp and headachy. She had been up half the night, dreaming and waking, listening to the wind sigh and moan outside her window. She missed Sigmund and longed to hear his voice, but perhaps it was better that he wasn't here right now to question her decision.

She watched as the nurse filled a clear glass bottle with chloroform and placed it on the metal table next to a small wooden box.

"Do we know how far along we are, my dear?"

"Well before the quickening, around two months."

"You're lucky, indeed, to have Dr. Gerringer. He's very selective, only takes women of substance. And extremely discreet."

"Oh . . ."

"Some of the ladies try oil of savin first . . . very dangerous," she said, pulling the curtains closed. "I've seen violent reactions, and deaths. And let me tell you, afterward, in the postmortem, the body oozes the smell of savin, like poison."

"There must be a misunderstanding," Minna said, trying not to look terrified. "I've canceled the procedure. Didn't the doctor tell you?"

"Now, now, dear. It's normal to be nervous," she said, as she began to remove some instruments from a velvet-lined oak case that reminded Minna of a tiny coffin. The steel-plated, ebony-handled instruments were easily recognizable: a scalpel, a blunt hook, a pair of forceps, and needles of varying sizes. Also, a spool of silk sutures to repair lacerations and an instrument that looked like a long steel crochet needle.

"Just relax. When you wake up, your little problem will be all gone."

Minna sat up abruptly.

"Excuse me. I don't have a 'little problem.' I'm here solely for a prenatal examination."

"Calm down, Fräulein."

"I want the doctor!"

"As you wish," she said, leaving, slamming the door behind her.

A few minutes later, the doctor appeared wearing a white linen medical coat that fit him like a dinner jacket. He had a reassuring face with deep-set eyes, and a sense of reserve, as he gently took her hand in his.

"I'm so sorry, Fräulein Bernays," he said. "I neglected to inform the nurse of your change of heart. Shall we proceed with the examination?"

Minna turned her head toward the opposite wall and focused

her eyes on the rough texture of the paint, as she felt the doctor's smooth fingers prodding her abdomen and then the edges of the cold, metal speculum between her legs. She tried not to cry out as she felt a sharp jab of pain inside her belly.

"Everything is fine, my dear. It looks as though you're eight weeks along, which is still safe to do the procedure, if you change your mind. But don't wait too long, or my hands are tied."

"I won't. My mind is made up," Minna said, summoning up as much grace as she could manage.

Minna spent the next few days planning her trip to America. She wrote her brother, asking him to send her a ticket, without explaining why. He had been urging her to visit for the past several years and he wouldn't ask a lot of questions. She made a list of the things that she would have to do before the trip. Even though she'd like to just disappear, there were so many details that must be dealt with first. She must apply for the necessary papers. God willing, that wouldn't take too long. Her brother had mentioned something about an expedited process. She thought about her travel trunk still sitting in the Freuds' storage closet. And her room full of belongings. She would, at some point, have to go back there to pick them up, maybe she'd schedule it when Sigmund was at class. In any event, she'd never forgive herself if she didn't say good-bye to the children.

She fell asleep that night with a premonition that something was wrong. Maybe it was just the hastily thrown-together plans of a woman in trouble. Was she taking into account all the complications that might arise? She couldn't possibly anticipate them all.

. . .

She woke up chilled, her heart beating quickly, the residual effects, she thought, of a nightmare. She could hardly catch her breath, as she felt a dull ache in her lower back and abdomen descending to her hips and thighs, passing around to her legs.

She pulled the cord near her bed, ringing for the attendant, who suggested hot compresses and tea.

"These are probably just false pains," she told Minna. "We see it all the time. They'll last for some hours. Wearisome, but not harmful."

She placed a small horsehair cushion under Minna's knees, drew the woolen curtains aside, and opened the bedroom windows. Then she chatted on, blaming Minna's discomfort on fatigue, mental excitement, or perhaps a disturbed condition of the bowel, for which she recommended a tablespoon of castor oil and a warmed-over pint of barley water.

"Some fresh air, a bit of slumber, and by and by you'll feel better."

A few hours later, Minna awoke to tremors so violent as to shake the bed. Severe cramps began, and nausea coursed through her body. She pressed her hand on her back in an attempt to stop the shooting pains as she made her way to the commode. The last thing she thought of as she fell to the ground and lapsed into unconsciousness was that she hoped there would be no damage to the child.

43

. . .

ow long have you been here?" Minna asked.

"I don't know. A few hours," Justine said, rising from her chair. She laid aside her needlework, slipped her stocking-feet into her satin pumps, and walked through the darkening room to Minna's bedside table. Her thick blond hair was piled up with pins, and her usual lighthearted demeanor was more disciplined now, her green eyes fixed on her task. She fumbled with the candle and relit it, then covered up Minna's arms, which were jutting out of the covers. Minna was told that five days had gone by and she had spent them sleeping, enveloped in a sickening combination of medication and misery.

"You look better. Your color is back."

Minna stared at her, then realized through her narcotic haze why she was in bed. She rose on her elbows and tried to focus. The pain of losing the child hit her as powerfully as if it had just happened.

Justine began fussing with the metal bed warmer, placing it under the covers and adjusting the blankets around it. Then she brushed Minna's hair off her face. She was about to tell her that it was time she got out of bed, but Minna looked so fragile lying there, her eyes ringed with dark circles, that she decided to wait.

"I just finished reading *Jane Eyre*," Justine said, trying to lighten the mood. "Didn't think it was quite as good as—"

"I don't want to talk about books," Minna said, her voice trailing off. They sat there for a few minutes half facing each other, not saying anything.

"Minna, you have to pull yourself out of this. . . ."

"I don't *have* to do anything."

"You can't stay here forever."

"As if I'd want to . . . I was moving to America, you know. I had it all planned."

"I know. You told me."

"I did?"

"Twice."

"Must be the medication. Hand me a cigarette, will you?"

"It's not allowed," she said with a slight smile as she pulled a tin of Egyptian cigarettes from the pocket of her dress. She gave Minna one, lit it for her, and watched as she inhaled deeply.

"It wouldn't have worked," Justine said.

"What?"

"America. It's not what you think it is. New York and Boston are brutal. They don't like foreigners, divorcées, bohemians. A woman in your position ends up with a ragtag life . . . the child a constant heartache."

"I don't believe you."

"It's true. I've been around. I've heard stories. Urban squalor, tenements, people with strange accents and appalling diets, gangs of vigilantes, and bodies dumped in the Hudson like dead fish."

"I'd go west, then."

"And who do you think you're going to meet out there besides savages and farmers? Scratching out a living on some parched piece of earth on a godforsaken prairie . . ."

"Are you finished?"

"Not quite . . ." she said brightly, relishing the picture she was painting. "Wondering if you and the child would make it through the winter without dying from typhus or consumption or the pox— vultures picking at your bones."

"Well, that was comforting," Minna said, amused in spite of herself. Justine's descriptions were elaborate to the point of being comical.

"I try," she said, adjusting the pins in her hair.

"A bit theatrical."

"Listen, I talked to your doctor this morning. I suggested that since your miscarriage was precipitated by his rough prenatal exam, you *certainly* shouldn't be charged for your stay here."

"You didn't!"

"Oh, yes, I did. He denied it, of course. But I checked later at the desk and they said that Dr. Freud will be given a full refund."

"Sigmund will be happy."

"I'm sure he will. In my experience, I've found that most doc-tors are . . ." She hesitated, and raised her eyebrows—"How to say this politely . . . ? Cheap bastards."

They heard a loud, rattling cough as a patient walked by Minna's half-opened door.

"Jesus! These people. You'd think they'd have the decency to cover their mouth," Justine said, slamming the door shut.

"I don't know what to do," Minna said after a long silence.

"If it were me, I'd go home," Justine said.

Home, Minna thought. Just where was that? Her mother's house?

God forbid. Her sister's? How could she go back there after all that had happened?

"Although," Justine added, lighting a cigarette, "I'm not the ideal person to give advice."

Minna sat up, slowly moved her legs over the side of the bed, and put on her dressing gown. She ignored the slight dizziness as she walked out on the balcony and carefully settled herself in a chair, watching the purple light spread across the horizon.

Justine threw a wool shawl over Minna's shoulders and sat down next to her.

"I'm leaving in the morning," Justine said. "I was supposed to be in Vienna a few days ago, but I wanted to make sure you were all right."

Her friend's voice was low and soothing. Minna leaned her head back and closed her eyes. She felt a wash of emotion but couldn't risk the embarrassment of tears.

"I don't deceive myself that we'll see each other again. . . ." Justine said softly.

Minna took her hand for a moment and pressed it to her cheek, then held it in her lap. The two women sat in silence, silhouetted by the fading light.

"Do you want me to call the nurse?" Justine said.

"No."

"Would you like me to order dinner from downstairs?"

"No."

"Shall we get really drunk tonight?"

"I'd like that."

Justine sat back in her chair and blew wavering rings of smoke into the air.

"Good. I would, too."

44

. . .

Vienna, November 1896

Dear Minna,

I hate to be the bearer of bad news, but we buried Jakob yesterday, following yet another severe pulmonary edema. Even though we knew this was inevitable, Sigmund is inconsolable. My dear Minna, he is not himself. He sits alone in his study, staring at the walls, and wanders the apartment, quite uprooted. I found him the other day in the parlor, staring into space. And he seems to have no interest in his practice or in his research.

Yesterday, he learned that a colleague at the university declined him as a consultant, telling the others that Sigmund could not be taken seriously. Surely another crushing setback for him. Now, you know what a fit he usually has when something like this happens. But he just looked up at me and shrugged. He seems to be doing nothing but reading about Bismarck, who, he tells me, was born on the exact same day as Jakob.

My dear Minna, I must also tell you that I have to leave the children and go to Hamburg. Mother is ill and has written a

*flurry of letters begging me to care for her. So unless you would
rather take care of her (and I know the answer to that), I told her
that I would come, and then, since Sigmund tells me you're much
improved, it's only fair that you come here to care for the children.*

*I looked up the schedule for the Brenner line of the Murano
central rail and made a reservation for you on the four o'clock
train Thursday. If I can, I'll meet you.*

*I wish my news were better. But it is what it is. I'll be happy
when life is back to normal and we're all together again.*

   Your loving sister,
   Martha

Minna couldn't help but note her sister's predictable division of
labor. Martha's tone was affectionate but clear that Minna would be
shirking an imperative duty toward the family should she say no.

Here was the solution. Handed to her on a silver platter. If only
it were that simple. Yes, she would be fulfilling an obligation, but
also returning to Freud. Her sister had offered her a home once
and she had ruined it. This time, she would not make the same
mistakes.

45

. . .

It was midafternoon when Minna stepped off the train at Wien Westbahnhof and found Martha waiting for her on the crowded platform. Her sister was wrapped in a dark red cloak, her hair, as usual, pulled tight in a small, neat bun, and she brightened when she spotted Minna through the burst of billowing steam.

"Martha. What an unexpected sight," Minna said, her voice barely heard above the racket of the passing porters hauling suitcases and the surge of travelers rushing by. She tipped the porter walking beside her and took her small, worn valise from his hand.

"You needn't have come—so much trouble for you. I could have taken the omnibus."

A gust of wind hit them, carrying the acrid smell of smoke and exhaust, and Minna shivered in her light serge jacket and walking skirt.

"I wanted to see you before I went to Mother's," Martha said, kissing Minna on both cheeks and picking up her bag. "My goodness, this is heavy. You shouldn't be lifting, should you? I'm on the five o'clock to Hamburg, so there isn't much time. How are you, my dear? Your lungs are clear?"

"Don't worry, Martha. I'm doing fine."

"I can see that. I have just enough time for a coffee."

Martha took her sister's arm and steered her through the terminal, toward a café near the entrance. The late-afternoon sun streamed through the long, vaulted hallway, and Minna shielded her eyes from the glare. She must have left her hat on the train.

The journey from Meran had been long and tedious, and she hadn't slept a bit. There had been wild jolts of train cars latching and unlatching at station stops, and she had hardly looked at the landscape skimming past the windows.

She had boarded the first train at the ungodly hour of six and was looking forward to seeing the children, exchanging a few pleasantries, pleading exhaustion, and going straight to bed. But Martha was so attentive, she could hardly show any reticence. Still, she found herself feeling ambushed as Martha chatted on about Emmeline's condition (beastly) and then launched into a detailed schedule of the household events for the next few weeks.

This was not at all what she had expected. She thought Martha would be home a few days before she had to face him alone. Good God. She'd have to deal with him tonight. What could she say? That she had decided to have the baby. That she had planned to leave him, after all. That the miscarriage had ended everything.

"Martha, must you leave today? Why don't you wait at least until I settle in? Mother's waited this long, she can wait a few more days."

"That's rather harsh, my dear. Especially considering her condition. In any event, it's all arranged. I have my ticket and I'm going."

It was no use trying to convince her sister otherwise. Martha *never* changed her plans unless someone was at death's door. They sat down in the café next to a group of fashionable women in big hats and ordered *Kaffee mit Schlag*. Then Martha called the waiter back and added two servings of strudel.

"None for me," Minna said. "I ate on the train." The thought of warmed-over oozing strudel made her stomach turn.

"Don't be silly. Bring two strudels," she repeated to the waiter. "You look thin. You *are* up to this, aren't you?" Martha said, examining Minna's face. "You can handle things until I get back?"

"Of course I can."

"I've written everything down and put the list in your room. Sophie now goes to the speech therapist on Tuesdays instead of Thursdays. Mathilde's tutor comes every afternoon at four. Martin will beg to go skating, but don't let him."

"I'll be fine. It's not that complicated."

"I'm sure . . . but if you're still feeling weak, I can get Edna to bring in her sister. Shall I do that? I don't want this to be a strain."

"No. I don't want Edna's sister. Stop worrying."

"Well, you look tired," Martha said.

They sat in silence for a few moments while the waiter served the coffee and strudel. Minna studied her piece of cake, pushing it around with her fork.

"You haven't asked about Sigmund. . . ." Martha said, carefully bringing up the subject they had danced around for the past half hour.

"How is he?" Minna asked softly, not looking up.

"He's still in a state, if can you believe it. And there's nothing to distract him. Frau Andreas-Salomé flew the coop last week, and the parting was *not* amicable."

"Oh, that's too bad."

"Yes, isn't it? My sentiments exactly," Martha said, with a slight smile. "The woman showed up hysterical, and I don't mean this clinically. There were *actual* tears. And of course, Sigi was nowhere to be found, so I had to deal with her."

"You showed her the door."

"In a very kind way."

"I'm sure."

Their eyes met for a moment.

"Minna," Martha said, in a more serious tone, "my worry is that he's so low right now. He'll lure you down to his study again, and you're simply not up to it. Six children. It's a difficult schedule even if you were well and rested. I hope you'll temper your time with him, for your *own* sake."

"But, Martha, I'm not coming back with the intention of—"

"Of course not," Martha interrupted, obviously not willing to hear more, "but when he gets his momentum back, and of course he will, he's likely to behave the same way he always has. . . . Do you understand me?"

No one could fail to understand her. The gravity in her tone was palpable. Minna nodded.

"I've seen your disappointment when he ignores you. You must try to adopt a bit of my philosophy when it comes to Sigmund. Enjoy him when he's civilized; pay no attention when he's a lout. What other choice do we have?"

Minna was speechless. And completely at a loss as to whether Martha knew. At the very least, she was acknowledging Minna's true feelings, but as Sigmund's lover? Or as simply another casualty in a long line of confidantes who were tossed aside? Minna appraised her sister, hoping for some insight, but Martha's face was unreadable, her color did not change. Her unique talent had always been to maintain a kind of infallible self-sufficiency of the soul, a daunting and enviable trait. She could maintain her even keel quite efficiently, despite the lacerating facts, and had, without saying it, invited her sister to do the same.

"Martha, I'll take care of things while you're gone, but I'm only staying a few weeks."

"I won't discuss this with you now. You're not yourself. But I *will* say that, in general, we shouldn't let our emotions get the better of us. And, specifically, there's no reason to give up everything over something so transitory."

"What are you saying?"

"Simply that everyone in the house knew Sigmund hurt your feelings. That's what he does. . . . You must get over it."

Minna gazed at her sister's implacable face. Tears fell on her cheeks and ran down her neck.

"Hush. Don't cry. It doesn't suit you. I'm through talking now. And so are you. We've both had our turns."

Martha reached her hand across the table toward Minna's in a gesture of mutual comfort. They embraced before she left for her train, and then Minna sat in the café awhile longer, gazing out the window at the cloudy sky. She felt a pang of loneliness that had not been there before and thought about her sister. She could still hear Martha's voice filled with passive resilience and acceptance and the promise of something good if they all just carried on, made the best of things, and took care of each other.

The trees along the avenue were starting to lose their leaves and soon they would be bare. All one would see was the gray block of apartment buildings across the street. It seemed that fall had arrived in Vienna without her. So much had happened since she left. She felt as if she'd been away for years.

She paid for her coffee, put on her coat, and walked outside, looking for a cab. She breathed deeply and listened to the wind rustle the trees. The house waited for her. Perhaps, she thought, she'd stay.

But only for a while.

EPILOGUE

...

Minna arrived at Berggasse 19 as a young woman and stayed on for over forty years. Now she was dying.

It was a dreary morning when Martha went upstairs to check on her sister. The garden was covered with a sprinkling of fresh, wet snow, and a stagnant cloud of mist hung over the city. The moment she walked into Minna's room, she knew. It would not be long now. Her sister's hands were crossed over her chest in supplication, and her breathing was raspy and labored. The doctor said that Minna's heart condition had worsened in the past few days, and there wasn't much left to do except keep her comfortable.

Minna seldom left her room since Sigmund's death a little over a year before. He had endured a long, drawn-out battle with throat cancer, and Virginia Woolf, who visited Sigmund shortly before he died, had likened him to "a half-extinct volcano." But he had always said that, like King Macbeth, he would rather "die with harness." And he did just that. He spent his last days in his study, working and reading in his favorite chair in front of his office window. And, in his final hours, Martha and Minna were at his bedside. Where else would they be?

Martha pulled an extra blanket over her sister and turned up the radiator, which hissed and knocked in protest. She didn't think Minna even noticed she was there at first, but then Minna turned her head slightly and smiled. Some days were better than others, and perhaps today she would be in the mood to talk. Yesterday she actually sat up and read for a while.

Martha heard an explosion in the distance and the window-panes rattled in their frames. The air raids were continuous now and there were blackouts every night. It was impossible to sleep, and every time she heard a blast, she would rush upstairs to check on Minna. One had to have nerves of steel to stay in this city.

Before the Freuds moved to their new home in London, life in Vienna had deteriorated dramatically. The chancellor had resigned, and Hitler's troops descended on Austria. Martha had watched through their parlor window as the Nazis marched down the Ringstrasse, cheered on by jubilant crowds. She had locked their door, fearful of the mobs who were breaking into Jewish homes and businesses.

As the Anschluss progressed, Sigmund was singled out as an enemy of the state. The Gestapo ransacked their apartment and confiscated their passports. Anna was arrested briefly, and friends began to disappear. Sigmund finally agreed that they must flee their home. But he had waited too long. Only through the help of highly placed friends and officials, including the American ambassadors in Paris and Berlin, President Roosevelt, and the U.S. State Department, were they allowed to leave. They made it clear to the German government that any mistreatment of the now-world-famous scientist would create an international incident. At this point in his life, Sigmund's hard-won reputation was without dispute.

The news from the Continent continued to horrify. Sigmund's four younger sisters had been deported to concentration camps, and Martha feared the worst. But never in all her imaginings had she thought that it would come to this.

"Minna, would you like some hot tea?" she asked. "The maid is bringing up a tray."

Minna nodded, so Martha gently raised her to a sitting position and plumped the pillows behind her back.

"Do you feel like talking, my dear? I didn't sleep very well last night—did you? Another visit from the bombs," Martha said, placing Minna's shawl over her sister's shoulders.

"They never stop, do they?" Minna said, with little interest. It was a question from someone who was surrendering this world and floating into another.

"Getting worse, I should think. One of the windows in the house next door completely shattered. Thank heavens, we've had no damage. Some mornings I'm surprised the house is still standing."

Martha stared at Minna's sharp shoulder blades and skeletal frame. She looked so fragile, pale as bone, as if she were being swallowed up by the bed. She'd always been too thin, and now even more so. Who was that old woman? Martha was losing her sister, the one person with whom she had shared everything. They had lived together for so long and endured so much. And through it all, there were the three of them. She silently wrestled with competing emotions—gratitude, sorrow, envy, and love—more than she could bear. But, if the heavens should reverse themselves, and she was given the opportunity to relive her life, she knew that she would make the same decisions.

The maid rapped lightly on the door and entered with a tray of tea and biscuits. Martha took it from her and placed it on the bedside table. Then she handed Minna a cup of tea, pulled up a chair, and sat down next to her.

"Eat your biscuits," she said with concern.

"You eat them, I'm not hungry."

"Minna dear, you must have something in your stomach. I'll leave it here, you might want it later," Martha said, pausing for a moment. "You know, I've been cleaning out Sigmund's study. Cataloging all the books and antiquities and storing the important papers. Saving everything of historic value. So much work."

"I'm sorry I can't help you. It must be difficult to go in there."

"It isn't easy but it's such an eyesore. You know how everything was everywhere. In any event, I have something for you."

Martha put her hand in her skirt pocket and produced a thick bundle of yellowed envelopes tied up tightly in twine. The contents obviously had not been touched in years.

"It's your correspondence to Sigmund. He must have kept it all this time," she said.

Minna handled the letters gingerly, then dropped them on the table, as though they were white-hot. She scanned Martha's face for any sign of anger but there was none.

"That's odd," Minna said, a catch in her voice. "I thought they were destroyed in Vienna. He told me he burned everything of a personal nature."

"Apparently not everything. When you're up to it, you might want to go through them."

Martha took a deep breath and slowly let it out. She spoke of the letters as if they were a bit of business for the morning, a trifle. After all these years, if any feelings of recrimination still existed, they were muted now. She attempted a smile as she readjusted her sister's pillows and drew up the bedcovers.

Minna looked at her sister without blinking.

"Do you remember that young American who came to Vienna and offered Sigmund a book contract for his autobiography?" Martha asked. "When was that? Ten years ago?"

Minna nodded.

"I think it was summer, right before we went on holiday. It was stifling. I felt sorry for the poor boy, all dressed up in a wool suit. Sigmund was incredibly rude. In fact, I don't know why he agreed to the meeting at all. He had no intention of ever writing the thing."

"They wouldn't pay him enough. That's what it was," Minna said.

"No, it wasn't. He told me it would be an utter betrayal of everyone—family, friends, enemies—everyone. That's why he spent his life destroying letters. He said that autobiographies were all worthless lies and would require, on his part, so much indiscretion that the consequences would be unthinkable."

"For his patients alone," Minna said, in little more than a whisper.

"Yes. For his patients alone," Martha agreed. "Now, why don't you get some rest?"

Minna stared out the window, her face distant and far away. Then she solemnly gathered the letters from the bedside table and called for her sister.

"Martha dear," she said in a flat tone. "Would you mind disposing of these for me?"

"You don't want to read them?" Martha asked carefully.

"No," Minna said, sinking back into her pillows, "and they're of no historical value."

Martha slid the letters into her pocket and left her sister's room. It was her firm belief that there are some things in this life that should remain hidden. She would do anything to protect her husband's reputation. And she knew her sister would do the same. Countless accommodations were made. But even though these things were never mentioned or acknowledged, and even though time had altered their impact, it didn't mean they never happened. And it didn't mean she never knew.

.   .   .

Freud's Mistress is a novel, based on the love affair between Sigmund Freud and his sister-in-law, Minna Bernays. The book portrays the period beginning in 1895 when Minna first came to live with the Freuds in Vienna. She stayed with them for more than forty years, and never married or had children of her own.

The Freuds escaped Nazi-occupied Vienna and fled to London in June 1938. Sigmund Freud died of throat cancer on September 23, 1939, at his home in Maresfield Gardens, with Minna and Martha at his bedside. Minna died a year later from heart failure. It was reported that, following Freud's death, she rarely left her room. Martha Freud lived in London, surrounded by her children and grandchildren, until her death in 1951, at the age of ninety.

For more than seventy years, rumors have circulated among biographers and historians concerning the nature of the relationship between Sigmund Freud and Minna Bernays. Tantalizing questions arose. Did they or did they not have an affair?

In 1989, Peter Gay, one of Freud's foremost biographers, set out to officially resolve, once and for all, this controversial mystery. The eminent scholar's research began in the Library of Congress, where he pored over a cache of letters between the two of them that had been recently released by the Freud Museum in London.

"I had the pleasure—every scholar will know what I felt—of being the first to go through the precious bundle," he wrote in an article published in *The New York Times* on January 29, 1989.

The story behind the letters' release began in 1972, when Freud's youngest daughter, Anna, turned over a significant number of letters to the manuscript division of the Library of Congress. Notably, she withheld certain letters, offering the explanation that they were of a personal nature and not for public scrutiny. The cache remained at 20 Maresfield Gardens, Freud's final residence in London (now the Freud Museum), until four years after Anna's death, when the director of the Freud Archives personally transported them to the United States.

Gay wrote that as he sat in the grand, silent manuscript room, staring at Freud's familiar German script, a puzzling and unexpected setback occurred. It seemed there was a significant gap in the collection of letters, and it struck him that there was "something odd about the missing portions." It appeared that someone had taken on the task of numbering the letters chronologically, and the numbers 93 through 161 were removed and unaccounted for. Those lost letters would have covered the years 1895 to 1900—the exact years that Minna and Freud were rumored to have had an affair.

That rumor was substantiated fifty years later by Swiss psychologist and former Freud disciple Carl Jung, who in 1957 stated that Minna Bernays confessed to him that she and Sigmund Freud were having an affair. The revelation appeared in an interview published by the *Andover Newton Quarterly*.

> *Soon I met Freud's wife's younger sister. She was very good-looking and she not only knew enough about psychoanalysis but also about everything that Freud was doing. When a few days later, I was visiting Freud's laboratory, Freud's sister-in-law asked me if she could talk with me. She was very much bothered by her relationship with Freud and felt guilty about it. From her I learned that Freud was in love with her and that their relationship was indeed very intimate. It was a shocking discovery to me, and even now I can recall the agony I felt at the time.*
>
> CARL JUNG, Interviewed by JOHN M. BILLINSKY,
> *ANDOVER NEWTON QUARTERLY* 10 (39–43), 1969

Most Freud scholars rejected Jung's claims as "sour grapes" from a rival. It was well known that the two men had a bitter falling-out over Freud's sexual theories. Gay eventually concluded that the letters between Sigmund Freud and Minna Bernays no longer existed, and that anyone who might shed light on the tampering was probably dead. Even if the letters were found, he argued, it was "exceedingly unlikely that they would substantiate the rumor" of an affair.

This was the general assumption until the summer of 2006, when a German sociologist found proof that on August 13, 1898, Sigmund Freud, then forty-two, and Minna Bernays, thirty-three, traveled to a fashionable resort in Maloja, Switzerland, where they registered at a hotel as husband and wife. The worn, leather-bound ledger showed that they occupied room 11 on the third floor and signed in as "*Dr. Sigm. Freud u Frau*"—Dr. Sigmund Freud and wife.

The evidence was apparently persuasive enough for Gay to change his opinion. On December 24, 2006, in a subsequent *New York Times* article, he said, "It makes it very possible that they slept together." It now seems certain that Minna Bernays was not only Freud's "closest confidante," playing a critical role during his most significant years of discovery, but she was also his lover.

While Freud scholars may now agree that Sigmund Freud and Minna Bernays had an affair, very little is known about Minna Bernays. But it is clear that she was a fascinating character in her own right.

Freud's Mistress is based on fact, but it is a work of fiction. In that vein, we took some dramatic license, such as with the children's ages and historical events that occurred several years before or after the time period covered in the book.

SELECTED SOURCES

. . .

The ongoing controversy about Sigmund Freud's affair with Minna Bernays began in 1957 with Carl Jung's claim that Minna confessed to him that she was having an intimate relationship with Freud. Again, in 1982, the controversial Freud researcher Peter Swales argued in an article in the *New American Review* that Minna Bernays not only had an affair with Freud but had become pregnant and underwent an abortion. Swales's theory met with heated debate over the next few years, particularly from eminent Freud scholars Peter Gay and Paul Roazen. But with the discovery of the Swiss hotel log by Franz Maciejewski in August 2006, major scholars reassessed the facts, and there was a gradual reckoning that Freud indeed had two wives. The genesis for this book sprang from the subsequent articles in major newspapers and periodicals, some of which are listed below.

Blumenthal, Ralph. "Hotel Log Hints at Illicit Desire That Dr. Freud Didn't Repress." *The New York Times*, December 24, 2006.

Bond, Alma H., Ph.D. "Did Freud Sleep with His Wife's Sister? An Expert Interview with Franz Maciejewski, Ph.D." *Medscape*, May 4, 2007.

Follian, John. "Analyze This: Freud 'Bedded Sister-in-Law.' " *The Sunday Times*, January 7, 2007.

Gay, Peter. "Sigmund and Minna? The Biographer as Voyeur." *The New York Times*, January 29, 1989.

Maciejewski, Franz. "Freud, His Wife and His 'Wife.'" *American Imago* 63 (4) (2006), 497–506.

Roazen, Paul. "Of Sigmund and Minna" (and Peter Gay's response). *The New York Times*, April 9, 1989, letters to the editor.

Silverstein, Barry. "What Happens in Maloja Stays in Maloja: Inference and Evidence in the 'Minna Wars.'" *American Imago* 64 (2) (2007), 283–89.

We would also like to acknowledge a host of other, indispensable sources that formed the historical background for this book. First and foremost are the biographies of Sigmund Freud written by two acclaimed historians: *Freud: A Life for Our Time* by Peter Gay, and *Freud: Darkness in the Midst of Vision*, by Louis Breger. In addition, straying from official memoirs of the time is Paul Roazen's comprehensive and illuminating study of Freud's relationships with others, *Freud and His Followers*. These writers paint a vivid and detailed portrait of this brilliant but flawed man.

Enormously useful to our understanding of Freud's life was a visit to the Freud Museum (formerly the Freud home) in Maresfield Gardens, London. The Freud family moved to England in 1938 after they fled Nazi-occupied Vienna, and virtually all of Freud's possessions were smuggled or shipped there afterward by close friends and family—his library, antiquities (the statue of Athena), paintings, furniture, photographs (including one of Lou Andreas-Salomé), carpets, and the famous couch, a gift from a former patient. Today, the rooms, including his opulent study and consulting room, have been painstakingly preserved, untouched by time. Even Freud's spectacles remain on his desk, as if they were just laid down by the doctor himself.

Providing insight into Freud's personality, creativity, and thought processes were the surprisingly frank, intimate letters he wrote to his family, friends, and colleagues, especially the large volume of letters between Freud and Wilhelm Fliess, his then closest friend: *The Complete Letters of Sigmund Freud to Wilhelm Fliess, 1887–1904*, translated and edited by Jeffrey Moussaieff Masson, and *Letters of Sigmund Freud*, edited and selected by Ernst L. Freud.

We used as direct sources those works written by Sigmund Freud during the time period of this novel, particularly *The Interpretation of Dreams*, and the more easily understood version, *On Dreams*. In addition, we consulted *Freud on Women: A Reader*, edited by Elisabeth Young-Bruehl, *The Psychopathology of Everyday Life*, and *Five Lectures on Psycho-Analysis*.

Other biographies and writings about Sigmund Freud valuable to our research include *The Life and Work of Sigmund Freud*, by Ernest Jones; *Sigmund Freud: Man and Father*, by Martin Freud; *The Death of Sigmund Freud: The Legacy of His Last Days*, by Mark Edmundson; *Berggasse 19: Sigmund Freud's Home and Offices, Vienna 1938*, by Edmund Engelman (photographs); *Martha Freud: A Biography*, by Katja Behling; *The Freudian Mystique: Freud, Women, and Feminism*, by Samuel Slipp, M.D.; "Jung and Freud (The End of a Romance)" by John M. Billinsky, *Andover Newton Quarterly* 10 (1969), 39–43; and *The Freud Journal*, by Lou Andreas-Salomé, translated by Stanley A. Leavy.

Within the confines of a work of fiction, we have attempted to make this book as historically accurate as possible regarding fin de siècle Vienna, including the political and social environment surrounding the Hapsburg Empire before its eventual collapse.

The following books were particularly useful. *Fin-de-Siècle Vienna: Politics and Culture*, by Carl E. Schorske; *Schnitzler's Century*, by Peter Gay; *A Nervous Splendor: Vienna 1888–1889*, by Frederic Morton; *Wittgenstein's Vienna*, by Allan Janik and Stephen Edelston Toulmin; *Pleasure Wars: The Bourgeois Experience: From Victoria to Freud*, by Peter Gay; *The Habsburgs: Embodying Empire*, by Andrew Wheatcroft; *Austria-Hungary Handbook for Travellers*, by Karl Baedeker; *Alma Mahler-Werfel: Diaries, 1898–1902*; *Fräulein Else*, by Arthur Schnitzler; and *The Radetzky March*, by Joseph Roth.

Finally, most helpful in re-creating the details of a bourgeois Viennese doctor's home were the following: *Inside the Victorian Home*, by Judith Flanders; *English Women's Clothing in the Nineteenth Century*, by C. Willett Cunnington; *Mrs. Woolf and the Servants*, by Alison Light; *Beeton's Book of Household Management*, edited by Mrs. Isabella Beeton; *Victorian and Edwardian Fashions from "La Mode Illustrée,"* edited by JoAnne Olian; *The Writer's Guide to Everyday Life in Regency and Victorian England from 1811–1901*, by Kristine Hughes; and *Cooking the Austrian Way*, by Ann Knox.

ACKNOWLEDGMENTS

. . .

First and foremost, we would like to thank Molly Friedrich. Without her guidance and tireless efforts on our behalf there would be no book.

To Amy Einhorn, our editor, whose exceptional insights and literary instincts brought this book to life.

Also, for their hours of attention and skill, we'd like to thank Lucy Carson, Molly Schulman, Nichole LeFebvre, and Elizabeth Stein.

To everyone at Putnam—the cover artists, the talented publicity team, and the extraordinarily knowledgeable copy editors—we are grateful for their support and expertise.

ABOUT THE AUTHORS

. . .

Karen Mack, a former attorney, is a Golden Globe Award–winning film and televison producer. Jennifer Kaufman was a staff writer at the *Los Angeles Times* and a two-time winner of the national Penney-Missouri Journalism Award. Both reside in Los Angeles.